A Life of Joy

Theresa Hupp

ISBN for paperback edition: ISBN: 978-0-9853244-9-0

ISBN-10 for paperback edition: 0-9853244-9-X

Rickover Publishing

A Life of Joy

Cover illustration adapted from *Young Woman Writing a Letter* (1874), oil on canvas, by Federico Zandomeneghi (private collection)

Back cover image by E.S. Glover and A.L. Bancroft & Company, 1879. Library of Congress, https://www.loc.gov/resource/g4294p.pm007220/

Frontispiece adapted from Oregon History Project, https://www.oregonhistoryproject.org/articles/historical-records/fire-area-portland-1873/

Dedication

This book is dedicated to all the writers in the Sedulous Writers Group and the Kansas City Writers Group who have encouraged me as a writer and helped me improve my craft. None of my books would have been possible without them.

Cast of Characters, as of September 1872

The McDougall Family: *(all ages as of opening of the novel)*
 Caleb (Mac) McDougall, age 51
 Geneviève (Jenny) McDougall, age 39
   William (Will) McDougall, age 24
   Maria McDougall, age 22
   Caleb (Cal) McDougall, age 20
   Nathan (Nate) McDougall, age 18
   Eliza McDougall, age 16
   Lottie McDougall, age 15
   Maggie McDougall, age 10
   Andrew McDougall, age 7
   Geneviève (Evie) McDougall, age 6
   Eddie McDougall, age 2

Owen McDougall, Mac's older brother in Boston

Hortense Peterson, Jenny's mother
   Jacques (Jack) Peterson, Jenny's half-brother, age 25

McDougall & Company Employees:
    Amos Higgins, head accountant in Portland
    Bayliss Beck, Sacramento branch manager
    Samuel Cassidy, San Francisco branch manager
    Zhuang Li, clerk in Portland

***The New Northwest* Staff:**
    Abigail Duniway, owner and editor (historical figure)
    Robert Taylor, typesetter
    Daisy Wilson, clerk

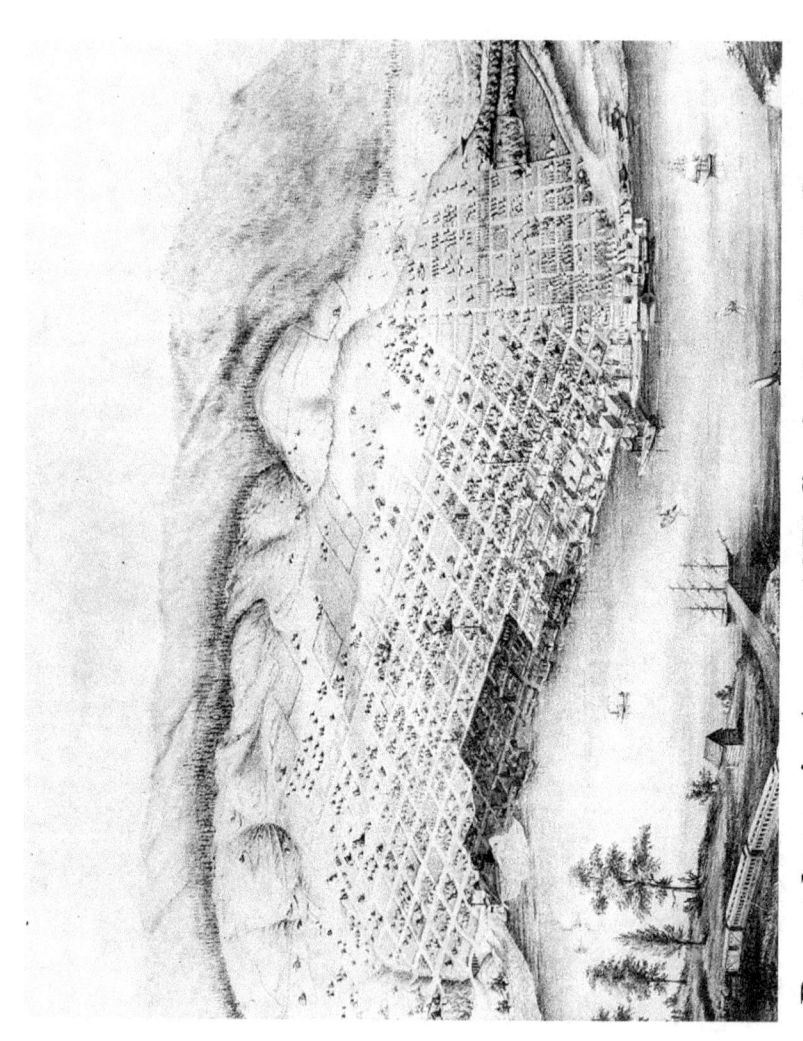

Burned area in August 1873 fire in Portland, Oregon

Chapter 1: Maria Wants a Job

Maria McDougall strode along the downtown Portland boardwalk to the offices of *The New Northwest* newspaper. Glancing at her reflection in the front window, she adjusted her hat to its most flattering angle, then stepped inside.

A man setting type looked up. "Yes, miss?"

"I'm here to see Mrs. Duniway." Maria tried to show confidence she didn't feel.

The man jerked his head toward an office behind him. "Back there."

Careful to keep her voluminous skirts away from the ink-stained type cases and frames surrounding the man, Maria approached the office. "Mrs. Duniway?" she said to the older woman inside. "It's Maria McDougall."

"Why, Maria. How nice to see you again. Please, have a seat."

Maria perched on the chair across from Abigail Duniway. Before she lost her nerve, she said, "I saw your solicitation in last Friday's paper. About needing writers. I'd like to apply."

Mrs. Duniway pursed her lips. "There must be a misunderstanding. I don't have any openings. I buy occasional articles from writers, but my staff is quite small." She paused. "But tell me, why do you want to work for my paper?"

"I-I read *The New Northwest* every week as soon as it comes out," Maria said, flushing. How had she misinterpreted the ad? It ran every week, soliciting "a competent corps of writers." She'd been sure the newspaper had open positions. "I attended the lecture you hosted for Susan B. Anthony last year. Then my mother and I traveled to Salem to hear her speak again. I've become a firm proponent of women's suffrage."

Mrs. Duniway smiled. "Mrs. Anthony's lecture tour in the West certainly aided our cause. Though women have not won the right to vote in Oregon. Not yet." Her gaze sharpened. "Why are you looking for a job? I've known your family for years. You do not need to earn wages. And why now?"

"Why shouldn't I work?" Maria countered, sitting taller. "I want to do something meaningful. Something more than helping Mama all day. I suppose the anniversary of Mrs. Anthony's lecture—it was last September, wasn't it?—has me reflecting. Then I noticed your advertisement—"

"With all the children in your family, there must be plenty for you to do at home."

Maria shifted to the edge of her seat, ready to stand. Clearly, her visit to the newspaper had been a mistake. "I'm sorry, ma'am. I just wanted to support women's suffrage. And to do something interesting with my time. I thought your paper—"

"Sit, girl, sit." Mrs. Duniway said. "Let's talk further. But first, you struggled when you assisted with my school in 1865. Why should I think you'd do better at writing?"

"I was fourteen then," Maria said indignantly. "Now I'm twenty-two. I've grown up."

Mrs. Duniway's gaze swept over Maria's fashionable hat and dress before meeting her eyes. "Indeed, you have. My students liked you. Why not try teaching again?"

Maria shook her head. "As you said, ma'am, I don't need to earn a living. And I want to help advance women's rights—your paper's mission."

"I advocate for *human* rights, my dear, not only women's rights." Mrs. Duniway peered over her spectacles as she spoke. "You used to have a fine hand at penmanship and excellent spelling. I trust those skills have not atrophied."

"No, ma'am."

Mrs. Duniway sighed. "I can't afford to take on a full-time employee. My newspaper is not yet profitable. But I could try you out as a part-time clerk. Two dollars a week is all I can pay. Your mother's housemaid probably earns more. Still, you'll learn how the newspaper operates. And if I assign you a piece to write or if you submit an article I agree to publish, I will pay you for that on top of your clerk's wage. Is that acceptable?"

Maria smiled and nodded. "All I want is a chance, Mrs. Duniway. Thank you."

"I'll start you next Monday, September 16. Our office opens promptly at eight."

"Yes, ma'am. I'll be here."

Maria grinned as she exited the newspaper office. She'd done it—she had a job. She would do her best to convert the clerk's position into a reporter's role on Mrs. Duniway's paper. Perhaps she could even meet Mrs. Anthony if the renowned suffragist returned to Oregon.

Now, she had to convince Mama—and more importantly, Papa—to let her take the position. She might be twenty-two, but they still treated her like a child.

Lifting her face to the sunny September day, Maria strolled down the boardwalk. In the east, Mount Hood watched over the city. In her hurry to get home, she nearly collided with a man. "Pardon me, sir—"

"Miss McDougall?" It was Amos Higgins, Papa's chief accountant. Maria recognized him, but didn't know him well. "Might I be of assistance?"

"No, thank you, Mr. Higgins. I'm on my way home." She smiled politely. He was a handsome man of around thirty, though in the past he'd seemed overly solicitous. Maria strove to be civil but distant. "I don't need an escort."

"I'm headed there myself," he said. "To meet with your father. May I accompany you?"

She shrugged. "If you wish."

Mr. Higgins remarked on the weather. She agreed it was a fine day. He asked after her mother's health. She responded her mother was in excellent health. He mentioned the new horse-car line that would soon start construction. She observed it would make travel downtown faster.

Soon they reached her family's grand three-story mansion. The McDougalls had moved there from Oregon City two years earlier, shortly after the birth of Maria's youngest brother Eddie. Maria opened the front door and asked the maid to inform Papa of Mr. Higgins's arrival.

Maria went upstairs and found Mama in the nursery rocking Eddie. "He has a cold, poor dear," Mama whispered. "I'm trying to get him to sleep. How was your day?"

"I asked Mrs. Duniway for a job on her paper," Maria blurted.

Mama raised her eyebrows.

"She offered me a position as a clerk," Maria said. "The pay is modest, but I'll learn a great deal. And I can write articles for publication if I want."

"I had no idea you wanted a paid position," Mama said. Rising, she laid Eddie in his crib. "Let's go talk with your father."

"Papa's busy with Mr. Higgins," Maria said. "Let me tell you first."

The two women went downstairs to the morning room that Mama used to manage the household affairs. Mama sat and picked up her mending.

"I want to be useful," Maria said, sitting near her mother.

"You're useful here," Mama said. "I don't know what I'd do without your help with the children. Especially Eliza and Lottie. Your sisters would run wild without your guidance."

"But Mama—"

"Abigail Duniway has been a friend to our family for many years. You could learn a lot from her. But your father will have an opinion, and we must let him weigh in." When Mama took that tone, Maria would not argue. She would need to plead her case to Papa.

Chapter 2: Parental Concerns

At supper that night, Maria tried several times to ask Papa about the newspaper job. Each time, Mama changed the subject. Finally, when Maria opened her mouth again, Mama said, "Wait until after dinner, Maria. When we can talk in peace."

Mama was right—it was impossible to have an adult conversation with all the children at the table. Will, the only sibling older than Maria, was working in Boston after graduating from Harvard College in 1869. Cal, the brother next in age after Maria, was enrolled at the recently created University of California in Oakland, California.

But all her younger siblings—Nate, Eliza, Lottie, Maggie, Andrew, Evie, and Eddie—filled the house with noise and chaos. They ranged from eighteen-year-old Nate down to Eddie at age two. Maria sometimes felt as if she were a second mother to the younger ones, rather than their oldest sister. She chaperoned Eliza and Lottie on their shopping trips downtown, and she settled squabbles between the little ones.

After the younger children were in bed, and Nate, Eliza, and Lottie settled in the parlor with books, Mama said to Papa, "Mac, Maria has something to discuss with us. Shall we adjourn to your library?"

None of the children could enter the library unless Papa issued an express invitation. Now, Papa nodded, took Mama's arm, and motioned for Maria to follow them.

Papa surprised Maria by sitting beside Mama on the divan rather than behind his imposing desk. Maria sat in a chair across from them, dreading this inquisition more than her interview with Mrs. Duniway.

"What is it, Maria?" Papa asked.

Not sure if Mama had said anything to him before supper, Maria began slowly. "I wish to make myself useful in the community," she said. "I spoke with Mrs. Duniway today about writing for *The New Northwest*. She offered me a position as a clerk."

"A clerk?" Papa said. "At her paper? And how much will that pay?"

"Two dollars a week," Maria said.

"That's hardly worth your time. Do you need me to increase your allowance?" Papa asked. "You don't need to work—"

"It's not about the money, Papa. I want to support women's suffrage."

Papa took Mama's hand. "Your mother has never wanted the vote."

"Perhaps I do, Mac," Mama said. "I trust you to represent my interests, but many women lack the support of a good man. The suffrage movement is necessary for them. As Abigail says—"

"Abigail Duniway is a fine woman," Papa said. "And I know many men do not take care of their wives and children the way they ought. But many women do not have the education to vote intelligently."

"And you think all men have the intelligence to choose wisely?" Mama said. "Then why is the state of politics as debased as you often claim?"

Papa snorted.

"I told Mrs. Duniway I would begin next week," Maria said.

"Without obtaining our approval?" Papa's voice rose.

"Papa, I am twenty-two. I know my own mind."

Papa sighed. "I worry about you, Maria. You know that."

Maria's muscles tensed. She understood what he meant. She wasn't her parents' natural daughter. When she was just an infant, Papa adopted her in California after her birth mother—a woman of Spanish and Indian descent— died, then brought her to his home in Oregon. Though Mama and Papa treated her as their own, Oregon society was not so kind. Maria had been belittled and teased during her school years, and she still suffered the sting of how others in Portland snubbed her. Papa tried to protect her from the insults.

"This is important to me," she told Papa. "I need to stand on my own."

Papa studied her, his face softening. "You may take the job," he said. "But if it becomes too much, or if you cannot help your mother when she needs it, or if you are mistreated or in any danger, you must resign. Do I have your agreement on that?"

Maria didn't think working at the newspaper would be dangerous. "Yes,

Papa," she said, smiling. She would start work at *The New Northwest* now and worry about any difficulties later.

For the rest of the week, Maria tried to help Mama as much as possible. She canned vegetables with Mrs. O'Malley, the housekeeper. She escorted Eliza and Lottie to town to buy hats and other accessories for their fall wardrobes. She stayed in the nursery one night with Eddie when his breathing worsened so Mama could rest. But throughout the week, she smiled whenever she thought about starting at *The New Northwest* on Monday.

On Saturday morning, Papa and Nate took the steamship to Oregon City, planning to visit the family farm outside of town. "I have a young horse to train," Papa said. "A two-year-old stallion who shows a lot of promise."

"Be careful, Mac," Mama said. "You're not so young anymore."

"Don't worry, Ma," Nate said, slinging an arm around her shoulder. He towered a foot above Mama. "I'll make him take it easy."

Mama gave Nate a stern look. "I worry just as much about you, young man. Let the trainers do their job."

Papa scoffed, and Nate grinned. Maria shook her head—neither of them would listen, and Mama would fret all weekend.

"You must be home by Sunday evening for Andrew's birthday supper," Mama said. Andrew would turn eight on Monday, and Mama made a big occasion out of every child's birthday. Monday was Will's birthday as well, but he was in Boston, and Mama couldn't fuss over him.

"We'll be home in plenty of time," Papa promised.

Saturday passed slowly after Papa and Nate left, as Mama and Maria did their chores. While the family was at supper that evening, the door knocker sounded, and Maria answered it. "Telegram for Mrs. McDougall," the boy at the door announced.

Maria gave him a coin and took the telegram to Mama. Mama looked at it and shrieked, collapsing into her chair. Maria then read:

DATE: 14 SEPTEMBER 1872
FROM: NATHAN MCDOUGALL OREGON CITY
TO: GENEVIEVE MCDOUGALL PORTLAND
PA FELL OFF HORSE HURT BAD COME QUICK

Chapter 3: Coping With the Accident

After her initial panic upon reading the telegram, Mama took Maria into her morning room to plan what to do. For as long as Maria could remember, Mama had handled catastrophes with ease. But Papa had never been badly hurt before.

"I must go to the farm in the morning," Mama announced, pacing the small room. "The steamboat doesn't run on Sunday, so I will have to take the carriage."

"Why not the train?" Maria asked.

"I might need the carriage to bring Mac home," Mama said. "Though it will take most of tomorrow to reach the farm."

"Let me come, too, Mama," Maria urged. She'd nursed the younger children through plenty of scrapes and bruises. Surely, she could help with Papa.

"No, you must take care of the children and household," Mama murmured, her brow wrinkled in thought. "Mrs. O'Malley can't manage alone. I'll take Eliza."

"Oh, Mama, Eliza is so flighty," Maria said.

Mama made another lap of the parlor. "Perhaps. But she's old enough to drive the carriage if need be."

Her decision made, Mama went upstairs to pack and talk to Eliza. Maria followed. "Likely your father is fine," Mama said. "Nate is probably exaggerating." But her voice quavered.

After Mama explained her plan to everyone, Maria ushered the younger children downstairs—all but Eliza, who stayed with Mama. "Let's play charades," Maria said, when they entered the family parlor. She kept them occupied until bedtime.

At dawn, Maria waved as Mama and Eliza left in the carriage, a basket of food from Mrs. O'Malley tucked in beside them. "Send a telegram when you know how Papa is," Maria pleaded. Her stomach churned as she watched them disappear—both because she worried about Papa and because of the responsibility Mama had left her with.

Her parents most likely would not be home before she needed to start work with Mrs. Duniway on Monday. But she couldn't worry about that now.

Sunday evening, another telegram arrived:

DATE: 15 SEPTEMBER 1872
FROM: GENEVIEVE MCDOUGALL OREGON CITY
TO: MARIA MCDOUGALL PORTLAND
FATHER UNCONSCIOUS MULTIPLE BROKEN
BONES SEND HIGGINS IMMEDIATELY

Maria's heart sank—Papa's injuries were serious. Poor Papa. Poor Mama, having to nurse him.

Her newspaper job would have to wait.

Monday morning right after breakfast, Maria left the younger children with Mrs. O'Malley and the nursemaid and walked to the McDougall & Company building on Fourth Street in downtown Portland. "Is Mr. Higgins here?" she asked the man at the front desk.

As she spoke, Amos Higgins came out of a back office. "Miss McDougall," he said. "How nice to see you."

"Papa's been hurt in Oregon City," she said without greeting him. She showed him the telegrams. "Mama needs your help."

He nodded and bowed. "I'll leave immediately. The train will have me there by midafternoon." Then he frowned. "Are you all right?"

"I'm fine," she said. "Just worried."

"Is there anything I can do for you before I leave?" He seemed more concerned about her than about Papa.

"I can manage. Just help Papa. Please."

"I'll send word to you as soon as I learn anything," he said, bowing again. She smiled her thanks, then left the building.

Her next stop was at *The New Northwest*, where she asked to see the editor. She explained about Papa's injury, ending, "I won't be able to start work today. I'm sorry. But I still want the job."

Abigail Duniway expressed her sympathy. "If your situation changes, dear, let me know. But your family must be your priority." She didn't seem upset that Maria could not begin her role as clerk that morning. Maria wondered if Mrs. Duniway had any meaningful work for her to do.

As she walked home, Maria realized today was Andrew's birthday. They'd done nothing about a birthday supper last night—the children had been too worried about their father. She would have to make the meal special tonight.

And it was her older brother Will's birthday, too, Maria remembered. Today he turned twenty-five. When they were children, she'd always looked up to Will. If he were home, she could count on him to help, but he was a continent away in Boston. She missed him.

Will needed to know about Papa, she decided. And Papa would need help with his business as he recovered—Will was the only one who could manage the business for Papa. It was time for Will to return to Oregon.

She turned back downtown and went to the telegraph office.

DATE: 16 SEPTEMBER 1872
FROM: MARIA MCDOUGALL PORTLAND
TO: WILLIAM MCDOUGALL BOSTON
PAPA HURT HORSE ACCIDENT COME HOME I
NEED YOU

Chapter 4: Will Gets the News

Will McDougall leaned over his desk, drafting yet another contract for Uncle Owen. Despite Will's three years at the Boston branch of McDougall & Company, his uncle still treated him like a new clerk. Will enjoyed the work and learning about the family business, but he longed for real responsibility.

Late in the day, the firm's errand boy burst into Will's office. "Telegram, Mr. McDougall," he said, waving a paper before tossing it on Will's desk. "Sounds serious." The boy read everything before delivering it. Will hoped the lad didn't gossip outside the business's headquarters.

Will picked up the telegram—from Maria. They corresponded regularly, but she'd never sent him a telegram. His stomach knotted as he read her message. How badly was Pa hurt?

And why was Maria summoning him home? Mama and Maria had coped with many injuries and illnesses over the years. Still, Pa was getting older. Perhaps, as the errand boy had said, this was serious.

He called the boy back. "Send a reply. Say 'How bad is Pa? What can I do?' And hurry."

The lad nodded and vanished, leaving Will to sink his head in his hands, worried about Pa and about what Pa's injury might mean for Will.

He'd been in Boston for seven years now—four at Harvard College, then three working for Uncle Owen. His uncle had taught Will to draft contracts and financial documents. He'd learned how banks assessed loans, how to determine whether land and buildings would be profitable to sell or keep, what inventory was most likely to be profitable, and which documents were needed before money or property changed hands.

Will had also learned how the Boston branch of McDougall & Company operated and how it related to the Oregon and California branches Pa handled. The Boston business started in banking and later expanded into financing commercial real estate. Pa's West Coast locations focused on warehousing, supplying merchants, and transportation. Uncle Owen helped Pa find clients on the East Coast to buy timber and other goods from the West, and also developed East Coast sources for Pa to buy from. The branches, all operated under the name McDougall & Company, were managed separately, but sought to maximize the profits of the entire enterprise.

There'd been three McDougall men in Pa's generation—Uncle Owen, another brother who died before Will moved to Boston, and Caleb (Will's father, the youngest of the three). Pa traveled to Oregon in 1847, and he'd rarely returned to Boston in the quarter century since. In fact, the first time Pa returned to Boston was in 1865 to bring Will to Harvard. Then, Will's parents and Maria made one trip to Boston in 1869 to see Will graduate. Despite Pa's distance—or maybe because of it—Uncle Owen treated Will as a proxy for his younger brother.

Will had not returned to Oregon in seven years. Other than the visit in 1869, Will's only contact with his family had been through letters. Mama and Maria wrote weekly about the family. Pa wrote less frequently, but his letters contained more substance about what Will should be learning in Boston. At Mama's prodding, Will's younger siblings wrote occasionally. But he hadn't seen them in years. He'd never met his two youngest siblings.

Now Maria's telegram had shattered the distance. Was it time for Will to go home?

Will left the office early, Maria's telegram still weighing on his mind. He'd almost forgotten it was his birthday. His grandmother—Pa's mother— had planned a lavish celebration for that evening. Will had lived with her since he graduated from Harvard. Tonight, despite his worry over the telegram, he would have to don formal attire, eat a rich meal, and mingle with her guests. Then, after the festivities, he would break the news to Grandmother McDougall that her youngest son was injured.

The evening unfolded as expected. Uncle Owen and his family were present, of course, as were business associates and their wives and daughters. For the past three years, Grandmother urged Will to marry one of these eligible daughters, but none of them appealed to Will.

Will smiled as the guests toasted his health and wished him many happy returns. Finally, everyone left, and he was alone with his grandmother.

"Happy birthday, William," Grandmother McDougall said, patting his cheek. "I hope you enjoyed the evening. I'm getting too old for such festivities. You need to choose a wife and settle down, so I don't have to parade these silly girls in front of you any longer. They get younger every year."

"Thank you for the party, Grandmother," Will said, offering a slight bow. "It was a nice evening." He paused. "I have news from home—"

"Home?" Her expression soured. "This is your home. Oh, you mean Oregon. Did you have another letter from your mother?" Grandmother still disapproved of her son's marriage to a woman from outside the Boston social elite—a woman of Southern and French heritage who was many years younger than Pa. And Grandmother didn't know the full story of how Pa and Mama had met—a story Will would never tell her.

"No," Will said. "A telegram from Maria." Grandmother despised Maria's Spanish heritage even more than Mama's French lineage. If Grandmother learned Maria was part Indian, she would suffer a fit of hysterics. "Pa's been hurt."

"A telegram? About Caleb?" Grandmother sounded concerned about her youngest son, despite their past quarter-century estrangement. "What happened?"

"The telegram gave no details. Only that he was injured in a horse accident."

"What a foolish boy," Grandmother said. "He was always careless with horses."

Pa was over fifty and the finest horseman Will knew. "I wired back, asking for more information. But Maria wants me to come home."

"You can't go," Grandmother declared. "You're needed here. Your uncle depends on you. And who would keep me company?"

"Perhaps I should go, Grandmother," Will said gently. "He's my father."

She sniffed. "Caleb ignored his own father for years. And me. Why should you owe him anything?"

Will closed his eyes. If only Grandmother knew—he owed Pa everything. "I'll wait for Maria's response," he said. "Then I will decide."

That night as he prepared for bed, Will thought about Maria's telegram. He worried about his father. Pa was a vigorous man, but fall from a horse could fell anyone.

He worried about his mother—he'd thought Mama could handle any domestic mishap. Her own growing-up years had not been easy. And she'd lost a child and overcome that devastating loss.

His parents were the closest couple he'd ever known. He'd always hoped to find a woman to love as much as they loved each other.

Maria. She'd been his cherished childhood friend. At one point when they were younger, he'd wondered if she might become more. She was adopted, and they had no blood connection. He still wondered.

Chapter 5: Papa Comes Home

Around noon on Tuesday, Maria heard a shout from outside. The McDougall carriage pulled up to the side portico, and Eliza and Nate climbed out. Nate hitched one horse to a post and hefted his and Eliza's satchels out of the carriage.

"Mama and Papa are taking the steamboat," Eliza told Maria. "They'll be here later. Papa insisted we come home today, though he could have remained in his hotel suite in Oregon City."

"How is he?" Maria asked.

Eliza shrugged. "In pain. Mama, Mr. Higgins, and the doctor are with him. The doctor thought the steamboat would be the easiest way to bring Papa home. They'll need a wagon from the dock, but Mr. Higgins said he'd manage everything."

"How bad are Papa's injuries?" Maria pressed. The telegrams had given no details.

"Leg broken in two places. Cracked pelvis. Also broken collarbone," Nate said, passing her as he carried the satchels into the house. "I'm famished. And he got quite a bump on the head."

"Lead the horses to the stable," Maria told Nate. "And ask the stable boy to curry and brush Pansy and Petunia." Their sister Lottie had named the mares several years ago when they were fillies.

"Would you do it?" Nate said. "Mama made us leave at dawn. I haven't had breakfast."

Maria sighed and unhitched the team. Nate would give her no peace if she didn't handle the chore. "I'll be back in fifteen minutes."

When she returned, Eliza and Nate were ensconced in the kitchen, each with a plate of bread and butter. Mrs. O'Malley muttered as she fried ham and eggs.

"Telegram just came," Eliza said. "From Will. Did you wire him?"

"Yes," Maria said, scanning the message. "He wants to know more about Papa."

"Pa will be furious," Nate said. "He doesn't want anyone to fuss over him. He won't like you told Will."

"What does Mama think?" Maria began drafting a response to Will in her head.

"She's worried," Eliza said. "It'll be weeks before Papa can walk again."

"If he ever walks," Nate added. "He had quite a fall."

Maria stared at Nate, wondering if he exaggerated. "I'd better wait until Papa gets here before I answer Will."

"Mama said to make up a bed in Papa's library." Eliza said, buttering another slice of bread. "He won't be able to manage stairs for weeks."

Maria peered out the window repeatedly, but the wagon and its occupants didn't arrive from the dock until midafternoon. It took Nate, Mr. Higgins, and the doctor from Oregon City to carry Papa inside to his library, where Maria had prepared a makeshift bed for him. Mama tucked a blanket over Papa once he was settled, while Maria and the younger children watched from the doorway.

Papa dropped off to sleep almost at once. Maria whispered to Mama, "How is he?"

"Stubborn," Mama said. "He hurts, but the doctor will only give him the smallest dose of laudanum. Mac was unconscious for hours, and the doctor is still concerned about his head injury."

Maria gasped.

Mama shook her head. She led them out of the library, leaving only the doctor with Papa. "If Mac's testiness is any indication, his head is fine. I worry about his bones knitting. We need to get a Portland doctor to examine him now that he's home."

"Shall I send for him?" Maria asked.

"Yes, thank you," Mama said, collapsing into a chair in the parlor. "The Oregon City doctor said he would consult with the local man before he left."

"Let me retrieve the doctor now," Mr. Higgins said, bowing to Mama and Maria.

An hour later, the Portland doctor arrived. Mama ushered him into the library, where Papa was now awake. Maria and Mama watched as the doctor felt Mac's limbs.

"You had quite a fall, Mr. McDougall," the doctor said. "But your bones appear to be well set." He nodded at the man from Oregon City. "Fine work, sir."

"I seen many a farm accident in thirty years," the country doctor responded. "Set my share of bones." Then he bid goodbye to Papa and Mama. "With your leave, I'll catch the late train back to Oregon City. He's in good hands now."

After Maria showed the doctor out, she returned to the library. She needed to confess to Mama about contacting Will before Eliza or Nate blurted out the news.

"Come in," Mama called in a hushed tone when Maria tapped on the door.

Maria entered and whispered, "How is he?"

"Sleeping again, thank goodness," Mama said from the chair beside Papa's pallet. "He barely dozed on the boat. The doctor just gave him more laudanum before leaving."

Maria sat beside Mama. "I sent Will a telegram."

"You did what?" Mama's voice was loud enough that Papa stirred.

"I thought he should know." Maria twisted her apron nervously. "Now Will wants to know about Papa's injuries. How should I answer him?"

"Why ever did you telegraph Will?" Mama said. "He's happy in Boston. His letters are full of his work and friends. You shouldn't have bothered him."

"You know he'd be a comfort here," Maria said, putting a hand on Mama's arm.

"Did you ask him to come home?" Mama's voice rose.

"Yes."

"You shouldn't have." Mama's next breath sounded like a sob.

"I don't know if he'll come," Maria murmured.

Mama looked at her. "He'll come. Will won't refuse you anything. Nor me. He loves us both. And he loves his father."

"That's why I asked," Maria said. "Because he loves us all. What should I tell him now?"

Mama sighed, staring at Papa. His chest rose and fell evenly. "Just tell him Mac is home. Let Will decide what he wants to do."

DATE: 17 SEPTEMBER 1872
FROM: MARIA MCDOUGALL PORTLAND
TO: WILLIAM MCDOUGALL BOSTON
PAPA HOME SEVERAL BROKEN BONES BUT
RESTING COMFORTABLY

Chapter 6: Will Is Torn

When Will arrived at work Wednesday morning, the errand boy handed him another telegram. "Your pa's home," he crowed. "Broke some bones."

Another missive from Maria. Why hadn't Mama written? "Broken bones" told him nothing about how badly Pa was hurt. And in this communication, Maria didn't ask him to come home. Was he needed in Oregon or not? Her vague response left him in a quandary.

He sat at his desk, staring at the telegram, and barely noticed Uncle Owen stride into the office.

"William, we have a new project. A construction loan on a building downtown. The customer is on his way here now to discuss terms. I want you there. You'll draft the documents."

"Yes, sir." Will picked up a folio of paper, a pen, and a bottle of ink, and followed his uncle to the meeting room. Dithering over whether to return to Oregon would have to wait.

The meeting lasted until noon, then Will and Uncle Owen walked to the Parker House to discuss the deal over steak and lobster.

"Do you think the construction company will complete the building on schedule?" Will asked.

"It won't matter to us," his uncle replied. "We have adequate security on our loan with pledges on their other buildings. If they don't repay their loan on time, we can foreclose on those properties. I'm surprised they agreed."

"They had little choice," Will said. "They need the funds, and your interest rate is reasonable."

"Can you draft the documents before you leave tonight?" Uncle Owen asked.

"I can complete my part, but then the clerks must copy my work. It'll probably take them a good part of tomorrow to make the requisite copies."

"Keep after them," his uncle said. "I want everything ready for signature by the end of the day tomorrow."

Will drafted the loan documents and handed them to the clerks before he went home that evening. The clerks must have worked until well after sunset, because the loan agreement and lien papers were ready for Will's review when he returned Thursday morning. He found two errors, had a clerk rewrite those pages, then took the completed package to Uncle Owen by midmorning. "Ready for signature," he said.

"Good," his uncle muttered. "The builder will be here in—" He glanced at his pocket watch. "Half an hour." He motioned for Will to sit. "Mother tells me you've been summoned back to Oregon."

"I should have told you sooner," Will said. "Summoned is too strong. But Pa was injured in a horse accident."

"You should go," Uncle Owen stated.

Will raised his eyebrows, surprised at his uncle's opinion. "Grandmother doesn't want me to leave."

"You've always been on loan to us," Uncle Owen said. "Unless you made your own decision to remain here. Your father wanted you to learn from me. Now, with your knowledge of the Boston operations, you can help Mac and me build closer connections between his business in the West and ours here."

Will was unaware Pa and Uncle Owen had discussed his career. "Pa never told me that."

"You were eighteen when you started at Harvard." Uncle Owen leaned back in his chair. "Way too young. Your father and I have corresponded through the years."

"Do you really think I should leave now?"

"If not now, when?" Uncle Owen eyed Will. "What more do you think you can learn here?"

Will shrugged. "I've drafted every type of document you need. Unless you turn over some of the deal-making to me, there isn't much more I can learn."

"Best to cut your teeth on the smaller deals in Oregon," Uncle Owen said. "California is already catching up to the East in terms of trade and construction. But Oregon is still a backwater."

Will opened his mouth to take exception to his uncle's words, then closed it. After seven years away, he didn't know what was happening in Oregon.

Uncle Owen continued, "If your father's been hurt, he'll need your help."

"But Pa has agents in California, and he told me his head accountant is a strong second in command," Will said. "And he never listened to my opinions in the past."

"Again, you were only eighteen when you left." Uncle Owen frowned. "Your brother Cal is in California, I hear."

"Yes," Will said. "Studying at the University of California."

"Then he's not ready to move into the business. Your father's agents in California are capable, but they aren't family." His uncle paused. "Take the train to Sacramento, then spend some time at the California branches before you head north. It's too bad there's no train from California to Oregon yet."

"It'll come," Will said.

Uncle Owen snorted. "Men have been working to build a railway up the West Coast for years. But no one has put together the financing yet. Without a rail line to San Francisco, Oregon will never capitalize on its resources."

"What about Grandmother?" Will asked. "She doesn't want me to go."

"Ignore her," Uncle Owen said of his mother. "She'll fuss whenever you leave. And unless you marry one of the 'suitable girls' she parades in front of you, she'll fuss even if you stay."

At dinner that evening, Will raised the topic of his departure with his grandmother. "I had another telegram from Maria today," he began.

Grandmother McDougall buttered a bite of her roll. "How is your father?"

"He's home now. All I know is he broke some bones."

"If he's home, he must be improving."

"I hope so." Will took a sip of wine, bracing himself for the coming argument with his grandmother. "Uncle Owen thinks I should return to Portland." It seemed strange to think of Portland as being his family's home now—they had lived in Oregon City when he left for Harvard.

"Owen? What does he know?" Grandmother dismissed her eldest son with a delicate wave of her soup spoon.

"He thinks I can build connections between our Boston and West Coast branches."

Grandmother sniffed. "How, without your father's support? Caleb never cared about building connections. He let your grandfather die before he returned to Boston. Caleb always pursued his own whims."

Will let her disparagement of Pa pass. "But Pa needs me. I've had good training here. I should go."

Grandmother sighed. "I'll speak to Owen. But I see no reason for you to leave me."

After dinner, Will went upstairs to his room. It was three times the size of the small room he'd had in his parents' house in Oregon City. He wondered whether his parents' Portland home would have space for him. If not, he could find a place of his own to live. At twenty-five, he was plenty old enough.

He gazed about the room, cataloguing in his mind how many trunks his possessions would fill. Should he ship some of his belongings to Oregon by sea? Or take everything with him on the train?

Will smiled, thinking of his parents' trek west in 1847—he'd found their journals years ago and read them avidly. They had fit everything needed for a six-month journey into one covered wagon. Neither had planned to join a wagon train, but circumstances had forced them into it. Circumstances unknown to anyone in Boston.

Tomorrow, he would investigate train schedules.

Chapter 7: Papa Weighs In

"You did what?" Papa shouted at Maria Thursday morning from his makeshift bed in the library.

"I telegraphed Will." Maria stood up straighter and faced her father. She wouldn't let Papa's words upset her—he didn't mean them. He was in pain, and that's why he was crotchety. He was usually so kind and patient.

"Mac," Mama said, softly but firmly. "Don't shout. It's bad for your head, and Maria doesn't deserve—"

"I don't need coddling," Papa snapped. "My head is fine, and my bones will heal. What can Will do for me, even if he returns to Oregon?"

"You'll need someone to run the business," Maria said.

"I have Higgins," Papa growled, grimacing as he shifted his weight on the pallet. "He knows the ledgers, the men working for us, everything. He's perfectly capable."

"Will is family. He'll care more than any hired man," Maria said. She was unaware of Amos Higgins's abilities, but Will would work out of love, not because he got paid.

"When is Will coming?" Papa asked.

"He hasn't said," Mama replied. "Shall we send another telegram?"

Papa's frown deepened. "Fine," he muttered. "But tell him to stop in Sacramento and San Francisco. I'll write my agents there. Will should meet them before heading north, so he can assess those branch operations. I've been away from California for too long. Higgins is the only oversight they've had in the last year." He winced again. "And send for Higgins. Until Will gets here, I want to meet with Higgins every morning."

"Yes, Mac," Mama said.

"What about you?" Papa said, glaring at Maria. "How's your job at the newspaper?"

"I told Mrs. Duniway I couldn't start—not until you're better."

"That's another thing you shouldn't have done," Papa barked. "You wanted the job, then you backed out? Not putting your best foot forward."

"You're more important than the newspaper," Maria replied, her voice steady.

"Talk to Abigail Duniway again," Papa said. "Tell her you'll start next Monday. Surely, you and Jenny can have the family and household in order by then."

"Does Papa really think I should take the job, Mama?" Maria asked during the noon meal. The older children were at school, and Evie and Eddie ate in the nursery, leaving Mama and Maria alone in the dining room.

"Yes, Maria, I believe he does." Mama looked at her. "And I do, too. You shouldn't abandon your dreams because of your father's accident. Neither of us wants that."

Maria sighed. "I don't know if it's a dream—"

"Then why do you want to work for Abigail?"

"I want to make a difference," Maria said, shrugging. "And if I could help women get the vote . . .." Her voice faltered.

Mama's voice gentled. "Voting is that important to you?"

Maria nodded. "There are so many things I haven't been able to do—because of who I am. But if I could vote—"

"What do you mean 'because of who you are'?" Mama's voice turned sharp.

"Because I'm part Indian," Maria said, picking at her food. "People look down on me."

"I thought we settled that nonsense long ago," Mama said. "You are Mac's and my daughter. A McDougall—part of a well-respected family in Oregon."

"You and Papa think so," Maria said. "But not everyone accepts me as such."

"Well, they should." Mama stood from the table. "I need to write a note to Amos Higgins. You can take it downtown, then visit the newspaper. Tell Abigail you'll start on Monday."

Maria left the house an hour later, her hat pinned securely against the wind. Mama's note to Mr. Higgins and Papa's text for a telegram to Will were tucked in her reticule. As she walked downtown, Maria mulled over Mama's words during their meal.

Mama and Papa had never let her heritage affect their love for her. She was their eldest daughter in every respect. But outside the family, it had been different. All her life, Maria had suffered slights in school and at social events. She might be the adopted daughter of Mac and Jenny McDougall, but others knew she was part Spanish, and even worse, part Indian.

And if they'd known her natural mother was a prostitute! Her adoption was common knowledge in Portland. Rumors were that Papa was her natural father, though he assured her he was not, and Maria believed him. But if society discovered her mother's trade, Maria would become a social outcast.

Then Maria's thoughts turned to Will. He featured in all her earliest memories—the big brother who played with her and taught her and protected her. He'd been her best friend in childhood.

But when she was fourteen and Will was sixteen, Will kissed her. Not a brotherly peck. A lover's kiss. She hadn't known what to think, what to feel. She only knew her world shifted. A few months later, her parents sent Maria to help Mrs. Duniway run a school, and then Will left for Harvard.

Before he traveled east, Will asked her whether she could think of him as more than a brother. She couldn't answer him then, and she still couldn't. They'd written many letters in the past seven years, but they'd only seen each other once in that time—a magical month of dances and parties in Boston three years ago. Will had seemed both foreign and familiar to her, a sophisticated adult with the boy's grin she'd known as long as she could remember.

Now he would likely come home. Would he be the boy she'd grown up with or the stranger she'd encountered in Boston? She loved him dearly. But how did she love him? And did he still care?

Maria sent the telegram to Will, then walked to Papa's office and handed Mama's note to Mr. Higgins. He was solicitous, as always. "Is there anything you need, Miss McDougall?"

"We're fine, thank you."

"And your father? Is he growing stronger?"

She laughed. "His voice is certainly stronger—issuing commands as he usually does. Be on your guard, sir, when you visit him tomorrow."

Mr. Higgins smiled and bowed as he held the exit door for her. "Thank you for the warning."

Maria next walked to the newspaper office to see Mrs. Duniway. "Might I begin work next Monday?" she asked.

"How is your father?" the older woman asked. "Are your parents in agreement with your working for me?"

"Papa is improving, ma'am," Maria said. "Both he and Mama encouraged me to talk to you."

"I'm surprised at your father's eagerness to have you support the cause of women's suffrage."

"He is more forward-thinking than he seems." The words surprised Maria even as she spoke. It was true. Despite his gruffness and protectiveness, Papa was a fair man. If Maria wanted something, he let her pursue it, regardless of his own opinions.

Chapter 8: Will Decides

On Friday morning, Will received another telegram, this time from Mama, dated the previous day.

> DATE: 19 SEPTEMBER 1872
> FROM: GENEVIEVE MCDOUGALL PORTLAND
> TO: WILLIAM MCDOUGALL BOSTON
> FATHER IMPROVING TRAVEL YOUR
> CONVENIENCE VISIT CALIFORNIA BRANCHES EN
> ROUTE

He sighed. Apparently, Pa (or Mama) agreed with Uncle Owen—they all wanted him to stop in California before reaching Oregon. But Mama didn't demand his return. She didn't even sound eager. What did "travel your convenience" mean? Still, he felt he should go.

He strode down the hall to his uncle's office. "What if I left for Portland in a week or two?" he asked. "Can you part with me that quickly?"

Uncle Owen motioned to a chair. "Is that what you've decided?"

Will handed over the telegram, then sat. "Mama doesn't tell me much."

Uncle Owen frowned. "Telegrams are not the best medium of communication. People don't spend their coins on clarity. Do you have any more details on your father's condition?"

Will shook his head. "And Pa is so bull-headed he won't admit to any infirmity."

His uncle chuckled. "Mac was always a mystery to me. So much younger that we barely knew each other. After he graduated from Harvard, he only worked here for a year before traveling. First, to Europe, then out West, where he met your mother and stayed." Uncle Owen raised an eyebrow. "How did they meet, anyway? I've never heard."

"I don't really know," Will said. He knew the important parts of the story, but he wouldn't tell his uncle. "Sometime before they joined the wagon train." He squirmed in his chair. "So, about my leaving?"

"Suit yourself," Uncle Owen said. "If you can pack your belongings in a week, I can part with you then. You should be able to update the clerks on your projects in that time."

"And Grandmother—"

"As I said, I'll handle her."

"I'll gather my files this afternoon and summarize them by the end of the week," Will said, standing.

He returned to his office and summoned a clerk. "Bring me the files on all the open matters I'm handling."

The clerk gaped. "All the files, sir?"

"Yes."

An hour later, his office floor lay buried in paper. He hadn't realized how many deals and lawsuits he had pending. His stomach sank. He would be lucky to get through it all in a week.

As Will returned to his grandmother's mansion that evening, thoughts of his family weighed on him. Now that he'd decided to leave Boston, he could focus on what lay ahead. It would be good to see them all—Mama and Pa, Maria, his younger siblings—and to meet the two youngest born during his seven years away.

Maria's face came to mind most often. They'd been close ever since Pa brought her to Oregon as a baby.

When Will was five, Pa moved the family from his homestead claim to a house in Oregon City. Will thrived in school and got along with most of the boys, but Maria's school days were harder. The other students mocked her Spanish and Indian blood. Will urged her to ignore their teasing, but he understood it wounded her deeply.

As they matured, Will began to view Maria as more than a sister. She became a lovely girl he longed to kiss—and one day, he did. Mama and Pa were angry when they learned of it—or perhaps confused, though no more confused than Will was. He wasn't Maria's brother, not by blood, and he didn't regret kissing her. But he couldn't deny it altered everything—the way he saw Maria, and perhaps the way she saw him. Before leaving for Boston, Will asked Maria whether she could ever love him as a man, not a brother. She didn't say yes, but neither did she say no.

During their years apart, Will and Maria wrote friendly letters about their activities, family, and friends, but never hinting at anything deeper. Will only saw Maria once since leaving home—when she was eighteen and visited Boston with Mama and Pa. By then, she'd grown into a breathtaking beauty, flashing dark eyes and smooth sable hair, with a dazzling smile she showed too seldom. They spent a month together under the watchful gaze of their parents. Will had just graduated from Harvard and was eager to prove himself in the family business. He danced with Maria, but treated her as no more than a sister.

Now, as he prepared to return home, the confusion of their first kiss returned to him. How would he feel when he saw her again? How would she feel? In all his time in Boston, no other girl had captivated him. He'd escorted many young women Grandmother McDougall paraded before him, and even kissed a few. But none held a candle to Maria. He was ready to find out how she might love him now.

During dinner that evening, Will told his grandmother, "I'll be leaving for Oregon as soon as I can pack—both here and at the office."

With a rare lack of decorum, Grandmother's fork clattered to her plate. "Oh, William." Her face sagged.

Will hadn't realized his presence meant so much to her. "I'm sorry."

She sighed. "I will miss you." After a sip of wine, she said, "I don't see what there is for you in Oregon. Such a backward place."

"Oregon has been a state for over a decade," Will said.

"But what of the social life?" Grandmother replied. "How will you find a young woman to marry worthy of a McDougall?"

"I haven't found anyone in Boston."

"You haven't looked," she countered. "Was there someone in Oregon you never told me about? But how could there be? You were only eighteen when you left."

"I had no commitments," Will said, though Maria came to mind again. "Portland's society can rival Boston's these days, I believe."

She sniffed. "I doubt it."

"Pa needs my help," Will said. "Uncle Owen agrees. He told me I can be more useful to McDougall & Company in Portland than here."

"But I will have to walk these halls alone." Her voice wavered. "Sit by myself every evening."

"Ask one of Uncle Owen's daughters to stay with you," Will said. The truth was, Grandmother McDougall's snobbery drove everyone away. But Will hoped to part on good terms, so he bit his tongue.

She sighed. "At least let me hold a farewell party for you. I'll send you off in grand style. You can't go sneaking away like your father did twenty-five years ago. I never understood why he left."

Will's jaw tightened. He wasn't sure what had estranged Pa from his family, though he knew what happened after Pa left Boston.

Chapter 9: First Day at Work

On Monday, September 23, Maria entered *The New Northwest* offices full of anticipation. A new chapter in life awaited her—a chapter in which she would be valued for her intelligence and productivity. Mama and Papa had always praised her, but it was different when someone outside the family—someone who would pay her—thought highly of her.

"Is Mrs. Duniway here?" she asked a man setting type, the same man she'd seen on her first visit to the paper.

"No, miss," he said, not even looking up from his type case. "No one here but me."

"Do you know where she is?"

"No, miss. Likely arguing with her brother. He visited earlier, then stormed out. She followed him." He raised his eyes to look at her. "Who are you?"

"Maria McDougall. I'm starting work today." Maria didn't know what to do in Mrs. Duniway's absence. "What usually happens on Monday mornings?"

"I'm Robert Taylor," he said, nodding. "Ain't no usual. Reporters come and go, though Mrs. Duniway writes most of the articles herself. I set type for advertisements and any serials early in the week. Late news must be set by Thursday morning. We print that afternoon, and the paper gets distributed on Friday."

"Are any articles planned for this week?"

"You'd best talk to Mrs. Duniway."

At that moment, Abigail Duniway burst through the door. "That brother of mine thinks he's always right. Just because he edits *The Oregonian*—"

She stopped, glaring. "Oh. I'd forgotten you." Brushing past Maria, she ordered, "Come along."

Maria followed the editor into her office and waited while Mrs. Duniway hung up her cloak and hat.

"I might as well make use of you." She handed Maria a stack of newspapers from her desk. "Read these. Mark any articles worth reprinting. Daisy usually handles this, but she's ill today."

"W-what types of articles do you want to reprint?" Maria stammered.

The editor frowned. "I thought you said you read my paper."

"I do, ma'am."

"Then find pieces similar to those you've seen in past issues." Mrs. Duniway shrugged. "Whatever interests you. I need a column's worth. Maybe more. Anything I can't print this week might be useful next week."

Maria took the stack of papers to a chair and table by the window in the front room and started reading. The newspapers came from all over the nation. She found a blurb from the *Boston Journal* about a calf that got caught in a tent—it made her laugh, so she marked it. Another piece from the *Willamette Farmer* on how women could refine men's coarseness that she thought might appeal to Mrs. Duniway. Maria didn't know any coarse men, other than her younger brothers, but she hoped her association with them improved their characters.

By noon, Maria had read the entire stack and marked ten or twelve articles. She gave them to Mrs. Duniway, who skimmed them. "This'll do. That's all for today. Come back tomorrow."

"You don't have any work for me this afternoon?" Maria asked.

Mrs. Duniway sighed. "I told you it was a part-time position. Go home. Try your hand at writing something yourself. Maybe I'll use it."

Maria trudged home from the newspaper office. She'd hoped to return to her parents with tales of writing her first article for *The New Northwest*. Instead, all she'd done was browse through other newspapers. Most of the articles were drivel, whether she'd found them in Oregon papers or in periodicals from the East. Papa bought the better papers, including *The Oregonian*, which had the largest circulation in Portland. He subscribed to *The New Northwest* as well, mostly for Mama and Maria, though Maria had seen him reading it on Friday evenings when it arrived.

Maria ate a late lunch in the kitchen with Mrs. O'Malley. Mama was at an afternoon tea with friends, and the younger children were still at school. Evie and Eddie in the nursery wouldn't care about Maria's morning, so she picked at her food silently, disappointment killing her appetite.

Her thoughts drifted to Will. He hadn't responded to Mama's telegram. They didn't know whether he was coming home, and, if so, when. Surely, he would tell them. Maybe a telegram had arrived that morning.

After she finished eating, Maria knocked on the door of Papa's library.

"Come in," he called.

"Good afternoon, Papa." She kissed his forehead. He was propped up on pillows today, but still on the pallet. She sat beside him. "Is there any word from Will?"

"No." Papa sounded tired. "Where's your mother?"

"Still out," Maria said. "I don't remember who is hosting this week's tea."

"She's gone so much," he muttered.

"No more than usual," Maria said. "But you're used to being out and about yourself. Can I bring you anything?"

"Would you read to me?" He gestured toward his desk. "There's a pile of correspondence I should answer. Higgins brought it this morning. But my head hurts."

Maria read the first letter to Papa, then asked, "Do you want me to draft a response?"

"Write what I dictate," Papa said, rubbing his forehead. "Higgins can clean it up later."

Maria spent her afternoon helping Papa. Taking his dictation felt more like proper work than what she'd done at the newspaper.

At supper that evening, Mama asked Maria to tell the family about her day at work. Maria tried to make the mundane tasks sound interesting. Nate hooted when she described the article about the cow stuck in the tent. Eliza and Lottie lorded it over their brothers at the idea that women could make men less coarse.

"You hear, Andrew?" Lottie said. "Boys need girls around. The paper didn't say girls need boys."

Andrew stuck his tongue out.

"Andrew," Mama chided. "Perhaps the article was correct."

Later, the children settled in the family parlor while Mama checked on Papa. When Mama joined them after a bit, she asked Maria, "So, did the day pass quickly for you?"

Maria shook her head. "There wasn't much for me to do. Perhaps tomorrow will be busier."

"Well," Mama said, "every job has dull moments. Abigail Duniway does important work in advocating for women's suffrage. Someday, she will be proven correct."

"Do you want to vote?" Maria asked. She noticed the other children listening, particularly Eliza and Lottie.

"As I told you and your father, some women have no one to protect them. They need the vote to protect themselves. Those of us who are more fortunate must do what we can to help." Mama patted Maria's hand. "And I'm proud of you for wanting to do your part."

The family worked silently for a while—on schoolwork and sewing. Maria knitted a scarf. Only tonight had she realized the yarn she handled was Will's favorite blue. The thought of Will made her ask Mama, "Do you think Will is on his way?"

Mama sighed. "I suspect not yet. I'm sure he will telegraph before he leaves."

"Is Will coming home?" Andrew asked.

"We hope so," Mama said. "We told him Papa was hurt."

"I don't even remember him," Andrew said.

"No," Mama said, smiling at Andrew. "You were only a baby when he left."

Chapter 10: Daily Grind

Maria's work at *The New Northwest* dragged into a second week with little change. She met Daisy Wilson, a plump, bespectacled woman about the same age, and they divided the work of sifting through other newspapers for articles to reprint. She also learned to lay out advertisements from Robert Taylor. "We don't make much off these ads," he told her. "Best you cut your teeth here. Ain't like these merchants'll go elsewhere—other papers charge more."

Mrs. Duniway passed by as he spoke. "But many of Portland's female readers subscribe to our paper," she said. "Millineries and other stores catering to women will advertise as long as we avoid errors. So perfection is our goal."

"Do you have any articles for me to write?" Maria asked Mrs. Duniway, as she did every morning.

"Not today," Mrs. Duniway said. "Have you written anything on your own?"

Maria shook her head. What did she have of interest to write about, sheltered as she was at home? And her afternoons were now spent working with Papa on his correspondence, so she had little time for herself. "I'm sorry, Mrs. Duniway," she said. "I'll keep thinking. Surely, an idea will occur to me."

Mrs. Duniway paused, then said, "This Wednesday, I am meeting Winema Riddle, who wishes to speak to me about the rights of native peoples. There might be something in her words worth publishing. You should join us for lunch."

Maria smiled—finally, Mrs. Duniway had suggested an intriguing topic.

"I shall be delighted," she said. "Though I know nothing about Mrs. Riddle."

"Winema Riddle is a member of the Modoc tribe," Mrs. Duniway said. "She works with her husband, a white settler in Klamath County, to advocate for the welfare of tribes on the Klamath Reservation. She is visiting Portland this week."

An Indian woman helping her tribe. Maria wondered why Mrs. Duniway selected her for this assignment, rather than a more experienced reporter. Did Mrs. Duniway think the topic unworthy of much space in the paper? Or did she think Maria would relish the assignment because of her native blood?

"I have a file of my correspondence with Mrs. Riddle in my office," Mrs. Duniway said. "Read it before Wednesday, so you are prepared to speak with her."

Daisy stared at Maria through her spectacles. "She must like you," Daisy whispered. "She ain't never offered me a chance to meet anyone. Though why she'd think you'd want to meet an Indian, I don't know."

Maria hadn't revealed her ancestry to Daisy. And she wouldn't. Not yet.

Maria spent the rest of Monday morning poring over Winona Riddle's letters to Mrs. Duniway, along with clippings from *The Oregonian* describing conflicts in Southern Oregon. White farmers in the area did not respect the boundaries of the Klamath Reservation. As American settlers seized fertile fields and hunting grounds, the native population grew increasingly militant, which threatened the whites. In addition to these racial tensions, the tribes in the area fought among themselves.

"Why don't Americans honor their agreements with the tribes?" Maria asked Mrs. Duniway when she returned the file.

"Money," the editor said. "And land. Settlers want the fertile valleys for farms and the mountains for mining gold and silver. Indians want the fish and game, but the farmers drive the Indians' food away. Plus, the government has ignored centuries-old conflicts between the tribes."

When Maria returned home that afternoon, she sought Papa's opinion. "I'm supposed to interview Winema Riddle on Wednesday," she told him. "She fights for her people's rights, but the natives' interests are contrary to those of American pioneers."

Papa nodded. "It's been that way ever since white people came west," he said. "The settlers' desire for land is in direct opposition to the native way of life."

"So, who is right?" Maria asked.

"There should be land enough for all," Papa said. "The Army negotiated treaties with the tribes to give them land, and if the natives would stay on that land, American farmers could grow their crops in peace."

"But Mrs. Duniway says whites don't follow the treaties."

"Some don't," Papa acknowledged. "Many white men simply ignore the reservation boundaries. And when gold or silver is found, miners stream into the land and drive off all the game. That leads the tribes to seek their food elsewhere. There is much wrong on both sides."

"Then is there really land enough?" Maria asked. She felt uncomfortable questioning her father on a topic in which he had more expertise than she had. But for the first time, she sympathized with her native forebears. She wondered if her birth mother's ancestral tribe in California had experienced similar troubles to those now facing Oregon tribes.

The next morning, Amos Higgins brought ledgers from McDougall & Company for Papa to review. That afternoon, after Maria drafted a few letters for Papa to sign, her father said, "Come, let me show you how we keep our accounts."

He grimaced as he opened one of the large books she placed beside him and pointed to a column of numbers. "As each customer pays his bill, we enter it as a credit in this cash receipts ledger. And we make a corresponding debit in our accounts receivable ledger." He pointed to another book on a table nearby.

"Why enter it twice?" she asked. "The shopkeepers in town only have one account book."

"They use a simpler system," Papa said. "But our business has grown enough that we use double entry accounting. It's a system that's been used for centuries." He opened another ledger. "Let's take the example of goods in our Portland warehouse. When we receive the goods, we make an entry here in our inventory account. That's an asset. And we add a balancing entry in the McDougall & Company ownership ledger because the business now owns more property. Does that make sense?"

She nodded. "I think so."

"Then, when we sell the goods, we take the amount out of inventory and add the money received for the goods to our cash account—cash is also an asset. Or, if the customer doesn't pay, then instead of adding the sum to the cash account, we create an account receivable and leave that on the ledger until we get paid. Then we move it from accounts receivable to the cash receipts ledger I showed you."

"That seems awfully complicated."

"Perhaps," Papa said. "But it allows us to track where our goods and money are. And there are checks and balances so my staff cannot steal as easily."

"You think your employees might steal from you?" Maria asked in surprise. She'd always enjoyed meeting the men who worked for her father.

"I hope not," Papa said. "But it is good business to discourage theft. These ledgers help."

"Could someone still steal, even with double entries?" Maria asked.

"Yes," Papa said. "How do you think it could be done?"

Maria hesitated, then said slowly, "If the same person handled both cash and inventory, then he could falsify both entries and keep some of the money."

"That's one way," Papa said, patting her hand in approval. "That's why we count our cash on hand every evening. And we audit our inventory regularly. Amos Higgins and his department manage the ledgers, but each man has his own responsibilities."

He turned to the ledger on his lap. "Now, let's see which customers paid their bills this week." And he ran his finger down the accounts receivable ledger.

"Pa! Pa!" Nate burst into the library while Maria and Papa were working, waving a paper. "A telegram. From Will. He's leaving Boston today."

Papa reached for the telegram, then read aloud:

DATE: 30 SEPTEMBER 1872
FROM: WILLIAM MCDOUGALL BOSTON
TO: CALEB MCDOUGALL PORTLAND
LEAVING BOSTON 1 OCTOBER VIA RAIL ARRIVAL
PORTLAND NOT KNOWN

At the news, Papa grinned as broadly as Maria and Nate. Maria looked over Papa's shoulder to read the words herself.

Mama followed Nate into the office at a more sedate pace. "Will's coming," Mama said unnecessarily, her voice happy, though there were tears in her eyes. "He'll be home in a few weeks."

"Maybe sooner," Pa said. "Perhaps in just days, if he takes the Transcontinental Railroad straight through—it's less than a week from Omaha to San Francisco."

"Oh, Mac," Mama said, clasping her hands. "Do you think he will?"

Pa shook his head. "If I were his age, I'd make an adventure of it. Take my time to see the country. We told him not to rush. Besides, I instructed him to meet my agents in California."

Mama and Maria both sighed. "I wish he were here now," Maria murmured.

Papa chuckled. "Didn't you enjoy our discussion of the ledgers? You're a quick study with numbers."

"But I want to see Will," Maria said.

At her words, Mama and Papa exchanged a glance, their expressions unreadable.

Chapter 11: Winema Riddle

Maria set out for *The New Northwest* office early Wednesday, eager for the meeting with Winema Riddle. She'd read wonderful stories in Mrs. Riddle's correspondence with Mrs. Duniway. Maria hoped their discussion today would lead to a published article.

Shortly before noon, Mrs. Riddle arrived. She was a full-blooded Indian, short, with long dark hair hanging loose down her back. She wore a Western dress and hat, but kept a plaid Indian blanket draped over her shoulders. Maria wondered if the woman wanted the comfort of her native wear, even in the heat.

Mrs. Duniway introduced Maria and Mrs. Riddle, then led them next door to the St. Charles Hotel. "My brother will join us," the editor said. Her mouth turned down as she spoke, and Maria wondered if Mr. Scott had invited himself to this meeting.

The St. Charles was one of the largest hotels in Portland, a four-story brick building. Maria had been to the St. Charles for tea with Mama, but had never attended a business meeting there. At the hotel's restaurant, the three women occupied themselves in small talk. Soon, Harvey Scott, Mrs. Duniway's brother, joined them. "My apologies," he said with a smile. "The press of the press, you know. How nice to meet you, Mrs. Riddle." He gave Maria only a brief nod.

When their meal arrived, Mr. Scott asked Mrs. Riddle, "How goes the relationship between the Klamath and the Modoc tribes?"

"How would you expect, Mr. Scott?" she responded in a steady voice. "The Modoc and Klamath tribes have fought for generations. Yet, the United States Army thinks it wise to move my people, the Modocs, from our ancestral land to a reservation for the Klamaths. As a Modoc woman, I cannot condone the taking of our land, nor the commingling of my people with our ancient enemies. The Modocs are not safe on the Klamath reservation." She sighed. "Still, I work for peace between our peoples."

"Tell my brother of your work with the Army at Fort Klamath," Mrs. Duniway suggested.

Mrs. Riddle shrugged. "There is little to tell. When an argument arises between the Modoc and Klamath tribes, I tell the fort commander. Captain Knapp, the former commander, cared more for his whiskey than for settling tribal disputes. I hope the new agent, Mr. Thomas Odeneal, will be more sympathetic."

"But the Modoc must move to the reservation," Mr. Scott said. "Otherwise, they will be at the mercy of miners and settlers traveling between Oregon and California. The traditional Modoc land is on the primary route from here to California."

Mrs. Riddle looked like she wanted to spit. "The Army sends troops to force the Modoc onto the reservation. But trouble will come from this."

The rest of the lunch was uncomfortable, with conversation limited to their food and the weather. Mr. Scott did not press his point any further, but both Mrs. Riddle and Mrs. Duniway sent malevolent glances his way. Maria didn't know enough to say anything.

After the meal, Mr. Scott excused himself. When he was out of earshot, Mrs. Duniway sighed deeply. "I am sorry, Winema. I did not think he would be so blunt. My brother has political differences with the new owner of *The Oregonian*. Harvey takes his frustrations out on everyone around him."

Mrs. Riddle shook her head. "He says what I hear every day. From the Army. From the whites near the reservation. They do not understand the deep hatred between the Modoc and the Klamath tribes. All I can do is warn the Army. But I fear there will be war." Then she turned to Maria. "What do you think, Miss McDougall?"

"M-my father tells me if the white men would abide by their treaties, the Indians would treat them fairly. He thinks most of the problems are because the settlers are greedy."

Mrs. Riddle nodded. "Your father is a wise man."

"Yet he has benefited from the development of Oregon and California," Maria blurted. "He was a miner in California, and now he owns a farm and timberland in Oregon. He has invested in steamships and railroads. How does his business fit with what the tribes have experienced?"

"There should be room for all," Mrs. Riddle said, echoing what Papa had said. "But white men take more than they need, which leads to trouble. Native peoples—regardless of tribe—take only what they need for survival."

Maria nodded, but she wondered—had Papa taken more than he needed? Their family was rich by most standards. Yet other families in Portland had more ostentatious houses, fancier carriages, and more lavish trappings of wealth. How much was too much?

She said softly, "I have Indian blood, Mrs. Riddle. I am adopted, but my mother was part Indian. I do not know which tribe, nor where in California she lived."

Mrs. Riddle studied her. "I noticed your dark hair and eyes," she said. "You are a lovely young woman by any people's standards."

Maria blushed.

"Do not be ashamed of your heritage," Mrs. Riddle said.

Maria nodded. What would Mrs. Riddle think if she knew Maria's mother had been a prostitute? Maria was ashamed of her mother, though she was beginning to understand her Indian blood came from people with long and admirable traditions.

Maria returned home after the meal with Mrs. Riddle, eager to talk to Papa about the meeting. Instead, he wanted her to review his ledgers again. It was almost supper before she could tell him about the luncheon.

"I met Winema Riddle today," she began. "She advocates for her tribe with the Army."

"What tribe is she?" Papa asked.

Maria explained about the Modocs and their long dispute with the Klamaths.

Papa nodded somberly. "I fear those tribes cannot live together peaceably. The Army sets aside more and more land for settlers and the railroads. That pushes the native populations into smaller and smaller sections of the state. And enemies like the Modoc and Klamath are forced to live together."

"What can be done to help them, Papa?" Maria asked.

He shook his head. "Whites make more productive use of the land than the natives. They deserve a sizable portion of it. To take their proper share of it, the Indians will need an education. Some attend white schools and adopt white standards. But others insist on sticking to their old ways of life. There should be some room for that. But each side must accommodate the other, and there are men in both groups who refuse all accommodations."

Maria sat silently. What accommodation was possible between two cultures that were so different? "And what about the disputes between the tribes?" she asked.

"It would be best to leave those to the tribes to resolve," Papa said. "However, if the Army forces the two tribes to occupy the same land, the Army will have to manage their arguments. Unfortunately, soldiers are not trained to be mediators. They are used to resolving disputes by force. The Indian agents are in a better position to mediate the tribes' differences, but many of them are political appointees and know little about Indian culture."

"Mrs. Riddle seemed to like the current agent, a Mr. Odeneal," Maria said.

Papa shrugged. "Then let's hope he can handle the festering chaos on the Klamath Reservation."

Maria spent all day Thursday drafting an article describing Winema Riddle's visit for Mrs. Duniway. But Friday was Mama's birthday, so Maria and Mrs. O'Malley also had to plan a supper and birthday celebration for Friday evening.

Maria turned in the article to Mrs. Duniway on Friday morning, then hurried home in early afternoon to finish the birthday preparations. She cajoled Papa into joining them in the dining room for dinner—his first meal with the family since his injury.

Nate wheeled Papa to the table, and Papa lasted through the meal. But his lips were white by the end, and he gestured for Nate to take him back to the library as soon as the cake had been served.

"I'm sorry, Mama," Maria murmured to her mother as the other children enjoyed their dessert. "Next year, perhaps you'll have more to celebrate."

"I'm happy enough," Mama said. "Mac is healing, though slowly. And Will is on his way home."

Chapter 12: Will Leaves Boston

Will spent the next week discussing his work with Uncle Owen and the clerk who would take over the files. And he spent every evening sorting through his belongings at Grandmother McDougall's house—deciding what to bring on the train, what to ship to Oregon, and what to leave behind.

"I wish you'd wait, Will," Grandmother told him on Monday, September 30, the day before his departure. "Why can't you stay through the winter? Your father is healing, is he not?"

"I think so," Will said. Mama's last telegram reported Pa was improving but still could not walk. Will had wired Mama he would leave Boston on October 1, and he wouldn't break his promise to her. "But Mama expects me soon."

When he mentioned Mama, Grandmother frowned. But she refrained from her usual comments about his mother's lack of Yankee pedigree. In a plaintive tone, she asked, "Are you sure you should take the train?"

"It's far faster than sailing," Will said. "The Transcontinental Railroad has cut travel across the nation to mere days."

"But trains are so loud and dirty."

"I prefer the soot to the mosquito-infested Isthmus," Will said. "I traveled by ship to get here, and I have no desire to repeat the experience if I don't have to."

"Then you leave tomorrow for Chicago." Grandmother said "Chicago" as if it were the gates of Hades.

"Yes," Will said. "I have a sleeper car booked for the first night, so I'll be comfortable at least to start with. I don't know what accommodations are available in the West."

That evening, before retiring for the last time in Grandmother's house, Will took out a new notebook. He planned to keep a journal of his travels, like Mama and Pa had on their wagon train trip.

September 30, 1872. Leaving tomorrow. What will I see along the way? And what will I think when I see my family in Oregon?

Maria, he thought, but did not write. What would he think when he saw Maria?

Before dawn the next morning, Will oversaw the loading of his trunk and smaller bags on Grandmother McDougall's carriage. Her cook had provided him with food to last him until he reached Chicago.

To his surprise, Grandmother came downstairs to see him off. When the luggage was loaded, he turned to her. "Thank you for opening your home to me for the past three years."

"Nonsense, dear boy," she said, patting his cheek. "That's what family does."

Will bit his lip. Family—if she only knew. "Yes, Grandmother," he said. He leaned over to embrace her—the first time in seven years she permitted the familiarity.

She clung to him briefly, then said, "Write when you arrive in Oregon. And tell me the truth about how your father fares."

"Yes, Grandmother," Will promised. He kissed her cheek, climbed into the carriage, and signaled the driver to leave. With a crack of the whip, the horses were off.

At the station, Will supervised the unloading of his luggage and settled into his first-class car. Soon, the train steamed along, and Will gazed at the Massachusetts towns and farms racing past him. Would he ever return to the East? He'd enjoyed his years in Boston, though at first it seemed so strange. The changes he'd encountered at Harvard and then working for his uncle caused him to grow up fast.

Before coming to Boston, Will had only been away from his family once. He and his friend Jonah Pershing had run away and joined a militia unit. But Will had had Jonah and Jonah's older brother with him. He'd never been entirely alone until he enrolled at Harvard.

Grandmother McDougall and the rest of the McDougall clan had been strangers to Will when he arrived in Boston. She was opinionated and set in her ways, and there was so much Will couldn't tell her. Starting with the fact that he was not Pa's son by blood. Will was conceived when Mama had been raped by three men. Pa rescued her by bringing her to Oregon. Few knew that story, and Will never told anyone in Boston.

Throughout the day, as he watched Massachusetts pass by, Will ate from his basket of food when he was hungry. Toward evening, when the train reached Albany, New York, he changed from the Boston & Albany line to the New York Central, where he boarded a Pullman car for the overnight trip to Buffalo.

Once settled, Will lit an oil lamp and jotted down a few impressions of what he'd seen that day in his journal. But soon he was ready to bed down. The porter created a bunk from the chairs in his car, and after Will drank a nightcap from the flask in his basket, he slept. His first day of travel was over.

The porter interrupted Will's sleep before dawn the next morning, bringing him a steaming bowl of water and towels. Will washed and ate again, finishing just in time to change trains in Buffalo, where he boarded another first-class car on the Lake Shore line to Chicago.

When he settled in his new compartment, he tried to read, but the view out the windows was more interesting. He watched a blur of fields busy with harvest activity pass by his car. The wheels clicked and clacked, interrupted by stops at various stations. Occasionally, he saw the rear cars far behind him when the train rounded curves in the tracks.

Will ate the last of Grandmother's provisions, then tried to nap. But without the bunk made up, he couldn't get comfortable. He resolved to hire a sleeper berth whenever he could on this trip.

Finally, the train rounded the southern end of Lake Michigan—or so the porter said. Will stared at the enormous lake, which appeared as large as the ocean. And he marveled he had traveled almost a thousand miles in the course of two days.

Will thought again of Pa's diary of his trip on the Oregon Trail. Pa had taken the train part of the way in 1847, but switched to steamboats in Ohio, then traveled by boat to Independence, Missouri. He'd stopped only once—

when he traveled by horseback through Mama's hometown of Arrow Rock, Missouri. That's where Pa met Mama, already pregnant with Will. Pa killed one man who might have fathered Will. Another died in Oregon in 1864— hung for murder. And the third—Mama's stepfather—died of illness sometime while Will was at Harvard.

Mama's birthday was later this week, Will realized—October 4. He made a quick calculation in his head. She would turn forty. He would look for a gift for her in Chicago—if not for her birthday, then for Christmas.

Chapter 13: Beyond Chicago

Will disembarked in Chicago with all his baggage. It was after dark, but travelers still roamed the station, most looking as dazed and confused as Will felt. He needed to transfer to another train bound for Omaha. Omaha, on the western bank of the Missouri River, marked the start of the true Transcontinental Railroad. From there, he would head to California.

Will entrusted his luggage to a porter and went to the window to purchase a ticket to Omaha. A big board showed the train schedule from Chicago to points in all directions—back East, west to Minneapolis and then Omaha, and south to St. Louis and other points in Missouri.

Missouri. That's where Mama was from. Her family still lived in Arrow Rock. On a whim, Will asked the agent how to get to Arrow Rock.

"Arrow Rock? Ain't no station there. It's a river town, train don't go there. I can only get you to St. Louis."

"How do I get from St. Louis to Arrow Rock?"

The agent shrugged. "Have to ask the agent in St. Louis." He looked past Will at the line of travelers waiting for tickets. "You wanna go to St. Louis or somewhere else?"

"How do I return to the Transcontinental line if I go to St. Louis?"

The agent huffed impatiently. "St. Louis to Kansas City, then to Denver and Cheyenne is the fastest. Takes a couple of days longer'n goin' to Omaha from here. But that route'll get you there."

"All right," Will said. "I'll take a ticket to St. Louis."

The man took Will's money. "Train leaves at dawn for St. Louis. You can get a hotel room or sit in the station until morning."

His decision made, Will arranged for the porter to load his trunk onto the train to St. Louis the next morning. "Is there a hotel nearby?" he asked the man.

"Most of the better hotels burned in last year's fire," the porter replied. "Little Sherman House has reopened at Madison and Clinton. It's about a mile's walk or take a carriage."

Will tipped the man, then took a small valise and set out to find a room. After the cramped train ride, he wanted to stretch his legs. As he walked, he saw the ravages of a fire that had swept through Chicago the year before. New construction was only beginning to replace burned buildings.

He strode along the boardwalk, browsing in the windows of the few shops that were still open. A display in one window of small pillboxes and *etuis* caught his eye. Mama always had a sewing basket at hand. She surely kept it well stocked, but the little sewing cases were attractive. One *etui* was brass, with a lapis stone on the front. Lapis blue was Mama's favorite color. Will entered and picked up the lapis *etui*. The cool brass fit neatly in his hand. Perfect for Mama.

Another *etui* sat next to the one he fancied for Mama, this one with a small red stone that made him think of Maria. He'd always thought she was prettiest dressed in red, the bright color contrasting with her dark eyes and hair. He could give both Mama and Maria the *etuis* for Christmas.

He purchased them both and put them in his pocket.

The Little Sherman was small, but adequate. He registered, then arranged to have bath water delivered to his room before dinner. Grandmother McDougall was right—train travel was dirty.

Later, after a long soak in the tub, Will savored steak and fresh vegetables at the Little Sherman. He finished his meal with apple pie and cheese, then sipped an aged single-malt Scotch as smooth as anything Pa ever bought.

Nursing his Scotch, Will had second thoughts about detouring to Arrow Rock. His years with Grandmother McDougall had taught him relatives were not always a comfort. Would meeting Mama's mother—his blood relation— be any easier?

And there was her son Jacques to meet as well. Mama's mother had given birth to a child with her second husband shortly before Will was born. That boy—a man now—was Will's half-uncle. And perhaps his half-brother—Mama's stepfather had been one of her rapists.

His glass empty, Will paid his bill and returned to his hotel room, where he pulled out his journal:

October 3, 1872. At the Little Sherman in Chicago. Headed to St. Louis tomorrow, then I'll try to find my way to Arrow Rock. Will I learn about the past or only stir up trouble?

Will spent a short restless night, then struggled to rouse himself before dawn. Bleary-eyed, he returned to the train station and boarded the train for St. Louis, still wondering whether his detour was a mistake. Maybe he should have wired Mama to ask before he made his plans.

He stared out the window as the train chugged along the eastern bank of the Mississippi River. The tracks crossed the river over the Rock Island Bridge, the first bridge to span the Mississippi. The train chugged over the narrow channel between Illinois and Rock Island, rolled across the island, then clicked and clacked over the wider river channel to Iowa. Will peered at the swirling current below as the train swayed above the river. Though the bridge had endured for fifteen years, the thought of it collapsing quickened his pulse.

Around midafternoon, the train steamed into St. Louis. After another inquiry with another station agent, Will learned he could take a train to Sedalia, Missouri, the closest stop to Arrow Rock. That line continued to Kansas City.

"How do I get from Sedalia to Arrow Rock?" he asked.

"Stagecoach, maybe, if it suits your schedule. You'll get to Sedalia about supper time, so you'll probably need to spend the night there."

Will hesitated.

"Or do you ride?" the man asked. "You could rent a horse. Think it's about four or five hours on horseback. Then you ride back to Sedalia and get on the next train to Kansas City."

"And my trunk?"

"Take it with you, or send it ahead to Kansas City now."

When Will still hesitated, the man asked, "Train to Sedalia leaves in fifteen minutes. Do you want a ticket?"

It was his last chance to back out of the detour to Arrow Rock. But Will said, "All right. I'll go to Sedalia. Send my trunk to Kansas City."

On the train through Missouri farm country, Will stared out the window, wondering how far beyond the horizon Arrow Rock was. His stomach churned at the thought of meeting Mama's relatives, but he was committed now to the attempt.

October 4, 1872. Mama's birthday. I worry I have made an unwise decision to travel to Arrow Rock. Mama rarely speaks about her mother, and they only correspond a few times a year.

But Mama's mother and her son were Will's only blood relatives, other than his family in Oregon. He resolved to meet them and decide for himself whether to stay in contact.

The train passed through fields of wheat, corn, and a plant Will didn't recognize. "What is that?" he asked a fellow passenger.

"Hemp," he was told. "Makes ropes and rough clothing."

Will had seen hemp ropes on ships, but he'd never seen it growing in a field.

"Sedalia," the porter called out around midday.

Will pressed his face to the window. A bustling country town came into view. When he disembarked, he saw farm wagons, drays loaded with commercial goods, carriages, and men on horseback, all vying for space in the muddy streets.

"Where can I find a room and a livery?" he asked the porter.

"Ives Hotel is right here at the depot," the man replied. "And the hotel clerk can point you to a livery."

Will booked a room, then arranged to rent a horse early the next day at a livery a block away.

The next morning at dawn, Will ate, then returned to the livery. The horse the stable hand gave him was a decent riding mare. She would carry him well, and he strapped his valise and a meal he'd purchased from the hotel behind the saddle.

After questioning the stable hand about the best route, Will set off. It was a fine early October morning. Farmers along the way harvested their crops, and he passed a few wagons loaded with hay bales and shucked corn. Otherwise, the route was quiet.

He and the mare got to know each other. She proved a docile companion and seemed happy to be out of the stable. Soon, he began a conversation with her. "I don't know if I should be doing this," he told her. "I'm off to meet a grandmother who treated her daughter abysmally."

The mare tossed her head and whinnied.

"That's how I feel," Will said. "But I want to know who I come from. I know so little." He sighed. "I have been well raised by my parents, but I often feel alone in the world. And I'm never sure if my father trusts me. Does he see my villainous sire, or does he see me?"

The mare did not respond.

"You probably know more about your antecedents than I do," Will concluded. "Though perhaps you care less."

Then Will thought about Pa. He'd also stopped in Arrow Rock on horseback, mounted on an Andalusian stallion he'd brought from Boston. "Pa's life changed in Arrow Rock," Will told the mare. "Will mine?"

About midday, a sign along the road proclaimed "Arrow Rock 2 miles". He ate his lunch under a shady tree, then rode on until a small country town came into view, a town far smaller than Oregon City, a town with only a few streets. A fire had hit Arrow Rock recently—charred buildings rose from burned foundations, and much of the ashy debris remained. For the first time, Will worried whether the Petersons still lived in Arrow Rock.

"How long ago was the fire?" he asked a man walking along the main street.

"August," the man replied. "Burned half the town. Tavern's still standing, though. You can get a bed there and a decent meal."

When the man mentioned the tavern, Will remembered Mama's stepfather had owned it at one time. She'd been assaulted there, and he loathed the idea of entering the building. But someone in the tavern would likely know where the Petersons lived.

Chapter 14: Another Grandmother

Will rode toward the tavern at the east end of the main street. It was a two-story brick building. After bracing himself for what he might encounter, he doffed his hat and went inside. "Do you know where I can find Hortense and Jacques Peterson?"

The man at the reception desk gestured toward the back room. "That's Jack in the black vest." A man about Will's age, but shorter and heavier, sat with other men, each with a tankard of ale.

Will approached. "Jacques Peterson?"

One of Jacques's companions guffawed, nudging Jacques. "So, it's Jock now, is it?"

"Who wants to know?" Jacques asked.

"I'm Will McDougall."

With a screech, the man's chair scraped on the wood floor as he shot to his feet. "McDougall? What're you doin' here?"

"I'd like a word, if you have a moment," Will said.

Jacques grabbed his tankard and told his companions, "Next time." He gestured to an unoccupied table in the corner, signaling the waiter to bring another ale for Will.

When they were seated, Jacques said, "I go by Jack." Then he was quiet, waiting for Will to speak.

Will sipped his ale and scrutinized Jack, seeking some resemblance to himself. If they looked alike, would it be because Jack was Mama's half-brother, or did Jack and Will also share a father's blood? The ale churned in Will's stomach.

"I'm traveling from the East to Oregon," Will began. "I wanted to meet you and your mother."

Jack eyed Will over his tankard. "Why now?"

Will shrugged. "This is the first trip I've taken west in seven years. My first opportunity to meet you."

"What good'll it do you to see my ma?" Jack's tone was as flat as his expression.

Unable to tell if Jack was hostile or merely reserved, Will frowned and said, "She's my grandmother."

"Your ma ain't never seen fit to come back to Missouri. She ran away and left us high and dry."

"Maybe she had good reason." Will didn't know what Jack knew, and he wasn't about to tell the man they might be half-brothers. Jack must have been told Mama left Missouri in a hurry, and that was enough to cause his resentment.

The two men stared at each other. Finally, Jack said, "Ma's at home. You got a horse?"

"Yes," Will said. "Will you take me to your farm?"

Jack stood, threw a few coins on the table, and motioned for Will to follow him. Outside, Will mounted his mare, while Jack mounted a stunted gelding, then Will followed Jack down a dusty road.

Jack was silent, so Will focused on the land along the road. Corn stubble dotted some fields, others bore crops still waiting to be harvested. Some farmhouses looked well-maintained, others had sagging shutters and overgrown lawns.

After about half an hour, Jack turned up a narrow drive. A two-storied brick house came into view, its sagging porch spanning the entire front of the structure on both levels. Vines clung to one wall, their tendrils eating into crumbling mortar.

"Is that your home?" Will asked. "Where my mother grew up?"

Jack grunted an affirmation.

The stable looked worse than the house, its yard cluttered with debris. As they dismounted, Jack instructed a Negro man to take their horses.

Jack led Will toward the back of the house. They entered through a kitchen, where Jack dumped his hat. An ancient Negress stirred a pot on the stove. She nodded at Jack, then her eyes widened when Will caught her gaze.

"*Mon Dieu!*" she said, crossing herself.

Jack passed into the hall, where he told Will, "Leave your bag here. We'll see to it later."

Will didn't know whether that meant he would stay the night or be sent back to town. Maybe Jack didn't know either.

Jack led him into a front parlor. "Someone's come to see you, Mama," he announced. "Will McDougall."

Will heard his grandmother gasp before he saw her. When he entered the parlor, he saw a short, stout woman dressed in the pre-War style. White curls escaped the cap on her head. She couldn't be over sixty, but she seemed ancient.

"William?" Her voice trembled. "William Calhoun McDougall? My Geneviève's William?"

"Yes, ma'am," he said, bowing to her. "I'm Will."

"My dear boy," she murmured. "I never dreamed I'd see your face. My oldest grandson." She patted the cushion beside her. "Please, sit with me."

Will perched on the edge of the settee. "I'm honored to meet you, Grandmother."

"*Grandmère*," she said. "You must call me Grandmère. Do you speak French?"

"A little."

She scrutinized his face. "You are the spitting image of my dear first husband, my William."

"That's what Mama tells me."

"He was so handsome," Grandmère said. "Such a sorrow to me when he died."

Grandmère launched into a torrent of French. Will only caught fragments, enough to get the gist of what she said. Something about Mama abandoning Grandmère in her grief, Mama writing so seldom, never bringing her children to meet their grandmother, and leaving Grandmère alone in Missouri.

As the old woman spoke, Jack's face stiffened. It seemed Grandmère Peterson was as self-centered as Grandmother McDougall, neither woman caring how their words affected those around them. Jack must surely resent Grandmère's dismissal of her second husband, Jack's father. Why had she married the man—a brute who raped his stepdaughter?

"Tell me," Grandmère said, switching to English as she patted Will's hand. "How long can you stay with me?"

"Only this afternoon, I'm afraid," he said. "I am on my way home to Oregon. My father is injured, and I must return to look after him."

"Pfft, your father," Grandmère said. "Surely, he would not begrudge me more time with my grandson. You remind me so of my dear William."

"I promised Mama—"

"Pfft, your mother," Grandmère said. "She has had you all these years, never a visit to her own mother. You owe me—"

Will became more resolute. "I'm sorry, Grandmère. I must leave tomorrow."

"Jacques," she said, turning to her son. "Have Letitia prepare our best room for my grandson. He will stay the night."

Jack muttered something under his breath and left the room.

A short time later, the old black woman Will had seen in the kitchen entered the parlor and curtsied. "The room be ready, ma'am," she said to Grandmère.

His grandmother waved a hand. "Show him upstairs, Letitia."

The old Negress nodded at Will, and he followed her. She picked up his valise, but Will took it from her. "I'll carry it." She smiled, then led him up the stairs.

When they reached the doorway of a bedroom and Will started to enter, Letitia stopped him with a hand on his arm. "You be William?" she asked.

"Yes, ma'am. William McDougall."

"You be 'bout twenty-five years old?"

"Yes. Next week, in fact." Surprised, Will wondered what else she knew.

Her face softened, and she asked gently, "Your mama, she was carryin' you when she left Missouri?"

Will nodded slowly.

"Your *père*, your father, the man she married—he's a good man?"

"Yes, ma'am," Will said. "He is."

Her smile widened. "You tell Mam'selle Geneviève, old Letitia glad for her. Glad she found joy. She ain't deserved the evil what happened after her *père* died. Old Massa Calhoun, he be a good man. You's named after him."

"Yes, ma'am. So my mother told me."

"You looks like him, too." Letitia squeezed his arm. "You tell your mama I's proud of her. She didn't let the evil win."

Will swallowed, his throat suddenly tight. "I will, ma'am. I'll tell her

Letitia remembers her fondly."

After washing up and changing his shirt, Will returned downstairs. He entered the parlor to find Grandmère and Jack waiting. "Dinner is ready," Grandmère said. "Please, William." She took his arm, and he escorted her to the dining room across the hall.

Will seated his grandmother, then took the chair she indicated on her right. Jack settled stiffly on her left.

Letitia brought in the soup. She was the only house servant Will had seen. When she left the room, he asked, "How long has Letitia worked for you?"

Grandmère laughed. "When has Letitia not worked for my family? She was born a slave in my father's household in Louisiana—my nurse first, and then my maid. He gave her to me when I married. She was freed, of course, during the War, but where would she go? She must be close to ninety now."

Will gritted his teeth. The matter-of-fact tone in which his grandmother spoke of owning another human being rankled. Both Mama and Pa abhorred slavery and taught Will to do the same, though many in Oregon had supported the South during the War Between the States. He hadn't realized Mama's family had been slaveholders, though since they came from Louisiana, he shouldn't have been surprised.

Jack asked Will about his father's business, which led to a discussion about the McDougall & Company enterprises in Oregon, California, and Boston. Jack's eyes grew wide as Will described the family's investments in warehouses, steamboats, railroads, office buildings, and banks.

Grandmère watched Will closely, her gaze calculating. "Then your father is wealthy?" she interrupted.

"His businesses provide well for our family," Will said. "He works hard and expects the same from his employees."

"Perhaps Jack and I should accompany you west," Grandmère said.

Jack frowned. "I have no interest in Oregon, Mama. Our farm is adequate."

"The house is falling down around our ears," Grandmère said. "The fields produce less and less each year. We no longer have slaves to work the land, and the men we hire are lazy and demand high wages. Why not see what my daughter Geneviève can do for us?"

Will squirmed in the face of Grandmère's overt greed. He did not want them to travel to Oregon with him.

"What do you think, William?" she asked. "Would my daughter welcome our arrival?"

Put on the spot, he said, "Perhaps it would be better to wire ahead. Let Mama know your plans, so she can welcome you appropriately. I have not seen their house in Portland, so I cannot vouch for its accommodations."

"Surely, Geneviève would have room for her mother," Grandmère said.

"No doubt," Will said. "But unfortunately, I must stop in Sacramento and San Francisco on business before I travel north. I would not want to lengthen your travels."

"We should discuss it further, Mama," Jack said. "It's harvest season, and I can't leave now. Perhaps in the spring after planting."

When Will retired to his room, he took out his journal and wrote:

October 5, 1872. I'm glad Pa took Mama away from Arrow Rock. Her life here would have been miserable, catering to Grandmère's selfishness, let alone being at the mercy of her stepfather. I pity my half-uncle Jack, stuck in a shambling farmhouse with Grandmère.

Not only had Pa saved Mama from this fate, he'd saved Will as well. Will wondered what would have happened to him had Mama stayed in Missouri.

Will tossed and turned through the night. The old farmhouse felt dank and his bed lumpy. He'd bid Grandmère farewell before bed, planning to leave for Sedalia before breakfast. At dawn, he arose, packed his valise, and went to the stable to saddle his rented mare.

The old black man staggered out from a back room. "Shoulda tol' me last night you'd be wantin' the horse early," he grumbled.

"I can saddle her myself," Will said. "I don't want to be a bother."

Between the two of them, they readied the mare, then Will rode to Sedalia. When he arrived, he returned the mare to the livery and strode to the station to await the train to Kansas City.

Chapter 15: Lunch with Mr. Higgins

On Monday, October 7, Mrs. Duniway summoned Maria to her office and handed back the draft of her article about Winema Riddle. It was covered with corrections in a bold script. "Let's discuss your writing," she said. "You must learn to lead with your most important facts."

"But I need to describe Mrs. Riddle's background to explain why she has such strong positions," Maria said.

"Perhaps. But a newspaper editor will often need to cut your drafts to fit," Mrs. Duniway explained. "If you put the salient information first, the editor's job is easier, and your work is more likely to be accepted. Now, rewrite this, and I want another look."

"Will you publish it then?" Maria asked.

Mrs. Duniway shook her head. "We will not print a paper this week because I am leaving for the state fair in Salem tomorrow. By the date of our next issue, your piece will be old news. Still, you must learn to rewrite your own work. That is how you learn to write correctly the first time." She smiled. "And I'll be more likely to publish your next piece."

Maria sighed as she left the editor's office.

"Why the glum face?" Daisy asked.

Most days, Maria and Daisy chattered cheerfully as they worked. Daisy's family needed every penny she earned at *The New Northwest*. But though their circumstances were different, the two young women had become friends, and Maria was frank about her disappointment. "Mrs. Duniway wants me to rewrite my article, but she won't publish it."

Daisy shrugged. "At least she takes an interest in you. She views me as a charity project. She only gave me a job because my ma needs my wages."

Maria spent the afternoon at her task. She started with Mrs. Riddle's warning that war between the tribes was likely, then wrote about Mrs. Riddle's background as the Modoc wife of a white settler. She stayed late to finish—maybe Mrs. Duniway would change her mind about publishing it. At the end of the day, she took her rewritten draft back to Mrs. Duniway.

"Leave it on my desk," the editor said. "I'll look at it when I return from Salem."

Maria's heart sank—Mrs. Duniway would not change her mind. "Thank you," she said, swallowing her frustration.

On Wednesday, as Maria left for work, Papa handed her a packet of letters. "Please deliver these to Amos Higgins on your way to the newspaper," he requested. "He'll know what to do with them."

"I could write your responses when I get home this afternoon," Maria offered.

Papa shook his head. "Higgins knows these customers. He can manage."

"Yes, Papa." Papa didn't want her help any more than Mrs. Duniway did.

At the McDougall & Company building, she asked for Mr. Higgins, who greeted her with a warm smile and a slight bow. "Good morning, Miss McDougall. How can I help you?"

"My father would like you to respond to this correspondence."

"Of course." Mr. Higgins hesitated. "Might I invite you to tea this afternoon, Miss McDougall?"

It was Maria's turn to hesitate. Should she have tea with him?

Before she could answer, he added, "I might have documents for you to take to your father."

She nodded. "All right. I am usually done at the paper shortly after noon."

His smile widened. "Well, then. Perhaps we could make it a meal. Shall I meet you at the St. Charles Hotel next door to *The Oregonian* at half past twelve?"

"That would be fine, Mr. Higgins." Maria inclined her head, then left. Another meal at the St. Charles. She was becoming a businesswoman indeed.

After Maria finished yet another tedious morning, with no one else in the office except Daisy, she walked to the hotel next door. Amos Higgins waited in the lobby, carrying a small packet of papers tied with string.

Mr. Higgins bowed. "Miss McDougall."

She nodded. "Mr. Higgins."

"Shall we be seated?" He led her to the restaurant, then helped her into her chair.

They ordered their meal, then Mr. Higgins handed her the papers he'd brought. "These are for your father. But they need not interrupt our lunch. He will understand my notes easily enough."

Maria tucked the packet in her reticule. "Thank you."

Mr. Higgins asked her about the newspaper, seeming interested in her responses. He asked about her family and chuckled when she recounted Andrew's latest antics. "At eight," he said, "I was quite the rapscallion. I believe it comes with the age."

"Do you have brothers and sisters, Mr. Higgins?" Maria asked.

"Alas, no," he said.

"And your parents?"

He shook his head. "Both died when I was young. I have been on my own since boyhood."

Maria felt sorry for him. Her family might annoy her sometimes, but she loved them all dearly. She would not want to be alone in this world. Out of sympathy, she asked, "Would you care to come to supper with our family some night, Mr. Higgins?"

He smiled. "Perhaps the invitation should come from your parents. I would hate to presume."

Maria sat up straighter. "My friends are always welcome in my parents' home."

"I am glad to be considered your friend," Mr. Higgins said. "But, as your father's employee, I think it best if I defer to his wishes."

"Papa is always kind to his employees," Maria said. "But I shall ask him. I do not want to make either of you uncomfortable."

As their meal concluded, Mr. Higgins rose and bowed again. "And now, might I escort you home?"

"Thank you," Maria said. "But there is no need." She stood. "I have taken more than enough time from your workday."

As Maria and Mr. Higgins exited the hotel, a voice from across the street called, "Maria!" Maria turned to see her sister Eliza rushing over to them.

"Mama wondered where you were." Then Eliza turned to Mr. Higgins with a coy smile. "Good day, Mr. Higgins."

"Mr. Higgins had papers for me to bring to Papa," Maria said. "He was kind enough to offer me lunch."

"I see." Eliza's smile broadened. "I've been shopping downtown, but I'm on my way home. Are you coming, Maria?"

"Of course." Maria turned to Mr. Higgins. "Thank you for the meal," she said, dipping a slight curtsey.

"The honor was mine, Miss McDougall." He bowed, then turned to Eliza and bowed again. "Good day, Miss Eliza?"

Eliza giggled. "And to you, Mr. Higgins."

He tipped his hat, then said, "I will leave you ladies here. Good day."

As he departed, Eliza linked her arm with Maria's and whispered, "How ever did you get him to buy you lunch?"

"He offered." Maria would have to tell Mama or Papa about the lunch as soon as she reached home, or Eliza would spin an elaborate tale about finding them outside the hotel. "As he said—he had papers for Papa."

Eliza skipped as they walked—not behavior fitting a young lady of almost seventeen. "He is so handsome, isn't he? Though a tad old for you."

"I suppose he is handsome enough." Maria really hadn't noticed. Mr. Higgins's coloring was almost as dark as her own, and she'd always preferred men with lighter hair. Like Will.

"How old is he, anyway?" Eliza asked.

"I don't know," Maria said. "Perhaps you could ask Papa."

As soon as Maria and Eliza got home, Maria went straight to Papa's library. "May I come in?" she asked as she knocked on the door.

At his shout, she opened the door and gave Papa the bundle of papers. "Mr. Higgins sent these letters home with me."

"Higgins?" Papa said absent-mindedly as he shuffled through the documents. "Today's correspondence. I wonder why he didn't bring them himself."

"He invited me to lunch," Maria said. "I thought it polite to accept. I wanted to save him the trouble of coming here."

"Lunch?" Papa peered at her over the papers. "You had lunch with Higgins?"

"Yes, Papa."

"I suppose there's no harm in him," Papa said. "Be sure to tell your mother."

"I will." She took a breath, then said. "Papa, I'd like to understand how your business fits with what Will has done in Boston."

Papa leaned back in his seat. "That's complicated, pet."

"But I want to know," she said.

"Very well, I'll tell you the basics," Papa said. "You know I left Boston and the family business behind when I came to Oregon."

"Yes, and you didn't contact them for years," Maria said. Though she didn't know the cause of the estrangement.

"But then, when I took Will to Harvard," Papa said, "I reconciled with my brother Owen, and we discussed how we might work together."

"I thought the Boston business was mostly banking."

"My father started in banking," Papa said. "But Owen later wanted to invest in businesses and real estate in the East. I understood how trade worked on the West Coast, so I told Owen what I knew. We agreed we could support each other financially when it made sense. We've referred customers to each other over the years, and we agreed we would both use the name McDougall & Company to bolster our connection."

Maria wrinkled her brow. "But how does that work? The distance between Boston and the West is so great. How do you work together?"

"With the improvements in communications—the telegraph, faster steamships, and now the transcontinental railroad—it is easier," Papa said. "We share funds when one of us can help the other. Sometimes we actually move gold, but usually we send each other commercial paper—like bank drafts, only private. And, of course, Owen's bank can issue drafts as well."

"And other people recognize these papers?" Maria asked. "Aren't they taking a risk that the papers are false?"

"Of course," Papa said. "That's why bank drafts are typically sold at a discount." He grinned. "Owen and I agreed not to discount each other's drafts. So, we save a bit there."

"Has Uncle Owen expanded the Boston business as he planned?"

Papa shrugged. "More or less. He invested in real estate in Boston, but he only dabbles in mercantile. Whereas, here on the West Coast, I own warehouses in California. I keep them stocked with grains and hides from the West and with silks and other goods from Asia. Most of my goods I sell to stores in California and Oregon, though I send an occasional shipload to

Owen."

"You don't have any warehouses in Oregon, do you?"

"Just one in Portland," Papa said, grimacing as he shifted his weight in his chair. "Most of the warehouse business is in California. In Oregon, I mostly finance farmers and small stores in Oregon City. I've also invested in steamboats, and I've supported some rail operations, too. But rail is slow to take off in Oregon. The terrain is mountainous, and river travel is easier."

"All of this has made you wealthy, hasn't it?"

"We are comfortable, Maria. And God help me, I intend to keep us so. I will never be a commercial baron like some men in Portland. But my business is profitable. I manage my risks for the security of our family, and I help my neighbors when I can. Friendship and peace of mind are more important to me than accumulating wealth."

Chapter 16: Dinner with Mr. Higgins

Maria hurried to Mama's morning room right after her talk with Papa, but Eliza had already spread the news. "I hear you lunched with Mr. Higgins," Mama said, her needle gliding through the hem of Evie's pinafore.

"Yes, Mama. He had papers for me to deliver to Papa."

"Hmm."

"He was very polite," Maria said. "I felt sorry for him—he's alone in the world, orphaned, with no brothers or sisters."

"I see."

"I invited him here for supper some evening," Maria ended in a rush. "Would that be all right?"

"Did you ask your father what he thinks of Mr. Higgins?" Mama asked.

"He said to talk to you. I didn't mention supper."

"I'll talk to Mac," Mama said. "If he approves, I'll issue the invitation myself."

"Thank you, Mama." Maria exhaled, relieved to put the matter in Mama's hands.

"Now," Mama said, "what shall we do for Eliza's birthday next week?"

Maria thought for a moment. "She thinks she is all grown up now, turning seventeen."

"Yes." Mama sighed. "Though her friends are flighty as sparrows. And we're trying to keep the house quiet for your father, so I hate to propose a musicale or dance here."

"What about a concert or theatrical downtown?" Maria suggested. "Just you and Eliza. It would be nicer if Papa could go, but he isn't ready to leave the house." It had only been four weeks since Papa's accident. He could now sit in a wheeled chair for short periods, and he usually joined the family for meals. But otherwise, he stayed in his library.

Mama chuckled. "I could dragoon Nate into escorting us."

"Poor Nate," Maria said with a giggle. "He would hate it."

"Well, maybe there is a theatrical he would enjoy." Mama sighed. "The New Market Theater opened recently. It's too bad Will isn't home already. He'd gladly take us."

Maria blinked, surprised. When she told Will she needed him home, she hadn't thought of him as an escort. Then she remembered dancing in his arms at gatherings in Boston. He would make a splendid escort.

Once Mama set her mind to something, she made it happen. By Friday morning, Mr. Higgins had an invitation to join the family for supper the next evening. Mama also scoured the Portland papers to see what events were occurring in town in the next few weeks. There was a performance of *Pygmalion and Galatea* scheduled for October 23, a week after Eliza's birthday. Mama purchased three tickets—for Eliza, herself, and Nate.

"You don't mind staying home?" Mama asked Maria.

Maria nodded. "Eliza would sulk if I went. She's always measuring herself against me."

Mama smiled. "She's jealous because you're older. She looks up to you and wants to do everything you do. But you're right—she would like it better if she got to do something special just for her."

Saturday evening, Mr. Higgins arrived promptly, presenting flowers to Mama as he bowed. "Thank you for your kind invitation, Mrs. McDougall." Although he addressed Mama, his eyes found Maria's. He bowed to her next. "Miss McDougall."

Mama led him into the parlor, where Nate, Eliza, and Lottie were gathered. "The younger children will relish a noisier supper in the nursery," Mama said. "Where no one will tell them to keep their elbows off the table."

After small talk, they moved to the dining room, and Nate wheeled Papa in from the library. Mr. Higgins inclined his head respectfully. "Mr. McDougall, I appreciate your hospitality. I hope my presence is not an imposition."

"Glad for the company, Higgins," Papa said. "I am a caged animal here at home, a beast too maimed even to pace my cage."

Mama seated Mr. Higgins on Papa's right and Maria on his left. Through the soup course, Papa quizzed Mr. Higgins about affairs in the Portland office. Then he asked, "And what do you hear from Sacramento? Any word of my son Will's arrival?"

"Not yet, Mr. McDougall," Mr. Higgins said. "I'm sure young Mr. McDougall will let you know as soon as he is in California."

Maria smiled, imagining Will's reaction at being described as "young Mr. McDougall." Surely, Will would demand more respect from an employee than that. Of course, Mr. Higgins had never met Will. As she listened to Papa and Mr. Higgins talk, she was impressed with Mr. Higgins's knowledge of the business. He answered any question Papa asked easily and affably.

When Mrs. O'Malley brought in the main course, Mama declared, "Enough business talk, Mac. Tell us, Mr. Higgins, have you been to the New Market Theater?"

"No," Mr. Higgins said, shaking his head. "But I hear the company is performing *Pygmalion and Galatea* next week. Perhaps I shall purchase a ticket. I've always enjoyed the tale of Pygmalion and his creation of Galatea."

"Yes," Mama said. "The play received great reviews in New York, and I hope our company does it justice."

Mama didn't mention that she, Eliza, and Nate would be attending. Instead, she led Mr. Higgins into a discussion of the mythical story. From that, they segued to the merits of Mr. Sullivan's writing. Mr. Higgins seemed very well read for an accountant, Maria thought.

After dessert, Papa began to flag, and Mama suggested coffee and tea be served in the parlor.

"Thank you, Mrs. McDougall," their guest said. "But I shall take my leave. I do not want to tire my superior." He smiled at Papa, who nodded back.

"Perhaps a whiskey in my library before you depart?" Papa offered.

Mr. Higgins wheeled Papa's chair into the library, where the men remained for a brief time. When Mr. Higgins left, he thanked Mama for the dinner, then Maria showed him out, and he bowed over her hand.

Chapter 17: Heading West

Will sighed as the train left Sedalia. He was ready to leave Mama's family behind, just as Mama had. He didn't care for Grandmère, and Jack seemed sullen and uneducated. All he wanted was to get home to his family. To check on Pa. To see Maria.

The train rolled west through more farmland. After about four hours, it reached Kansas City where he needed to change trains to reach Denver. None of these communities existed when Pa and Mama had traveled by wagon. Then, Kansas City was merely a river landing called Westport, with only a few trading posts between there and Oregon.

Will got off the train. As the clerk in St. Louis promised, his trunk awaited him. "When's the next train to Denver?" he asked.

"Leaves late this afternoon," the porter said. "Want your trunk on it?"

"Yes, please."

The agent eyed him. "You'll want a sleeping compartment."

"The train runs through the night?" Will asked.

"Yes, sir. Reaches Denver late tomorrow. Ain't much to see in the dark."

"Then, yes. A sleeping compartment." Will paid for the ticket.

"You got food? It's two nights and a day on the train. You can get off at some stops, but most folks bring their meals," the man said. "And you can eat here afore you leave."

Will's stomach growled. "Where's the best restaurant?"

"Pacific House," the man said. "Fourth and Delaware. 'T'ain't far."

Will nodded his thanks and set off to find the hotel.

The agent's recommendation was a good one, and Will slaked his appetite with a large pork chop and grits, chased with a mug of cider. As he drank coffee after the meal, he pulled out his journal:

October 8, 1872. As I sit in a comfortable train and stop at fine restaurants, I think of Mama and Pa in their wagon. They had only the food they carried with them and a few pots in which to cook over an open fire.

Will bought a basket of food to take with him and returned to the station. He ensured his trunk was aboard, then settled into his compartment. The train to Denver rumbled across the Hannibal Bridge—the first bridge to cross the wide Missouri River. His parents had traveled south of the river to avoid crossing it, though other wagon trains forded or ferried the river well north of Kansas City.

That evening, Will watched a spectacular sunset streak brilliant orange and purple lines above the prairie. Off in the distance, black dots marked the prairie. He thought they must be buffalo. Once again, Will's thoughts turned to his parents' journey, and he added to his earlier entry:

My parents took months to cross the prairie that the train crosses in a day. Yet the prairie sky and buffalo must look the same. Some men hunt the beasts from trains for sport these days. But Pa taught me to kill only for food or hides.

Later, the rhythm of the wheels rocked Will to sleep. The next morning, as he ate breakfast from his basket, he saw snow-covered peaks on the far horizon. They were still many hours from Denver, but the Rocky Mountains rose above the plains, like a dark wall with brilliant white caps.

The train reached Denver on time. Again, Will found a hotel room, this time at the newly opened Everett House. The next morning, he again ordered a basket of food to take with him, then returned to the station.

As he waited in the chill autumn air on the platform, he read *Roughing It* by a man named Mark Twain. Mr. Twain's stories didn't depict the West as Will had experienced it. Of course, the author had a rollicking sense of humor, and he no doubt exaggerated. Will was glad he traveled by train and not by stagecoach, like Mr. Twain. Train travel was dirty, but it beat the cramped, bone-rattling coach trips Will had taken.

Finally, with a shrill whistle, the train to Cheyenne arrived, and Will boarded. His compartment this time was less plush and polished, but he would arrive in Cheyenne by evening. He hadn't bothered to book a private compartment and sat in a first-class car with other passengers.

Cheyenne was even smaller than Denver, little more than a stopping point on the Transcontinental Railroad. "When does the train to Sacramento depart?" Will asked the agent as soon as he disembarked in Cheyenne.

"Train's late," the man said. "Got a telegram sayin' it won't be here for another two hours. Won't leave here until tomorrow morning. And it'll only take you to Promontory. There you switch from the Central Pacific to the Union Pacific."

"I'd like to book a sleeping compartment," Will said.

The man frowned. "Most sleepers are booked in Omaha."

Will didn't want to sleep sitting up in a car with other passengers. "But I detoured through Missouri for family reasons. Surely—"

The agent shrugged. "Sorry, sir. Telegraph only tells me the arrival time. Don't say nothin' 'bout what cars are available. I can't sell you a sleeper ticket till the train pulls in."

Will's stomach sank. "And if there isn't a sleeping compartment?"

"You can buy a cheaper ticket. Then sit here in the station all night or get a room in town. Either way, you board tomorrow morning."

It was already dark. "Where can I get a room?"

"Boardinghouse a block away. But if you get a sleeping compartment, you can sleep on the train tonight. No need to pay for a room in town."

Will took a seat outside the agent's office, bracing himself for the possibility of an uncomfortable night at the station. He finished reading *Roughing It*, then had nothing to occupy his time. Another man sat nearby. Out of boredom, Will asked the man where he was from.

"Sacramento. Heading home on the next train."

"What brings you to Cheyenne?" Will asked.

"My brother was mining in these parts. He recently died of typhoid."

"I'm sorry," Will said, only then noticing the man's black armband.

"I'm taking his body back to bury in California," the man said. "Our mother wants him home."

When the train pulled into the station, both Will and the man from Sacramento rushed to the counter. "Is there a sleeper compartment?" the California man asked.

"Only one." The agent nodded at Will. "And this man was first to ask."

The California man looked crestfallen.

Feeling sorry for the man, Will said, "You can have it. You have more reason to hurry to California than I have." He looked at the agent. "When's the next train?"

"Tomorrow afternoon," the agent replied. "Unless it's late, too. It'll head west after a quick stop here."

"Do I have your word I'll get the first sleeping compartment available on that train?" Will asked.

The agent nodded.

"Then I'll go look for a bed in town for tonight," Will said.

The Sacramento man shook Will's hand and handed him a calling card. "My name is Ambrose Jones," he said. "If you need anything in Sacramento—anything at all—I will do my best to help. I got a warehouse on the American River."

"William McDougall," Will said. "My father owns warehouses in Sacramento, too."

"Not Caleb McDougall—is he your father? I was acquainted with a Caleb McDougall a long time ago."

"That's him," Will said. "I'm headed to Sacramento to meet with his agent now."

"Bayliss Beck is your agent, isn't he? I know him well," Jones said, his expression neutral. "I'll hope to see you in Sacramento."

Will's kindness earned him an uncomfortable night in the boardinghouse. He shared a room with two strangers, but at least he had a bed to himself. After the landlady's hearty breakfast, he had the day to spend alone until the train arrived. And he might have to return to the boardinghouse for another night—unless he secured a sleeping compartment.

He roamed the streets of Cheyenne, which didn't take long. In one store, he bought eagle feathers and Indian beads for his younger siblings. He checked at the train station twice, but the agent could tell him nothing until the train arrived.

He took the opportunity to send a telegram home.

DATE: 9 OCTOBER 1872
FROM: WILLIAM MCDOUGALL CHEYENNE
TO: CALEB MCDOUGALL PORTLAND
REACHED CHEYENNE HOPE TO HEAD WEST TONIGHT

He wouldn't explain his detour to Arrow Rock—that he needed to do in person. He wasn't sure how to tell his parents about the odd reception he'd received from Grandmère.

That afternoon, when the train arrived, he bought a ticket for a sleeping compartment with no problem. After seeing to his trunk, he boarded and gratefully closed the door of his compartment.

Chapter 18: On to Sacramento

The train left Cheyenne, swaying back and forth as it climbed through the hills. Will wondered if he would need to get his land legs back after disembarking, as he did after sailing. He took out his journal to describe his surroundings:

October 9, 1872. The forests are evergreen like in Oregon, and the hillsides as steep as any I saw in the Owyhee Range. How long until this vacant land is as settled as Oregon and California?

Late that evening, as Will readied himself for bed, the train stopped near Fort Laramie. He remembered that's where Pa bought Mama the little Indian mare she named Poulette. Will learned to ride on Poulette, and her colt Shanty was the first horse he thought of as his own.

When Will left for Boston, Mama still had the buffalo hide Pa bought her at Fort Laramie. For many years, it warmed her children's feet on chilly winter mornings. He wondered if the old hide still lay on the nursery floor.

The next morning passed in tedium as the train climbed upward through barren desert dotted with sagebrush. He recalled Mama telling him how she tried to season prairie hens with sage from the dry bushes, but sagebrush was not the same as sage herbs. And Pa described the need to protect the oxen and mules from alkali soil and poisonous water. The inhospitable land made no difference to Will's train, which chugged steadily across the desert.

Once, a caravan of canvas-covered wagons lumbered alongside the tracks—Mormons on the way to their promised land. But the train soon left the wagons far behind. The emigrants would make about fifteen miles this day, while the train would travel hundreds.

As the train climbed into the mountains, it passed by coal mines—a critical resource for the railroad. The whistle blew when the engine crossed the summit and began speeding down the Pacific side. Again, Will reflected on his parents' elation when they reached the downward portion of their journey. Though more tribulations later awaited them. Not until they reached the Willamette Valley had they felt secure.

The train didn't reach Promontory, the terminus of the Central Pacific Railroad, until late that evening. A Union Pacific train headed to Sacramento waited for passengers to transfer, but it wouldn't leave Promontory until morning.

Will arranged for another sleeper car and moved his belongings to the next train. His fellow passengers included unwashed miners, nattily dressed businessmen, and a few Chinese with their hair braided in long queues. He'd seen Chinese in Boston, though only a few. But Pa had written California was full of Chinese workers who came to work on the railroads, and most of them stayed. Some even migrated north to Oregon. In fact, Pa wrote he employed a few Asians in the Portland office.

Will decided he should alert his brother Cal to his arrival in California. Will hadn't seen Cal in seven years. He and Cal, who was next in age after Maria, had sparred frequently as boys. Cal now attended the University of California in Oakland, and Will wondered whether his brother had changed as much as Will had since they last spent time together. Perhaps they could find their way to an amicable relationship as adults. After all, as the two oldest boys in the family, they would likely need to work together for decades to come.

Before the train departed in the morning, Will found the station's telegraph desk. "I'd like to send a telegram," he told the operator.

DATE: 10 OCTOBER 1872
FROM: WILLIAM MCDOUGALL PROMONTORY
TO: CALEB MCDOUGALL JR OAKLAND
ARRIVING SACRAMENTO SATURDAY WILL
ADVISE SAN FRANCISCO ARRIVAL

Will spent a restless night on the train fretting about what to ask his father's agents. Plus, there was his brother to deal with. Meeting Cal worried him more than meeting the agents.

The train passed through the dry Humboldt River Valley, then it slowed as it climbed the Sierra Nevada range to Truckee. Will remembered Pa telling him about the Donner Party's ill-fated journey through these mountains in 1846. Lurid tales of cannibalism still surfaced whenever anyone mentioned their tragic fate. Pa told Will that if he'd heard about the Donners before he headed west, he might not have made the trip.

After the train passed the summit of the Sierras, it descended until it reached the broad valley between the Sacramento and American Rivers. Finally, the whistle blew, and the train chugged into the Sacramento station around dusk on Saturday, October 12.

Will gathered his possessions and left the train in search of a hotel. McDougall & Company business with Cal and the company agents would keep him in California for several days, but he hoped to sail north to Portland in a week or so.

Chapter 19: The Sacramento Agent

Sunday morning after breakfast, Will strode toward the main McDougall & Company warehouse in Sacramento. The mid-October weather was sunny and crisp, a perfect day for walking. When he arrived at the warehouse on the bank of the American River, he knocked.

After a few minutes, an older man opened the door. "We ain't open today."

"I'm William McDougall, Caleb McDougall's son. Could you direct me to the home of Bayliss Beck?"

The guard squinted. "McDougall, you say?"

"Yes." Will handed over a calling card, but the man put it in his pocket without a glance. "Please," he said, "I've come from Boston, and I need to meet with Mr. Beck as soon as possible."

"It's Sunday."

"Yes," Will said. "But Mr. Beck knows I'm coming. I thought to get a head start on my business by seeing him today. Might I have his address?"

The man stared at Will, then shrugged. "He lives on N Street. Between Eighth and Ninth. Big brick house with green trim."

Will tipped his hat, then set off. When he arrived at the block where Beck supposedly lived, he sighed—two brick houses with green trim. He walked to the first and knocked. A maid answered.

"Is Mr. Beck home?" he asked.

"Who might I say is calling?"

At least he hadn't bothered the wrong household on a Sunday morning. "William McDougall."

She led him into the foyer. "Wait here, sir."

McDougall & Company must pay Beck a good salary, Will thought as he looked around the well-appointed foyer. The maid returned. "Mr. Beck says for you to join him in the breakfast room." She led Will down a hallway.

"Will, my boy," said a stout man in a booming voice. Beck, Will presumed. The man rose from his chair and extended his hand in greeting. "Get the lad some coffee and pastries, Maisie."

The maid curtsied and complied.

"Have a seat," Beck told Will after they shook hands. "I hadn't expected you today. You just got in last night, didn't you?"

"Yes, Mr. Beck," Will said. "But I'm in a hurry to get to Portland."

Beck looked concerned. "Your father isn't worse, is he? I've heard nothing since Higgins—do you know him?—wired me right after Mac's injury."

"I know little myself," Will said. "Which is why I'd like to get home."

"If you're headed north," Beck said, "I will have a packet of materials for you to take straight to your father. I'm not sure if Higgins passes on everything I convey in my letters."

"I'll take anything you wish to send with me," Will said. "My father requested I talk to you about the business here in California."

"Happy to tell you everything, my boy," Beck said. "Let's meet at my office tomorrow morning."

"I'll be stopping in San Francisco as well," Will said. "To talk with Samuel Cassidy."

Beck frowned. "Cassidy? Of course. He and I meet regularly. Though the bulk of the company's inventory is here in Sacramento."

"Might I look through the warehouse this afternoon?" Will asked. "I don't want to waste your time with that tomorrow. Would you give me a letter of authorization for the guard?"

"A letter." Beck guffawed. "Old Chester can't read." He laughed again. "Why don't I meet you at the warehouse this afternoon? Say about one o'clock?"

Will nodded. "All right. I'll leave you to your breakfast now and meet you there at one."

Will wandered back to the warehouse to wait for Beck. His first impression of Beck hadn't been favorable, and he wondered if Beck would try to beat him to the warehouse. After an hour, a carriage drove to the warehouse, and Beck got out.

"Mr. Beck," Will called. "You're almost as early as I am. Perhaps we can start our tour now."

The agent's face turned red, but he nodded. "Yes, yes, of course. Come in." He grunted at the guard as they entered, then turned to Will. "Wait here."

Instead, Will followed him into a large office. With a quick glance at Will, Beck hurried to the desk and swept a stack of papers into a drawer. "Let's go, then." He led Will to the inventory space on the first floor, pointing out large piles of leather goods and barrels of grain. Will questioned him about the value of the merchandise. Beck answered vaguely, even when Will pressed for clarity.

As they ascended to the second floor, Beck asked, "What did your father ask you to look for?"

"He wants me to understand the company operations in California."

"I thought you were destined for the Boston office," Beck said.

Will shrugged. "I might return East, but until my father recuperates, I intend to remain in Portland."

They inspected the second floor, then Beck said, "The only thing on the third floor is old records. Ledgers from decades past and the like. No need to go up there."

"I'll just take a peek," Will said. "No need to accompany me."

Beck grumbled, but followed. Dusty floors told Will no one had been up to the third floor in months. The contents appeared to be what Beck had said—old files and ledger books.

Back on the first floor, Will couldn't think of a reason to remain at the warehouse. "I'll meet you here in the morning," he said. "Thank you for your time today."

Beck nodded curtly, his eyes narrowing as Will left.

Will wondered how to occupy the rest of his Sunday. Hands in his pockets, he turned toward his hotel. His fingers touched a card in his pocket, and he pulled it out—Ambrose Jones.

Jones had told Will he was well acquainted with Bayliss Beck. Uneasy after his meeting with Beck, Will decided to seek Jones's opinion. The man's office address was nearby, and Will headed there.

When he arrived at Jones's office, he was surprised Jones himself answered the door. "I'm Will McDougall. We met in Cheyenne—"

"Yes, of course," Jones said. "Come in."

"I hate to intrude on Sunday," Will said. "Particularly when your family is in mourning."

Jones nodded. "Thank you. We buried my brother yesterday. I am catching up on work today."

"Then I won't take your time now," Will said. "Perhaps we could meet tomorrow."

"No. I must repay your kindness in Cheyenne," Jones said, ushering Will into a small office. "What can I do for you?"

Will sat, then said. "I met my father's agent, Bayliss Beck." He hesitated. "He seemed evasive. Not eager to show me the premises."

"I see."

"You said you knew him well."

"Beck has been active in Sacramento for over twenty years."

"He has worked for my father for close to a decade, I believe," Will said. "Though this was my first meeting with him."

"Does he represent others as well as the McDougalls?" Jones asked, steepling his fingers against his mouth.

"I don't think so," Will said. "I've been in Boston, so I've never seen the contract between Beck and my father. But Pa usually demands exclusivity. He wants to avoid conflicts of interest."

"I suggest you check the contract and talk to your father," Jones said. "Because Beck holds himself out in Sacramento as representing several companies." Jones placed his hands on the desk between them. "I have used the man myself in the past, but I will not do so in the future."

Will raised his eyebrows. "Why is that?"

"Like you said—conflicts. Beck will broker a deal between two companies and take a fee from each. I want my agents focused solely on my interests. Your father probably has the same inclination."

"Thank you for your candor, Mr. Jones." Will rose to leave. "Could I buy you dinner at my hotel tomorrow evening? I will meet with Mr. Beck tomorrow, and I might have more questions after I speak to him."

"I would be honored," Jones said. They shook hands, and Will left, his misgivings about Beck deepening.

Armed with warnings from Ambrose Jones, Will met Beck again on Monday morning. Will asked to see the contract between Beck and

McDougall & Company. Beck showed it to him, and indeed, Pa had demanded exclusivity. Will then asked to see Beck's agreements regarding the purchase and sale of inventory and inquired about Beck's relationships with the other parties. Beck denied representing any other party, though he said many agents in Sacramento did business that way.

"Thank you," Will said at the end of the meeting. "I will report on all this to my father."

Standing, Beck said, "I will have my correspondence to Portland delivered to your hotel tomorrow. When do you expect to travel north?"

"I don't know," Will said. "I must meet with my brother and our San Francisco agent before I book a steamship berth."

"I wish you safe travels," Beck said. "And I shall write your father to report on our visit."

Will wondered how self-serving Beck's letter to Pa would be.

That evening, Will dined with Ambrose Jones. When Will described Beck's responses to his questions about the purchase and sale contracts, Jones said, "That is what I would expect him to say. Many agents in Sacramento will make a profit from anyone and everyone they can. But there are agents who work more ethically, who will focus on the interests of their principals. Let me make a list of those I trust implicitly for you to take to your father."

"How do you feel about our San Francisco agent?" Will asked. "Mr. Samuel Cassidy."

"I have heard of him, though I have not worked with him," Jones said. "I cannot tell you anything. You will develop your own opinion, of course."

Jones took a bite of beefsteak and a long swallow of wine. "I have a thought," he said. "There is a young Chinese man I know in San Francisco heading to Portland to work with a branch of his family there."

Will waited for Jones to chew another bite.

Then Jones continued, "He worked for me here, then moved to San Francisco when his family opened an importing business there. And now the family is opening a branch in Portland."

Will smiled. "The Chinese are as enterprising as we Americans."

"Many are more so," Jones said. "Zhuang Jin is the young man's name. His father came to California to work on the railroad about ten years ago. He saved enough money to open a store catering to other Chinese and has since brought other family members here from China to work with him. The store expanded into a thriving import business. Now, many Americans buy silks and other luxuries from him."

"Why do you think Mr. Jin—"

"It's Mr. Zhuang," Jones said. "The Chinese put their surnames first. The Zhuang family operates the import company."

Will nodded his thanks at the correction. "Why do you think I should meet him?"

"Jin's cousin Zhuang Li works for your father," Jones said. "Li is an accountant. I don't know if Li will stay with your company after the Zhuang family opens its Portland branch. But you should get to know Li when you reach Portland. I trust the Zhuang family."

"Give me Jin's address," Will said. "I will seek him out in San Francisco. Perhaps we can travel north together."

Chapter 20: Meeting Cal

Tuesday morning, Will boarded a local train from Sacramento to Vallejo, where he transferred to a ferry bound for San Francisco. As he shepherded his trunk from train to ferry, he marveled that his luggage had stayed with him through his travels. He hoped his good luck would continue all the way to Portland.

On the ferry deck, Will stood gazing at the bay. The brilliant waters shimmered in the afternoon sun through the strait to the Pacific Ocean—it truly was a "golden gate." Pa's tales of ships abandoned in the bay during the Gold Rush filled his head, though now San Francisco's harbor rivaled Boston's in activity and prosperity.

Will fretted about seeing his brother Cal, who would turn twenty-one in another month. Cal had wired he would meet Will at the ferry terminal in San Francisco. Will hoped Cal would travel to Portland with him, but he didn't know if his brother would agree.

He mulled over his meetings with Beck and Jones. He didn't feel comfortable with how Beck managed the company's interests in Sacramento, but he couldn't put his finger on why. If Cal wouldn't travel north, maybe he would keep an eye on Beck for the family.

The ferry docked, and Will found a porter to deal with his trunk.

"Will!"

Will turned to see Cal—changed from the lad he'd last seen seven years ago, but unmistakably Cal. He rushed to embrace his brother. They thumped each other on the back, then Will told the porter to take his baggage to the Palace Hotel at Market and New Montgomery Streets. "You'll stay there with me, won't you?" he asked Cal.

"Of course." Cal added a small valise to the porter's load. "I can stay for a day or two. How was your journey?"

"Too much to tell," Will said, grinning. "Let's find the hotel and talk over dinner. I'm famished."

The brothers hired a carriage to the Palace Hotel, chatting about family as they rode. Cal knew no more about Pa's condition than Will did.

The Palace Hotel was huge—seven stories high, with many sitting rooms and courtyards where men gathered to smoke and drink. The bridge from the Palace across New Montgomery Street to the Grand Hotel made both buildings seem even bigger than they were—more imposing than any hotel Will had seen in Boston.

After checking in and refreshing themselves, Will and Cal made their way to the gentlemen's grill room. Once seated, with whiskeys in hand and steaks ordered, Cal asked, "How long will you be in San Francisco? I can only stay two nights, then I must return to my studies."

Will frowned. "I'd hoped you'd travel to Portland with me. Pa needs our help with the business."

Cal shook his head. "I'm in the middle of the semester at the University. I cannot leave Oakland. And you don't know what Pa needs."

"But surely family comes before classes."

"In future years, perhaps," Cal said. "But not now. I will finish my course of study next spring, then I will be ordained as a minister. I plan to preach to the tribes in Oregon. That is what God is calling me to do with my life."

Cal had never seemed like a missionary when they were boys. "You don't intend to work for McDougall & Company?" Will asked. "I always thought we'd work there together, though maybe not in the same branch." As boys, the brothers often butted heads, but Will trusted Cal more than any hired agent. Cal might minimize the importance of family, but Will was sure his brother felt it as deeply as he did.

"No." Cal peered down at his glass. "You can have it, Will. Pa thinks you have a knack for business. He never thought I did."

"That's only because you're younger. If you put your mind to it—"

"I don't want to put my mind to it," Cal snapped. "I want to forge my own path. Ministering to the tribes would do more good than amassing wealth for our family. We have enough."

"You could work in Sacramento," Will pressed. "I have concerns about the agent there."

Cal laughed. "And you think I can fix whatever is wrong? I know nothing about ledgers and contracts. Maybe *you* should stay in California."

"I've got to check on Pa," Will said. "And Mama. And Maria."

"Maria?" Cal said. "Why do you worry about her?"

"She hides her feelings sometimes," Will said. "Mama leans on her for help, but who can Maria lean on?"

"Well, you'll sort them out," Cal said, a wry smile on his face. "You always do."

"I suppose." Will stared into his glass. He hadn't expected he'd have to run McDougall & Company alone. "I guess I'll have to talk to Pa about how to handle Sacramento."

The next morning, Will left Cal still sleeping. After a sumptuous breakfast at the Palace, he set out to see Zhuang Jin, the Chinese man Ambrose Jones had mentioned. The young Asian man was at work at the address Jones had given him.

Will explained what Jones had told him about the Zhuang business and Zhuang Jin's plan to move to Portland.

"You go Portland, too?" Jin asked. "When you leave?"

"In two days, if all goes well," Will said. "I must meet my father's San Francisco agent tomorrow. But once my business with him is concluded, I plan to sail north."

"I take steamer on Friday," Jin said. "My cousin Zhuang Li, he work for your father."

"Yes, Mr. Jones told me. Will he be joining your family business when you expand into Oregon?"

Jin shrugged. "Depend how fast business grow. Until then, Li work for McDougalls."

"I look forward to meeting him," Will said. "And I hope you and I can travel together to Portland."

That evening, Will and Cal dined in the main restaurant of the Palace Hotel—another elegant venue with rich food. Will argued with his brother again, but Cal remained adamant he would not leave the university.

Will shook his head. "As a boy, you dreamed of being a soldier. Never a minister."

"The Catholics call their Jesuits soldiers for Christ," Cal replied with a grin. "Perhaps I'll be a Methodist soldier." He turned serious. "Write me as soon as you know Pa's condition. I care about him, but I cannot interrupt my studies."

"Could you at least visit the Sacramento branch on your next school holiday?" Will asked. "By then, I should have talked to Pa and his accountant about Beck. You could investigate for us."

Cal shrugged. "I cannot make any guarantees. It will depend on whether I feel prepared for my exams."

That night, Will wrote:

October 15, 1872. Cal has no interest in working for Pa. How can he, who is Pa's blood son, pass up this opportunity? I want nothing more than to gain Pa's approval to succeed him someday.

Chapter 21: Eliza's Birthday

When Maria came downstairs on Wednesday, October 16, Mama and Mrs. O'Malley already had a huge breakfast prepared for Eliza's birthday.

"No cake?" Eliza asked with a laugh when she sauntered into the dining room.

"There'll be cake for supper," Mama assured her. "And presents. But I wanted you to start the day off knowing I am thinking of you."

"Not like my birthday," Andrew said mournfully. "Maria forgot my birthday until supper."

"I'm sorry," Maria told her younger brother for what was probably the hundredth time. "I only forgot because of Papa."

After breakfast, Maria left for the newspaper office. Although her work was often dull, she enjoyed the debates among the staff about politics and what to publish in the next issue of *The New Northwest*. Maria discovered she was more knowledgeable than her friend Daisy, but not as well-informed as Robert, the typesetter.

"The national election is less than three weeks away," Abigail Duniway announced. "We must print everything we know about the results in that week's issue."

"With the telegraph, we should have results from Washington by Friday, shouldn't we?" Maria asked. She recalled Papa's frustration in the years before the telegraph reached Oregon—then it took two weeks for papers from the East to reach California and Oregon.

"That depends," Mrs. Duniway said. "Some outcomes might not be reported right away."

"What do you mean?" a reporter asked her.

"We shall have to see."

It was unlike Mrs. Duniway to be so secretive, Maria thought.

Later that morning, Mrs. Duniway called Maria into her office and handed her a letter. "Read this. It is from my dear friend, Susan Anthony."

The letter was dated a few weeks earlier. Maria read the first page, then came to the shocking ending:

> . . . *Several of us involved in our righteous cause have decided to take a stand for women's suffrage. I plan to vote in the election on November 5, and no man can stop me.*
>
> *Will you join me and other women around the nation?*
>
> > *Yours truly,*
> > *Susan B. Anthony*

Maria gasped and her eyes widened as she looked at Mrs. Duniway. "Will you do it?" she asked. "Will you try to vote?"

"Yes, and I want an article ready to print in *The New Northwest*," the editor said. "Can you draft the story without telling anyone, not even your parents? I do not want any leaks before the election."

Maria gulped. "Y-yes, ma'am, I think so."

Mrs. Duniway looked at her sharply. "There is no thinking so, young lady. If you work for this paper, you must keep my confidences."

"Yes, Mrs. Duniway," Maria said. "I can keep it secret. But you didn't like my earlier article. Why are you letting me write this one?"

"Your writing shows promise," the older woman said. "Though you need practice. I will probably revise your draft thoroughly. Moreover, I will publish it under my name—I am the editor of this paper, and I will be the one casting a ballot." She sighed. "Unless I am in jail, which is why I need another reporter involved." She leaned forward. "If I am arrested, tell your father to send a competent attorney to defend me. I would ask him to represent me himself, but for his injury."

Maria gulped. A woman voting violated the law. "How should I begin?"

"Use Mrs. Anthony's letter. Review my recent pieces in the paper about women's suffrage. From those sources, you should be able to draft an editorial that sounds like me. Bring it to me by week's end. I will revise it before the election. Then I will give it the finishing touches after the election when we know whether my efforts were successful."

"Then you are really committed to casting a vote?" Maria whispered.

"I am committed to trying. Whether I will succeed remains to be seen."

Maria gathered back issues of *The New Northwest*. Mrs. Duniway wrote about suffrage in almost every issue. She would need to take the papers home to review, so she could begin drafting her article tomorrow. Tonight was Eliza's birthday supper, and Maria would have no time to write.

But Mrs. Duniway had more surprises for her that day. Shortly before noon, the editor called Maria into her office again. "Maria, I'd like you to meet someone. Sarah, this is Maria McDougall. Maria, this is Mrs. Sarah Winnemucca Bartlett. She is a member of the Paiute tribe."

Maria bobbed a curtsey. "Mrs. Bartlett."

The Indian woman, not much older than Maria, smiled. "Mrs. Duniway has told me about your family. You were born in California?"

"Yes, ma'am," Maria said. "But I've lived in Oregon with my adopted parents since infancy."

"I was born in Nevada Territory," Mrs. Bartlett said. "But I attended school in California while living with a white family. Soon I'll travel to the Malheur Reservation to live with my tribe."

"And your husband, Sarah?" Mrs. Duniway asked. "Will he join you on the reservation?"

Mrs. Bartlett's expression saddened. "I do not think so. I have not seen him for some time."

"I'm sorry," Mrs. Duniway said.

"The marriage was a mistake," Mrs. Bartlett said bluntly. "I have his name, but nothing more. I shall live with my people. They need an interpreter, and I speak English fluently. I read and write it as well."

"Thank you, Maria," Mrs. Duniway said. "Let's talk tomorrow about the article I assigned you."

Maria recognized the editor's dismissal. "Yes, ma'am." Maria packed up the back issues she'd gathered and went home. As she walked down the street, she wondered why Mrs. Duniway wanted her to meet the native women who came through the office—first Winema Riddle and now Sarah Winnemucca Bartlett.

But her thoughts didn't linger on the Indian women for long. She had an important piece to write for Mrs. Duniway. And Eliza's birthday supper to attend.

In between helping Mama and Mrs. O'Malley prepare the birthday supper, Maria pored through suffrage articles. Mrs. Duniway argued vehemently that women should vote—if only to protect themselves when their husbands or fathers did not. Many of her articles described harrowing abuses men piled on their wives and daughters—primarily their wives.

Maria thought gratefully of her father's support. He treated Mama with love and respect. He never raised a hand against his children. Though more protective of his daughters than his sons, he'd allowed Maria to work for the newspaper. And he had never treated Maria—or Will, for that matter—any differently than his children by blood.

Few people were aware Will was not Papa's son. Maria didn't think any of their younger siblings knew. Maria learned the truth at the same time Will did—when a man from Mama's past invaded their home and assaulted Mama and Will. Brandishing Papa's rifle, Maria forced the man to leave. But not before the assailant revealed he might be Will's father. Mama later told Maria about the terrible assault she'd suffered in Missouri.

Will never spoke of his parentage. But she wondered if he worried about his natural father the way she worried about her natural parents. She sighed and pushed the family's dark past out of her mind, so she could focus on Mrs. Duniway's articles.

Eliza's birthday supper was even more sumptuous than breakfast. "You must think I'm a toothpick," Eliza exclaimed, clapping her hands when she saw the feast. "Or do you want me to be as fat as a cow?"

Tonight, even six-year-old Evie and two-year-old Eddie joined them in the dining room. Maria placed herself between the youngest two, ready to assist them, while Eliza sat beside Papa at the head of the table.

After the meal ended, including birthday cake covered in lemon frosting, the family adjourned to the parlor. The younger children gave Eliza wood carvings or pictures they'd painted. Maria's gift was a shirtwaist with a pintucked bodice and embroidered cuffs. She'd labored on it for weeks. Eliza hugged each sibling as she thanked them. Perhaps Eliza was growing up, after all, Maria thought.

Then Mama handed Eliza an envelope, said, "We want your birthday celebration to continue for days to come."

Eliza opened the envelope. "*Pygmalion and Galatea*," she exclaimed. "At the New Market Theater. Oh, Mama!"

"I regret I cannot accompany you fine ladies," Papa said. "I have not recovered enough to sit through a theater performance. But Nate has agreed to take my place."

With a grimace, Nate bowed to Eliza. "I shall don my finest coat and cravat," he said. "And do my best to escort you and Mama."

Eliza looked at Maria, eyebrows raised. "Then you aren't going?"

Maria shook her head. "This is your evening, Eliza. Mama wanted the special time with you."

Eliza's face beamed, and she hugged Mama. "Thank you. I so look forward to it."

"The tickets are for next Wednesday," Mama said. "A week from tonight."

Chapter 22: The San Francisco Agent

After bidding Cal farewell Thursday morning, Will headed for the McDougall & Company office near the San Francisco wharves. The company's chief agent was a man of about thirty-five named Samuel Cassidy.

Mr. Cassidy had been hired about a year ago. Pa had written Will about the new manager, but after the initial announcement, neither Pa nor Uncle Owen ever mentioned the San Francisco agent again. After dealing with Beck in Sacramento, Will feared the worst.

But he was pleasantly surprised. Unlike the evasive and condescending Beck, Cassidy was courteous and deferential. After introductions, Cassidy's first words were, "How is your father?"

"I wish I knew," Will said. "I haven't heard from home in about a week."

"Would you care to send a telegram now?" Cassidy asked.

"Thank you, but I'll wait until I return to the hotel. There might be word waiting for me." Besides, Will thought, he might want to mention Cassidy in his telegram.

Cassidy showed him around the warehouse, opened the ledgers, and discussed the inventory values. "Our inventories are low at the moment," he said. "When harvest finishes, we'll buy more grain and ship it east."

"Is more of our business with the East Coast or with the Orient?" Will asked.

"We ship in both directions," Cassidy said. "But since completion of the Transcontinental Railroad, we send more grain to the States. We buy silks from the Orient and ship them to the East Coast, too."

"I met an enterprising young man from the Zhuang family yesterday,"

Will said. "Their business is expanding into Oregon."

"So I've heard," Cassidy said. "They will be formidable competitors. McDougall & Company should consider an alliance with them."

Surprised, Will asked, "You think we should join forces with the Chinese?" In Boston, very few American companies partnered with Chinese businesses.

"The Zhuangs are fair traders. They mostly hire their own," Cassidy said. "But I understand one of them is working for the McDougalls in Oregon."

"Zhuang Li," Will said, nodding. "I will have to meet him when I get to Portland. Tomorrow, I'm traveling north with his cousin, Zhuang Jin."

"I know Jin," Cassidy said. "He is respected here. A shrewd bargainer, but he meets his obligations—his goods are high quality and delivered on time."

"Not much more you can expect from a trading partner," Will said.

"No, sir." Cassidy sighed. "The Zhuangs bring more relatives to San Francisco from China each year as their business grows."

"I thought they started as railroad workers," Will said.

"They did. But serving the Chinese laborers is more profitable than laboring themselves."

Will chuckled. "That's what my father discovered—he made most of his fortune catering to miners, not by digging gold."

"Exactly so." Cassidy grinned. "Men of every nation learn the same lessons."

Will invited Cassidy to dine with him that evening at the Palace Hotel. After dinner, Will sat in the smoking room nursing a whiskey and a cigar. He reflected on the two agents he'd met, then pulled out his journal and wrote:

> *October 17, 1872. Our two agents are quite different. I will tell Pa that Beck needs watching, if not replacing. But I think Cassidy is a good man. I wonder if Cassidy could manage both the San Francisco and Sacramento branches. I will discuss the matter with Pa.*

Then there was Cal. Will did not write again about his brother, but he wondered what Pa thought of Cal's interest in the ministry. And what did Mama think? If anyone could change Cal's mind, maybe it was Mama. Had Cal even discussed the matter with their parents?

Will closed his journal and blew a smoke ring as he let his thoughts drift to Maria. He would see her in just a few days. He remembered her flashing smile as they waltzed in Boston, her red skirts swirling around their legs, her bare shoulders gleaming under candlelight. Would she still be the most beautiful girl he'd known? Would she still be as agreeable as she'd always been?

If so, maybe he should ask her to marry him.

The next morning, Will stopped at the telegraph office in the hotel to notify his family he would be home soon.

DATE: 18 OCTOBER 1872
FROM: WILLIAM MCDOUGALL SAN FRANCISCO
TO: CALEB MCDOUGALL PORTLAND
LEAVING SAN FRANCISCO TODAY SS
OREGONIAN ARRIVING PORTLAND MONDAY 21

After sending the telegram, he took a carriage to the steamship dock and boarded the *S.S. Oregonian*, a flagship of the Oregon Steam Navigation Company. Pa had invested in steamships for years, though recently he put money into railroads. But Pa's letters revealed frustration at the slow pace of rail development in Oregon. Perhaps Will could help manage the family's rail investments for Pa—maybe that could be his niche in the business. He itched for some responsibility to call his own.

Will made sure his trunk was in his cabin, then stood on deck as the ship pulled away from the dock. He'd stood with Pa on a similar deck seven years earlier when they'd traveled to Boston. Seven years—an eternity, it seemed. He'd grown in ways he'd never imagined.

Again, his mind turned to Maria. She, too, might have changed a lot since he saw her last. But surely, she would be the same Maria. Still lovely. Still devoted to Will, as she had always been.

"Mr. McDougall," a man behind him said.

Will turned. "Zhuang Jin. Good to see you." He smiled and offered his hand, and Zhuang shook it. "Shall we see if the bar is open yet?"

Zhuang shrugged. "I second-class passenger. Maybe they not let me."

"Nonsense. You are my guest," Will said. "Come on."

But when they arrived at the bar, the *maître d'* glanced at them and said, "I'm sorry. We're not yet open." Will peered inside the smoky room, where many gentlemen sat drinking. He opened his mouth to object, but thought better of it, and said, "Then, Zhuang Jin, let us find some deck chairs."

"You see," Zhuang said, when they had seated themselves on the breezy deck. "Chinese not welcome."

"I didn't realize there was so much animosity against the Chinese in California," Will admitted.

"Portland same," Zhuang said. "So my cousins say."

"Then why are you heading north?" Will asked.

Zhuang waved a hand. "Money. My family large. Life here better than in China. Only rich have hope in China. In America, poor man can hope, even if he is despised."

Chapter 23: Reaching Home

The ship steamed north toward Portland. Though Will did not suffer seasickness, Zhuang Jin was not so fortunate. Will saw little of the Chinese man during the voyage.

Midmorning on the fourth day, October 21, the ship reached the mouth of the Columbia River. But an autumn storm blew in, churning the Pacific into a frenzy as it collided with the powerful river current.

"We can't go upstream today," the first mate told the passengers. "Captain says the current's too dangerous."

"I'm expected in Portland tonight," Will protested. "I haven't been home in seven years."

"Sorry, sir," the mate said. "Too many ships have broken apart on rocks and sandbars 'round here. We won't be one of 'em."

Zhuang Jin was on deck to hear the message, his face pale. "Stay in the fresh air," Will told him. "Let me find us some tea and pastries."

"Tea, yes," Jin said. "No pastry."

Will returned with tea and cookies, settling in a deck chair beside Jin. "How's your cabin?"

"Cabin mate sick, too," Jin said. "Room smell bad. But better than lower decks."

After their snack, Will returned to his first-class cabin and took out his journal.

October 21, 1872. I am grateful for this cabin, which sits above the water and has a window I can open. And for the privacy of not having a roommate.

By evening, the storm passed, and the captain announced they would attempt to enter the Columbia's mouth at dawn.

Although the winds abated, the ocean waves still clashed with the river current as the *S.S. Oregonian* steamed past Astoria. Will marveled at the breadth of the Columbia's mouth—six miles as the crow flies from the Oregon bank, where the old shipping and fishing town of Astoria sat, across the river to Washington Territory.

Standing next to Will, Zhuang Jin muttered, "Graveyard of Pacific. That what crew say."

Will laughed. "Yes, that's its nickname. But since the coming of steamships, there have been fewer wrecks. The old schooners couldn't manage winds and current, but our steam engine can power us through."

"Some steamers still sink," Jin said morosely.

"Look at the sunshine," Will said, gesturing at the sky. "It's a fine day. And I'm ready to get home."

"I must find cousin's family in Portland."

"Don't they know you're coming?"

"I sent letter weeks ago. But they not know which boat I take."

"You'll find them," Will assured him. "Portland's Chinatown isn't that large." Then, curious, he asked, "They live in Chinatown, don't they?"

Jin shrugged. "Where else?"

Where else indeed? Will thought. Prejudice against the Chinese left few options.

The steamship passed the Columbia Bar into calmer waters. "Not long now," Will said. "We'll reach Portland soon."

The *S.S. Oregonian* finally steamed up the Willamette River, and the crew tied her to the dock in Portland. Will talked to a porter about conveying his trunk and other luggage to his parents' home—the last time for that task, he hoped.

"It'll take a while, sir," the porter said. "Lots of bags to unload."

"I don't need to stay here, do I?" Will said. "I'm ready to get home."

"No, sir. You go 'bout your business. We'll get your luggage to you by tomorrow morning."

Will looked for Zhuang Jin, but didn't spot the Asian. So he made his way down the gangplank.

"Will! Will!"

He scanned the crowd on the dock. Maria! She was more lovely than when he'd seen her last. Beside her stood three other young people, who must be Nate, Eliza, and Lottie—all grown so much since he'd left seven years ago.

Will rushed toward them, and Maria's arms enveloped him in a fierce hug. "Oh, Will. It's so good to have you home," she said, her voice muffled against his chest.

He returned the embrace and kissed her soft cheek, inhaling her lavender scent. "It's good to be home."

Then he greeted his younger siblings and asked, "Where's everyone else?"

"No room in the carriage for more," Nate said. "We claimed our rights as the oldest. Mama let us skip school when we found out your ship would arrive today."

Will laughed. "Is there space for me to ride home with you?"

Together, they made their way to the family carriage. "How's Pa?" Will asked as he handed Maria and the younger girls inside.

"Improving," Maria said. "But he tires easily. That's another reason he and Mama didn't come. But they are anxiously awaiting you at home."

After wending their way through the crowd on Front Street, they sped through town to a street of stately mansions. "Goodness," Will said, as the carriage pulled under the side portico of a grand three-story house. "This is where we live now?" The home was every bit as imposing as Grandmother McDougall's in Boston.

"Mama said we outgrew the Oregon City house," Eliza said. "This one has five bedrooms for family—six now that you're here, as Mama has given you a room of your own. And there are still three more rooms for guests, the nursery, and quarters for Mrs. O'Malley, a nursemaid, and a housemaid. The stable boy lives above the horses."

Will remembered his little room in the Oregon City house, not much bigger than a closet. But his earliest memory of home was of the old log cabin on Pa's homestead where he and Mama lived while Pa was in California during the Gold Rush. "I'm sure I will be happy wherever Mama

103

puts me," he said.

Eliza prattled on—Maria had her own room, Eliza and Lottie shared a room with Maggie on a trundle bed, Nate and Andrew shared, and Evie and Eddie were still in the nursery. "But after Evie's next birthday, she and Maggie will get a room, and Lottie and I won't have to share with Maggie anymore."

"Well," Will said, "let me see Mama and Pa, and then you can give me the grand tour." He followed his sisters into the house.

Mama shrieked when she saw him. For a little woman, she had a monstrously hard hug. "Will," she said, clasping his face in her hands. "Let me look at you. How were your travels? Are you hungry?"

He hugged her back, noticing a few gray hairs in her light brown bun. "I'm fine, Mama. Glad to be home." He kissed her cheek. "Where's Pa?"

Mama led him to a room furnished as a library, though the desk was pushed aside to make space for a bed. "Will is home," she announced.

Seeing his father shocked Will—Pa seemed so small and frail, and he struggled to sit up.

Will hurried over. "Don't get up, Pa," He held out his hand for Pa to shake, but Pa pulled Will over into a bear hug. "Good to have you home, son," Pa said in a choked voice.

Two younger children rushed into the room—ten-year-old Maggie and eight-year-old Andrew, he surmised, though he hadn't seen them since they were toddlers. Maggie came right up to him for a hug, but Andrew hung back until Will approached him and offered the lad his hand. "Hello, I'm Will. You must be Andrew."

The boy nodded with a shy smile.

"You were still in skirts when I left," Will said. "But now you're a young man."

At that, Andrew's smile broadened.

Then a maid brought in two younger children. "This is Evie," Mama said. "She's six now." Mama took the baby out of the maid's arms. "And this is Eddie, our youngest. Meet your brother Will." Evie hung on the maid's skirt as she bobbed a little curtsey, while Eddie hid his face against Mama's shoulder.

"We'll have plenty of time to get to know each other," Will said.

"Shall we have supper?" Mama asked, handing Eddie back to the maid. At Mama's nod, the maid took Evie and Eddie away. "I thought it would be too much commotion for them tonight," Mama continued. "Though Evie now has some evening meals downstairs."

Over supper, Will described his journey, though he refrained from mentioning his stop in Arrow Rock. He wanted to discuss that with Mama and Pa in private first. For now, he was just happy to be home.

After supper, Will noticed Pa was tiring. "May I wheel you back to your library, sir?"

"Please," Pa said. "And stay a while if you would. We have much to discuss."

Will settled Pa in his bed and poured them both whiskey. "Just a short one," Pa said. "Your mother is convinced it slows my recovery."

Will chuckled and handed Pa two fingers, then filled his own glass with three fingers.

"Now, tell me what you learned in California," Pa said.

"I met with both Bayliss Beck in Sacramento and Samuel Cassidy in San Francisco," Will began. He summarized the two visits, concluding, "Beck barely answered the questions I put to him. Cassidy, however, was open and cordial. I trusted him."

"Cassidy hasn't been with us long," Pa said.

"That may be," Will said. "But he opened his ledgers and showed me his inventory without hesitation. Beck couldn't get me out of the warehouse fast enough."

Pa frowned. "Perhaps I'll send Higgins south," Pa said. "He's been an enormous help since my accident."

"Higgins?" Will asked. "The accountant?"

"Yes, Amos Higgins. He manages the accounting function here in Portland, and he's run the Portland office since my injury. I've relied on him heavily. He is also handling our communications with Beck and Cassidy. And some with Boston. Did you read his correspondence to Owen?"

"No," Will said. "Uncle Owen mentioned Higgins once or twice, but that's it."

"I'll introduce you to him later this week. You can hear his take on Beck and Cassidy." Pa sipped his whiskey. "How were my mother and Owen when you left?"

"Both well," Will said. "Grandmother seemed sorry to see me go."

"You made a fine impression on them both, Will. I'm glad you got to know my family."

Will paused, then confessed, "I stopped in Arrow Rock to meet Grandmère Peterson and her son Jacques."

Pa raised his eyebrows. "Why the devil did you do that?"

"I-I was curious."

Pa glowered. "Does your mother know?"

"Not yet," Will said. "But I'll tell her."

"How are they faring?"

"Their farm seems to have fallen on hard times," Will said. "Though Jack was doing the best he could."

"Talk to your mother soon," Pa said. "I want her to hear it from you. And I won't keep a secret from her."

"Yes, sir." After Pa's negative reaction to his Arrow Rock detour, Will wondered what Mama would say.

Chapter 24: Theatrical in Portland

Mama had gone to bed by the time Will left the library, so he didn't see her until breakfast the next morning. Mindful of Pa's instruction, Will asked to speak to her privately.

"Let me get the older children off to school and the little ones settled," Mama said. "Then I shall join you in my morning room."

Maria came through the dining room and grabbed a pastry. "Off to work, Mama," she said, kissing her mother's cheek.

Surprised, Will asked, "You have a job? Where?"

"At *The New Northwest.*"

"What's that?" he asked.

"A newspaper published by Abigail Duniway," Maria said. "We'll talk later. I'm late."

Will vaguely remembered a friend of Mama's with that name. He frowned—Maria had never expressed an interest in writing when they were growing up.

He finished his coffee, then found his mother's morning room—a small, bright room with a view of the garden, furnished with striped furniture and a small escritoire. While he waited for Mama, Will paced from window to window and perused the bookcase.

"There you are," Mama said, when she entered about a quarter of an hour later.

"Why is Maria working for a newspaper?" he asked.

Mama sat on the settee and patted the cushion beside her. "She wants to be useful. Mrs. Duniway publishes a paper devoted to human rights, including women's suffrage."

Will chuckled as he took the seat Mama indicated. "Does Maria believe in that sort of thing? Women's suffrage?" Maria's letters had never mentioned anything political.

"She's grown in the years you've been away." Mama smiled. "You said you had something to tell me."

"Yes, Mama." Will hesitated, wondering how she would react. "On my way home, I stopped to meet your mother and brother. I spent a night at their farm."

Mama's smile froze into a startled expression. "You did what? You met my *maman*? And Jacques?"

"I'd spent years with Pa's family," Will said. "I wanted to meet yours."

Mama opened her mouth as if to speak, then shut it. Finally, she murmured, "But you know I parted on bad terms with my mother."

"Yes," Will said. "But you write her. I didn't think you would mind."

"I don't," Mama said, too quickly. After a pause, she asked, "How is she?"

"She seemed well," Will said. "She asked me to call her Grandmère. She is definitely a Southerner, as well as French. But she was kind to me."

"She was not kind to me before I left."

"No," Will acknowledged. He knew why his mother left Missouri. "Their farm was run down. Jack was sullen, but he seems like a decent fellow. And Letitia asked me to wish you well."

"Letitia?" Mama's eyes lit up. "She's still alive?"

"She is old, but she still keeps house for them."

"Letitia was a better mother to me than my own." Mama sighed. "I suppose I will have to write and thank my *maman* for her hospitality to you."

"She mentioned visiting us here."

Mama gasped. "No." Then she shook her head. "I cannot see her enduring such a journey. She was never one to expose herself to hardship."

"It's not so arduous anymore," Will said. "Only a couple of weeks."

Mama rubbed her temples. "Perhaps I should visit her. Though I have no desire to return to Missouri. Letters are enough." Mama shook her head as if to clear it, then patted his arm. "Tell me, would you like to go to a theatrical tonight?"

"A theatrical?" Will said, surprised at the change of subject.

"Last week was Eliza's birthday. Mac and I gave her tickets to *Pygmalion and Galatea*, which is playing at a new theater downtown. I'd asked Nate to escort us, but he'd gladly give up his seat to you."

"What about Maria?" Will asked.

"This is a special event for Eliza," Mama said. "Maria understands."

Will didn't like the idea of leaving Maria at home. "I'll go if Maria goes."

Mama frowned. "It's settled. Maria agreed. We only have three tickets."

"But I want her there," Will said, imagining Maria in an evening gown like she'd worn in Boston. "I'll walk downtown this morning to inquire about another ticket."

Will donned his greatcoat against the morning chill and headed downtown. He'd only spent a little time in Portland before moving to Boston and the town had grown in the last seven years, so he needed the directions Mama gave him. He found the New Market Theater just where Mama said it would be and easily purchased another ticket for the evening's performance. Then he wandered to the wharf, but learned his baggage was already on its way to the house.

On his way home, a sign for *The Oregonian* newspaper offices caught his eye. Mama said Maria worked in this building. On a whim, he stepped inside, then opened a door labeled *The New Northwest*. He discovered Maria leaning over a galley sheet with her dress sleeves covered in ink-smeared protectors. "Hello," he said, grinning.

She startled, then smiled. "Will, what are you doing here?"

"What are you poring over so diligently?"

"I'm proofreading the copy for this week's advertisements." She shrugged. "It's not glamorous work, but we must keep our advertisers happy."

"I bought you a ticket for this evening's theatrical."

She frowned. "But it's Eliza's birthday. Nate is going with them."

"Mama drafted me to take Nate's place. And I thought you'd enjoy it."

"I would, but—"

"Then it's settled." Will said, patting the ticket in his pocket. "I'll see you later."

Maria called to him as he exited the office, "Please be sure to compliment Eliza."

That afternoon, Eliza beamed at the news Will would be her escort for the evening.

"And I'm glad not to put on my fancy clothes," Nate said, grinning.

But Eliza's expression dimmed when she learned Maria was accompanying them. "I thought this was my birthday gift."

Maria shrugged. "Will insisted. I shall stay safely in the background and let you shine, Eliza."

Will didn't think that was possible—Maria was far prettier than Eliza, who he thought was too young to attend an evening theatrical.

After supper, the four of them dressed—Will in a black suit newly pressed to rid it of wrinkles from his trunk, Mama in a fashionable navy gown, Eliza in a light blue frock trimmed with lace, and Maria in a striking red dress that made Will catch his breath.

As they waited for the McDougall carriage to pull to the portico, Will bowed to Eliza. "I shall be the envy of every gentleman at the theater." Though he bowed to Eliza, his eyes met Maria's. Maria smiled, and Eliza giggled.

They arrived at the theater, found their seats, then awaited the beginning of *Pygmalion and Galatea*. Eliza squirmed, staring at the finery of the ladies around them, while Maria and Mama whispered together. Will sat silently, wondering whether this performance could match the theatricals he'd seen in Boston.

When the curtain rose, he was surprised at the professionalism of the cast. They brought the myth to life. Will stole a look at Maria's entranced face, a slight smile showing her appreciation.

At intermission, Will stood. "Would you ladies like some lemonade?"

"Why don't we all get some air in the lobby?" Mama suggested. They filed up the aisle to the lobby, and Will went to fetch drinks.

When he returned with a tray of glasses, a handsome, well-dressed gentleman was talking with Mama, Maria, and Eliza. "Will," Mama said, "This is Amos Higgins, an associate of your father's."

Will passed around the lemonade, then shook Higgins's hand. "I've heard of you, sir," he said. "You are the head accountant here in Portland—do I have that right?"

Higgins nodded. "I have the privilege of managing the business with your father."

"Mr. Higgins dined with us last week," Mama said. "He has been most helpful to your father since his injury."

Higgins bowed to Maria. "And I hope to escort Miss McDougall to some future event, at this theater or another."

Will's fingers tightened on his glass. Was Pa's underling courting Maria? In all his reveries, Will assumed Maria would be waiting for him when he returned. It seemed she not only had a newspaper job, but she might have a suitor as well. She wasn't the girl he'd left behind, nor even the girl who'd visited him in Boston.

Maria smiled. "Perhaps so," she told Higgins.

Did she welcome the man's attentions? Will spent the second half of the play seething, wondering whether he had a rival for Maria's affections.

Chapter 25: Maria's Conversations

On Friday, two days after the performance at the New Market Theater, Maria stayed at work longer than usual. Mrs. Duniway had been on a tear, stirred up about the coming election. It was midafternoon before Maria finally arrived home for lunch, which she ate in the kitchen, relishing a moment to herself.

Will came prowling into the kitchen. "I've been looking for you."

Pleased to have a chance to talk to Will, she gestured to the chair beside her. "Do you want anything to eat? There's bread and butter. And cider."

He shook his head. "You and I have spent no time together since I arrived."

"I've been busy," she said. "Working."

"Why did you take the job at the paper?" he asked, running a finger along the table's oak grain.

"I wanted to be productive. I like to write." She took a bite, chewed, then added, "I'm twenty-two years old. I've done nothing with my life except help Mama raise the younger children. She can afford nursemaids, and she doesn't really need me." She and Will used to talk about their deepest dreams and fears. Surely, he would understand.

"I'm sure she appreciates your help."

Maria sighed. "She may enjoy having me home, but she doesn't *need* me. You don't know what it's like not to be needed."

"Maybe I do," Will said. "I spent three years in Boston at McDougall & Company. Uncle Owen didn't need me. But I learned a lot. And now I'm ready to help Pa." He ran his finger along the grain again. "Though I don't know if Pa needs me either."

"Oh, he does," Maria said, wanting to reassure Will. "Papa is still recuperating. You'll be a tremendous help to him."

Will shrugged. "That Mr. Higgins of yours seems to handle things in the office just fine."

Maria laughed. "He's not my Mr. Higgins."

"Didn't look that way at the theater on Wednesday."

Maria raised her eyebrows. "What's that supposed to mean?"

"That man wants to court you, if I'm not mistaken."

Maria sipped her cider. "Maybe so. But that doesn't make him mine. Nor me his."

"Do you like him?"

"He's been very kind. To Papa, to Mama, and to me." Maria hadn't decided how she felt about Mr. Higgins. But she didn't plan to tell Will that. Some things were too personal to discuss, even with Will.

"Do you want him to court you?"

She shrugged. "If I don't see more of him, how will I know?" She frowned at Will. "What do you think of him?"

"I've only just met him," Will replied.

"You've been to the company offices the last two days. Haven't you talked to him?"

"Yes," Will said, drawing out the word. "He knows a lot about our Oregon business. And he has a good handle on California as well. I quizzed him about Sacramento and San Francisco."

"And?"

"Higgins took my concerns seriously," Will said. "About not liking the Sacramento agent. But he didn't express an opinion. I need to talk to Pa more about what I saw in California." He paused. "How is Pa—truly? He says he's fine, but I can see he's in pain."

Maria nodded, relieved to have left the subject of whether she liked Mr. Higgins. "He tries to hide it, but by the end of the day, his leg aches terribly. And he's frustrated he can't walk yet. He needs you, Will, even if you don't think so. Not an accountant. He needs his son."

Will sat quietly while Maria ate. Then he said, "Do you remember what I asked before I left for Boston?" he asked when she'd finished her meal.

"That was seven years ago," she said.

"I asked if you could love me as a woman loves a man."

Maria swallowed. Yes, she remembered. She'd thought about Will's question often, though each time she thought about it, she wondered if Will remembered. He'd written nothing about it—not once in seven years. "I remember."

"Well?"

"Well, what?" she countered.

"Can you?"

She sighed. Why should she respond when Will hadn't said how he felt? "I don't know, Will. We've been apart for so long. We've both changed a lot. Grown a lot. We need time to get to know each other again. How do you feel?"

He shrugged. "I've never met a woman I liked better than you."

She smiled faintly. "Let's see what happens." She stood and gathered her dishes to take to the scullery. "I have things I need to sort out—my job among them."

"And Higgins?"

"He's one of those things, too."

Over the weekend, Maria kept to herself—a difficult task in a large household full of children. Sunday afternoon, she sat reading in her bedroom when Mama knocked and entered.

"Are you all right, dear?" Mama asked.

"Yes, Mama," Maria said, looking up. "Why?"

"You've been pensive this weekend," Mama said, sitting on Maria's bed.

Maria closed her book. "Will says Mr. Higgins is courting me."

Mama smiled. "I think that's true, don't you?"

"Yes," Maria said slowly.

"How do you feel about it?"

"Will doesn't like it."

"That's not what I asked," Mama said gently. "I asked how you feel."

"I barely know Mr. Higgins," Maria said. "That's what I told Will." She sighed. "I also told Will I need to get to know Mr. Higgins better before I can say whether I want him courting me."

"A wise answer." Mama plucked at her skirt, but said nothing more.

Maria had always been open with Mama, so she said, "Will asked me whether I could love him."

Mama sighed. "I wondered how he felt about you now."

Maria played with the bookmark in her novel. "He didn't say. He only asked how I felt."

"So how do you feel about Will?"

"At this point, I don't know him any better than Mr. Higgins," Maria said, her voice rising. "We've barely seen each other in seven years."

Mama moved to sit on the footstool beside Maria's chair. She cupped Maria's cheek. "Don't worry, dear girl. Give it time. Don't rush—neither with Mr. Higgins nor with Will. Wait until you know your heart."

"You had it so easy," Maria murmured. "You knew Papa was the one for you as soon as you met."

Mama's expression became unreadable. "You think so?"

"He rescued you from Missouri," Maria said. "And then you married him and came to Oregon."

Mama paused, a long pause. "That's not the full story."

Maria stared at her mother, waiting.

"Mac and I didn't marry before we traveled to Oregon." Mama took Maria's hand. "He asked, but I wasn't sure of him. I wasn't sure I could ever love any man at that point. We didn't wed until Mac came back from California—with you."

"You weren't married all that time?" Maria whispered. "For three years?"

Mama shrugged. "Mac was away for almost two of those years. When he came back, he asked me to marry him the first night he returned. We wed the next day. Very few people here in Oregon know that."

"Why did you marry him then?"

Mama's face lit up. "I knew by then I loved him. I wished I had married him before he left." She shook her head. "But if I had, he probably wouldn't have gone to California. He wouldn't have made his fortune there. Who knows where we'd be now? And he wouldn't have brought you to me." She tightened her grip on Maria's hand. "The point is, wait. Wait until you know which man you love. It might be Amos Higgins, it might be Will, it might be someone you haven't even met yet. Wait."

Maria spent the rest of Sunday in a daze, and she thought again about her conversation with Mama as she walked to work on Monday morning. Her parents' marriage—the foundation of their family—had been far less certain than she'd believed.

She'd known Mama was raped and Will was the result, but she'd romanticized Mama's and Papa's meeting and their journey to Oregon.

Papa's departure for California was what many men had done in 1848—a quarter of all men in Oregon had headed south after gold was discovered.

What if Papa hadn't returned? What if he'd stayed in California with Maria? What if Mama hadn't agreed to marry him when he came back? These possibilities were too strange to contemplate.

When Maria arrived at *The New Northwest*, Mrs. Duniway asked her to review a new set of newspapers from the mail. "Write up any interesting stories you find, Maria," Mrs. Duniway instructed. "Then give your summary to Robert to typeset."

"Don't you want to see it first?" Maria asked.

"You've learned this task well," the editor said. "I trust you. Prepare one column's worth of material. That should be plenty."

"Yes, Mrs. Duniway." Maria turned to start her assignment, then hesitated. "Do you think I have promise as a newspaper writer?"

Mrs. Duniway studied her for a moment. "I do." She paused, then continued, "You're an intelligent young lady. You are capable of accomplishing whatever you set your mind to. You merely need to decide what you want and work for it."

Maria beamed. "Thank you, Mrs. Duniway."

"Your draft of my article about the election next week was solid," the editor said. "I hope it can be published as is. But if I end up in jail—"

"Surely not," Maria protested.

"Remember what I told you. Ask your father to send me a reputable attorney. But say nothing to him in advance."

"Yes, ma'am."

"And just because I believe your writing shows promise doesn't mean success will come to you quickly." Mrs. Duniway sighed. "A woman's life is not easy, particularly if she wants to work in a man's world. And make no mistake—it is a man's world."

That gave Maria more to ponder through the day. Did she want to work in a man's world?

Chapter 26: Dealing with Business

Will had gone to the office daily since his return. He met with employees and scrutinized the ledgers so he could understand the Portland operation. He also wanted to confirm his views of the California managers.

After a few days of poking about on his own and talking with Pa, Will realized he needed a lengthy conversation with Amos Higgins. He wasn't eager to meet with the accountant, but Higgins seemed to be the most knowledgeable employee in the office.

He stopped by Higgins's office late Tuesday morning. "Do you have time to talk?"

"Certainly." Higgins shut an open desk drawer and stood. "Though I was about to go to lunch. Would you care to join me?"

Will shrugged. "Where'd you have in mind?"

"Why not the Pacific Hotel?" Higgins said. "It's next door to the newspaper. Perhaps your sister could join us."

The last thing Will wanted was to see Maria and Higgins together. "I'd rather discuss business," he said. "Let's keep it to the two of us."

After they settled in the hotel restaurant and ordered their meal, Will said, "I'd like your opinion on the Sacramento and San Francisco branches."

"You met Beck and Cassidy, didn't you?" Higgins said. "What was your impression?"

"You've worked with them longer," Will said. "You go first. Then I'll tell you what I noticed when I was there."

Higgins nodded. "Beck has been with the company longer than I have and has managed Sacramento throughout his employment. Your father hired him. I made a trip to California last year. That's the only time I've met Beck in person. Most of my information comes from his monthly reports, which have not given me any cause for concern." Higgins sipped his wine. "I wish he were more aggressive in keeping the warehouse full, but perhaps the mercantiles in California don't turn over their inventories as fast as we do here in Portland."

"The warehouse looked full when I toured it," Will said.

"Hmm." Higgins smiled at the waiter who brought their meals. "Cassidy is new. I hired him to manage the San Francisco operation when I was in California last year. In fact, the main purpose of my trip was to replace the former manager, who left our company for another position."

"How did you decide to hire Cassidy?"

Higgins stabbed his roast beef, an onyx ring on his right hand flashing as he did so. "Beck introduced us. Cassidy is young, but on Beck's recommendation, I agreed to give him a chance." After finishing a bite, he added, "It's probably time for me to make another trip south."

"I suggested that to my father," Will said, attacking his own meal. "I'll push it with him. One of us—you or me—needs to stay in close contact with the men in California."

Higgins rubbed his temple. "Why do you say that?"

Will chewed thoughtfully. How much did he want to reveal to Higgins? He wanted to trust the man—Pa seemed to. But given Higgins's interest in Maria, Will instinctively didn't like him. "Beck seemed evasive. Cassidy didn't."

Higgins chuckled. "Curious. I'd say the opposite. Beck's reports are thorough, if not as ambitious as I would like. He accounts for every sale and purchase. Cassidy is a little vague about the San Francisco operation." He took another bite. "But both branches are profitable, so I haven't worried about either." He pointed his knife at Will. "As you said, one of us should keep an eye on them."

After their meal, Will and Higgins returned to the McDougall & Company offices. "By the way," Will said as they entered the building, "doesn't a Chinese man named Zhuang Li work for us? I haven't met him yet."

"Zhuang Li?" Higgins asked. "How did you hear about him?"

"I traveled north from San Francisco with his cousin. Their family owns an import company, and Zhuang Jin—the cousin—is expanding their business in Portland."

"Really?" Higgins said. "Li is just a clerk. I didn't know he came from a Chinese merchant family."

"How did you come to hire Li?"

Higgins shrugged. "His skills are good. He's faster on an abacus than I am with paper and pen. And the Chinese work for less than white men. But I don't mingle with them socially."

"I'd like to meet him."

Higgins led Will to a back room where young men manned a row of desks. Higgins barked an order at one of them, then continued to a corner desk. An Asian man about Will's age sat there with a ledger and an abacus in front of him. "Li," Higgins said. "This is Mr. McDougall's oldest son, William McDougall."

Li stood and bowed. Though dressed in Western clothes, he wore his hair in a long queue down his back. "Honored, Mr. McDougall. Cousin Jin say he travel from San Francisco with you."

"Yes," Will said, nodding. "I was glad for his company. How is he?"

"Jin better now on land," Li said with a smile. "He not like sea travel."

"We'll all benefit when the rail lines enable us to avoid ocean voyages," Will said. "I don't want to interrupt your work, but I'm pleased to meet you. Please let me know if I can help you or Jin."

"Thank you, Mr. McDougall. And please you ask if you want me help you." Li bowed again.

As Will and Higgins left the back office, Higgins said, "Back to work, Li. No lollygagging till the work is done." Then Higgins turned to Will. "I maintain a firm hand over the bookkeepers. And our Chinese employees require more supervision than most."

Will walked along the Willamette River that evening, mulling over his conversation with Higgins and trying to form an unbiased opinion of the accountant. A man shouted, "Is that you, Will McDougall?"

He turned and squinted. A beefy man a few years older than Will approached from the wharf. "Noah Pershing," the man said. "Remember me?"

"Noah," Will exclaimed, extending his hand. "How are you?" Noah had been about four or five years old when his family traveled to Oregon with Will's parents. Will was born on that journey, as was Noah's younger brother Jonah. The Pershings and McDougalls remained close, and Jonah had been Will's best childhood friend. At the time, Noah lorded it over the younger boys, but his few extra years no longer mattered.

"Just fine," Noah said, pumping Will's hand and pounding him on the back. "You're home now, I see."

"Portland doesn't feel like home yet," Will said. "Though I'm glad to be with my family again. What brings you here?"

"Work. I'm a riverboat captain. My boat is docked here for the night."

"Not a farmer?" Will asked. Noah was orphaned as a child and raised by his older brother Zeke, who farmed land outside of Oregon City.

Noah grinned. "I got bored farming. Hired on with a steamboat soon as Zeke let me." He shrugged. "Now I have my own boat."

"Good for you," Will said. "Do you have time for a drink?"

Noah nodded and gestured toward a nearby saloon. It took them two pints each to catch up.

When Will got home, Pa was in a grumpy mood. "The doctor visited," Mama whispered to Will. "He poked and prodded and had Mac bending and twisting in every direction. Your father is worn out."

Will decided not to bother Pa that night. The next evening, however, Pa seemed much improved, and Will asked if they could talk after supper. Pa invited Will to join him in the library where Pa still slept.

"When will you be allowed upstairs?" Will asked as he wheeled his father into the library and helped him settle onto the bed.

"It's been six weeks," Pa said. "The doctor told me yesterday I could start walking with a cane. But damn it, it hurts."

"Don't push it, Pa," Will said. "I can handle matters at the office. In fact, that's what I want to talk about. Higgins and I talked at length yesterday, mostly about California. He thinks Beck is the better manager of the two, and I disagree, but we both think we need closer oversight of the branches."

"And the other manager? The new man—Cassidy?" Pa grimaced as he tried to adjust the pillows behind his back.

Will plumped the pillows. "I liked him, but Higgins thinks Cassidy is weak. One of us should make another trip to California. I'm happy to go if you want to keep Higgins here. But he volunteered to travel if you want me to stay."

Pa grimaced again. "You just got home. Your mother would be most unhappy if you left again."

"Then shall we send Higgins?" Will wouldn't mind keeping the accountant away from Maria for a while.

"The election is next week," Pa said. "Let him stay here to vote. We can decide about California later."

"Do you really think we should wait?" Will asked. "At least let me write Uncle Owen and ask what he knows about Beck and Cassidy. And about Higgins, for that matter."

"Keep Owen out of the West Coast business," Pa said, sounding both weary and testy. "I've managed Oregon and California just fine for decades without Owen's involvement."

"But Pa—"

"And now you're here," Pa continued. "You can be my eyes and ears in the office until I can get there myself. We don't need Owen."

Will sighed. Pa wasn't likely to change his mind tonight. "All right. We'll discuss California again after the election. In the meantime, I'll examine the correspondence files from Beck and Cassidy. Then I'll know what they've reported to Higgins. I'll let you know if I find anything odd."

"Higgins is a good man," Pa said. "If there was a problem in California, he'd have noticed. And told me."

Chapter 27: Election Day

On Tuesday, November 5, Maria awoke with a nervous stomach—it was Election Day, and Mrs. Duniway still intended to vote. Maria dressed and made a quick breakfast by stuffing ham into a sliced biscuit.

"It's still dark, Maria," Mrs. O'Malley said. "You'd best take the carriage."

"No time," Maria said. "I'll be fine." She bundled herself into her coat and nibbled on her biscuit sandwich as she walked.

At the newspaper office, men milled around *The Oregonian* presses debating the election. Oregon was heavily Republican, and most men wanted President Grant to earn a second term.

Maria had never asked Mrs. Duniway whom she planned to vote for—assuming she could cast a ballot. But the night before, Mrs. Duniway had enthusiastically endorsed President Grant at a political rally. Will had escorted Mama and Maria to the event, and Maria had been surprised at how many women had been in attendance.

Maria's article lay on Mrs. Duniway's desk, awaiting final changes. Maria peered inside the editor's office and saw Mrs. Duniway, dressed in a somber black dress and hat. "Are you ready, ma'am?" Maria asked.

"Quite," Mrs. Duniway said. "But I shall not cast my vote until after the noon meal. Three other women will accompany me, and we will vote together."

"May I come?" Maria asked.

Mrs. Duniway shook her head. "I have no desire to become a spectacle by bringing an entourage. We shall conduct ourselves with the solemnity that voting deserves."

That afternoon, Maria waited with Daisy for Mrs. Duniway to return. The editor stormed into the office, her face flushed. "We cast our ballots," she announced. "But the election judges protested our votes."

"What happened?" Maria asked.

"They refused to put our four ballots in the ballot box," Mrs. Duniway fumed. "The judge took mine from my hand and told me he was required to take it under protest." She took off her hat and threw it on her desk. "Protest!" She sniffed. "He claimed nothing in the law permitted him to accept my ballot. And I told him there was also no law prohibiting him from counting it."

"Then he didn't take your ballot?" Daisy said.

"Oh, he took it. He took all four of our ballots. But he did not put them in the ballot box. He put them under the box, and they will not be counted."

"At least he didn't throw you in jail," Maria said.

"Some things are worth incarceration," Mrs. Duniway said, her eyes flashing. "Now, let's get to work on our story. I have been promised space in *The Oregonian* tomorrow to describe my attempt to vote. All of Oregon will soon know of the perfidy of our election officials."

The next morning, Maria ate a leisurely breakfast with her family before heading to the newspaper. "The Republicans won decisively," Will announced as he read *The Oregonian*. "Do you remember, Pa, when it took weeks to get the election results? Thanks to the telegraph, we know almost as much as they do in Washington."

"Humph," Papa said. "I'm glad General Grant will remain in the White House another four years."

"It says here your Mrs. Duniway voted," Will said, grinning at Maria. "But the judges wouldn't count her ballot."

"At least she tried," Maria said. "And at least the judges treated her civilly."

"What?" Papa said. "May I read that?" He held out his hand to Will for the newspaper. After he read it, he turned to Maria. "Did you know about her scheme?"

"My sources are confidential," Maria said, buttering her toast.

"Confidential, my foot," Papa snapped. "I am your father, young lady.

Did you know this in advance or not?"

"Yes, Papa."

"And yet you still went to work yesterday? There could have been violence."

"But there wasn't," Maria said. "Mrs. Duniway was treated peaceably, though she was disappointed in the result."

"I'm surprised at Abigail," Mama said. "I thought her a law-abiding woman."

"The law is unjust, Mama," Maria said.

"Maybe so," Mama said. "But there are ways to protest injustice."

"Which is what Mrs. Duniway did," Maria said. "Along with many other women—in Oregon and back East."

"How do you know what happened in the East?" Will asked. "*The Oregonian* doesn't mention female voters outside of Portland."

Maria sniffed and bit her toast.

"Has Mrs. Duniway been filling your head with tales?" Papa asked.

"They're not tales," Maria said. "Women will vote someday. Many women are pushing for suffrage now. Perhaps I shall vote next time." Will rolled his eyes at her last statement.

Mrs. Duniway arrived at *The New Northwest* offices just as Maria was hanging up her coat. "Did you see *The Oregonian* article?" she crowed, waving the morning paper.

"Yes," Maria said. "We discussed it at breakfast."

"They printed it exactly as I wrote it," Mrs. Duniway said. "I was afraid they would edit it."

Maria smiled. "Would they dare?"

"Unfortunately, yes." Mrs. Duniway spread the paper out on a table. "We shall reprint this in *The New Northwest*."

"But what about what we wrote earlier?" Maria asked.

"I want the facts put before Portland and the world," Mrs. Duniway said. "Just as I described them in *The Oregonian*." She sighed. "I suppose we over-thought the problem, worrying about whether I would be jailed."

Maria swallowed hard. She had hoped to see her words in the paper, even if under Mrs. Duniway's signature. "Will none of what I wrote make it into the paper?"

"I'll work in what I can," Mrs. Duniway said. "The part about my trip to

New York in May will probably still do, with a new introduction discussing the election results. Plus, I think your paragraph comparing the former vassalage of the Negroes to the disenfranchisement of women is good."

"Thank you, ma'am," Maria said, still disappointed.

"Now, Maria," the editor said, "I'd like you to comb through every other publication we receive today. I want to report on any other situations in which women voted and how their ballots were treated. We shall not print this Friday's issue until tomorrow afternoon. So please check the papers we receive in tomorrow's morning mail as well."

"Yes, Mrs. Duniway." But Maria chafed at the mundane assignment after being allowed to channel the thoughts of her editor.

By Thursday at noon, Maria had a column's worth of articles collected for the typesetter to reprint. Mrs. Duniway decided not only to reprint Wednesday's *Oregonian* article in full, but also to reference an article from the *Oregon Herald*.

"That should complete this week's edition," Mrs. Duniway said. "Thank you, Maria."

"When do you think we will hear about Mrs. Anthony's attempt to vote?" Maria asked.

"I do not know," Mrs. Duniway said. "Perhaps we will see something on the wires by next week if she was successful. It will be at least two weeks, I suspect, before I receive any correspondence from her. Most likely, she will write her local supporters before me."

Maria walked home for the noon meal and encountered Mr. Higgins on the street. "Miss McDougall," he said, tipping his hat. "It is a fine day for early November, is it not?"

"Very fine," Maria responded.

He fell into step beside her. "Is your father satisfied with the election results?"

"Yes," she replied.

"And you?"

"I am pleased that the Republicans won, Mr. Higgins," she said. She wondered how he felt about women's suffrage, so she added, "But I am not pleased that Abigail Duniway's vote was not counted."

"I saw *The Oregonian* article," he said, shaking his head. "She is certainly a woman of conviction."

"Yes," Maria said. His answer didn't tell her anything about what he thought. "Perhaps I will join her in the next election."

"Miss McDougall," he said, "I am sure you are also a woman of conviction."

Chapter 28: Will Seeks Responsibility

Once the election results were in—Republican victories in both the U.S. Congress and the Oregon Legislature—Will redoubled his focus on McDougall & Company. He read through correspondence from the two California branch managers, Bayliss Beck and Samuel Cassidy. Neither file raised any concerns. As Higgins said, Beck's profits were modest, but steady. Cassidy's results were more erratic. Will also examined recent copies of the California ledgers, but without being able to conduct a physical inventory or see the actual invoices, there was no way to know what was accurate.

"We need to compare the information we have with what the California bookkeepers record. And we also need to do a full inventory of the warehouses," Will told his father that Thursday evening.

"Do you mean to treat our agents as criminals?" Pa asked.

"No," Will said. "I merely mean to hold them accountable. Any honest man would appreciate confirmation his records are accurate."

"Have you talked to Higgins about making the trip?"

"Not yet, Pa. But if you agree he should go, I'll raise it with him."

"Invite him to take the noon meal with us soon," Pa said. "We'll talk with him then."

Will saw no reason to delay, so on Friday, he asked Higgins to join the McDougalls at noon. He explained why Pa wanted to talk to him.

"I will be most happy to undertake the trip to San Francisco and Sacramento," Higgins responded.

At midday, Will and Higgins left the office. Higgins steered them past *The Oregonian* offices, saying, "I thought we might escort your sister home."

Will raised his eyebrows but remained silent. He entered the newspaper office and looked for Maria. She was putting on her coat, and Higgins rushed to help her.

"We're heading home," Will said. "Pa wants Higgins to join us for lunch."

Maria smiled at the accountant, then at Will. "Then we should leave. Mama won't want the meal to be cold."

When they arrived home, Will made a point of assisting Maria with her coat, if only to avoid letting Higgins have the honor. In the dining room, Will sat on one side of Pa, while Higgins sat on the other.

"No business until after the meal," Mama said. And she directed the conversation toward the weather, current theatricals, and other topics she and Maria could also discuss.

After they finished eating, Will wheeled Pa into his library, and Higgins followed. "Now," Pa said, shrugging Will away when he moved to adjust the cushions, "What do you think of Will's notion of auditing the California operation?"

"It's always good to keep men on their toes," Higgins said. "Based on my prior dealings with Beck and Cassidy, they will bemoan the time spent on the audit, but they will be glad to build their relationships with the Portland office."

Something in the way Higgins spoke made Will think Higgins had additional information on Beck and Cassidy. "Have you had private correspondence with these two gentlemen?" Will asked. "More than what is in the office files?"

Higgins rubbed his temple as if trying to remember. "I sent Cassidy a letter congratulating him on his marriage shortly after he started work with us." He frowned in thought. "I don't recall any personal letters to Beck, only correspondence about the business."

"Well, then, it's settled," Pa said, passing a hand wearily over his face. "Higgins, you will go to California to inspect our branch offices. When can you leave?"

Higgins shrugged. "With Will here in Portland, I can leave any time." He looked at Will. "Do you feel comfortable supervising the operations here?"

"He can ask me if there are any problems," Pa said testily. "I haven't lost my faculties yet."

Higgins looked at the calendar on Pa's desk. "Why don't I leave next Wednesday? If the steamboat stays on schedule, I will be in San Francisco that weekend, and certainly by Monday. I'll plan a week in California, perhaps two weeks—" He thumbed through the calendar. "And be back in Portland sometime around December 6."

"Sounds fine," Will said.

"I will purchase my steamboat ticket tomorrow," Higgins said. "And wire Beck and Cassidy."

"Don't wire them," Will said. "Let your arrival be a surprise."

Higgins's eyes narrowed, and he glanced at Pa.

Pa shrugged.

"As you wish," Higgins said.

That evening after supper, Will approached Pa again. They sipped their whiskey and rehashed the conversation with Higgins. "Do you trust Higgins to make this California trip?" Will asked.

"If I didn't," Pa said, "then I shouldn't employ him. He's my head accountant. I have no reason to doubt his abilities or his character."

Then Will asked what he really wanted to know. "What do you see my role being in the company? I want to run a part of it, to be as trusted as you seem to trust Higgins—both for my abilities and my character."

Pa studied Will for a moment. "Your character is not in question, son. But you've only been home a few weeks. Owen sent me excellent reports on your work, but I must see how you interact with our employees and customers here in Portland before I give you more responsibility."

"But you do intend to turn over the business to me someday, don't you? Cal doesn't seem to want to share the responsibility."

Pa gave a wry smile. "When I can no longer oversee the company myself, I suppose I will have to. And if the younger boys want a part of it once they are grown, I will find roles for all of you." He tipped his whiskey glass toward Will. "But as of now, I still have a brain, even if my legs do not work as I want, and I intend to remain in charge."

Before he went to bed that night, Will sat in his room, staring at a book on his lap. He'd read the same words over and over, his mind replaying the conversations of the day. Something about Higgins didn't sit right with him, and he wondered if he should have insisted he travel to California instead of Higgins. But perhaps he just didn't like the man's interest in Maria.

Higgins was better acquainted with the California operation than Will, so he should be able to ferret out whatever shenanigans Beck was up to. Will really didn't think Higgins would find any fault with the San Francisco branch—he had no suspicions after Cassidy's candor when they met. But as long as Higgins was in California, he obviously should review both offices.

Would Pa ever give Will the responsibility and independence he craved? Or, once he could return to the office, would Pa look over Will's shoulder to scrutinize and critique every move he made?

He couldn't answer any of his questions. All he could do was worry. Finally, Will closed his book, extinguished his oil lamp, and tried to sleep.

Sunday afternoon, as most of the McDougall family engaged in quiet activities in the parlor, a knock sounded on the front door. Will answered it. "Telegram," the boy outside said. Will gave him a coin, and the boy handed over the paper.

Will read:

DATE: 10 NOVEMBER 1872
FROM: OWEN MCDOUGALL BOSTON
TO: CALEB MCDOUGALL PORTLAND
FIRE DOWNTOWN BOSTON LOSSES UNKNOWN

"Pa!" Will shouted, rushing into the library where his father lay napping. "Uncle Owen says there's been a fire in Boston."

Pa startled awake. "What?"

"What is it, Will?" Mama said, entering the library with Maria and Nate behind her.

"A fire in Boston," Will said. "Telegram from Uncle Owen."

Pa took the telegram from Will and read it. "This doesn't tell us anything." He looked at Will. "What properties does the company have in downtown Boston?"

"The only downtown property we own outright is the office building," Will said. "But we hold liens on several other offices and warehouses that we've financed. The losses could be significant."

"Send Owen an inquiry first thing in the morning," Pa ordered.

"Of course," Will said.

"Is the company adequately insured against loss?" Pa asked.

"The building we own is insured," Will said. "For the buildings we've financed, our contracts require the owners to maintain insurance. But whether they do and in what amounts, I cannot say."

"Don't our contracts specify how much coverage our clients must carry?" Pa demanded.

"Usually." Will sighed and shook his head. "But whether we followed up to be sure the owners complied is another matter." He paused, wondering if this was the time to raise his interest in railroads with Pa. "I think the Boston branch has become too invested in real estate. We should have diversified—in Boston and here in the West. After my recent travels, I am convinced the nation will soon be crisscrossed with rails, and I think we should invest in railroads."

"Railroads have been slow to come to Oregon," Pa said. "I thought the same as you a decade ago. But here we are, still with no tracks finished to California. Only short lines around Portland. And now is no time to speculate. We need to proceed cautiously, at least until we know what we lost in Boston."

"The long-distance rail lines will come," Will insisted.

"Maybe," Pa said. "But when?"

Chapter 29: Business Problems

Monday morning, Will was at the telegraph office when it opened.

DATE: 11 NOVEMBER 1872
FROM: WILLIAM MCDOUGALL PORTLAND
TO: OWEN MCDOUGALL BOSTON
CONDOLENCES ON FIRE SEND IMMEDIATE
REPORT DETAILING LOSSES

It was late Tuesday afternoon before Uncle Owen's response arrived.

DATE: 12 NOVEMBER 1872
FROM: OWEN MCDOUGALL BOSTON
TO: WILLIAM MCDOUGALL PORTLAND
OFFICE UNHARMED FIVE INVESTMENT
PROPERTIES DESTROYED INSURANCE UNKNOWN

When Will showed the telegram to Amos Higgins, Higgins said, "Perhaps I should delay my trip to California tomorrow. This new situation—"

"You've purchased your ticket already, haven't you?" Will asked.

"Yes, but I can exchange it if—"

"There's nothing you can do from Portland about Boston," Will said. "Insurance may cover our losses. Besides, I know the Boston business better than you do."

Higgins reached into the bottom drawer of his desk and pulled out a flask and two tumblers. "Drink?" he asked.

Will nodded.

Higgins poured whiskey into the tumblers, then frowned as he handed one glass to Will. "Insurers will be overwhelmed with so many properties destroyed. The same insurance companies will have covered many of the burned buildings."

Will sipped his drink. "We won't know for weeks how much exposure McDougall & Company has and whether our clients can continue their loan payments. You might as well spend your time in California."

"Bankers rarely escape from disasters unscathed. And the Boston business is mostly banking, isn't it?" Higgins said.

"More financing at this point than banking," Will said. "We make loans to real estate investors. But yes, after the fire, the Boston branch may well struggle. All the more reason to understand what's happening in California. Our West Coast operations may have to carry the company for the next couple of years."

"I suppose so," Higgins said. "Then I shall leave tomorrow as planned."

"What's your opinion on railroad investments?" Will asked. "My father seems reluctant."

Higgins nodded. "I've discussed rail proposals with him in the past. He's hesitant—says rail development here is too slow."

"When I was a boy, Pa was excited about the prospect of rails. But he seems to have soured."

"Many men in Portland have lost fortunes on Oregon railroads." Higgins shook his head. "I still believe railroads will have their day. But when? Perhaps your father is right to be cautious."

"Or perhaps we're missing an opportunity," Will said.

The next morning, Will stood at the dock to see Higgins off on the *S.S. Oregonian*, the same steamship Will had taken north a month ago. "Wire me when you have a sense whether there could be a problem with Beck."

"Or with Cassidy," Higgins said. "I know you liked the man, but I will form my own judgments based on what I find."

"As you should," Will said. "My father and I will expect a full report when you return to Portland. Take the time to have a copy made of any records you think we might need."

"I hope to only be gone a fortnight," Higgins said. "But I shall do what I can."

"Also, please look in on my brother Cal," Will said. "Perhaps you can convince him to get involved in the family business, though I could not."

"I look forward to seeing Cal again," Higgins said. "I'll invite him to go with me to the branch offices. My correspondence with Beck and Cassidy has always been cordial, and I have no reason to think they will not be candid with me. But having a McDougall along cannot hurt."

"Thank you," Will said, extending his hand.

Higgins shook it, then reached for his valise. "Please give my regards to your mother and sister."

"Which sister?" Will asked, though he knew well enough.

"To Miss Maria, of course," Higgins said. "I shall call on her when I return."

Will turned to leave as Higgins walked up the gangplank. He was sure the accountant intended to court Maria. But for at least the next two weeks, Will could pursue her himself. He needed to determine if she was the same girl he'd loved as a boy.

That evening after dinner, Will joined his father in the library. "When will the doctor let you try stairs?" he asked.

"Don't tell your mother," Pa said. "I've been trying a step or two every day. Hurts like the devil. But a little less each time."

"Don't rush it, Pa," Will said. "It's only been two months since your accident. And I'd hate to see you fall."

"Then don't watch, son," Pa said, settling into a chair. "I will get better. I will walk on my own. I might never ride a horse again, though I'm not ruling that out yet."

Will poured them each a drink. He wondered why Pa didn't invite Nate to join them—Will had been younger than Nate when Pa first offered him an after-dinner drink. But then, Will's militia experience had caused him to grow up quickly.

"Have you thought about making another railroad investment?" Will asked as he sat near Pa. "I mentioned it to Higgins today. He agrees railroads will have their day."

"Yes, railroads will have their day," Pa said. "But will it be in my lifetime?"

"Don't be morbid, Pa." Will sipped his whiskey, savoring its burn down his gullet. "What was your last foray into rail investments?"

"Men approached me last year," Pa said. "I have yet to see the right opportunity."

"Who did you talk to?"

"Ben Holladay. He's pushing for a rail line from Roseburg south to California."

"I've heard of Holladay," Will said. "He started the stage line in California before the War, didn't he?"

"Yes," Pa said. "Sold it to Wells Fargo in sixty-six. Made a fortune. Moved to Oregon in sixty-eight, and he's pursued rail lines here ever since. He's nosing around for local money, but he's also reeled in several German investors."

"Should I talk to Holladay?" Will asked. "Ask him what his plans are?"

Pa shrugged. "Talk to him if you like. Just be careful. The man is too clever by half. And he's a rude, unscrupulous son of a bitch."

Will nearly choked on his whiskey. Pa rarely cursed. Was he acting the curmudgeon because he was in pain? Or were his words a warning about Holladay for Will to heed?

Will decided he would wait to approach Ben Holladay until Higgins returned. Higgins would probably have a perspective on the railroad tycoon.

In the meantime, Will delved further into the McDougall & Company history, using Higgins's absence to comb through files kept in the accountant's office. Will also rummaged through the attic and cellar, uncovering dusty records back to the 1850s. When he'd left Oregon, he'd been too young to pay any attention to Pa's business. Now, he read its history with great interest. Pa had started in Oregon City, but as the state's fortunes shifted to Portland, so too had Pa's investments. The company also owned significant assets in the state capital of Salem, with scattered investments elsewhere in Oregon.

By Friday noon, Will had been through every nook and cranny on the premises, everything except the locked drawer in Higgins's desk where he kept his whiskey.

Satisfied with the week's effort, Will set out to enjoy himself. He stopped by the New Market Theater on his way home and purchased two prime tickets to a concert playing that evening, intending to invite Maria to accompany him. He wanted to see her in her red dress again, all fiery finery and molten eyes. With Higgins away, this was his chance to court her.

Chapter 30: Another Theater Outing

Maria heard Will call her name as she sat in the parlor sewing with Mama, Eliza, and Lottie. After a busy morning at the newspaper, she was enjoying a leisurely Friday afternoon—if mending Evie's pinafore could be called leisure.

Will burst into the room, grinning. "Maria, I have tickets for the concert tonight. Will you join me? It's an operetta that's been a sensation in Boston."

She laid the pinafore in her lap and smiled. "How lovely."

"Wear your red dress," he said, then turned to leave.

"What about the rest of us?" Eliza asked.

"I only have two tickets," Will said over his shoulder. "Maybe next time, Eliza."

Eliza huffed and pouted.

"Now, Eliza," Mama said, "Will and Maria have been working hard. They deserve an evening of fun."

Eliza's expression did not change.

Maria put on her red dress before supper, and she was pleased to see Will's gaze linger as she took her seat. Mama frowned at them both.

After dinner, Maria went upstairs to finish preparing for the theater. Mama followed her into her room. "Be careful, Maria," Mama said. "In the eyes of our neighbors, Will is your brother."

Maria's throat tightened. "I know, Mama."

"I want you and Will to enjoy yourselves," Mama said. "And I know you and he want to see how you feel about each other. But you mustn't jeopardize this family. I love you both, and I will not let the two of you break this family apart."

"How could we—?" Maria began.

"Before Will left, you and he were too young to know your hearts. Now you are old enough to determine your futures. But decide based on who you are today, not on childhood memories. And in the meantime, you must behave with decorum."

"Yes, Mama." Maria thought she understood what Mama meant, but she didn't want to worry about the future tonight. She simply wanted to enjoy Will's company for an evening. Just one evening.

The music was enthralling. Maria closed her eyes and listened—sobbing violins, laughing flutes, wailing oboes. She felt Will's shoulder against her own and leaned toward him, sensing the strength and tension in his arm.

His hand clasped hers on the armrest between them. She opened her eyes and smiled at him, squeezing his hand as she settled a little closer.

At intermission, Will stood and helped Maria to her feet. "Would you care for lemonade?" he asked.

"Please," she replied. He placed his hand on the small of her back as he guided her toward the lobby.

"Maria," a voice called. She turned to see three former classmates approaching, their fans fluttering. They greeted her, then smiled at Will. "Who is this?" one asked.

"My brother William," she said. "Home from Boston at last." And she introduced them to Will.

"Your brother?" a second girl asked, eyebrow arching. "Very pleased to meet you, Mr. McDougall. Maria has spoken of you often."

"Always favorably," the third girl said. "But she never mentioned you were so dashing."

They made small talk during intermission, while Will brought them glasses of lemonade.

When the concert was over, Maria let Will lead her through the long line to find their family's carriage. As he settled inside the vehicle beside her, she said, "Thank you, Will. I had a wonderful time."

"So did I," he said. "And I enjoyed meeting your friends."

Maria shook her head. "They weren't so friendly when we were in school."

"Were they some of the girls who teased you so badly?" he asked, then shouted at the stable boy to set off for home.

She nodded. "But that is all in the past now."

"Was it so terrible?"

"For a while," she said, then shrugged. "But I grew not to mind." She smiled at him. "You helped."

"How did I help?"

"By being my friend," she said. "By treating me with respect. You and our parents."

"I hope I will always be your friend," he said, his voice husky.

She patted his hand. "You are."

"I'd like to be more," he said. He leaned over and touched his lips to hers, murmured, "Do I have any hope, Maria?"

His lips felt soft and gentle. His tongue touched her lower lip, and she opened to him. He deepened the kiss and pulled her close. It felt heavenly. She touched her tongue to his, and she felt his groan throughout her body.

Maria let him kiss her and kissed him back until she remembered Mama's words. "It's too soon," she said, pulling back.

Will let her go. "Too soon for what?"

"Too soon to know how I feel," she said. "We can't do this."

"Do what? Kiss?"

"Not like that," she said.

"How will we know how we feel if we don't spend time together?" he asked.

"I will spend time with you," she said. "I want to." She used Mama's words to explain. "But we must decide based on who we are now. Not on long-ago memories. And we need to be careful because the world thinks we are brother and sister."

Will took a deep breath and moved away from her.

"Beyond all else," Maria said, "you are my friend. I couldn't bear to lose that." If she lost Will's friendship, she would be lost herself.

The household was dark when Maria and Will entered through the side door. The stable boy waved as he drove toward the carriage house. "Thank you, Will," Maria said. "It was a lovely evening."

"It was," he said, as they walked upstairs. He paused at her bedroom doorway and brushed his lips against hers again, this time with only a whispery touch. "Goodnight."

She entered her room and leaned against the door, listening to Will walk down the hall to his room. She put a finger where his lips had been.

Mama was right. She would have to be careful, particularly if she wanted to remain friends with Will, no matter what. But what if she didn't want to just be friends? What if she wanted more from Will? Could it work?

She touched her lips again. She could feel more than friendship for him. It would be so easy. But what would it mean for the family? What would it mean for her work?

Chapter 31: Zhuang Li Raises a Problem

Will spent the weekend after the concert following Maria about the house. There were too many people around for him to speak with her privately, and she told him she was too busy to walk with him. On Sunday afternoon, she turned to him and said, "Will, please quit pestering me. I must get letters written to friends in Oregon City. I'm writing the Pershings—do you have news for me to pass along?"

Will shook his head, then retreated to Pa's library with a book. But he couldn't read. He didn't want to moon over Maria, but he wondered if she thought of their evening together as much as he did. He remembered the kiss they'd shared. As she'd molded herself to him, she was everything he'd imagined she would be—beautiful, passionate, enticing. He would pursue her until she agreed to marry him, Higgins be damned.

On the Tuesday after Higgins left for California, Will sat at his father's massive oak desk at the McDougall & Company offices reviewing customer correspondence. Zhuang Li came to the doorway and bowed. "May I speak, Mr. McDougall?"

Will looked up and gestured at a chair. "Of course, Li. Come in."

Li entered, holding a bound volume. He approached the desk but remained standing. "I find problem."

Will frowned and gestured again for Li to sit.

Still standing, Li said, "Wrong numbers in ledger."

"Wrong?" Will said. "How so?"

"Some October numbers in ledger not match what clients pay." Li seemed

140

hesitant. "I total invoices paid every day. Other clerks later write payments in ledger. Ledger not match my daily totals."

Li's pidgin English was hard to understand. "Please explain." Plus, Will didn't like looking up at the man. "And sit down."

At Will's direct order, Li sat. "Each day, I add invoices customers pay that day. On abacus. I keep running total. Other clerks enter payments into ledger. After month end, clerks make summary of invoices and payments. Mr. Higgins review, then give to your father. October summary not done before Mr. Higgins leave, so I review today. Ledger not match my daily total. Summary match ledger, but not my tally."

After parsing through what he thought Li said, Will summarized, "You mean the cash ledger that the clerks keep doesn't match the amounts you calculated through the month. And the summary prepared from the ledger doesn't match your daily tally either."

Li nodded. "Yes."

"How can you recall amounts from several weeks ago?" Will asked.

"I keep daily total. Abacus very fast, very accurate. Numbers not match." Li showed Will a list of handwritten numbers on a sheet of unruled paper. "Here my daily total." He opened the bound volume full of columns of neatly written numbers. "Here ledger. All invoices for October. Many pages." Then he pulled out another paper with a list of numbers. "Here October summary of ledger from clerks. Numbers in ledger and summary match. Numbers not match my daily total. My total higher."

"How can you be sure your calculations were correct?" Will pressed.

"Abacus not lie."

Will thought for a moment. "Where are the invoices marked paid? Don't we keep them?"

Li shrugged. "I not know. Clerks not know. Mr. Higgins give invoices to clerks to write in ledger, then he take them back. Don't know what he do with them."

"You don't know where Higgins puts them?"

Li shook his head. "No."

"I'll look through his office," Will said. "I was researching our old contracts in there, and I didn't see any recent invoices. But they must be somewhere."

"Thank you, Mr. McDougall." Li stood. "Look soon."

"Do you suspect any wrongdoing? Or do you think it was an accounting error?"

Li lowered his head and mumbled, "All I know—ledger wrong."

The Asian man clearly seemed to suspect wrongdoing, but Will doubted Li would say so directly. "Thank you, Li. I'll investigate the matter."

Li bowed as he left.

Will immediately went to Higgins's office and rummaged through drawers and stacks of papers. He found no invoices, no strange lists of numbers, nothing suspicious. Nothing to indicate receipts or expenses had been altered. Perhaps it was a simple accounting error. Or perhaps Li's daily tallies were wrong.

Frustrated, Will strode to the clerks' office and asked one of them for the file on an October order of lumber a customer had purchased from the McDougall warehouse in Portland.

The clerk handed him the file.

"Did we receive payment for the lumber?" he asked.

"Yes, Mr. McDougall," the man replied. "The week after delivery. The receipt's in the file."

Will examined the receipt, which appeared in order. "Thank you."

Then he reviewed a few other files from October. Those, too, appeared to be accurate. Short of reviewing every file for the past month, there was no way to verify what Li had told him. Li only had daily totals, not a list of every invoice received—and Will only had Li's word the sums didn't match.

That evening over their whiskey, Will asked Pa, "What do you think of Zhuang Li?"

"I barely know him," Pa said. "A bright young man, I think. Higgins manages the clerks. I rarely deal with them directly."

"Li thinks the cash ledger was off in October." Will swirled his glass, watching the amber liquid reflect the library's fire. "Have the books always balanced in the past?"

"Off?" Pa said. "What do you mean off?"

"Li says he adds up our daily cash receipts, then someone else records them in the ledgers. He says the October ledger doesn't match his totals."

"How can he know that?" Pa said.

"I asked him that very question." Will sighed. "He says his calculations are accurate. He uses an abacus."

Pa grinned. "I've seen him with that thing. His fingers move so fast I can't follow them. I don't see how he can know his original sums were accurate."

"I wondered," Will said. "Higgins does the monthly summaries for you, doesn't he?"

"Yes," Pa said. "I've never had a reason to doubt him. If there's a discrepancy, it's probably because someone else did this month's report. Do you have it?"

Will found the monthly summary he'd put on Pa's desk when he got home that afternoon. "Li said he prepared this. I checked a couple of invoices, and they matched the ledger and this report."

Pa leaned back. "Not much we can do until Higgins gets back. Have you heard from him?"

"Only a one-line telegram saying he arrived in California," Will said.

"Wire him back," Pa ordered. "Ask if he saw any issues with our receipts in October. Maybe he knows what Li is talking about. And tell him to report on the California branches as soon as he can."

The next morning, Will sent a wire:

DATE: 20 NOVEMBER 1872
FROM: WILLIAM MCDOUGALL PORTLAND
TO: AMOS HIGGINS SAN FRANCISCO
FATHER REQUESTS CALIFORNIA UPDATE
SOONEST POSSIBLE DISCREPANCY IN OCTOBER
PORTLAND LEDGER CAN YOU EXPLAIN

Will didn't expect an immediate response, so he settled into a routine. He spent mornings reviewing old files and answering questions from the staff. He met businessmen around Portland for coffee and sometimes stayed downtown for lunch. Other days, he walked home for the noon meal, then spent an hour updating his father.

Each day, he asked Zhuang Li to show him his daily tally of receipts. He checked the ledgers the following day after the clerks entered those same receipts. Everything matched. He decided Li must have made a mistake in October. He wouldn't worry about the problem until he could talk to

Higgins.

Meanwhile, at home, he and Pa continued their daily discussions, which centered mostly on their potential losses in Boston.

"I wish we would hear from Owen," Pa fumed, drumming his fingers on his library desk.

"How long do letters typically take from Boston?" Will asked. "Two weeks, give or take?"

Pa nodded. "About that. A week on the Transcontinental train to California, then another four or five days on a ship or coach north to Portland. But Owen knows we want the information—he ought to have written by now."

"With a fire that size, it might take time to determine which businesses were underinsured," Will said. "We may just have to be patient."

"Yes." Pa shut his eyes, fatigue showing on his face. "But without the information, we can't make plans to invest our funds here. We don't know whether Owen will need our support for the East Coast operation."

"Have you thought any more about investing in railroads?" Will asked.

Pa shook his head. "I told you before—now is not the time."

Will bristled at Pa's abrupt dismissal of his idea. But Pa looked too tired to argue. Still, Will wondered again how he could create a significant role in the family business for himself. Could rail investments provide that opportunity?

By the following Tuesday, November 26, Will still hadn't received a response from Higgins. It was Cal's birthday, and Will sent his brother a telegram:

DATE: 26 NOVEMBER 1872
FROM: WILLIAM MCDOUGALL PORTLAND
TO: CALEB MCDOUGALL OAKLAND
HAPPY BIRTHDAY SUGGEST YOU MEET AMOS
HIGGINS SAN FRANCISCO OFFICE SOONEST

That afternoon, Will had a response from Cal.

DATE: 26 NOVEMBER 1872

FROM: CALEB MCDOUGALL OAKLAND
TO: WILLIAM MCDOUGALL PORTLAND
THANK MAMA FOR SWEATER WHO IS HIGGINS

Upon reading the telegram, Will sighed. Clearly, Higgins hadn't involved Cal, as they had discussed. Frustrated, he sent another wire to Higgins:

DATE: 26 NOVEMBER 1872
FROM: WILLIAM MCDOUGALL PORTLAND
TO: AMOS HIGGINS SAN FRANCISCO
AWAITING UPDATE REQUESTED 20 NOVEMBER

Higgins's lack of responsiveness gnawed at Will, but for now, all he could do was wait.

Chapter 32: Modoc War Begins

When Maria came downstairs for breakfast on Wednesday, December 4, Will and Papa were already at the table discussing the news. "What's in *The Oregonian*?" she asked, dropping a kiss on her father's head.

"There's been a skirmish between the Army and the Modoc tribe," Will said. "Near Fort Klamath, where I was with the militia in sixty-four."

"The Modocs?" Maria turned from filling her plate at the sideboard. "That's Winema Riddle's tribe."

"Who?" Papa asked.

"Winema Riddle. She's a friend of Abigail Duniway." Maria took her seat. "I met her in October. She's living with the Modoc now."

"Then she might be caught up in this problem," Papa said, his face grim. "The Modoc are refusing to move to the Klamath Reservation."

"Was anyone hurt?" Maria picked at her eggs and toast, worried about Mrs. Riddle.

"Soldiers and natives both," Papa said. "The Army retaliated and captured some of the Modocs. I hope Mrs. Duniway's friend wasn't among them."

"Then white vigilantes in Klamath burned another Modoc village," Will said. "It's an ugly situation."

Maria put down her fork, unable to continue eating. "What started it?"

"Hard to tell from the newspaper," Papa said. "Early shots came from both sides."

"I pray Mrs. Riddle is safe," Maria murmured.

But Papa and Will moved on to another topic. "When does Higgins get back?" Papa asked Will.

"He planned to leave San Francisco on Monday's steamboat," Will said. "He never sent the report I requested. We won't hear anything until he returns."

"That ship will arrive on Friday, won't it?" Papa said. "That's just two more days."

Maria learned nothing more about the Modoc War beyond what was in *The Oregonian*. That evening at supper, Will and Papa discussed a report on the impact of the Boston fire on the East Coast branch of McDougall & Company. Curious, Maria asked Will to tell her more about the Boston operation. She understood most of what he explained because of what Papa had taught her.

"Is the damage severe?" Maria asked Papa.

He shrugged. "We can weather it. We have assets beyond those destroyed in the fire. But Owen won't have any extra capital to help finance new investments here in the West for a long time. We will have to bankroll our new projects on our own."

"Then our family is all right?" Maria asked.

Papa smiled indulgently, as he had when she was a little girl. "We'll be fine, poppet. No need to fret."

She didn't like him treating her like a child. "I'm not fretting, Papa. I just want to understand our business."

"Leave that to Will and me," Papa said. "And your Mr. Higgins."

Will shifted in his chair, his mouth opening as if to say something.

But Maria spoke first, her cheeks flaming. "He's not my Mr. Higgins," she said, catching Will's eyes. "He's cordial, but that's all."

The following Monday, when Maria arrived at work, she combed through the day's newspapers looking for more information about the Modoc conflict. Still no news.

"Have you had any word from Mrs. Riddle?" she asked Mrs. Duniway. "Is she with her people on the reservation?"

"I believe so," Mrs. Duniway said. "I've heard nothing since her visit here two months ago. I fear the conflict will become a full-scale war. The Army was embarrassed to lose men to a rag-tag group of tribesmen. And the Modocs are furious over the burning of their village. A Modoc woman perished in the flames."

"How dreadful," Maria murmured. "What do you think will happen?"

Mrs. Duniway sighed. "The Army will fight until they win. Otherwise, they would be humiliated. And the Modocs are starving and have few weapons. But they will not leave their homeland and move to the reservation, which would preserve the peace. It could become a full-scale war."

Later that day, as Maria left work to return home for the noon meal, she found Mr. Higgins waiting for her outside the newspaper office. He must have returned over the weekend, as Papa predicted.

"Good day, Miss McDougall," he said, tipping his hat.

"Why, Mr. Higgins," she said, smiling. "Did you have a pleasant journey from California?"

"Fortunately, I am not plagued by seasickness," he said, falling into step beside her. "Though travel is tiring. Do you recall our discussion some months ago about the horse-car line?"

"Yes."

"It is now operating. Have you ridden it yet?"

She shook her head. "Not yet."

He bowed slightly as he walked. "Neither have I. I would be pleased if you would take a ride with me. It would be a first for both of us."

"I am headed home to eat, and the line runs on First Street, away from our house."

"We could ride to the end of the line, then back," he said.

She shrugged. She would be late for the meal, but she could eat in the kitchen, as she often did. "All right."

They walked to the nearest stop, Mr. Higgins paid their fares, and they boarded. The seats faced sideways, and Mr. Higgins sat beside her. The horses trotted from stop to stop, pulling the car along the rails.

"Isn't this pleasant?" Mr. Higgins said. "Portland is as advanced as any Eastern city now."

"We're not moving any faster than if we were walking," Maria said. "The horses stop every couple of blocks."

"Perhaps," Mr. Higgins said. "But we can save our breath for talking."

Maria laughed. "I suppose. Tell me about your trip to California."

Mr. Higgins obliged with a description of San Francisco and then of the coastal sights from the steamship back to Portland.

When they arrived at the end of the line, they boarded the return car, getting off at the stop closest to the McDougall mansion. Mr. Higgins escorted Maria to her front door. "Won't you come in?" she asked. "We could find you something to eat."

Mr. Higgins shook his head. "Not without an invitation from your parents." He took her hand. "Though I appreciate your offer." He leaned over and kissed her cheek. "I very much enjoyed our conversation."

Maria blushed as she turned toward the house. From the porch, she saw Will watching from the front parlor window.

Chapter 33: Higgins Returns

The morning after Amos Higgins's expected arrival, Will was at the McDougall & Company offices early, determined to talk to the accountant first thing. Higgins walked in just as business hours began.

Without preamble, Will demanded, "What did you learn in California? You never responded to my father's request for a report."

Higgins dropped his hat on his desk and took off his coat. "Might a man sit before being interrogated?" He sank into his chair with a sigh, rubbing his temple.

Will sat across from the accountant's desk. Higgins opened his portfolio and handed Will a sheaf of papers. "I wrote my findings on the steamship. Plenty of time to think without interruption."

"Give me a summary," Will said as he took the papers. "Is Beck involved in any shenanigans?"

"Beck?" Higgins shook his head. "No, not Beck. The Sacramento operation looked strong. But Cassidy is pulling the wool over our eyes."

"Really?" Will said in surprise. "He didn't strike me as dishonest."

"You only spent a few hours with him," Higgins said. "I spent three full days in his company. And I heard plenty from other employees in our San Francisco branch. I suspect he overstates his expenses."

"Which expenses?"

Higgins waved at the papers he'd given Will. "It's all there. Read my report, then we'll talk."

Will stood. "I'll show it to my father as well. Let's meet at the house first thing Monday morning, and the three of us will decide how to proceed."

The accusation against Cassidy trumped Will's concern about the

Portland ledgers. He'd raise that matter later.

Will perused Higgins's report, which was thorough and well written. The accountant detailed his conclusions about both the San Francisco and Sacramento branches.

Higgins had started in San Francisco with Cassidy's operation. Cassidy's income reporting seemed solid, but Higgins thought the purchase prices of grain and lumber were overstated. He also wrote that the cost of Asian imports was high—"above what we pay in Oregon," he wrote.

Will frowned. Couldn't purchase prices be verified? If the costs were real, Cassidy might be a poor negotiator or a poor manager, but high expenses didn't mean he'd defrauded the company, as Higgins hinted.

Turning to the report on Sacramento, Will was surprised to find it began with a description of Beck's family—Higgins noted Beck's wife had been seriously ill during Will's visit. Beck apologized to Higgins for rushing Will's warehouse tour and told Higgins he'd been worried his wife might die.

Perhaps he'd misjudged Beck, Will mused, though he'd found the man more pompous than distraught. If Beck had mentioned his wife's illness, Will would certainly have understood. He wondered why Beck hadn't explained himself at the time.

Higgins found no concerns with the income or expenses in Sacramento. Both were lower than in San Francisco, but Sacramento was a smaller market, so Higgins wrote it was reasonable for prices to be lower. Will couldn't disagree.

Will dug into the numbers Higgins included in his report. The net profit in Sacramento was less, but, as Higgins pointed out, that didn't mean Beck was mismanaging the Sacramento operation.

Will gave Higgins's report to Pa. "Here," he said. "Read it, then we can talk. Higgins will be here Monday morning to discuss it."

Will and Pa spoke briefly Sunday evening, both agreeing the report was thorough, but they needed to probe the details with Higgins. They were ready with questions when Higgins arrived on Monday at nine.

"Tell me, Higgins," Pa began, "did you have any concerns about Beck or Cassidy?"

Will thought Pa should have confronted the accountant more directly. He wondered why Pa started with such a broad question.

Higgins shook his head. "Not really. Beck is a seasoned manager. He keeps the warehouses well stocked and buys inventory at reasonable prices. I'd like to see a higher net return to McDougall & Company, but he is probably charging as much as the Sacramento market can bear."

"So the numbers seem to indicate," Pa murmured. "And Cassidy?"

Higgins shrugged. "He's younger, less experienced. San Francisco is the largest market on the West Coast—it dwarfs Portland. His costs to purchase goods are higher, but so are his sales prices. I wonder if he couldn't press harder for lower costs, look harder for bargains, but maybe he's doing a reasonable job."

"Then you wouldn't replace either of them?" Pa asked.

"Not now." Higgins looked at Pa. "But we need to keep an eye on Cassidy—"

"And Beck," Will interjected, not ready to abandon his initial negative impression of Beck. "Both California branches bear watching."

"Of course," Higgins said, continuing to focus on Pa. "We must supervise them both. Do you agree, Mr. McDougall?"

Pa nodded. "I appreciate your efforts in California. I trust your travels went smoothly?"

Higgins smiled. "I'm a homebody at heart. But I go where I'm needed." He rose. "Thank you for your time this morning, Mr. McDougall."

"I will see you out," Will said. At the front door, as Higgins donned his hat and coat, Will said, "I'm sorry if my assessment of the California managers caused you to travel unnecessarily."

"Not at all," Higgins said, offering his hand. "As we agreed before I left, oversight of the company's branches is essential. You or I should visit California regularly, now that your father cannot travel easily."

Will watched the accountant stride down the walk to the street. He still hadn't brought up the October discrepancies with Higgins. He wondered how to do so, given that Zhuang Li had no proof that any discrepancies existed. Plus, Higgins seemed to have an answer for everything.

Will puttered around the house through the morning, deciding not to go into the office until after the midday meal. As noon approached, he prowled the front parlor, pacing in front of the windows.

"Gracious, Will," Mama said as she sat sewing. "Won't you sit? You make me nervous."

"Sorry, Mama," he said. He turned to take a seat, but froze when he saw Higgins and Maria approaching the front door. Why were they together? He peered out the window.

Higgins clasped Maria's hand and leaned over to kiss her cheek. Will's fists clenched. What the devil was the man about? And why had Maria permitted such liberties?

Maria entered the house, stopped to greet them, then went upstairs. Will itched to rush after her, but that would not be wise. Not while he was angry.

Throughout the meal, Will glowered across the table at Maria. She didn't seem to notice. When they finished eating, he asked, "Want to take a walk, Maria?"

She tilted her head as if puzzled, but said, "You can walk me back to the newspaper office. Let me fetch my hat and cloak."

They met in the hallway, and Will opened the door for her. She smiled and preceded him down the front steps. "A fine day, isn't it?" she said, lifting her face to the wintry sun. "Mr. Higgins took me on the horse-car this morning. But I much prefer walking when the weather is nice."

"What were you doing with him?" Will said, trying to stay calm.

"He escorted me home. We'd discussed the horse-car weeks ago, and he wanted to treat me to a ride."

"I saw him kiss you," Will blurted.

Maria stopped and stared at him. "Were you spying on us?"

"You were on the porch, in plain sight of the parlor window. Anybody could have seen you. Mama was there—she could have seen you."

Maria shook her head. "You can't act this way, Will. We have to be able to live in peace, whatever we decide about our future. I won't break our family apart. And I won't let you do it either."

Will looked into her eyes. Such pretty brown eyes. Eyes he wanted to see glowing at him in love, not in disgust as they did now. "Do I have a chance with you, Maria?"

She turned away. "I don't know, Will," she said. "But acting jealous is not the way to find out."

They walked the rest of the way downtown in silence.

The morning after he spied Maria and Higgins on the porch, Will strode into Higgins' office and said, "I need to talk to you."

Higgins motioned at a chair.

But Will remained standing, and only by force of will did he keep himself from pacing. "Zhuang Li came to see me while you were gone," he said through his teeth.

Higgins raised his eyebrows. "And?"

"You didn't respond to my wire asking about discrepancies."

"Discrepancies? What discrepancies?" Higgins rubbed his temple. "I don't recall that telegram."

"You didn't get it?" Will's anger flared higher. Was Higgins lying?

"Get what?" Higgins sighed. "Why don't you tell me what this is about?"

"Li said our ledgers don't match his daily tallies of cash receipts."

Higgins frowned. "Why was Li keeping daily totals of our cash receipts? That's not one of his assignments."

"Well, he came to see me in good faith," Will said. If Higgins didn't know what he was talking about, there was no point in this conversation. "I'll ask Li to pull the information together again, then we'll come talk to you."

Higgins shrugged. "Whenever you're ready."

Will stormed out of the office, still angry. He'd had no satisfaction from Higgins about the discrepancies Li claimed to have found. And even less satisfaction about the man's interest in Maria—a topic he couldn't even raise.

Chapter 34: Christmas Preparations

Maria was so vexed by Will's reaction to her walk with Mr. Higgins that she avoided him as much as possible for the rest of the week. In turn, he scowled at her during every meal, until Mama told him to smile so he wouldn't frighten the younger children. After that, Will seemed to avoid Maria as much as she avoided him.

She threw herself into both her work at the newspaper and Christmas preparations. Maria helped Mama and Mrs. O'Malley make cakes and candies, hams and applesauce. Eliza and Lottie lent a hand when school was out, but Maria bore the brunt of preparing for the holiday celebration.

Maria brought some McDougall family recipes to Abigail Duniway and asked if she could publish them. "Mama's lemon dumplings are a cherished holiday treat," she said. "And we've been making sugar biscuits and cheesecakes as well. If we need filler for this week's issue, I could have the recipes set in type."

"Excellent idea, Maria. We have space for half a column of recipes. And perhaps there will be room for more next week."

When she had a minute to herself, Maria finished the socks and gloves and scarves she was knitting as gifts. She had something handmade for everyone in the household, including Mrs. O'Malley and the maids.

She hesitated over what to give Will. Even though they were having a tiff, she wanted to give him something special. Most of his clothes were the latest Boston fashion, including bespoke jackets and well-polished boots. Would he appreciate a handmade gift? She'd found a blue wool yarn in a local mercantile that just matched Will's eyes, and she knit him a scarf. It was all she had to offer him.

One afternoon, she took his cashmere scarf off the rack in the front hall to measure for length. "What the devil are you doing?" Will asked as he passed by.

"Never you mind," she said, raising her chin.

"That's my scarf."

"It's almost Christmas, silly," she said. "Don't ask questions."

He grinned. "Then you're not so angry you won't give me a present?"

"It's Christmas," she repeated. "I can't skip your gift. Mama would notice."

He chuckled. "Well, then, I guess I'll give you something, too." He gave her a sideways hug, then walked off, leaving her to wonder if their quarrel was over.

Mrs. Duniway traveled frequently around Oregon. One week in December, she traveled to Yamhill, where she had once run a school. The next week, she was in The Dalles, a river town on the Columbia.

But on Wednesday, December 18, she was in Portland and arrived at the newspaper office early. "Maria," she said, "summarize the report from the annual meeting of the American Women's Suffrage Association. I want to print a full account."

Almost every week, *The New Northwest* contained a lengthy article about women's suffrage meetings around the nation. The attempts of women to vote in the East and in Oregon gave Mrs. Duniway plenty of fodder to include.

As Maria began her assignment, Mrs. Duniway added, "Also write about the earthquake in Washington Territory last Saturday. People in The Dalles were all agog," the editor said. "The Cascade Mountains in Washington aren't that far away, and people here in Portland felt it, too, though not as strongly as in The Dalles."

"Yes, ma'am," Maria said. "I remember Mount Hood spewing steam in sixty-five. I was terrified, but Papa told me it was only a minor eruption."

"Indeed," Mrs. Duniway said. "But it seems we live in a land that is still untamed, no matter how we seek to control it. The earthquake in Washington Territory is but one more example of our wild surroundings."

"Papa said he felt last week's quake in our home," Maria said. "No one else did, but he was resting in his library, so perhaps he was more susceptible to the tremors."

"Perhaps," Mrs. Duniway said. "Now, please work on the article quickly. It must be done before day's end so we can set type by noon tomorrow."

As Maria donned her coat to leave, Mrs. Duniway emerged from her office waving a letter. "I've heard from Winema Riddle," she said. "She's mediating between the Army and the Modoc tribal leaders. She cannot travel to Portland this month, as I had hoped."

"Is she safe?" Maria asked. "Or is she in the middle of the hostilities?"

Mrs. Duniway smiled wryly. "Knowing Winema, she is in the middle of it. The Army is attempting to force a Modoc chief to relocate to the Klamath reservation. The soldiers and local militia tried to disarm the natives, which sparked a skirmish." She looked at Maria. "My words, not Winema's. Tempers flared, and a few men on each side were killed. She is trying to calm the tribesmen, though I wonder if she will have any luck."

"She seemed sympathetic to the Modocs," Maria said.

"They are her family." Mrs. Duniway sighed. "But she is married to a white man, so she also has reason to placate the Army."

"I am sorry she cannot visit us." The Modoc woman had intrigued Maria. She wondered if the native members of her natural mother's family were involved in the conflict. Perhaps one day she could go to California and find her tribal ancestors. Maybe Papa would help her.

"I would like to hear her accounts firsthand," Mrs. Duniway said. "But her work on the reservation is vital. If anyone can reduce the tensions between the Modoc and the Army, it is Winema."

That evening, Maria followed Papa to his library after supper. "Papa," she asked, "what do you know about my Indian ancestors?"

He frowned. "Your Indian ancestors? Why would you want to know about them?"

She shrugged. "The stories about the Modocs make me think about my background. You said my mother's father was Indian. What tribe was he?"

Papa shook his head. "I don't know. Consuela—your mother—never said. All I know is that her mother's family owned a hacienda and ranch in the hills southeast of San Francisco. Perhaps we could locate them, but I don't know if anyone on the ranch would still remember Consuela or her parents. I doubt they know of your existence."

Maria sighed. "Oh."

Papa sat on the divan and patted the seat next to him. After Maria sat, he said, "You are not a part of them now, Maria. You are a McDougall. Jenny and I have raised you as such, and that is who you are."

"Yes, Papa." But that wasn't the whole truth. She might bear the McDougall name, but anyone who looked at her could see her Spanish and Indian heritage. She had tried to escape it, but the girls at school had teased and shunned her. It was easy for Papa to say she was not a part of any tribe, but he didn't see the looks she got as she walked down the street.

Maria left the library and went upstairs to finish Will's scarf, the last present she needed to complete before Christmas. As she knit, her thoughts drifted to Will. He never looked down on her. He never hinted he thought less of her because she was part Indian. In fact, he'd always told her she was pretty. Even when he was angry with her, she knew he cared about her.

Come to think of it, she realized, Amos Higgins didn't seem to look down on her either. He, too, behaved like a gentleman toward her.

If two good men thought she was worthy of courting, perhaps she could reconcile the various parts of her heritage in her own mind. Winema Riddle and Sarah Winnemucca were courageous and intelligent women. Maria decided she, too, could do anything she set her mind to.

Chapter 35: Fire

Will could not avoid dealing with Higgins, much as he wanted to after seeing the accountant kiss Maria. Higgins understood the McDougall & Company operation in Portland inside and out, and he also was acquainted with many men in the Portland business community.

Higgins steered Will toward investors in Oregon railroads. Because of Will's teenage militia experience in the Owyhee range, he had a particular interest in rail development in Southern Oregon. The rail line from Portland now extended as far south as Roseburg, but progress toward California had stalled there. Will remembered the wilderness around Roseburg—craggy mountains and stark desert traversed by roiling creeks and alkali lakes.

"Why hasn't the railroad pushed farther south?" he asked Higgins late one afternoon when he stopped by the accountant's office. "Surely the people of Portland want easier transportation to San Francisco."

"Yes, but infighting among investors has stopped all progress," Higgins replied, pulling out a flask from his desk drawer and pointing it at Will. "Each man thinks his competitor should bear more risk. And the Indian wars in Southern Oregon make the potential for loss even greater."

Will nodded at the flask and took a seat. "So, no one will step forward."

"Just so." Higgins frowned. He poured two drinks and offered one to Will. "Has your father mentioned Ben Holladay?"

"Yes," Will said. "Pa told me Holladay is a leading advocate for rail expansion in Oregon."

"He is," Higgins affirmed. "But Holladay is a bold fellow primarily interested in lining his own pockets."

"Have you talked to him?"

Higgins took a sip of his whiskey. "I have, but he is reluctant to deal with an underling like me. Holladay would prefer to work with your father, but Mr. McDougall doesn't trust him."

"What if I meet with Holladay?" Will asked. "I think McDougall & Company should invest in Oregon railroads, assuming we can do so profitably. We've been a part of Oregon commerce since 1850. Our funds are tight now because of the Boston fire, but we shouldn't pass up a good opportunity."

Higgins nodded. "Holladay will treat you with respect. You bear the McDougall name, and you have your father's ear. But be careful, Will—don't let him play you for a fool."

Will met Ben Holladay for lunch on Friday, December 20, at a restaurant near Holladay's office. Will waited until Holladay had eaten and drunk his fill before raising the topic of rail investments.

As Holladay lit a cigar and sipped his brandy, Will said, "I hear you are the lead man on railroad development in Portland."

Holladay's eyes narrowed. He puffed the cigar, then said, "Some say so. Why do you ask?"

"I recently traveled from Boston by rail. The journey was fast, reasonably comfortable, and the timetables generally accurate." Will shrugged. "Trains are subject to the vagaries of weather and mechanical failures, but they are far superior to stagecoach or sea travel."

"True." Holladay exhaled a cloud of smoke.

"Our company has interests in California, and I'd like to see faster travel time between there and Portland."

"So would I." Holladay pointed the cigar at Will. "But the California route is dangerous—difficult terrain, the region populated by savages, and terrible weather in the winter. I see Portland becoming a rail hub linking towns in Oregon. I already own spur lines around the city, and I want that network to expand. Plus, men of Oregon should fight for Congress to make Portland the western terminus of a second transcontinental line. What does McDougall & Company think about that?"

"I haven't talked to my father in depth," Will admitted. "But with our interests in Boston, a line directly to Portland from Chicago would help our business."

Holladay grinned. "See what your father thinks of both investments—the lines around Portland and to the north, as well as the line to California. Then we'll talk further, young man."

Will ambled home after his lunch with Holladay, deep in thought. He hadn't told Pa he was meeting with Holladay, and he wondered how Pa would react. Will hadn't liked the man—both Pa and Higgins had warned him not to trust Holladay, and now Will understood why. Holladay seemed focused solely on his own profits.

Yet, if Holladay was the leader of rail development in Portland, McDougall & Company should work with him. Will was convinced there was money to be made from railroads. He just didn't know where to start.

When he got home, he went straight to Pa's library and announced, "I talked to Ben Holladay today."

Pa looked up with raised eyebrows. "And?"

"He wants to develop rail lines around Portland, as well as to California. Have you talked to him about local investments?"

Pa shook his head. "I've made my own investments in local lines. No need to involve Holladay."

"He says the route to California is too risky."

"Then he is sticking to the Portland area?" Pa asked.

"Not necessarily. But he wants Portland to become the terminus of another transcontinental route."

Pa nodded. "There's talk of another transcontinental railroad. And Portland is the biggest city north of California. But we'll have to see."

"I'd like to talk further with him," Will said. "Find out more about his schemes. Maybe there's a role we can play in his plans."

"It doesn't hurt to talk," Pa said. "But do not make any commitments before speaking with me. Holladay will do his best to pocket the profits, leaving others with the risks."

The day after his lunch with Holladay, Will dug into his trunk and pulled out the gifts he had purchased on his journey from Boston. With Christmas just days away, he needed to wrap them. There were already piles of presents in the parlor which the younger children shook frequently.

He found Maria sitting in Mama's morning room. "I need some cloth. For Christmas wrapping."

She smiled. "Leaving it a little late, aren't you?"

He put his hand to his heart. "I'll have you know I bought you and Mama gifts before anyone else. Now, will you help me find some material, so you'll have a pretty package on Christmas morning?"

She led him upstairs to a linen cupboard and opened a drawer. "Take some of this." She picked up a length of muslin. "Mama and I were saving it to make Evie some pinafores, but you can have it. Or use butcher paper and string from the kitchen. Mrs. O'Malley can help you."

"Thank you," Will said, rummaging through some silk pieces.

"No," Maria said. "Not silk. It's too dear for wrapping. Stick with muslin or cotton. Or twill scraps for the boys if your presents aren't too big. Don't waste the better fabrics."

"Yes, ma'am," Will said.

After Maria left him, he chose what he wanted and returned to his room. As he tied up the gifts, he examined again the *etui*s for Mama and Maria. He remembered buying the garnet for Maria—he'd seen her in her red dress now, and she was everything he'd hoped for.

Early Sunday morning, clanging bells jolted Will out of a sound sleep. He rushed out of his room, shouting, "What is it?"

Nate stood in the hallway. "Fire bells. From downtown. I'm going to see." He returned to his room.

Will dressed quickly and met Nate downstairs. "I saw smoke from the window," Nate said. "Andrew wants to come with us, but he's too young." Their younger brother pouted in the doorway.

"Let's go," Will said.

The entire household was awake now. Eliza declared she wanted to go, and Maria seemed tempted as well. "I could write an article for the paper," Maria murmured. But when Mama said firmly Eliza could not go, Maria said no more.

Will and Nate joined a throng of men and boys, wagons and carriages, all rushing toward the smoke billowing near the river. When they reached Front Avenue, they could see flames rising from a building between Morrison and Alder Streets. Will asked a man nearby, "What's burning?"

"Chinese laundry," came the reply. "Damned Chinks store trash under their buildings."

Flames spewed skyward from a laundry that stood on wooden pilings to keep it above the Willamette River. All the buildings along Front Street sat on pilings, and most had trash and debris stored below.

A fire company fought the fire, which was contained in that one building. "They're all volunteers," Nate said. "But they'll do their best to put it out."

Unfortunately, a stiff wind blew from the south, and the fire spread to buildings north of the laundry. Men shouted and swore as the wind funneled flames around the pilings. The inferno shot upward into the commercial buildings throughout the block. More fire companies arrived, and the scene became chaotic.

"It's out of control," Nate shouted. "Everything's burning."

"Move back. We're too close," Will said, pulling Nate away.

As they retreated, Will saw Amos Higgins standing on a corner, and he led Nate over to the accountant. "What caused it?" Will asked Higgins.

Higgins shook his head. "Too soon to know. But the Chinese are careless about trash accumulating. And it started in the laundry. My apartment is only a block west of here." He pointed at a building near the furniture store. "If the furniture catches fire, my lodgings are doomed."

By now, the flames consumed the entire block where the laundry had been, and men ran in and out of buildings in neighboring blocks, scrambling to save their possessions. Wagons and horses clogged the streets, preventing firefighters from getting to the spreading flames. Soon the flames engulfed two city blocks.

"It's spreading north," Higgins exclaimed. "My apartment should be safe."

Militia and police officers arrived and shouted orders at everyone in sight. They herded spectators, including Will and his companions, away from the fire, where they milled around and continued to gawk.

Firemen wrapped in water-soaked blankets beat at the flames. "No water!" one of them shouted. "Ain't nothin' comin' out of the main. Cisterns must be dry."

A steamboat shot water from the river at the blaze, but it wasn't enough to quench the flames.

Woodard's Drug Store exploded. Screams pierced the air as several firefighters on ladders fell into the fire. More men were injured when a wall collapsed at First Avenue and Alder Street. Goods abandoned in the streets caught fire, as did wood in a lumberyard. The police rounded up Chinese men at gunpoint and forced them to pump water from the river.

"Serves them right," Higgins muttered, nodding at the Chinese pumpers. "Whether it's arson or negligence, they started it, and they should put it out."

"How do we know they started it?" Will asked.

"It's in Chinatown," Higgins replied.

Will saw Zhuang Li among the men pressed into service. Surely, the young clerk wasn't responsible for the fire. He wondered how to extricate Li from the press gang.

"Look," Nate said, pointing. "Firefighters and wagons from Vancouver and Oregon City have arrived to help."

The spectators watched helplessly as more and more men attacked the blaze. Finally, around noon, rain began to fall. The wind died, the air cooled, and the firefighters brought the flames under control.

Shivering in the wet and cold, Will turned to Nate. "Let's go home. I'm hungry." He invited Higgins to join them. "We haven't eaten all day. I'll bet you haven't either."

Higgins shook his head. "I want to check the company offices. Make sure everything is all right—no looters." For the first time, Will noticed a holstered pistol on Higgins's hip. "Then I'll head home."

"I'll come with you to the office," Will said, though he had no weapon to thwart any looters.

"No." Higgins nodded at Nate. "Take your brother home. And give my regards to your parents and Miss Maria."

As they walked home, Nate chattered about what they'd seen. But Will worried both about the possibility of looting at McDougall & Company— should he have accompanied Higgins?—and about whether the Zhuang family would be blamed for the fire.

That night, heavy snow fell over Portland. By the time Will headed to the office on Monday morning, the city was covered in pristine white. Throughout the burned area, the snow dusted charred timbers and blackened bricks, lending a frosty eeriness to the destruction.

"Everything all right here?" he asked Higgins when he arrived at McDougall & Company.

"No damage. Not from the fire, and not from looting or rioting," Higgins replied. "We were fortunate. But some of our customers were not so lucky. We may still incur losses."

"Where's Zhuang Li?" Will asked.

"Not in yet." Higgins shrugged. "I wonder if he'll show his face."

"Li and his family couldn't have had anything to do with the fire," Will said.

"Someone in their community did," Higgins said. "And if one Chinaman knows something, they likely all do."

Will settled into his office with a copy of *The Oregonian* and read:

> *Other cities may boast of having more experienced firemen, but none can claim superiority over the department of this city in the essential elements of courage, presence of mind, and willingness to do freely all that is possible for human beings to do. . . . They have proved themselves worthy of the title of firemen in the truest sense of the word.*

Will threw down the paper in disgust. Surely, more could have been done to be ready for such a conflagration. Portland may have courageous firefighters, but the city needed better preparedness—larger cisterns and a faster warning system.

And the Chinese should not be blamed without cause. He would have to find Zhuang Li and hear his story about what happened.

Chapter 36: Christmas

When Maria walked into the newspaper building Monday morning, the staffs of both *The Oregonian* and *The New Northwest* stood in the lobby discussing the fire.

"The blaze is finally out," one reporter said. "Though some buildings still smolder. Thank heaven for the rain and snow."

"Despite my emphasis on human rights," Mrs. Duniway said, "*The New Northwest* should print an article about the fire this week. What do we know about the cause?"

"Everyone says it was the Chinese," another reporter said. "Suspicion is falling hard on the laundry where the fire started."

"I doubt anyone would destroy his own business," Mrs. Duniway said.

"The Chinese are inscrutable," the first reporter said. "Westerners can't understand their ways."

"Poppycock," Mrs. Duniway said. "I want proof of their culpability before I print unfounded accusations."

"Your brother didn't have the same scruples when he ran our paper," one of *The Oregonian* reporters said. "As long as he had a man willing to be quoted, he printed the story. Too bad he didn't get along with our new owner and lost his job."

"Even the Chinese deserve human rights," Mrs. Duniway said, ignoring the comment about her brother. She turned to Maria and the other *New Northwest* staff members present. "If you learn anything definite, tell me. If we are to print a story, we need the facts by the end of tomorrow. Christmas is Wednesday, and we will not work then."

By late on Tuesday, there was still no evidence who started the fire, and

The New Northwest went to press without an article on the fire.

For as long as Maria could remember, Christmas morning had meant joyous pandemonium in the McDougall household. The children rushed downstairs to find their stockings filled with candy and oranges and an occasional small toy—marbles or a carved animal for the boys, and a new doll dress or hair ribbon for the girls.

The Christmas after Will left home, Maria told Mama she was too grown up to hang a stocking. But Mama insisted all her children, no matter how old, should take part in the custom. "Otherwise, the younger ones will suspect it is us, rather than Father Christmas," Mama argued. So every year, Maria followed the younger children down the stairs.

"Where's Will?" Maria asked.

Nate grinned. "Probably thinks he's too old for Christmas. He should know Mama better than that. And Eddie will have to wait until the nursemaid brings him down."

Just as Nate spoke, Eddie appeared at the top of the stairs. "Cwithmath!" the toddler shouted and ran after his siblings to the parlor.

Will didn't appear until the others had emptied their stockings and were occupied with their new toys. Maria sat on a stool by the fireplace with her candy and a new fountain pen with extra steel nibs. "Merry Christmas," she said, smiling up at Will when he entered the parlor.

"The McDougalls still arise early on Christmas morning, I see." Will grinned as he sat on the floor beside her. "Thank you," he said when Evie handed him his stocking.

"You know Mama," Maria said.

Will shook his stocking to empty it. A pen matching Maria's fell to the floor, along with wrapped toffees and peppermints. "I suppose we are still children in her eyes," he said.

Maria laughed. "I suppose we always will be."

After breakfast, the family returned to the parlor to exchange gifts. Maria unwrapped mittens from Eliza, a scarf from Lottie, and a whittled horse from Nate. "Remember the horse you carved for me?" she said to Will as they sat in a corner apart from the younger children.

"The one Cal hid and wrecked?" Will said. "It took me a long time to forgive him."

Maria smiled. "But you made me another."

"I never liked the second one as much." Will handed her a small package. "I didn't put this under the tree. Nor a similar one I bought Mama. I was afraid they would get lost."

Maria unwrapped his offering. "Oh, Will!" She held up a small brass *etui* with a bright red stone. "How lovely."

"I saw it in Chicago and thought of you," Will said. "I wanted you to think of me whenever you sew."

Tears sprang to her eyes. "Thank you." She hadn't expected such a lovely gift from Will, nor the sentiment he expressed.

"Mama's has a lapis stone," he said. "But the red one reminded me of you. You're so beautiful in red." He leaned over and kissed her cheek. "Like the red gown you wore to the theater." His thumb brushed her lips as he whispered, "Think of me admiring you whenever you use this."

She shivered at his touch. "Thank you," was all she could trust herself to say.

Will opened the scarf she had made for him. "It's not nearly as grand as the *etui*," she said.

"But you made it yourself," Will said. "I shall think of you whenever I wear it. Of your hands knitting the yarn. And I'll imagine you tying the scarf to keep me warm."

"The wool matches your eyes," Maria said. "That's why I bought it."

His smile lit up his blue eyes as he met her gaze.

After the gifts lay unwrapped around the parlor, most of the family bundled into the carriage and rode to church. Eddie returned to the nursery, and Papa didn't feel up to sitting in crowded pews.

Maria enjoyed the carols. Her own voice was nothing special, but Mama had a lovely soprano—she couldn't hit the highest notes any longer, but her tone was pure and rich. Will had inherited Mama's talent, and Maria listened with pleasure as Will's baritone harmonized with the melody.

Moments like this reminded Maria she had no blood connection to the McDougalls. Their shared traits—blue eyes, hair from golden to caramel—pointed out her differences—chocolate eyes, midnight-black hair, and skin that browned in sunlight if she forgot her bonnet or parasol. Despite what Will said, Maria didn't feel beautiful. When she stood beside her sisters or

Mama, she felt odd. She felt alien.

Those thoughts were too negative for Christmas, Maria decided. Papa reminded her often that she came from a good Spanish family in California, even if her natural mother had been part Indian and turned to prostitution to survive. Papa always emphasized Consuela had done her best after being abandoned by her intolerant family.

Maria wanted to respect the mother she could not remember. Still, she wished she could meet Will on equal terms. Despite their romantic moment that morning, she didn't feel ready to say she loved him as a potential husband. She didn't feel ready to marry any man. She needed to prove her worth before marrying.

After the service, Will announced he wanted to walk home. "Would anyone care to join me?"

"I will," Maria said.

As the family carriage set off, Maria took Will's arm, and they strolled toward home.

"Thank you for your part in our merry Christmas," she said.

He patted her hand on his arm. "And my thanks to you as well," he said. "It's good to be home."

"Does Portland feel like your home now?" she asked, searching his face. "Will you stay here?"

"I'll stay as long as you want me here."

"Then you will keep working for Papa?"

Will nodded. "He and I have our differences. He doesn't fully trust me yet. For both our sakes, I need to find a role where I will have my own responsibility and authority. But for now, he needs me as his eyes and ears. So, unless you send me packing, I will stay."

She squeezed his arm, but she looked at the road ahead of them. Would she someday send Will packing? If she did, would he leave?

Chapter 37: Talking to Zhuang Li

Will spent Christmas week at home with family. On Monday, December 30, he returned to McDougall & Company, ready for work. The prior week's fire had spared the McDougall-owned property in Portland. Moreover, unlike in Boston, where some of their loans would likely not be repaid, their Portland investments remained intact.

"That's because most of my investments and loans are in Oregon City and smaller towns," Pa told Will during the Christmas holiday week. "I haven't bought many properties here in Portland. I trust the farmers and shopkeepers who traveled with me to Oregon, and I prefer to support them."

"But you've also lent money to steamboat operators and railroads," Will said.

"I know many of the steamboat owners," Pa said. "And Oregon needs railroads. Though I won't get ahead of the rail construction. It's too much of a gamble."

"Like Ben Holladay," Will said. "He's a slick devil."

"Just as I warned you," Pa said. "If you see a promising venture, we should discuss it. But Holladay is a man who likes to spend other people's money. I don't want him spending ours."

Will entered his office and hung up his overcoat, hat, and new blue scarf. Zhuang Li appeared in the doorway. "May I speak, Mr. McDougall?" Li asked.

"Come in." Will sat behind his desk and gestured for Li to take a seat. "And call me Will."

Li hesitated before sitting. "What you hear about fire?"

Will frowned. "Everyone says the Chinese started it in the laundry."

"Not true," Li said.

"Oh?" Will didn't want to get involved in Chinatown rumors any more than in white men's rumors. He liked Li, despite his accusations against Higgins. Maybe a part of Will wanted those allegations to be true, if only to get Higgins away from Maria.

"Fire start in laundry," Li said. "Why Chinese burn their own business?"

Will shrugged. "I can think of lots of reasons one Chinese business might destroy another. Competition. A feud."

Li shook his head. "Not so. No one think so in Chinatown. Maybe railroad man."

"Why would the railroads want to hurt the Chinese? They need your labor," Will said. "And why talk to me? What do you expect me to do?"

"You good man. Your family have good name. I trust you. I tell you truth. You look at white men. Look hard."

"My family's interests weren't damaged. We don't have any reason to investigate."

"What you do about Mr. Higgins?" Li asked next. "You look for what I say?"

"That's between me and Higgins," Will said. "I can't talk about one employee to another."

"You look," Li said. "You find."

On his way home that afternoon, Will passed by the docks. He spotted Noah Pershing on a steamboat and strode over to the pier where it was tied. "I thought you'd be in Oregon City with family for Christmas," Will said.

Noah shook his head. "I didn't work Christmas Day. But I'm the junior captain, so I had to make a trip the next day. Been on the water ever since."

"Do you have time for a drink?" Will asked, gesturing toward a bar across the street.

"Come aboard," Noah said. "Let's see what I can find in my cabin."

He had a fine bottle of Kentucky bourbon. "Christmas present from Zeke."

Will nodded his thanks as Noah handed him a glass.

"How was your Christmas?" Noah asked, after sipping his own drink.

"Nice to be with family again." Will sighed. "Though it's strange, too."

"How so?" Noah asked, raising an eyebrow.

"Maria."

"Maria? What about her?" Noah seemed surprised. "I've always liked her."

"I do, too," Will said, staring into his mug. "I fancied myself in love with her before I left for Boston. I think I'm in love with her still."

Noah choked and slammed his glass on the table. "She's your sister!"

"She's adopted. She has no blood ties to my parents. Nor to me."

"My sister Esther always told me there was a secret behind your pa bringing Maria from California. But she never told me what she knew."

Will shook his head. "Maria's background isn't a secret. We just don't talk about it much."

Noah eyed Will over his mug. "So, do you love her or not?"

"I think so. But my father's chief accountant, Amos Higgins, is courting her, too."

Noah leaned forward with a grin. "Then the real question is whether *she* loves *you*."

Will sipped his bourbon. That was the question, all right.

That evening, Will talked to Pa about his conversation with Li. "What do you think? Are the Zhuangs likely to know how the fire started?" Will asked.

Pa shrugged. "The Zhuangs are involved in most happenings in Chinatown. If they say the Chinese didn't start the fire, they're probably right. But they could also be protecting someone. Or placing blame on someone they don't like."

"Why would Li mention the railroads?" Will mused. "I can't see any reason a rail investor or builder would want to burn down part of Portland."

"Which businesses were most damaged besides the laundry?" Pa asked.

"Everything on both sides of Front Avenue, from Morrison Street to Washington," Will said. "And it extended from the river to First Avenue."

"So Woodard's Drug Store was burned?" Pa asked.

"Yes," Will said. "You've read the papers. Maybe twenty-five buildings destroyed, and scores more damaged. I hear total losses of more than $400,000."

Pa rubbed his chin. "It could have been the Chinese. Or it could have been someone out to blame them. But I agree with you—I don't see why a railroad man would start the fire."

Will shifted the conversation to his desire to invest in railroads. "Do you still think we should stay away from Ben Holladay's plans?" he asked.

"I'm concerned our business will suffer this year," Pa said. "We might not have lost any assets, but some of our customers have, and they won't be able to buy from us."

Will argued his case, and finally persuaded Pa, who said, "Go talk to Holladay, if you insist. But don't make any commitments. Be careful of the man, son."

The McDougall family celebrated the New Year holiday on Wednesday, and on Friday Will met again with Ben Holladay.

"Damned Chinese," Holladay bellowed to one of his underlings as Will walked into his office. "Burn up half the town, and now I have to repair my horse-car line."

"I didn't think the fire damaged First Street where the horse-car runs," Will said. He didn't want to fuel the town's suspicion of the Chinese, but challenging Holladay's assertion outright would destroy any business relationship with the man before it started.

"All the firefighting traffic on First damaged the rails," Holladay growled. "Won't take long to fix, but it's the damned principle."

Will wondered whether Holladay had principles beyond making a profit, but all he said was, "My father and I are considering more investment in Oregon railroads. What financing are you seeking?"

Holladay peered at Will with a gleam in his eye—the prospect of profit trumped the rail tycoon's tirade against the Chinese.

"California line is stalled," Holladay said. "Damned mountains. Can't get around 'em. Can't go over 'em. Might have to tunnel through. Damned expensive."

"My father and I prefer to put our money in lines around Portland," Will said. "You've almost reached McMinnville to the west. Do you plan to build farther out?"

"Possibly," Holladay said. "What do you have in mind?"

"You're the rail expert," Will said. "How about north toward Astoria?"

Holladay shook his head. "No point to it. River moves traffic easily and cheaply to the north. What we need is to get around the damned mountains. But the damned Chinese can't be trusted, and they're the cheapest labor we have."

Will pushed Holladay for a while longer, but the man held his schemes close to his vest. "Keep McDougall & Company in mind when you develop

173

your plans," Will said as he stood to leave. "For the right return, we have money to invest in local rail projects."

"I'll do it," Holladay barked, lighting a cigar. "I'll take your money when I'm ready."

Chapter 38: A Third Theatrical

Maria settled into a routine after the Christmas and New Year holidays. She spent her mornings at *The New Northwest* doing Abigail Duniway's bidding. Occasionally, Maria was assigned a brief article to write, but most often she spent her time reviewing other publications or copying Mrs. Duniway's draft editorials for Robert to typeset.

At home in the afternoons, Maria assisted Mama with the younger children and household chores or sat with Papa to help him with paperwork.

"Shouldn't Will manage your correspondence?" she asked Papa one day. "I enjoy learning about the business and talking to you. But Will knows so much more."

"Will isn't nearly as patient as you are." Papa patted her cheek. "Nor as eager to accommodate an old man."

"You're not old, Papa," she protested. "And you're getting stronger every day." Papa could now climb the stairs, albeit slowly, and he could walk with a cane. Four months after his accident, he rarely slept in the library anymore.

"I still tire easily." Papa sighed. "I should return to the McDougall & Company office downtown, but it wears me out to tie my cravat and don a frock coat."

"Well, then," Maria said. "I will help you as long as you need me."

"Where are Owen's reports about the Boston losses?" Papa asked. "Let's see how much income we're likely to receive this spring."

Maria found the reports, and together they added up the expected receipts from Boston.

When they finished with Boston, they moved on to the Portland records. As they reviewed the company's Oregon holdings, Papa told Maria which loans would bring in greater payments in the new year and which California warehouses were full after last autumn's harvest. He talked to her about the business's major expenses, such as labor, inventory, insurance, and the like.

"Now you'll know as much as your husband after you marry," Papa said with a grin. "You'll be able to manage not only the household accounts, but you'll understand his business accounts as well."

Maria laughed. "If he'll show them to me."

Papa's face turned serious. "If he won't let you see his business accounts, then he's no husband for you, Maria. A husband should not hide his affairs from his wife."

Maria frowned. "But Mama doesn't spend any time on your business."

"I'd tell her anything she wanted to know." Papa leaned back in his seat. "When I first came back from California, I described everything I owned, everything I'd worked at while I was away. We had secrets enough between us before I left, and I didn't want there to be any more."

Mama had told Maria some of those secrets, but she didn't feel comfortable asking Papa why he hadn't married Mama before he left for California. As far as Maria knew, none of her siblings were aware of that fact.

"Do you talk to Will and Mr. Higgins like this?" Maria said. "About the company income and expenses?"

"Of course," Papa said. "They're of no use to me if they don't know what's going on. And they're also of no use if they don't tell me what they know."

On Thursday, January 9, Maria left the newspaper office and headed home. Soon, Mr. Higgins fell into step beside her. "Good afternoon, Miss McDougall."

She smiled. "Good afternoon, Mr. Higgins." It was a bright winter afternoon after a week of cold rain, and she commented on the weather.

"A fine day, indeed," Mr. Higgins said. "I hope you'll make it even finer. Would you do me the honor of attending the new theatrical with me next Friday? The seventeenth? Now that my travels are behind me, I hope to deepen our acquaintance."

An evening with Mr. Higgins sounded like a delightful break from her routine. "It would be my pleasure."

"Shall we say supper first? At the hotel opposite the theater? That way, we can avoid the carriage lines before the show."

She nodded. "That would be lovely."

"I shall call for you at seven. We'll dine, then walk to the theater."

"Thank you, Mr. Higgins."

"Don't you think you could call me Amos?"

Maria hesitated. Will wouldn't approve of such familiarity. "Yes, Amos. And please call me Maria."

That evening at supper, Maria mentioned Amos's invitation. Eliza was obviously jealous. Nate teased her about having a beau. Mama and Papa were carefully bland in their comments.

Will glowered, his jaw tense.

After the meal, Maria followed the younger children toward the parlor to read to them. Will caught her arm as she left the dining room. "Do you really mean to spend an evening with Higgins?"

"With Amos?" she replied. "Yes, I—"

"Amos?" Will hissed. "You call him Amos now?"

"I see no reason a friend and colleague of Papa's—"

"Colleague?" Will said. "He's our accountant. An underling."

"Papa trusted him enough to send him to California on a matter of some delicacy," Maria said. "That makes him Papa's colleague in my mind, even if you won't claim him as such."

"Fine. Go to the theater." Will stalked away. "See if I care."

Did Will care? Maria wondered. He'd asked her to declare her feelings, but never declared his own. She wanted to see if she liked Amos as much as she liked Will. Though she didn't much like Will when he was in a snit.

Amos arrived promptly at seven o'clock on January 17. He wore the same fine suit he'd worn to the theater in October. She wore a dark green silk evening gown, covered with Mama's black brocade cape trimmed in mink. Her hair was piled on top of her head, darker than the mink fur.

"You look lovely, Miss McDougall," Amos said with a bow.

Maria blushed. "I thought we were on a first-name basis now, Mr. Higgins."

He grinned. "I am awestruck, and I forgot, Maria. But I shall not forget again."

He helped her into the carriage he had rented, and they rode to the hotel. Amos had reserved a quiet table in the corner of the dining room—perfectly proper, yet they could talk privately.

"Tell me about your family," Amos requested. "I know your father and Will, of course, and your delightful mother. But I know little of your younger siblings."

Maria relaxed as she recounted her siblings' antics with affection.

From there, Amos led her to talk about her role at the newspaper. After describing the monotony of much of her work, Maria confessed, "I'd like to write bigger articles. Articles about important things."

"Women's suffrage is certainly important," Amos said. "And you help convey that information to the women of Oregon."

"Do you believe women should have the vote?" Maria asked.

Amos nodded. "Women are much more reliable than men. Educated women—like you—are as fit to vote as most men I know."

Maria smiled. "Thank you, Mr.—Amos."

Their conversation flowed easily until time to leave for the theater. Amos draped the mink-trimmed cape around her shoulders, then they walked across the street and took their seats.

The performance of *Blue Beard* was chilling. Maria shivered as the story of the wicked husband unfolded. His wife had access to every room in the house except one, which the husband told her not to enter. Of course, that was the room she wanted most to see. When she disobeyed, she discovered her husband's brutal past and soon was threatened with a grim fate of her own.

"Are you cold?" Amos murmured, leaning toward her.

"Haunted by the play," she whispered, wondering how a woman could go so wrong in choosing a husband.

After the horrors of the play, Maria stayed close to Amos's side as he fetched her cape and led her to the carriage. They rode mostly in silence toward her home. "I'm sorry the play was so frightening," he said.

"Not at all." She smiled. "I was familiar with the story—it's an old fairy tale. But these actors brought it to life. After our talk of women's suffrage, it was a cruel reminder that many wives are unfortunate in their marriages."

"Then I'm sorry the world's reality marred your enjoyment of the evening," he said. "Next time, we will attend a comedy."

Maria laughed. "Perhaps."

When the carriage stopped in front of her home, Amos leaned across the space between them. "I enjoyed tonight very much, Miss Maria." He touched his lips to hers.

She gasped lightly, then smiled. "I enjoyed it, too." She let him take her into his arms. He kissed her again, this time more passionately.

Chapter 39: Will's Reaction

Will waited in the front parlor for Maria to return. Finally, Higgins's rented carriage pulled up to the house and stopped. It stayed still for entirely too long before Higgins opened the door and helped Maria out.

Will seethed as the accountant escorted her to the porch, and he yanked the door open before either knocked. "Good evening, Higgins," he said through his teeth.

"Why, Will." Maria smiled. "You waited up for me. How thoughtful."

Will didn't want to be thoughtful. He wanted to punch Higgins in the nose. "I'll see you at the office, Higgins."

Higgins ignored him. "Thank you for accompanying me, Maria. I had a delightful time." He bowed over her hand.

"As did I, Amos," Maria said, her smile growing. "Thank you."

Amos gave a curt nod to Will, then left.

Maria followed Will inside, her smile gone. "You were rude, Will."

"I don't like him," Will blurted. Though spontaneous, he realized the words were true. Higgins had done nothing to cause it, but Will despised the man. "Did he pay you his attentions?"

Maria turned to him, frowning. "What do you mean—his attentions?" She handed Will her cape, and he hung it on a coat stand. "Amos was kind—a perfect companion. Which is more than I can say for you. You're brooding and jealous, and it doesn't become you." She started up the stairs. "Good night," she called over her shoulder.

Will cursed under his breath, then stalked to Pa's library—thankfully, Pa wasn't there—and poured himself a large brandy. He sat drinking, brooding and jealous, just as Maria had said.

The next morning, Will was at the office early, and he asked Zhuang Li for the company ledgers. If he and Pa decided to invest in railroads with Holladay, the business would need plenty of cash. Either that, or a strong balance sheet on which to borrow money.

As Will perused the ledgers, he noted the cash on hand was lower than in December. He looked through recent transactions—it seemed income was down slightly and expenses were far higher.

Will called Zhuang Li back to his office, and when the Asian man entered, Will gestured for him to take a seat. "I'm trying to figure out why our expenses were so high last month."

"Many reasons, Mr. McDougall."

"I told you to call me Will. What reasons?"

"Mr. Higgins's travel. California trip expensive."

"Yes." Will nodded. "But why were inventory purchases so high?"

"Some goods destroyed in fire," Li said. "Cost lots to replace."

Will frowned. "I thought our company hadn't suffered losses in the fire. Are we sure all the charges are valid?" He ran a finger down the ledger numbers. "Or are our vendors gouging us?"

"I take invoices. I record," Li said. "I don't know if correct."

"Who audits our invoices?" Will asked, frowning.

"Mr. Higgins. He see vendors himself. Sometimes he send clerk."

Will's scowl deepened. "I guess I'll have to talk to Higgins." He scanned the ledgers again. "Now, on the income side, I see receipts are lower in January than a month ago."

"Fire again," Li said. "Some borrowers not pay."

"Have we tried to collect?" Will asked.

"That Mr. Higgins's job. Clerks not talk to borrowers."

All roads led to Higgins. "Higgins handles collections, too?"

"Yes, Mr. Will." Li nodded, looking uncomfortable.

Everything Zhuang Li said made sense—Higgins was the head accountant. Ultimately, all the financial aspects of the business were his responsibility. Li was just a bookkeeper. "Thank you, Li," Will said, dismissing the man. Li bowed and left.

Will leaned back in his chair, putting his feet on his desk. He didn't like having the Oregon branch so dependent on Higgins. Was there a problem? Or was he simply too suspicious of Higgins because he didn't want the man courting Maria? Will needed to talk to Pa, but he had nothing concrete to report.

Who else could he trust? And given what the ledgers showed, were there sufficient funds for a major investment in railroads?

Later that day, Will searched for Higgins, whom he found in the attic, rummaging through old files. "What are you looking for?" Will asked.

"A local shop owner says he can't make his loan payment because he lost inventory in the fire," Higgins said, shoving a box into a corner. "I need his contract, so I'll be on firm ground when I discuss his penalties for nonpayment."

"That's what I wanted to talk about," Will said. "I reviewed this month's and last month's ledgers. Income is down and expenses are up this month."

"It's because of the fire mostly," Higgins said, confirming what Li had told Will. Higgins dragged another box out and thumbed through the contents. "Here it is—the Willis Mercantile contract. Willis owes a half percent surcharge every month he misses a payment. That's what I thought."

"Can we collect?" Will asked.

"First, I remind him of the penalties," Higgins said, waving the contract. "That's usually enough to get some money. Most mercantiles don't want to pay any more interest than they must."

"What if he can't pay?" Will followed Higgins downstairs to the main floor. "Didn't he lose inventory in the fire?"

"I'll still do my best to collect," Higgins said, entering his office. "Ultimately, I'll threaten to sue—and I might actually have to file suit." He squinted at Will. "Want to join me on my next call to Willis? He'll know I'm serious if I have a McDougall along. And there are other shops in the same position as Willis."

"All right," Will said, settling into a chair in Higgins's office. "But I see some of our income shortfall comes from California. That's not related to the Portland fire. What have Beck and Cassidy reported about their business this month?"

Higgins waved his hand, causing his ostentatious ring to flash. "Probably just seasonal. They may not have collected the year-end proceeds yet. I'd have to compare to last January to know if there's a problem."

"But what did they tell you when you visited?" Will pressed.

"Just as I said before," Higgins replied, rubbing his temple. "Beck thought everything was in good order, though business was down a bit. Nothing to worry about, in my opinion."

"And Cassidy?" Will asked.

"As I told you and your father, Cassidy seems to be overstating his expenses."

"Do you think he's stealing, or are his expenses just too high?"

Higgins threw up his hands. "Does it matter? Whichever, I'm of a mind to fire him. I didn't make that recommendation right away, because of the Christmas holiday. But if his January month-end report is as bad as December's, then it's time to be rid of him."

"Have you told my father?" Will asked, wondering if Higgins was going behind Pa's back.

"No." Higgins leaned forward. "You and I should be united in our decision. Let's wait for Cassidy's report. After we review it, then we'll present our case to your father."

What Higgins said made sense, though Will paused at not telling his father of the potential problem immediately. "All right," he said.

As Will walked home that evening, he considered what Li and Higgins had told him. There were reasonable explanations for the cash flow variances—both on the income and the expense side. But without a full-scale audit, Li had to rely on what Higgins told him. And rightfully or wrongfully, Will didn't trust Higgins.

He thought of Higgins lingering in the carriage with Maria. The vision of Higgins kissing her made Will's stomach churn. He understood Maria wasn't ready to declare herself to Will. He understood her commitment to preserving their family relationships if they did not ultimately marry. He even understood that she might need to meet other men before committing to him.

But why Higgins? Will's jealousy of Higgins complicated their business relationship. Should he tread carefully with Higgins so as not to offend Maria? And to offset his irrational dislike of the man? Or should he push Higgins harder to uncover any problems in the business?

How would he feel about the man if Higgins weren't courting Maria? He had no idea.

Chapter 40: Letters to Abigail

One morning in mid-January, Maria arrived at the newspaper office to find Daisy and Abigail Duniway laughing. "Look, Maria," Daisy said, gesturing at a paper the editor held. "A Wisconsin man has proposed to Mrs. Duniway."

"But you're married," Maria said, reading the letter Mrs. Duniway handed to her.

"He must think me a lonely spinster," Mrs. Duniway said. "I received this yesterday and took it home to show my husband."

"And what did he say?" Daisy asked, pushing her spectacles up her nose.

"Well, he objected to my accepting the proposal," Mrs. Duniway said with a grin. She handed Maria another paper. "Here is my draft response. What do you think?"

Maria read Mrs. Duniway's neatly handwritten prose to Daisy, " 'We laid your letter before our other half, who raised such decisive objections to an affirmative answer that, under the circumstances, we think it best to decline the honor you have so graciously tendered us.' " She laughed and said, "That should nip his romantic notions in the bud."

"Romantic notions, poppycock," Mrs. Duniway responded. "I imagine he was under the influence of moonshine when he wrote. But at least we now have filler for this week's issue."

"Less for Maria and me to do this week," Daisy said, chuckling.

On Friday, January 24, Maria found Mrs. Duniway waiting for her with a more serious subject to discuss. "I have a letter from Winema Riddle," the editor said. "Read this." She handed the letter to Maria, who read:

> *January 19, 1873*
> *My Dear Mrs. Duniway,*
> *You may have heard that war between the Modoc tribe and the U.S. Army exploded into battle on the 17th of this month. Soldiers attempted to attack the Modoc near Tule Lake but were defeated because of weather and the tribe's patient defense. Many soldiers died, though the Modoc lost no warriors.*
> *Peace negotiations are likely to begin soon, and I hope to serve as an interpreter. I endeavor to bring understanding to both parties, not recriminations of either the Army or the Modoc. Please keep an open mind on the conflict, without favoring one side over the other in your newspaper.*
> *Yours respectfully,*
> *Winema Riddle*

"Another battle," Maria said, returning the paper to Mrs. Duniway. "What will you report in *The New Northwest*?"

"Most likely, nothing," Mrs. Duniway said. "As Winema requests, I will not take a side at this point. And if I choose not to advocate a position, there is no need to publish anything. Unless I see the other Portland papers acting irresponsibly."

"As I review other publications, I'll keep an eye out for what they write," Maria said.

"Excellent," Mrs. Duniway said. "Summarize what you find. I do not plan to reprint articles from other sources. This isn't our war. I will keep my focus on women's suffrage and other family issues."

After hearing Mrs. Duniway's lack of enthusiasm toward the Modoc War, Maria wanted more than ever to write an article of consequence for *The New Northwest*. What could she write that Mrs. Duniway would publish? The editor was enamored with human rights issues. But Mrs. Duniway wrote her own editorials on those themes.

Was there another topic that Mrs. Duniway would find worthy of her newspaper's pages? Maybe something of local interest. Or perhaps Maria could write something she could sell to *The Oregonian* or another newspaper. She just wanted to see her words in print.

Maria had learned a lot through her clerical and administrative tasks. She'd helped Robert Taylor typeset the galleys, so she understood how the paper was printed. She'd covered meetings of the Temperance Society and other Portland groups, which taught her what was happening locally.

But she didn't feel her work was valued. She wanted to write something her family and friends would admire. Something they would be proud of. Something to convince Papa—and Will—that her work was as important as theirs.

That evening, Amos Higgins joined the McDougalls for dinner. Mama had invited him and seated him at Papa's right hand. Maria sat on Amos's other side, and Will sat on Papa's left. Maria was surprised when Mama allowed the conversation to turn to business.

Maria listened to Will and Amos spar as they both sought Papa's ear. Will challenged almost everything Amos said. Amos kept his voice level, but Maria thought Will's demeanor must perturb their guest.

Amos made veiled comments about theft in California, and Will responded with skepticism. Papa asked pointed questions of both men. "Tell me again why you think the San Francisco operation isn't up to snuff," Papa said to Higgins.

Higgins explained, describing high-priced purchases and low sales.

"But you told me that could just be the San Francisco market," Will objected.

"Yes, but month after month?" Higgins countered. "There's more going on."

Mama cleared her throat from the far end of the table, her sign she'd had enough men's talk during the meal.

"We can't resolve this tonight," Papa said, glancing at Mama. "Let's discuss the railroad opportunities."

Maria listened closely. Will seemed eager for the company to invest in railroads, while Amos was doubtful. Papa seemed to side with Amos, though he did not disparage Will's opinion.

Maybe Maria could write about railroad development. Will had fascinated the family with his tales of crossing the country. She agreed trains were the transportation of the future. "Have you traveled much by train, Amos?" she asked.

"Not as much as I'd like," he replied with a smile. He nodded toward Will. "Your brother is correct—railroads are crucial to the nation's future development. Not only can they transport both goods and people, but they will also enhance communications between peoples in all corners of the land. Telegrams are faster, but do not convey the nuances of letters. We need rapid delivery of correspondence to enhance commercial profitability."

"Then you agree we should invest in rails," Will said.

Amos nodded. "Yes. But we should be circumspect. Construction is costly in Oregon, and we should not invest beyond what railroads can build. Though Holladay will get the line to California finished eventually."

Will huffed. "Builders cannot construct what investors do not fund."

"No," Amos said. "And the opportunities for fraud are rampant in rail construction. But Holladay has the contacts needed to acquire the funds."

"How do you know whether someone is honest?" Maria asked.

Amos smiled at her. "There are many ways to hide money in a construction project the size of a railroad. An extra payment here, missing materials there. It happens in any large enterprise, and in the wilds of Southern Oregon, it would be all too easy to lose a load of lumber."

"Then people steal from the railroads?" Maria asked.

"It happens." Amos took a bite of his dessert, then complimented Mama on the meal.

"How can the thieves be caught?" Maria asked.

"That is another problem we will not resolve tonight," Papa said. He turned to Amos and added, "Would you care to join Will and me for a libation, or would you rather spend the evening with the family?"

Amos smiled at Maria. "If Miss Maria and her siblings will play whist, that would be a pleasant end to our evening."

They all moved to the parlor, and Eliza and Nate found the cards. Amos and Maria played against the younger two, while Will watched from the corner.

As Maria prepared for bed that night, she mulled over writing an article about railroads. If she could find evidence of theft in the rail industry, would Mrs. Duniway publish her story?

Women's suffrage was important, but women needed more than the vote. They needed to engage in all aspects of the world in which they lived. Not only family and home, but the business world as well.

Papa had explained his business to her. She understood how ledgers worked and how McDougall & Company made money. If she could understand Papa's business, then she could understand railroads. Perhaps she could interview a railroad man and find a story in what he told her.

Papa had always told Maria she could think as well as her brothers. It was time to prove it.

Chapter 41: Higgins and Li Have Concerns

On Wednesday, February 12, Higgins walked into Will's office waving a sheaf of papers. "We've got him," Higgins said. "Cassidy."

"What do you mean?" Will looked up from reading Uncle Owen's year-end report. McDougall & Company's Boston operation had lost significant revenue from uninsured clients ruined by last October's fire.

Higgins dropped the papers on Will's desk. "This is Cassidy's January report for the San Francisco branch."

"And?"

"The numbers don't match. His inventory levels are far lower than what I observed in December."

"But this is January, not December."

Higgins rubbed his temple, as if he found Will stupid. "Remember the December report? I said there were problems. I wired Cassidy. He said they would audit inventory in January, and it should all balance then. Well, it doesn't. He can't explain how merchandise vanished between what I saw in December and now."

Will sighed, not wanting to believe ill of Cassidy. He picked up the report. "Let me see. Bring me both Cassidy's December report and your report of your trip."

"Of course." Higgins turned to leave. "Look them over. You'll see. Cassidy will have to go."

Will put aside the Boston information and spent the rest of the day scrutinizing the San Francisco report. Higgins was right. The December and

January inventory tallies couldn't be reconciled with the sales that Cassidy reported, nor with the inventory Higgins had done when he was there.

Late in the day, he went to Higgins's office, where the accountant sat writing in a ledger. Higgins glanced up and slammed the ledger shut, his onyx ring flashing in the lamplight. "Well?" Higgins asked, slipping the ledger into a desk drawer.

Will slumped into a chair and shoved Cassidy's report toward Higgins. "You're right. The numbers don't agree. I can't make heads or tails of them."

"And neither the December nor the January numbers match what I saw with my own eyes," Higgins said. "We must fire Cassidy."

Will hesitated. He didn't want to agree with Higgins, but his initial favorable impression of Cassidy couldn't excuse mismanagement—or theft. Still, he wanted to argue. "Is he incompetent?" he asked Higgins. "Or is he embezzling?" He hoped Higgins would opt for sloppy management. Perhaps he could save Cassidy's job if they took him out of the branch manager role.

"Does it matter?" Higgins asked. "We can't keep him either way."

Will steepled his fingers against his lips, not wanting to admit he'd misjudged Cassidy. "Let me talk to Pa. I want him on board before we decide."

Higgins smiled. "Fine. Tell him I'll return to San Francisco to deliver the news to Cassidy in person."

Will nodded.

"And tell your father I suggest we give Beck the San Francisco business to manage, along with Sacramento."

"But you said his profits were weak," Will protested.

"He's a shrewd and experienced manager. He's doing his best in the Sacramento market. I want to see what he can do with the larger San Francisco branch."

That evening after supper, Will joined Pa in the library for whiskey. He described the discrepancies in the reports from Cassidy. "There's no way to reconcile what Cassidy sent us with Higgins's inventory count in San Francisco."

"And you're sure Higgins is correct?" Pa asked.

"You said you trust Higgins," Will said. "You've worked with him a lot longer than I have." He blew out a deep breath. "And I might be biased against the man."

Pa chuckled. "Maria."

Will's eyebrows shot up. "How did you know?"

"You're not subtle, son." Pa chuckled again. "And Maria talks to your mother, who talks to me."

Will gulped his drink. "I love her." So far, he'd only confessed his feelings for Maria to Noah.

Pa's face turned serious. "You're sure of that? Sure enough to marry her?"

"If she'll have me. But she's not ready to declare."

"Because of Higgins?" Pa asked.

Will nodded. "I think so. And I won't press her. At least not much."

"Good man." Pa sighed. "I love you both. Neither of you is a child anymore, and you need to find your own paths. Just don't hurt each other or your mother as you do."

They sat silently, sipping their whiskey, as the fire crackled nearby. Then Pa said, "To answer your question, I have no reason to distrust Higgins. He's a strict taskmaster as a manager, particularly with the Asian employees. But he has been honest with me. If he said he counted the inventory in San Francisco, I believe him."

"What about Cassidy?" Will asked.

Pa shrugged. "Never met him personally. I've trusted him thus far because Higgins hired him. If Higgins has changed his opinion, then we have no choice."

Will stared at the glass in his hands. "So, you agree we should give Cassidy the sack?"

"Yes," Pa said. He paused, then asked, "Higgins said he'd return to San Francisco?"

"Yes," Will said. "He'll fire Cassidy. Then he wants to expand Beck's authority to cover both Sacramento and San Francisco."

Pa nodded. "Makes sense. Tell him to proceed."

Will stood to leave. "What about Cal? He's in California—shouldn't we offer him a role in the business?"

"Cal shows no desire to be a part of McDougall & Company. He never has." Pa tossed back the rest of his drink. "I vowed long ago to let my children follow their own paths in life." He grinned ruefully. "Sometimes, it's difficult to accept their choices."

"What about Maria and me?" Will asked. "Do you approve?"

Pa eyed Will, frowning. "If you and Maria choose to become more than siblings, you will become the subject of gossip from those who do not know our family story. But I will support you both, whatever you choose."

The next morning, Will told Higgins about his conversation with Pa.

"I thought that would be the outcome. I already bought a ticket to leave for California tomorrow," Higgins responded. "No use in delaying. Then may I offer Beck the San Francisco branch?"

"Yes," Will said. "Pa agrees."

"Here." Higgins handed Will an envelope sealed with wax. "Please give this to Maria."

"What is it?" Will asked, as he pocketed the envelope.

Higgins grinned. "Do you pry into every gentleman's correspondence with your sister?"

Will thought he detected an emphasis on the word "sister," and his posture stiffened. He couldn't explain his feelings for Maria to Higgins. He said only, "I am protective of my family."

"Just give the letter to her, please."

"Of course," Will said.

That evening, Will handed Maria the envelope when he returned home. She thanked him without opening it, tucking it into a pocket.

When a knock sounded on the McDougall front door Friday evening after supper, Will answered it. Zhuang Li stood on the porch, carrying a portfolio stuffed with paper. "Zhuang Li, what brings you here?"

"I need speak to you. And father, too. Higgins leave today—yes?"

"As far as I know," Will said. "He had a ticket. Come in. Let me see if Pa is available." Pa was willing to see Zhuang Li, so Will led their guest to the library.

Pa struggled to his feet to shake Zhuang Li's hand. "What can we do for you, Li?" Pa asked, as the three men sat.

"Mr. Higgins," Zhuang Li said. "Your son tell you what I say?"

"About your abacus totals not agreeing with the ledgers?" Pa responded. "Yes, Will told me."

"More problems now," Li said. "I make copy invoices."

"Invoices of what?" Will asked.

"Invoices we pay. For last month," Li said. "Also daily totals from abacus. They match invoices. They not match payments we make."

Pa's eyes narrowed. "What do you mean?"

"I see invoices. I add daily. I keep list of what I add," Li said. "That all match."

"Then what's the problem?" Will asked.

"Today I check ledger. I add payments in ledger," Li said. "Ledger total not match." He took a sheaf of papers out of his portfolio. "I show you." He spread the papers out on Pa's desk.

Will stood behind Li as the Asian man pointed out numbers. Pa stayed seated, but leaned forward to see. Li had a list of invoices detailing amounts McDougall & Company owed vendors. He also had the daily totals from his abacus. Will added a couple days' worth of invoices, and the sum matched the abacus totals.

"See," Li said. "What I add all match. But here—" He brought out several invoices from the vendors on his list. "These not match. Invoice amount changed. See. Ink color darker. Four change to nine, so we pay ninety dollar, not forty. One change to seven, so we pay seven dollar, not one." He pointed out other discrepancies. "Here three change to eight. We pay eighty, not thirty."

"Do you know what we actually paid our vendors?" Will asked. "Where's the payments ledger?"

"Yes," Li said. "I bring ledger, too." He pulled a large book out of his portfolio and showed Will where the changed invoices were recorded. "Ledger show we pay larger amounts."

"But why wouldn't the vendors show a credit on the next invoice they sent us?" Pa demanded. "Unless you're saying our vendors are stealing from us."

"Maybe vendors. Maybe not," Li said. "Maybe someone inside McDougall & Company pocket difference."

"But who?" Will said. He knew Li suspected Higgins, but he wondered whether Li had any proof.

Li shrugged. "This not all. Our receipts also change. See." He pulled out another sheaf of papers and a last ledger to empty his portfolio. "Here McDougall bill to customer for fifteen dollar. Here ledger show payment for five dollar. One turned into dollar sign, so fifteen dollar become five. Most entries not show dollar sign. Where one changed to dollar sign, payment to

McDougall look less. Receipts look less."

"You're saying someone has systematically increased our payments to vendors and decreased our receipts from customers?" Will asked, wanting to clarify. The ink changes were subtle, but he could see them. Still, Li's allegations seemed preposterous. "Who would do this?" he asked again.

Li was silent.

"If you're claiming we have someone stealing from us," Pa said, "then we need evidence. Who has access to the ledgers? That seems to be where the entries are changed."

"Several people, Pa," Will said. "Higgins has access. But so do several of the bookkeeping employees, including Li and others in his department."

"Whom do you suspect?" Pa asked Li again.

"It's Higgins, isn't it?" Will said. "You still suspect Higgins. That's why you've brought us this information while he's away."

Li bowed.

"Do you have any proof?" Pa asked.

Li shook his head. "No proof. McDougall Company good to me. So I tell you."

Chapter 42: Maria Seeks a Source

"We must form a women's suffrage association in Oregon," Abigail Duniway announced to her staff one morning. "Our attempts to vote last November raised the dander of many women. Susan Anthony has been prosecuted for her courage."

"What good will a suffrage association do if we do not have the right to vote?" Maria asked.

"The association will fight to get us that right," Mrs. Duniway replied. "We will storm the legislature in Oregon. Many men are sympathetic to our cause, but we need a majority of the legislators on our side to make change happen. Persuading them will require concerted effort. Washington Territory has an association, and Oregon—which is already a state—should lead suffrage efforts in the Pacific Northwest. Mrs. Anthony believes Western men are more chivalrous than Eastern men, and I agree. The West will blaze the trail for women's suffrage. Wyoming Territory already permits women to vote in local elections."

"There are other issues besides the vote," Daisy said. "Women need property rights and the right to earn a living and keep their wages."

"True," Mrs. Duniway said, nodding. "But without the right to vote, all women's rights remain subject to men's whims. Some men are decent, but many are not. I know women who fear for their physical safety at the hands of their husbands. They do not have a voice even in their own homes."

"But don't you think women should address other issues of the day?" Maria asked. "Such as theft and injustice?" She didn't want to mention her plan to investigate embezzlement in the railroads. Not until her story was further developed.

"Certainly," Mrs. Duniway said. "But my cause is women's suffrage—women's rights, as a part of human rights. It is why I founded my newspaper and where my passion lies."

Maria swallowed hard. Mrs. Duniway sounded unlikely to support her idea. Maria would have to investigate embezzlement on her own, then submit a completed article after it was written.

Maria sought Papa out in his library when she returned home that day. "Papa," she began, "do you have time to talk about railroads?"

"Railroads?" He glanced up from a document he was reading. "Why do you want to know about railroads? Beyond their ability to transport us with great speed."

"I'm curious how they are managed," Maria said. "Who funds them? Who decides where to put the tracks?"

Papa gestured to the chair beside him, and Maria sat. "Each venture is a little different," he said. "When financiers decide to build a railroad, each investor puts in some capital. Early funds usually come from a small group of men. But at some point, the promoters usually issue stocks or bonds to obtain additional monies. They sell the shares or bonds to other men—sometimes to just a few men, and sometimes to the public. You know what a share of stock is, don't you?"

"It's a piece of paper, isn't it?"

"Yes, but that paper represents a share of ownership. If a company issues one hundred shares of stock, then each share represents one percent of the ownership. Any profits from that enterprise will be paid out in proportion to the shares a man holds."

"What about women?" Maria asked.

Papa smiled. "Well, if a woman can own property, then she can own stock, of course. Stock is simply a representation of ownership."

"So shareholders fund the railroads when they buy the shares?" Maria wanted to be sure she understood.

Papa nodded. "At the startup, yes. But most funding for constructing the line comes from land grants from the federal government. The railroad owners sell most of the land the government gives them, and the proceeds of those land sales buy the rails and cars and land improvements needed to get the railroad built."

Maria wrinkled her nose. "Why does the government give away its land?"

"Because Congress wants railroads built, and the federal government owns vast amounts of vacant land in the West. When the government fosters commerce across the nation, we all prosper. Undeveloped land isn't worth nearly as much as land with towns and farms and businesses—and the railroads tie these enterprises together to make them even more valuable."

"But don't the men who set up railroad companies want to keep as much profit for themselves as they can? How does that help the nation?"

Papa chuckled. "Yes, they do. But if they try to pull the wool over their investors' eyes, if they don't keep accurate records of their income and expenses, then their investors will sue them. All business is ultimately built on trust—whether the business is McDougall & Company or a railroad. Our company is owned only by family members—my brother Owen and myself—but he and I must trust each other. And our employees must trust both of us, as we must trust them."

"So that's why embezzlement is a crime?" Maria asked. "Because it's a breach of trust?"

"Exactly," Papa said. Then he frowned. "Now, why are you worried about embezzlement? Have you heard Will and me talking?"

"You and Will?" Maria asked in surprise. "No. Have you been talking about embezzlement?"

"Never you mind, poppet," Papa said. "Will and I have our company's business well in control."

Maria fretted all evening about her conversation with Papa. She wondered why he asked whether she'd overheard him talking with Will. Did they think there was someone embezzling from McDougall & Company? She was interested in railroad embezzlement because the entire community would care if thieves infiltrated railroads. Who in Portland would care about their family's business other than family?

The next morning, she asked Mrs. Duniway, "Do you know who the major railroad investors are in Portland?"

The editor raised her eyebrows. "Why do you care about railroads?"

"I'm just curious," Maria said. "Who in Portland knows the most about railroad operations?"

Mrs. Duniway shrugged. "Ben Holladay, I suppose. Though Mr. Holladay has an unsavory reputation." She shook her head. "There's no reason for this newspaper to talk to Mr. Holladay or his subordinates. We are focused on human rights, not commerce."

"Yes, Mrs. Duniway."

"Now," the older woman said, "what have you found for this week's edition? One of the merchants in town has not paid his bill, and I will not run his advertisement again until he does. I need to fill that space."

The conversation about railroads was over, and Maria turned her attention to the needs of the paper.

On her way home that afternoon, Maria debated whether to ask Will about Ben Holladay and other railroad investors in Portland. He'd been acting oddly around her ever since he gave her the letter from Amos Higgins on Thursday evening.

Amos wrote he regretted leaving town on Friday, which was Valentine's Day.

> *But urgent business for your family calls me away. Otherwise, I would have delivered a nosegay of flowers, even in the middle of winter, together with a box of candy, though your sweetness needs no augmentation.*
>
> *Dear Maria, know that I grow fonder of you by the day. I will hurry my work in California, and I look forward to resuming our friendship—dare I hope for more?—upon my return.*
>
> *Fondly,*
> *Amos Higgins*

Fondly? Maria wondered. Was she fond of Amos? She liked him. She'd liked his kiss. She wanted to know him better. Perhaps that was a basis for fondness to develop. Meanwhile, the less Will knew about Amos's letter, the better.

After supper, she found Will reading in Mama's morning room. "What are you doing here?" she asked. "The rest of us are in the family parlor. There's a roaring fire in there. It's much cozier."

"And much noisier," Will said, looking up from his book.

"Do you have a minute?" she asked.

"For you, of course." He clapped the book shut and sat up straight. "What is it?"

"I want to investigate railroads for the newspaper," Maria said. "And I need to talk to someone knowledgeable about how the finances work. Whom would you suggest?"

Will shrugged. "There are many railroad investors in Portland. But is this really something a women's paper would want to publish?"

Maria was surprised Will guessed Abigail Duniway's position on railroads. She stood as tall as she could, and said huffily, "*The New Northwest* is not a women's newspaper. It is interested in all human rights, and railroads are key to the future of Oregon."

Will grinned. "Well, then." He thought a moment, then said, "Ben Holladay prides himself on being the father of Oregon railways. I'm not sure he is, but he thinks he is."

"Have you met him?" Maria sat near the settee where Will lounged.

"Yes," Will said. "He's a crusty old bast—man, and you should not meet him alone. Mama and Pa would not approve. I could accompany you if you want to speak with him."

"But then you'd be privy to my interview," Maria said. "I need to write this article on my own."

Will shook his head. "Stay away from Holladay, unless Pa or I go with you."

Maria could tell Will would be stubborn about this. "All right," she said. "If I decide I need you to arrange a meeting, I'll let you know."

"Be careful, Maria." Will touched her arm. "Railroads are a cut-throat business. Several groups want the land grants between here and California. Stay out of their shenanigans."

"Do you know of any embezzlement in the industry?" she asked.

"Embezzlement?" His eyebrows shot up his forehead. "Is that what you want to write about? Then you really must be careful, Maria. No one will thank you for investigating theft. Thieves, of course, want to remain hidden. And victims will not appreciate being seen as fools. Keep your reporting to recipes and women's hats."

Recipes and hats! Maria stood and flounced to the doorway. "You've said your piece, Will. I can manage my newspaper work on my own."

Sunday afternoon, Maria sat sewing with Mama, Eliza, and Lottie. Eliza and Lottie sighed heavily as the pale winter sun lowered toward the horizon.

Finally, Mama told them to go upstairs and prepare for supper. The two girls rushed out of the room, leaving Mama and Maria alone.

"Mac and Will both say you've been asking about railroads," Mama said.

"It's for the newspaper," Maria said. "I'm writing an article."

"Did Abigail Duniway assign you this topic?"

Mama and Mrs. Duniway were friends, so Maria couldn't lie. Besides, she didn't want to lie to Mama. "Not really," Maria admitted. "But it's an interesting topic. I want to impress Mrs. Duniway. She says my writing shows promise."

Mama frowned. "Women have to be careful when they enter the business world. Abigail is fortunate. For all she complains about her brother Harvey, he would not let her come to harm in the business world. He has many connections after his years at *The Oregonian*. Plus, she has the full support of her husband and sons. No one in Portland would dare bother her."

"Papa and Will would support me, too," Maria said.

"Yes, dear," Mama said. "But you are young and unmarried. For you to write about suffrage and other women's issues is unobjectionable. But if you investigate a rough industry like railroads, particularly if you write about men's wrongdoing, you are asking for trouble. You might find yourself in a situation in which Mac and Will could not protect you."

Mama didn't understand the newspaper business, and Maria didn't want to explain her desire to prove herself. "I will be careful, Mama."

"Will tells me Amos Higgins sent you a letter."

What a tattletale Will could be! "Yes, he did."

"Was he overly familiar, Maria? Your father and I like the man, but we want you to proceed slowly. Get to know him well, and do not allow any liberties."

"Amos has been a gentleman, Mama," Maria said. "He has his career with Papa to think of, so I doubt he will act inappropriately."

"It is best if most of your meetings are here in our home," Mama said. "That is why Mac and I have invited him to dinner so often."

Maria sighed. "But how can we get to know each other if the younger children are hanging about?"

Mama laughed. "I understand, dear. You and Mr. Higgins need some time alone. Within reason."

Chapter 43: Telegram from Cassidy

Late on Thursday, the boy from the telegraph office brought a wire to Will at work. He read:

DATE: 20 FEBRUARY 1873
FROM: SAMUEL CASSIDY SAN FRANCISCO
TO: WILLIAM MCDOUGALL PORTLAND
HIGGINS SLANDERS ME COMING PORTLAND TO
DISCUSS

Well, thought Will, Higgins must have fired Cassidy. But why would Cassidy come to Portland? Would he try to defend himself? Would he plead for another chance? And what would Will do if he did?

Will liked Cassidy, but Pa had approved the man's discharge. Will had no clear role in the company and no basis for overruling Pa—or even for arguing with him.

He wanted Pa to rely on him. But since his injury, Pa depended on Higgins to run the Western operation. Will felt like a mere go-between. He'd tried to get Pa to invest more in railroads, but thus far, Pa hadn't listened to Will. As Pa's mobility increased, Will wouldn't even be a go-between. How could Will find the responsibility he craved? Will didn't see how he could find a place with Pa and Higgins both managing the business in Portland.

Maybe Will should return to Boston to work with Uncle Owen. After working in Portland, Will could be a better liaison between the family's East and West branches. Perhaps that was the way to develop his stature in the company.

What about Maria? Will didn't want to leave Oregon until they had resolved their future. She showed no signs of wanting to marry him, though they both enjoyed their kisses. And Maria was no longer the compliant girl he'd known as a youth—was she really the wife he needed?

Though his future was unresolved, Will knew one thing—he needed to find out from Higgins what had happened in San Francisco. He called a clerk into his office and dictated a telegram to Higgins.

> DATE: 20 FEBRUARY 1873
> FROM: WILLIAM MCDOUGALL PORTLAND
> TO: AMOS HIGGINS SAN FRANCISCO
> HOW DID CASSIDY TAKE YOUR NEWS

On Friday morning, a reply arrived at the house before Will left for the office.

> DATE: 21 FEBRUARY 1873
> FROM: AMOS HIGGINS SAN FRANCISCO
> TO: CALEB MCDOUGALL PORTLAND
> CASSIDY GONE ON MY WAY TO SACRAMENTO
> TO MEET BECK

Will shook his head. Higgins's telegram didn't answer Will's question about how the meeting with Cassidy had gone.

Will spent much of the day pacing his office floor, wondering about Cassidy and Higgins. Whatever happened in California was beyond his control. Finally, in midafternoon, he went for a walk to clear his head.

As he walked along the Willamette River near the docks, he saw two rough-looking stevedores shoving an elderly Chinese man.

"Hey," Will shouted. "What's going on?"

"Them Chinamen burned down the city," one sneered, spitting on the street.

"Dirty yellow bastards," said the other.

"Are you all right?" Will asked the Asian.

The old man nodded and sidled away from the two roughnecks.

"What did he do to you?" he asked the dock workers.

"They're all the same," one man growled. "Stinking food stinks up the whole of Chinatown."

"As long as it stays in Chinatown, what difference does it make to you?" Will said mildly.

"This ain't Chinatown. He needs to keep to his own kind," the other stevedore said.

"I might say the same to you," Will said. He turned to the Chinese man. "Go home. They won't bother you any more today." Then he said to the dock workers. "Fun's over, boys. Leave him alone. I'll have a word with Captain Noah Pershing if I see you acting like this in the future."

He ambled along the riverfront, then turned toward home. He wondered if his threat to involve Noah would make any difference. Will didn't know how Noah felt about the Chinese. And then he wondered if the Chinese man knew the Zhuangs. Maybe he should have asked.

When he arrived at work Saturday morning, he sought out Zhuang Li. "I saw a Chinese man being beaten near the docks yesterday. Does that happen often?"

Li shrugged. "Americans not like Chinese. December fire start in Chinatown. Whites think Chinese start fire so they beat us."

Will shook his head. "That isn't right."

Li frowned. "What you and your father do about Higgins?"

"Higgins?" Will said. "He's still in California. We can't do anything until he returns."

"My numbers don't lie."

"I'm not saying you lied," Will said. "But by themselves, your numbers aren't proof. They're no more proof than the rumors the Chinese started the fire." He hesitated, then asked, "Samuel Cassidy is coming to Portland. Do you know him?"

Li shook his head. "Only know name. Never meet."

"Higgins fired him for mismanagement."

"Why? What proof you have?" Li asked. "Proof from Higgins?"

"Yes," Will admitted. "Higgins says Cassidy's numbers were incorrect."

"You not believe my numbers," Li said, arching an eyebrow. "But you believe Higgins?"

The Asian man turned back to his desk, effectively ending their conversation. As Will walked back to his office, he wondered why he felt Li had put him in his place.

Monday morning early, Pa received a telegram from Higgins at home. Will answered the door and took the telegram. He fumed as he tipped the delivery boy—he'd sent the telegram questioning Higgins, but the man sent his response to Pa. Oh, well, Will thought, Pa is the boss.

He carried the telegram into Pa's library and read it to him:

DATE: 24 FEBRUARY 1873
FROM: AMOS HIGGINS SAN FRANCISCO
TO: CALEB MCDOUGALL PORTLAND
BECK AGREED TO MANAGE SAN FRANCISCO I
WILL WORK WITH HIM FOR TWO WEEKS MAYBE
LONGER

"I wonder why he wants to spend so much time with Beck," Will said.

"The San Francisco operation is our largest on the West Coast," Pa replied. "Higgins doesn't know it all, and Beck knows even less. It's probably wise for them to dig into it together. Meanwhile, we'll hear from Cassidy if he comes to Portland." He grimaced as he lowered himself into a comfortable chair. "It's about to rain. My bones can tell now."

Will chuckled. "It's Oregon in winter. It's always about to rain."

"I want to talk to Cassidy if he shows up," Pa said. "Don't try to shield me from whatever he's complaining about. You didn't hire him—Higgins and I were responsible. You shouldn't have to clean up our mess."

"All right," Will said. "But I want to hear Cassidy's story, too. I thought he was a straight shooter. And we only have Higgins's say-so that his reports were wrong."

"You still don't like Higgins, do you, son?"

Will shook his head. "I don't trust him the way you do, but I haven't known him as long."

"And he's interested in Maria." Pa scrutinized Will. "Have you told her you love her? Have you asked her to marry you?"

"She knows."

Pa harrumphed. "Have you *told* her?" he emphasized. "A woman needs to be courted. Are you courting her?"

"She says she's not ready."

"Is she letting Higgins court her?" Pa grimaced again as he shifted his weight. "Maybe you should take advantage of his absence."

"Do you want me to marry Maria? Or are you and Mama encouraging Higgins?" Despite his earlier conversation with Pa, Will wasn't sure how his parents felt about him and Maria.

Pa responded, "I want both Maria and you to be happy."

On Wednesday, Will took advantage of Higgins's absence, as Pa suggested. He went to *The New Northwest* office at noon and invited Maria to join him at the St. Charles Hotel to eat.

"Won't Mama expect us at home?" she said.

Will grinned. "Let me spoil you a bit." He thought a meal in the hotel restaurant would impress her.

But when they arrived, the *maître d'* nodded at her. "Miss McDougall," the man said with a bow. "How good to see you again."

She smiled and let Will help her into her seat.

They ate and made small talk about the family. Will asked her about her newspaper work, but Maria seemed hesitant to say much.

"Is there anything I can help you with?" he asked. "Information about people in town?"

She sniffed. "I've lived here longer than you have. And you and Papa won't tell me what I want to know."

"What are you working on now?"

"I'm trying to come up with a topic," she said. She seemed to have something on her mind, but she wouldn't discuss it with him.

"That dress becomes you," he said. "And the hat."

Finally, he got a smile from her. "The dress is two years old, though the hat is new. But thank you."

Will wondered what it would take to flatter her. And he wondered if she responded any better to Amos Higgins's compliments.

Thursday morning, Will received another telegram from Cassidy.

DATE: 27 FEBRUARY 1873
FROM: SAMUEL CASSIDY SAN FRANCISCO
TO: WILLIAM MCDOUGALL PORTLAND
DEPARTING SAN FRANCISCO TODAY EN ROUTE

PORTLAND

It had taken the man a week since Higgins sacked him to leave San Francisco. Will wondered what Cassidy had been doing since the prior Thursday when he'd sent the first telegram.

At noon that day, Will stopped by the newspaper office. "May I walk you home?" he asked when he found Maria at her desk.

She looked up and smiled. "Of course." She put on her hat, and he helped her into her coat.

Will offered her his arm when they exited the building, and they strolled toward home. Along the way, he asked, "Are you still interested in railroads?"

"Perhaps," she replied. "But I haven't found a good source."

"You shouldn't investigate them," Will said. "It's too dangerous. And there are enough shenanigans within McDougall & Company to make a good story."

"In our family business?" She stopped and stared at him. "What do you mean?"

"Higgins is in California dealing with inaccurate reporting in our San Francisco branch. He fired the branch manager, who is on his way north to talk to Pa and me."

"What inaccurate reporting?" she asked, her eyes narrowing. "I can't write a story without details."

"We don't know the details yet," Will said. "And I'm not sure who to believe. But either Higgins or the fired branch manager is lying to us. So, you can't write about it. Not yet."

"Amos wouldn't lie," Maria said.

"We'll have to see what Cassidy—that's the branch manager—says. And what Higgins has to say for himself when he returns."

"Why don't you like him, Will?" Maria asked, resuming the walk toward home.

"Why *do you* like him?" Will shot back.

"Are you jealous?" She smiled.

"I don't want to be," he said. "I want you and me to be friends, as we always have been. I want to see if we can be more than friends. I hope we can. I've backed off so you could spend time with Higgins, but I don't want to wait any longer."

She eyed him suspiciously but said nothing.

"Let me court you. Like you've let Higgins." That was the least she could do, Will thought in frustration.

She sighed. "How long will Amos be gone?"

"Two more weeks, he says." Will took her hand. "Come with me to Oregon City on Saturday. We'll explore our childhood haunts. Just the two of us."

She eyed him again. "If Mama says it's all right."

Will grinned. Now he had something to look forward to.

The next day, Will asked Zhuang Li to come to his office. Once there, Will asked Li, "What should I ask Cassidy when he arrives? If I'm trying to catch Higgins in a lie? Or Cassidy, for that matter."

"You need ledgers showing receipts and expenses. Like what I add each day."

"Higgins shouldn't have let Cassidy take any records with him when he was fired."

Li cocked an eyebrow. "Maybe Cassidy have numbers. Maybe not. But you ask."

"All right."

Li paused, then said, "I hear Higgins keep second ledger."

"A second ledger? On our business?"

Li nodded. "Just rumor. Someone say he see Higgins with strange book."

"Who told you?"

"Old man. He work here until year ago. He gone now, back East."

"That's convenient," Will muttered. "Why didn't you tell me before?"

Li was silent.

Will pressed, "But you think there's a second set of ledgers?"

"Maybe," Li said. "Only hear one time. Man gone now."

"I already looked in Higgins's office. Where else could he keep it?"

"Don't know." Li frowned. "At his home?"

"I can't break into his home," Will said. "And I've I searched his office thoroughly. Everywhere except his whiskey drawer."

Chapter 44: Maria Meets with Holladay

Will's plans for a trip to Oregon City that Saturday fell through. Mama had too many chores for Maria. "But I'll make sure you get a day away in the next few weeks," Mama told them.

Will smiled at Maria. "Then it's a date. You will go, won't you?"

"Of course," she said. "I'm looking forward to it. I haven't been to Oregon City since last summer."

While she handled Mama's chores on Saturday, Maria mulled over her plan to write an investigative article for *The New Northwest*. Her conversations with Papa and Will convinced her there were issues to write about in the railroad industry, though Will's comments about skullduggery within McDougall & Company also intrigued her. Which of these stories would most interest Mrs. Duniway?

The railroad story would have broader appeal to readers, Maria decided, so she would pursue that topic first. Perhaps if rail development disadvantaged women somehow, Mrs. Duniway would agree it fit her paper's purpose. But Maria believed women would benefit as much as men from faster, safer, and more convenient travel and shipping.

She resolved to interview Ben Holladay about his railroad. Her parents and Will had cautioned her against speaking with Mr. Holladay alone, and Maria thought about taking a man with her. Amos Higgins would likely accompany her anywhere, but he wouldn't return until mid-March, and Maria didn't want to wait that long.

She considered asking Will. But Will would condescend to her—Amos was more likely than Will to treat her with respect. Will treated her like a little girl, despite his claims he wanted to marry her. So her only option was to approach Mr. Holladay alone.

Monday afternoon, March 3, after her shift at the newspaper ended, Maria marched toward Ben Holladay's office building. She wore her best hat and walking dress, garments designed to be both severe and flattering. It couldn't hurt to try charm on the tycoon.

She climbed the stairs to the second floor and entered a suite filled with dark walnut furniture. "Is Mr. Holladay here?" she asked the man seated at the first desk.

"Who's asking?" the man said. He was in his forties, shabbily dressed, but with an imposing demeanor.

"Miss Maria McDougall, reporter for *The New Northwest*. I'm here regarding an article."

"Did he ask to see you?"

"No. Our paper is making inquiries into railroad developments."

The man chuckled. "The women's rag wants to know about railroads." He chuckled again.

Maria stood as tall as she could. "I fail to see the humor."

The man leered at her. There was no other word to describe his gaze.

"Is Mr. Holladay available or not?" she asked.

"No, miss, he is not."

Her stomach sank. She would have to return. "Might I leave my card?"

He extended his hand. She took a card from her reticule and gave it to him.

"Might I set up an appointment later this week?"

"I don't know if he wants to see you."

"Is he free Wednesday at two o'clock?" she asked. "I assume you have his calendar."

The clerk grinned. "Of course."

"Is he free?"

"Tell you what, Miss—" He glanced at her card. "—McDougall. I'll tell Mr. Holladay you'll be here at two on Wednesday. If he wants to, he'll talk to you. Or he'll tell me to send you packing."

Maria stared at him. She had no choice. "Very well. I'll return on Wednesday."

Two days later, Maria returned to Ben Holladay's office. "Is Mr. Holladay in, please?" she asked the same clerk.

"Who's asking?" he said, smirking.

Surely, he remembered who she was. "Miss Maria McDougall," she said with a huff.

"Well, miss, let me ask if Mr. Holladay can see you now." He disappeared through a door into a back office. She took a chair nearby.

When the clerk returned, he eyed her as boldly as he had on Monday. "Mr. Holladay will see you. Follow me."

She followed him into the inner office, trying to maintain her dignity.

"Mr. Holladay, it's Miss Maria McDougall." The clerk snickered and left her alone with a beefy, balding man with a long shaggy beard.

"Good afternoon, Mr. Holladay," Maria said. "I appreciate your taking the time to see me."

"Sit, Miss McDougall," he said, gesturing at a low chair across the desk from him. He hadn't stood when she entered the room. "I understand you have questions about my railroad."

"Yes, sir," she replied, sitting as instructed. "I am a reporter for *The New Northwest*—"

"What interest does Abigail Duniway have in me?" He squinted as he lit a cigar. "She has never spoken to me herself. Why has she sent you?"

"I write about a variety of topics for her paper."

"Does your father know you're here?"

Maria stuttered, "M-my father?"

"I know your father—Mac McDougall. And your brother, too. William."

"That is correct. But I'm here on behalf of the newspaper, not my family."

"So you said. But do your father and brother know what you're doing?"

Maria sat up as tall as she could in the short chair. "They know I am a reporter."

Mr. Holladay grinned. "Then you haven't told them." He leaned back and puffed his cigar. "Fire away, Miss McDougall."

"Tell me about your railroad holdings around Portland, please." She took a small notebook and a pencil out of her reticule.

"What's the point of your inquiry?"

"I want to understand how the business operates. I've been told you are the leading railroad man in Portland."

His grin widened. "And what story do you intend to tell in your paper?"

"I have wondered whether railroads might be vulnerable to theft."

Mr. Holladay chuckled. "My dear Miss McDougall, if I told you that, every Tom, Dick, and Harry would try to steal from me."

"Then please tell me as much as you are comfortable revealing." Maria poised her pencil over a blank page.

Mr. Holladay chuckled again, but then began talking about his ownership of rail lines around Portland. She took notes as quickly as she could. After a few minutes, she interrupted. "You mentioned safeguards in how you keep your ledgers. But even so, couldn't employees steal from you?"

He frowned. "Every business faces that risk, my dear. That is why we institute so many checks and balances. Surely, your father does the same."

"Yes," Maria said. "He explained double entry accounting to me."

"Did he?" Mr. Holladay grinned around his cigar. "Then even the upright McDougalls protect themselves."

"Isn't that the prudent thing to do?"

"Yes, it is, Miss McDougall." Mr. Holladay glanced at his watch. "I find myself in need of sustenance. Would you care to join me for a meal in the hotel next door?"

"Oh, no—"

"Then my time with you must end. For today. Perhaps we could continue our discussion. Would next Tuesday at four in the afternoon be acceptable? I can take a suite—"

"I'm afraid I cannot meet you at a hotel, sir. It would be most improper. Unless we are chaperoned. And then my reporting would suffer."

Mr. Holladay's leer matched that of his clerk. "What I had in mind would not benefit from a chaperone," he said as he stood. "Give it some thought, my dear, and send word if you change your mind."

Maria rushed out of Mr. Holladay's office, not meeting the eye of the clerk as he guffawed. She slammed the door behind her and shivered as she marched down the stairs to the street.

The audacity! Mr. Holladay was Papa's age or more, yet what he suggested was most decidedly improper. Whatever story she was going to write would have to make do without his information.

But there must be a good article related to his business. No man could act so foully toward women without having something to hide. How could she find out more about the Holladay enterprises?

She was still livid when she walked into *The New Northwest* office fifteen minutes later. "I thought you'd left for the day, Maria," Abigail Duniway said in surprise.

"I just met with Ben Holladay," Maria said.

"Holladay? I told you I'm not interested in railroad stories. Or was this an errand for your father or brother?"

"No," Maria admitted. "I hoped to find a story that would interest women readers."

"And did you?"

"No." Maria paced the floor, then spun on her heel to face her editor. "Mr. Holladay made a blatant request that I meet him in a hotel suite."

Mrs. Duniway's eyebrows rose. "I warned you—"

"*You* warned me. *Will* warned me. *Everyone* warned me. And who will do more than warn women? Who will stop men like Ben Holladay? *That* is a story that would interest women."

The editor sighed. "Maria, you're old enough to know women get blamed and shamed. Men do not. That is why women must protect their reputations. When you enter a man's world, you must expect some men will behave like Mr. Holladay. You should not have gone to his office alone."

"Then how am I to find a story?"

"I didn't ask you to write about Mr. Holladay. We should focus on public events, such as suffrage meetings, rather than approach men individually and question them behind closed doors. Through suffrage and other legal reforms, women can advance themselves. We cannot count on men to do it for us."

"So, I shouldn't pursue Mr. Holladay? He must be corrupt in his business dealings. How can a man behave honorably toward his partners and customers, yet behave so abominably toward women?"

"No, you should not pursue Mr. Holladay. If you are determined to write a business article, ask your father or brother for ideas. They are good men who will steer you toward a more savory story."

"I wanted to do this on my own."

"I know, my dear." Mrs. Duniway's voice was kind. "But we live in a harsh reality, not the world of our dreams."

Chapter 45: Cassidy's Visit

The door knocker sounded at the McDougall house about supper time on Wednesday, then the housemaid entered the parlor. "For you, Mr. Will," she said, handing Will a note.

He opened it and read:

> March 5, 1873
> Dear Mr. McDougall,
>   I have arrived in Portland, and I am staying at the St. Charles Hotel. I await a meeting with you at your earliest convenience.
>
>   Respectfully,
>   Samuel Cassidy

Will showed the note to Pa.

Pa handed it back after reading it. "You'll talk to him, won't you?"

"Yes," Will said. "But where? I don't want him in the office since he's been fired. Nor at the house until we know what he wants. And we need a private location, so rumors don't spread?"

"He's already at the hotel. Why not get a private dining room there?" Pa suggested.

Will had the stable boy deliver a response to Cassidy that evening:

> March 5, 1873
> Dear Mr. Cassidy,
>   I will meet you for breakfast tomorrow morning at 7:30

213

a.m. in the St. Charles Hotel restaurant. Please reserve a private room.

Cordially,
William McDougall

The next morning, when Will walked into the hotel lobby, Samuel Cassidy approached, his hand outstretched. "Mr. McDougall," he said. "I am glad to see you again." Cassidy carried a large portmanteau, which appeared to be heavy.

"You called me Will before," Will said, shaking the man's hand. "Let's see if we can keep our meeting amicable."

"I have a dining room reserved," Cassidy said, leading Will through the lobby.

They ordered coffee, steak, and eggs, then discussed the weather. Once their meal arrived, Will said, "Tell me why you made the trip to Oregon."

Cassidy paused, as if collecting his thoughts. "You know, of course, that Higgins sacked me as branch manager."

"We had concerns about your reports. And about the aggressiveness of your efforts on behalf of McDougall & Company." Will sipped his coffee.

"First, let me assure you I have always acted in the best interests of your company. I did not know of any concerns you or your father had with my work until Higgins spoke with me."

"The profitability of the San Francisco branch has been less than we expected," Will said calmly. "And less than that of Sacramento, even though San Francisco is by far the larger market."

"But competition in San Francisco is much stiffer than in Sacramento," Cassidy replied. "My branch cannot raise prices as easily. Though I wonder whether my results were really worse than the Sacramento branch." He paused. "I am not here to plead for my job back, though I believe Higgins discharged me without cause. The primary reason for my visit is to let you and your father know I suspect someone is stealing from you."

"Stealing?" Will said. "That's a serious accusation. Who is the thief?"

"I do not know the full scope of the theft," Cassidy said. "But I think the ringleader is Bayliss Beck. I suspect he is in cahoots with others."

Will hadn't liked Beck from the start. But he could do nothing without proof. "Tell me what you know," he said.

Cassidy pulled a large ledger out of his portmanteau and laid it on the table. "Higgins ushered me out of the office after firing me, so I took nothing that day, but I already had this book at my house. It is one of the official McDougall & Company ledgers, and I will leave it with you. It rightfully belongs to the company, and I wanted to return it to you or your father personally."

Will gestured at the book. "What does it show?"

"Of course, I do not have the original receipts," Cassidy said. "Those are in the files in San Francisco. But this is a ledger for the last quarter of last year. You can compare the entries with the reports you received from my branch. I suspect you will find discrepancies."

"What do you mean?" Will asked, opening the ledger. It looked like any other book of account.

"I believe my reports were altered before you or your father received them. I mailed the reports to Higgins, but I wonder whether he gave you my originals or whether he altered them."

"Altered reports?" Will said. "Why would Higgins do that?"

"To make me look bad. To find an excuse to get rid of me. So Beck and his associates can take over the entire California operation." Cassidy raised an eyebrow. "Isn't that what Higgins did—gave my role to Beck?"

"Then you suspect Higgins and Beck are working together? Will asked.

Cassidy nodded.

"Do you have any proof your reports were altered?"

"If my suspicions are correct," Cassidy said, "you can compare this ledger with the reports allegedly from me. There will be differences. You have three months' worth of entries here to compare with three reports."

"Your reports were often late, according to Higgins."

"They were not late leaving California," Cassidy responded. "Perhaps the delay was because someone needed time to alter the reports."

Will was confused. "I don't understand why anyone would go to this trouble. How would changing the documents benefit Beck or whomever else was involved? The McDougall & Company profits would still be in the San Francisco branch, would they not?"

"Unless someone is also stealing monies sent here from California. They would have to report lower profits to match the lower cash sent in case they were audited. They would have to keep two sets of books."

"Higgins did an audit in December."

"So he says." Cassidy leaned back in his seat. "I have given you what I have, Will. What will you do with it?"

"Do you have any other proof against Beck or Higgins?" Will asked.

"Nothing. Only my suspicions." Cassidy shrugged. "And I no longer have access to company records. The next step is up to you."

Will thought. Cassidy's allegations were serious. But without a detailed audit of the reports and this ledger, there was no proof of any wrongdoing. "I shall talk with my father immediately. Do you plan to stay in Portland awhile?"

"I must find a new position to support my family in San Francisco. I can only stay here for a week or two before I must return."

"I shall be in touch as soon as I can," Will promised.

Will returned home after meeting with Cassidy, mulling over what he had heard. Cassidy's claim was plausible—reports could have been altered either in California or in Oregon to match a theft of gold or bank certificates sent from San Francisco to Portland. Or from San Francisco to Sacramento—it didn't matter where the stolen funds landed, if the branch reports matched the funds received in Portland.

He would have to talk to Pa, but he wanted someone to review Cassidy's reports—or what Higgins said were Cassidy's reports—and compare them to the ledger. Whom could he trust to conduct such a review? Zhuang Li immediately came to mind.

Will went to Pa's library and recounted his conversation with Cassidy.

"Cassidy is accusing Beck?" Pa said. "And maybe Higgins, too? Zhuang Li also thinks Higgins is stealing. But Higgins has worked for me for years. Longer than either Cassidy or Zhuang Li. And neither of them has any proof."

Will shrugged. "I know you trust Higgins. I don't. Though we have no proof against him yet."

Pa frowned and opened his mouth.

"Don't say it," Will said. "You think I'm jealous of Higgins because of Maria."

"Or you simply don't know Higgins as well as I do. He's always done what I have asked." Pa rubbed his forehead. "But we must investigate. These allegations are serious."

"I thought Zhuang Li could do the audit."

"Will he be honest?"

"The records are what they are," Will argued. "He can find the discrepancies—"

"If there are any discrepancies."

"If there are any," Will continued. "The records either match or they don't. I will check everything Li does."

"We only have Cassidy's word that this is the real ledger," Pa said.

"That's true," Will said. "But if there are discrepancies, then at least we should question Higgins."

"All right." Pa sighed. "But I want to talk to Cassidy first."

"I'll bring him to the house tomorrow," Will said.

Will sent another note to the hotel, this time asking Cassidy to come to the McDougall mansion the next morning. When Cassidy arrived Friday morning and was escorted to the library, Pa began, "Please go over again what you told my son yesterday."

Will opened the ledger on a low table between the three men's chairs. Cassidy described the ledger and the reports again, pointed at a few figures, and answered questions from Pa and Will.

At one point, Maria poked her head in the study. "Papa," she began.

"Not now, Maria," Pa said. "I'll talk to you later."

"I'm sorry," she said. "I didn't realize you had company." Will wondered if she expected an introduction. He shook his head at her. Her mouth twisted in a moue, and she left.

Cassidy continued, "This ledger is part of the puzzle. But without the reports on the San Francisco operation, plus records showing the monies you received, there is no way to know whether there is a problem. I have strong suspicions, but I do not have proof."

Will sighed. Just like Zhuang Li—no proof. Somewhere there must be proof—either in Higgins's favor or against him. "I will have someone compare your ledger with the reports in our files and the bank drafts we have received from California."

"It's *your* ledger, Will," Cassidy said.

Will nodded. "I will start the review immediately. But I must ask you to stay in Portland until our clerk is finished in case there are questions."

"I will try," Cassidy said. "When do you expect Higgins back?"

"He said mid-March," Pa said. "But I could wire him to return sooner."

"Don't raise his suspicions, Pa," Will said. He hoped Zhuang Li would find problems, and he didn't want Higgins alerted.

Pa frowned. "I think I can request he complete his business quickly and return to meet with me without making him suspicious."

Cassidy rose. "Thank you both. I shall be at the hotel if you need me."

"Why don't you travel to Salem or Eugene?" Will suggested. "I don't want Higgins seeing you in town when he returns. Not until we're ready."

"I keep a suite at the hotel in Oregon City," Pa said. "You may stay there as my guest while we conduct our review. We will be in touch."

After Cassidy left, Will asked Pa, "What did you think?"

Pa sighed. "He has no proof."

"No. But do you agree we should ask Zhuang Li to compare the documents?"

"Only if he does so here at the house," Pa said. "I don't want rumors spreading through the office. Can your mother find a room for him to work here?"

"I'll see to it, Pa."

That afternoon, Will called Zhuang Li into his office. "I have an assignment for you," he said. "It must be done quickly and confidentially."

Li bowed.

Will explained what Cassidy had alleged. Li's eyes lit up when Will said Cassidy thought Higgins might be involved in skullduggery. "But it isn't necessarily Higgins. This could be all Beck's doing," Will added. "Or perhaps Cassidy has it all wrong—intentionally or unintentionally. To keep rumors out of the office, I want you to work at our house."

"I look into it, Mr. Will," Li said. "I pull California reports. Also receipts from California. I come to house tomorrow morning."

Saturday morning, Li appeared at the McDougall service entrance carrying a large sheaf of papers. Will took him to a table in the kitchen. Someone was usually in the kitchen, so Li would not be left unattended.

"You'll be warm here," he told Li. Will gave Mrs. O'Malley instructions to keep Li fed. "I'll check on you periodically."

Chapter 46: Maria Questions Zhuang Li

Maria fretted for two days about her meeting with Ben Holladay. She was no fool, and she knew she could not work with Mr. Holladay. Though his business might hold a story, she wouldn't be the one to write it.

What should she do instead?

She thought again of asking Will to help her. But he was far too protective. Perhaps she could wait for Amos to return—he would be more understanding than Will.

Then, on Friday, she overheard part of a conversation in the library between Papa, Will, and a man she didn't recognize. Something about a ledger and discrepancies in monies received in Portland. Papa told her to leave, so she didn't hear the full story. But she heard enough to suspect there was a problem at McDougall & Company, and the stranger was part of the problem.

She wouldn't get hurt investigating her own family's business. Plus, Will and Amos would surely help her. Maybe even Papa would help.

Saturday morning, Maria encountered a Chinese man sitting at Mrs. O'Malley's table in the kitchen, a stack of papers spread in front of him. "Hello," she said. "I'm Maria McDougall."

He stood hurriedly. "Zhuang Li, miss. I work for your father."

"What are you working on?" she asked, her curiosity piqued. Why would Papa have a Chinese man handling paperwork in their kitchen?

"Ask your father, miss."

She smiled. "All right, I will."

She went to find Papa, but Papa simply said, "It's a private business matter, Maria. Let Mr. Zhuang work in peace."

"Why isn't he working at the office?" she asked.

"As I said, it's a private matter."

It vexed Maria that Papa wouldn't tell her anything. He'd told her he was open about his business with Mama. But maybe Mr. Zhuang was handling a transaction that couldn't be made public yet.

After the noon meal, Will took her aside. "Please leave Mr. Zhuang alone, Maria. He's handling something confidential for Pa and me."

"That's what Papa said. What's so secret?"

"I can't tell you yet. We don't have any proof. And we can't jump to conclusions."

Now Maria was even more curious. Proof of what? Was Mr. Zhuang's work related to the conversation she'd overheard the day before? "What conclusions?"

"Just don't worry about it." Will refused to say anything more.

"Mr. Zhuang seems like a nice man," Maria remarked at supper that evening.

"You didn't bother him, did you, Maria?" Papa asked as he carved the roast beef Mrs. O'Malley set in front of him.

"No, Papa," Maria said.

"How long will Mr. Zhuang be here?" Mama asked. "We can make room in the kitchen, of course. But Mrs. O'Malley grumbled a bit this afternoon."

"Li is unobtrusive at the office," Will said. "I can't think he interferes in the kitchen."

"He didn't," Mama said. "But Mrs. O'Malley prefers things done her way."

"He shouldn't be here more than a week," Papa said. "Do you agree, Will?"

Will shrugged. "That sounds about right. Let's all pretend he isn't here. He wouldn't be at the house unless Pa and I thought it was essential."

Nate snickered. "It's hard to ignore a Chinaman in the kitchen. And hard to raid the pantry with him about."

Mama laughed. "You don't need to raid the pantry, Nate. Mrs. O'Malley will appreciate your staying out of her way for a few days."

"Will he be gone before my birthday?" Maggie asked. She'd turn eleven

220

later in the month.

"I expect so," Papa said. He passed a plate down the table to Mama. "What are we doing for Maggie's birthday this year, Jenny?" he asked.

The conversation shifted to Maggie's plea for six school friends to come to supper on her birthday.

"Six!" Eliza protested. "There won't be room for the rest of us."

Mama had to resolve the ensuing argument. Maria ignored the family squabble while she pondered why Mr. Zhuang's work was so "essential."

Maria grew certain something was brewing at McDougall & Company, something tied to Mr. Zhuang's work at the house, though she didn't yet know whether there was a story to be written. Pa and Will would not talk to her, so she would have to talk to another employee. Once Amos returned, she would ask him, but for now, Mr. Zhuang was her best source.

For the next few days, Maria made a point of greeting Mr. Zhuang in the kitchen every afternoon when she got home from the newspaper. She asked if he was comfortable, if he needed a drink.

"Cook give me drink," Mr. Zhuang replied. He was polite to Maria, but told her nothing.

His piles of paper moved from one side of the table to the other. "Do you have enough space, Mr. Zhuang?" she asked. "I could find you another table."

Mrs. O'Malley banged pots behind Maria and muttered the kitchen was already cramped.

"No, Miss McDougall. I fine." He rubbed his eyes.

"Do you have enough light? Should I bring you a lamp?"

"No, thank you, miss."

But the next day, she brought him an oil lamp, filled and trimmed. "This is an extra," she said. "Perhaps it will help you."

He smiled. "Thank you."

As he spoke, she peeked at the papers on the table—stacks of invoices and receipts. Directly in front of him was a large ledger of the type Papa had shown her. A strange device with beads also stood on the table.

"What's that?" she asked, pointing at the machine.

"Abacus, miss. How Chinese count."

She studied it. "How does it work?"

He showed her how each rod held five beads below and two on top of a middle bar. "Lower bead equal one. Top bead equal five. Right rod ones. Next rod tens. And so." He performed a few simple additions and subtractions until she understood its function.

"How unique," she said.

"Not unique," he replied with a smile. "Many people use in Asia and Arabia."

"Well, I've never seen one. You are so fast with it. What are you calculating?"

His smile faded. "Your father tell me not talk."

She wouldn't get any information from Mr. Zhuang. At least, not today.

Chapter 47: Zhuang Li's Conclusions

Wednesday evening, Pa handed Will a telegram. "I received this from Higgins," he said.

DATE: 12 MARCH 1873
FROM: AMOS HIGGINS SAN FRANCISCO
TO: CALEB MCDOUGALL PORTLAND
LEAVING SAN FRANCISCO STEAMBOAT
TOMORROW

"That's it?" Will said. "That's all he says?"

Pa shrugged. "Higgins did what we asked. He'll tell us more when he returns."

"But we requested a report."

"We're better off hearing him in person." Pa didn't seem concerned. "I reserve judgment until I have all the facts."

"Didn't you believe Cassidy?" Will didn't understand how Pa could accept both men's versions of the state of the San Francisco branch.

"What has Li found?" Pa asked, ignoring Will's question. "Anything?"

"He's still working," Will said. "I'll ask him how much longer it'll take. I hope he's done before Higgins returns." He left for the kitchen to speak with Li.

"Still working," Li said. "Friday I finish."

Will stifled a groan—two more days. But Higgins wouldn't be back until the weekend at the earliest, so they'd have Li's conclusions before Higgins returned. He wondered if Pa would accept what Li found.

After the noon meal on Friday, Will was back in the kitchen. "What have you found?" he asked Li.

Li rifled through his papers. "Here summary."

Will sat beside Li, ready to review the documents as Li presented them.

"Many problems," Li said. "See." He pulled out the ledger Cassidy had brought from San Francisco and pointed to an entry for gold sent from San Francisco to Portland. "San Francisco ledger show one hundred twenty dollars sent." Then he showed the report from San Francisco. "Report say one hundred dollars."

"And how much gold did we actually receive here in Portland?" Will asked.

Li tapped the Portland cash ledger he'd brought from the downtown office. "Portland ledger show one hundred dollars."

"How many discrepancies are there like that?" Will asked.

"Two, three each month. October, November, December." Li tapped the ledger. "This only ledger Cassidy bring. All errors lower San Francisco profits. All hurt McDougall & Company."

Will exhaled slowly. "Then it looks intentional?"

Li shrugged. "I not know intent. I know numbers."

"Do all the discrepancies involve gold transmissions?"

Li shook his head. "Bank drafts, too. Some drafts listed in San Francisco ledger. But not in Portland ledger. Missing."

"So, it looks like the bank drafts left San Francisco but disappeared before they were recorded on the McDougall & Company books here in Portland?"

"Yes."

"Who had access to the bank drafts and gold?" Will asked.

"Ask Cassidy and Higgins," Li said. "They know. I don't."

Will mused, "But presumably Cassidy had access on the San Francisco end, and Higgins here in Portland."

Li remained silent.

"Maybe other men also had access, but at least those two," Will said. "And Cassidy brought the problem to our attention, which makes him a less likely suspect."

Li still said nothing.

"All right," Will said, standing. "Let's talk to my father."

Will and Li took the books and papers to Pa's library. "Zhuang Li has finished his review."

Pa shook Li's hand, then bade them sit. Li walked Pa through the same documents he'd shown Will in the kitchen. After four or five examples, Pa held up a hand. "Are the other entries like these?" he asked Li.

"Yes, sir."

"To sum it up, you have found discrepancies, but you cannot tell whether the errors are in the San Francisco ledgers or in our Portland records?"

"Yes, sir." Li nodded.

"Then all you can say is Cassidy's reports match our actual Portland receipts—both in gold and in bank drafts, but both differ from the San Francisco ledger he brought us?" Will wondered why Pa had not spent more time in his legal practice when he was so good at cross-examination.

"Yes, sir," Li said. "San Francisco ledger come first. Cassidy's reports later. They not match."

"Do you have any explanation for how that could happen?" Pa asked.

"No good explanation," Li said. "Only theft."

"It couldn't just be a simple error?" Pa asked.

Li shook his head. "Maybe once. But all errors hurt McDougall & Company. Portland receipts always less than San Francisco ledger."

Pa rubbed his chin. "If Cassidy's ledger is correct, why would his reports show lower amounts being sent to us?"

"Someone take money. Write report to hide theft." When Pa questioned him further, Li refused to elaborate. He couldn't say whether the problem arose in San Francisco or Portland. He couldn't say who might have taken the money or changed the documents.

"Then all we know is that our records don't match," Pa said. "We don't know whether we have a thief, where that thief might be, nor who he is."

"But, Pa," Will said, "Cassidy brought the matter to our attention. Why would he do that if he's guilty?"

"He's out of a job," Pa said. "Perhaps he wants to shift blame, so we will rehire him."

"Sir," Li interjected.

"Yes?" Pa said, turning to the Chinese bookkeeper.

"Whoever do this must track what he take. Maybe Cassidy's original reports, if reports changed. Maybe notes of how much gold or bank drafts taken."

"And whoever has such documents is likely the thief," Will said. Finally, something he could try to do—he could look for other records. "Or at least he'd be in cahoots with the thief."

"Where would such records be?" Pa asked.

"I need to search Higgins's office again," Will said.

"Now, Will," Pa said. "Do not jump to conclusions." He turned to Li. "You haven't ever seen any other reports from Cassidy, have you? No documents you think someone might have forged?"

"No, sir."

Pa glared at Will. "We will wait until Higgins returns to pursue this matter."

Will glared back at Pa. "May I talk to Cassidy again? Perhaps he can shed light on these specific discrepancies?"

Pa sighed. "I suppose there's no harm in that."

After leaving Pa, Will found Mama in her morning room, writing menus for the week ahead. "You know Maria and I want to go to Oregon City," he said. "May we go tomorrow?"

Mama set down her pen. "Tomorrow? There's so much going on."

"I need to meet with Samuel Cassidy who is staying there. I thought Maria and I could make an outing of it."

Mama sighed. "Next Tuesday is Maggie's birthday."

"Surely, Eliza and Lottie can help you. You can let Maria have a day away."

"You don't plan to involve her in your business troubles, do you?" Mama shook her head. "She already has her head full of ideas about making a name for herself at the newspaper."

"Don't you support her reporting?" Will asked in surprise. He didn't like Maria spending so much time at the newspaper—she'd become enamored of women's suffrage and other such matters. But he'd thought Mama and Pa both wanted her to have the opportunity.

"I don't want her getting into trouble," Mama said. "You know, she talked to that dreadful Ben Holladay."

"Holladay?" Will's stomach dropped. He'd told Maria to stay away from the man, or at least to take Will with her.

"Yes, and he treated her rudely. That's all she told me."

"Let me take her with me tomorrow," Will said. "I'll get the story out of her and then thrash Holladay if I have to."

"I'm sure it won't come to that," Mama said. She sighed. "All right. Take Maria. You two enjoy yourselves." She looked sharply at Will. "But behave yourself, son."

"Yes, Mama."

As soon as he had Mama's approval, Will looked for Maria. "I'm headed to Oregon City tomorrow. Would you like to join me? We talked about an outing."

"Tomorrow?" she said, just as Mama had. "But Mama wanted me to—"

"I just spoke with her. She says we can go."

"Really? With Maggie's birthday next Tuesday?"

"Eliza and Lottie will help Mama," Will said. "You've been doing too much, especially with your work on the paper."

Maria hesitated. "Why can't we wait until next week?"

"I need to see Samuel Cassidy," Will said. "Before Higgins gets back."

"When is Amos returning?" Maria asked.

"He said he would leave San Francisco yesterday. He should reach Portland by the first of next week."

"Who is Mr. Cassidy?" she asked, frowning. "I've heard that name. Isn't he the San Francisco branch manager? Why is he here if Amos is in San Francisco?"

It seemed Maria hadn't heard of Cassidy's firing. "Cassidy used to be our San Francisco agent. He came to Oregon to talk to Pa and me. Zhuang Li has been looking at the books Cassidy brought with him."

"Is Mr. Zhuang finished?" Maria asked. "I thought I saw him here earlier today."

"He finished this afternoon."

"What did he find out?"

Will shook his head. "I can't talk about it, Maria. Not until Pa and I know what's going on."

"But you said Mr. Zhuang had completed his work."

"It was inconclusive." Will didn't want to say anymore. "I need to ask Cassidy some questions. But you and I can spend time together except during my meeting with him."

"It sounds like you'll be busy. Why do you want me there?"

"To spend time with you. We'll have the train ride together, and you can see some of your friends in Oregon City."

She looked at him. "Will I meet Mr. Cassidy?"

"I don't know. We'll see." Did she just want to get a story for her newspaper? Why was she so interested in Cassidy?

Chapter 48: Oregon City

Maria was ready early Saturday morning for the train ride to Oregon City. She and Will said goodbye to Mama, then rode the family's carriage to the station.

"The train's barely faster than the steamboat," Will remarked. "But it's warmer."

"And dirtier." Maria liked to watch the river flow by on the steamboat. Watching the vegetation change from spring through autumn was peaceful and soothing. But today was a dreary late winter day—spring had not yet arrived, and she was glad not to be traveling on the damp riverboat.

Will bought their tickets, then escorted her into a first-class compartment. A man and his wife soon joined them, but the rest of the seats remained empty. They could converse quietly without interruption.

Will made himself unusually agreeable, Maria thought. He asked her about her job at the newspaper, and she explained her desire to write a publishable article to impress Mrs. Duniway.

"She already thinks your writing is good," Will said. "She told Mama so."

"She told Mama?" Maria asked in delight.

Will grinned. "I overheard them talking last week."

"But I still want to do more than write about women's meetings."

Will's face turned serious. "I hear you met with Ben Holladay. I told you not to see him without me."

Maria shrugged. "I can't take you with me on interviews."

"I warned you—Holladay isn't a pleasant man," Will said. "Mama said you had a problem. Do I need to have a talk with him?"

"No," Maria said. "I won't meet with him again. I've decided against writing about the railroads."

"Then what will you write about?"

"I don't know yet," Maria said. She'd see what she could find out from Samuel Cassidy—she'd try her best to speak to him today, even if Will didn't want her to. "Tell me what you're working on now." Maybe Will would let something slip.

"I'm exploring railroad investments," Will said. "Rails will be key to Portland's future."

"What does Papa think?"

"He's interested," Will said. "But for the past decade and more, he has put a lot of money into steamboats. And Uncle Owen doesn't have funds to help us expand. His losses from the Boston fire were too great."

Will talked openly about railroad investments, which made Maria suspect that Mr. Cassidy's trip to Portland had nothing to do with transportation.

They arrived in Oregon City in late morning. "I need to meet with Cassidy now," Will said. "Can you amuse yourself until one? Then we'll have a late lunch at the hotel."

"Couldn't I sit in on your meeting?" she asked. "I thought we'd be spending the day together."

Will shook his head. "What Cassidy and I need to discuss is private."

Hands on hips, Maria said, "Private? It's about the family business, isn't it? I'm part of the family."

Will sighed. "Please, Maria, I can't tell you. I don't want to slander anyone until we have all the facts."

Slander? Maria raised her eyebrows. Something nefarious was going on. Who might be slandered? Mr. Cassidy? Mr. Zhuang? Amos? Surely not Will or Papa. "I'd really like to know what this is about."

"I know," Will said. "And I'd like to tell you. But I can't. Trust me."

Maria sniffed. "Trust you?"

"Please." He smiled.

She wouldn't get anywhere with Will today. She wondered again why he had bothered to bring her along. "Fine." She turned away. "I'll go shopping, then meet you at the hotel at one."

Maria had lived in Oregon City from the time she was an infant until they moved to Portland just a few years ago, so she knew the town well. She ambled along the main street with no purpose in mind. Finally, she entered the mercantile store the family had patronized for years.

"Maria McDougall," the woman behind the counter said with a smile. "How nice to see you. Is your mother with you?"

"No, ma'am," Maria responded. "I've come for the day with my brother Will."

"Is William back from Boston?" the clerk asked.

Maria satisfied the woman's curiosity about Will and the rest of the McDougall family. "Will has a meeting at the hotel," Maria ended. "I'm waiting for him to finish."

The clerk bustled about, showing Maria new merchandise, until Maria bought a few ribbons and pins to take home to Mama and her sisters. "I must be going," she said, after paying.

She ducked out of the store and headed back to the hotel. It was early, but she had no interest in making more small talk with other store clerks.

When Maria arrived at the hotel, Will and another man—the man she'd seen meeting with Papa and Will, who must be Mr. Cassidy—sat in the lobby with their heads close together in deep conversation. She walked over to join them.

Both men stood, Mr. Cassidy bowing when Will introduced them. "Miss McDougall," he said. "Your brother and I have had a most productive conversation. Please—" He gestured to a seat between them. "Join us."

She sat, then looked at Will.

"I'm sorry, Maria," Will said. "We will try to wrap up our meeting quickly."

Mr. Cassidy gave a small smile. "We were nearly done. Your brother agrees he must look into the discrepancies in the San Francisco—"

"Sorry to cut our conversation short, Cassidy," Will interrupted. "I promised Maria we would tour our childhood haunts in Oregon City before we catch the evening train home." He stood and shook Mr. Cassidy's hand. "You will be returning to Portland soon, will you not? I will see you then." Will held out a hand to help Maria up. "Shall we eat, Maria?"

As Will led her toward the hotel restaurant, Maria wondered what Mr. Cassidy had meant by "discrepancies." Maybe she could pry it out of Will later.

"What discrepancies were you discussing?" she asked Will after their meal was served.

"I told you," he said. "I can't talk about it yet."

"You mean you *won't* talk."

"Fine," he said with a sigh. "I won't. There isn't anything to say yet, anyway."

After their meal, Maria and Will spent a pleasant afternoon strolling around Oregon City. They walked past the school Will graduated from at age fifteen, as well as the girls' academy Maria attended briefly. "Did you hate it so much?" Will asked, gesturing at the building.

She nodded. "The girls acted as if they were better than me. I had no friends at school."

"But you got along well with the Pershing girls," Will said, drawing her arm tighter through his.

"Yes," Maria said, smiling. "They were friendly, but they lived in the country. Of course, Cordelia Pershing was sweet on you. She thought she could hook you by being nice to me."

Will laughed. "I hear she's happily married now. To some farmer whose parents emigrated to Oregon in 1843. One of the earliest settlers."

"Did Mama tell you that?" Maria asked. "I don't think I did."

"Not Mama. Cordelia's uncle Noah."

"The riverboat captain?" Maria asked.

"Yes. I've seen him several times since my return. He's told me all the Pershing news."

"His younger brother Jonah was your best friend growing up, wasn't he?" Maria and Cordelia had often tagged along after Will and Jonah, to the boys' great annoyance.

"Yes. Noah says Jonah's a farmer now," Will said. "He married not long after I left for Harvard."

"Don't you wish you'd married Cordelia and followed Jonah's example?" Maria teased.

Will looked at her seriously. "Not at all. I'm waiting for you to come to your senses. Then I'll ask you to marry me."

She frowned. "What do you mean, come to my senses?"

"Leave off newspaper investigations."

She huffed. "That isn't likely to happen."

They turned up the hill toward their old home. When they reached it,

Maria grew wistful. "It looks the same," she whispered.

"Yes," Will said. "The trees are bigger than when I left home, but it looks the same."

They talked of the games they'd played, of their school days and summer evenings. Of Mama and Papa and their siblings.

"Do you miss living here?" Will asked Maria.

"It's fun to remember the good times. But I never felt entirely a part of the family as a child."

Will turned to face her. "How can you say that? You were what made the family for me—you and Pa, when he brought you to Oregon. Before then, it was just Mama and me."

"Thank you," she said, smiling up at him. "You always made me feel whole. But . . ." Her voice trailed off. "But I never really knew who I was."

Will looked off into the distance. "I know. A part of me felt that way, too. Because I never knew who my natural father was."

Maria took his arm, and they walked away from the house. "We have that in common."

Will pulled her close. "But we'll always be each other's family."

They reached the train station shortly before time to board. On the return trip, they were alone in the car. Maria asked Will, "Was Mr. Cassidy dismissed as the San Francisco branch manager?"

Will shook his head. "I can't discuss it."

"But you called him the former branch manager. Did he quit, or was he fired?"

"That's a private matter," Will said.

"What did he mean by discrepancies? Were there errors in his documents?"

"Maria, I can't—"

"I'll find out eventually," Maria said. "Papa will tell me."

"I doubt it," Will said. "And don't you bother him. He still tires so easily. I'm dealing with the situation."

"He won't thank you for coddling him." Maria turned to look out the window at the passing fields. "Maybe I'll ask Amos when he gets back. He must know what's going on."

"Maria," Will said, exasperation written on his face. "Don't meddle in things you don't understand."

Maria glared. "How can I understand if you won't tell me anything?"

"Come now," Will said, putting an arm around her shoulders. "We've had a pleasant day. Don't spoil it now by arguing."

She leaned back against his chest when he pulled her to him. He was solid and comfortable, and she was tired. "Don't think I'll forget this," she murmured, though for now she would let it rest. Soon, the clickity-clack of the wheels against the tracks lulled her to sleep, safe in Will's arms.

Chapter 49: Higgins Returns Again

While Will was home for the noon meal on Monday, March 17, Higgins sent a note to Pa that he had returned. Will sent a response asking the accountant to come to the McDougall residence at four o'clock that afternoon. As the hour approached, Will paced the halls, wondering how to broach Zhuang Li's findings with Higgins.

"Let me handle him," Pa said when he saw Will pacing. "I'll decide what to tell him about Cassidy's visit. You'll make him feel like a cornered bear. It's better to let him talk. If a man has a hanging offense in his past, he'll eventually hang himself. And we want to know what he found in California."

"But, Pa—"

"You'll have your chance," Pa said. "Let me start."

When Pa gave an order, it was best to obey, though it went against Will's grain.

Higgins arrived late, irritating Will. Once the three men were seated in the library, Pa began, "Well, Higgins, tell us about your meetings with Cassidy and Beck."

Higgins described dismissing Cassidy. Cassidy had argued, but Higgins was firm and escorted Cassidy off the premises to be sure he took nothing with him.

"Do you know if he had any records at his house?" Pa asked.

"Why would he?" Higgins said. "Beck has reported nothing missing since he took over."

"And how'd it go with Beck?" Pa asked.

"Beck was elated at the prospect of overseeing both San Francisco and Sacramento," Higgins said. "More than twice the revenue to manage. He will expect his salary to increase proportionally."

"If he can hold expenses down," Will interjected. "Which Cassidy couldn't."

"Precisely," Higgins said. "If Beck's the manager I think he is, he'll do well, and so will McDougall & Company."

"Did you find any more problems in San Francisco after Cassidy was gone?" Pa asked.

"No," Higgins said. "Nothing more."

"No discrepancies between Cassidy's reports to us and the books there?"

"I left the details for Beck. I commended him for Sacramento's success, and I told him I expected the same from San Francisco now. We spent several days reviewing the operation, which is why I delayed my return here."

"Seems like you and Beck get along well," Pa said mildly. Will would have been more direct, but maybe Pa's approach would work better.

"We do," Higgins said.

"Do you still think he's the right man to run the entire California operation?" Pa said.

"I found no reason to change my opinion."

Will shifted in his seat, waiting for Pa to raise the various discrepancies Li and Cassidy had identified. But Pa meandered around the issue, asking Higgins about accounts in both San Francisco and Sacramento.

Higgins's answers were detailed about Sacramento, less so about San Francisco. "I told Beck to go over the books in San Francisco and look for opportunities to improve. We'll need to wait for his first report."

"Thank you," Pa said, rising stiffly. "We've kept you late enough, Higgins. I appreciate your willingness to travel, as well as your time this afternoon."

The younger men stood as well. "I shall leave you to your family supper," Higgins said, with a small bow to Pa.

After Higgins left, Will turned to Pa. "We didn't learn much, did we?"

"We learned Higgins and Beck are thick as thieves," Pa said. "If one is crooked, the other probably at least knows about it. But we still don't know if they've done anything wrong."

"You didn't ask him about Li's findings," Will said.

"There will be time," Pa replied.

"I'll talk to Higgins in the morning," Will said. "I'll confront him then."

"Go easy, son," Pa said. "Your mother always says you catch more flies with honey than vinegar."

The next morning, Will arrived at the office early, wanting to meet with Higgins as soon as the man walked in. He remembered Pa's admonition to "go easy," but he wanted to watch Higgins's face when he mentioned Cassidy was in Portland.

As soon as he saw the accountant in the hallway, Will called, "Higgins, do you have a minute?"

Higgins entered Will's office. "Yes?"

"Cassidy claims the San Francisco reports we received were wrong."

Higgins's eyebrows shot up his forehead as he plopped into a chair across from Will. "Cassidy? How do you know what he claims?"

"He came to Portland while you were gone." Will leaned back in his chair. "Naturally, he complained about being fired, and wanted to know if Pa and I had approved it."

"Did he talk to your father, too?"

"Yes." Will took a breath, then continued, "We explained his reports showed San Francisco wasn't as profitable as we expected. He wanted to see the reports. When we showed him, he said they weren't the reports he'd sent."

"What?" Higgins exclaimed. "That's preposterous."

Will shrugged. "He surprised me, too. I asked how that could be. He didn't know."

Higgins rubbed his temple. "Did he have any proof?"

"Proof of what?"

"That the reports we had were not what he sent," Higgins said slowly, as if speaking to a dullard.

"No." Will shook his head. "It was an odd story. When you audited the San Francisco operation in December, did you see any evidence of forgery? Or of theft within the branch?"

Higgins snorted. "How could I see anything when I didn't know there was a problem? I had no idea Cassidy would claim his reports were forged. He made no such claim when I fired him. This must be something he made up after the fact, something he's alleging to reverse his dismissal." He frowned at Will. "You didn't reverse it, did you?"

"No. As you say, he had no proof."

"Is Cassidy still in Portland?"

"I don't know," Will said. "Shall I make inquiries? Do you want to speak with him?"

"I sure as hell do," Higgins said. Will had never heard the man swear before. Higgins was usually in complete control of himself. "I want to hear face to face what he has to say and why he said nothing to me in California."

"I'll ask around at the hotels," Will said. "See if he's still here." He decided not to mention Li's findings. As Pa said, there would be time. Higgins was riled enough about Cassidy.

For the rest of the day, a somber mood prevailed in the office. Employees seemed to sense conflict brewing. Zhuang Li watched Will, while the other men kept their heads down.

Will left the office in midafternoon. He'd sent word to Cassidy in Oregon City that Higgins wanted to meet. If Cassidy was amenable, Will would talk to Pa about how to set up the meeting. Both men were more likely to be civil if Pa were present than with Will alone.

He wandered through downtown on his way home. Today was Maggie's birthday, and there would be giggling girls celebrating with her at supper. Will would have to put in an appearance to congratulate his little sister, but he wouldn't have to stay.

Then he remembered—Maria's birthday was March 30.

He passed a store that proclaimed on its sign "Clocks, Watches and Fine Jewelry." On a whim, he stepped inside—perhaps he'd find something special for Maria. Floor and table clocks dominated the shop, but one locked case held watches and jewelry. Will studied its contents through the glass cover.

"Are you looking for a watch, sir?" the bespectacled male clerk asked.

"No. Perhaps a small pin for a woman."

"A wife?" the man asked. "A sweetheart?"

"I hope she'll be my wife someday," Will murmured, more to himself than to the clerk.

"We have a few cameos," the clerk said, unlocking the case. "Direct from Italy. Or a ring. Are you ready to declare yourself? Would a ring be appropriate?"

"Let me see the rings," Will said with a sheepish smile. "I should know what's available."

The man showed him a small pearl ring, then a large sapphire that would not suit Maria at all, and then a garnet. In the back of the case, Will spotted a ruby ring set in gold, rimmed with tiny diamonds. The center stone was dark red, not ostentatious, and when he held it up to the light, it appeared flawless. It would look stunning with her dark eyes and warm skin tones, particularly when she wore her red dress. "How much for this one?" Will asked, holding the ring so it flashed in the light from the window.

The clerk named a price—more than what Will had intended to spend for Maria's birthday, but reasonable for an engagement ring. "I'll take it," he said. "Will you put it on account? I'm William McDougall. I'll bring you payment tomorrow?"

"For the McDougall family, of course," the clerk said, boxing the ring. "Will it need to be resized?"

"I don't know," Will said, pocketing the box. "Let's worry about that after she agrees to marry me. I'll be back tomorrow with payment."

Maggie's birthday celebration was as giddy as Will had feared. After he greeted the girls and ate his piece of cake, he escaped. He worried he'd been precipitous in buying the ring for Maria. But he could hold it until he was ready to propose. He didn't have to give her the ring for her birthday.

Will wanted Mama's advice, but Mama was too distracted by Maggie's birthday to have time to talk. He went to his room and hid the ring in a desk drawer with the journals he'd written on his trip from Boston.

When should he talk to Maria?

Chapter 50: After Maggie's Birthday

In the week after their trip to Oregon City, Maria noticed Will seemed distracted. She, too, was preoccupied—first by Maggie's birthday celebration, and then by events at the newspaper.

Mama had planned Maggie's birthday easily without Maria. Still, the supper with eleven-year-old Maggie and five of her school chums was chaotic. Six girls that age could never be silent for long, and Maggie's friends were among the giggliest girls Maria had ever met.

When Maria was Maggie's age, she'd been in school in Oregon City. As she'd told Will, the other girls taunted her about her Spanish and Indian heritage. Despite Mama and Papa telling her she was a McDougall and inferior to no one, Maria was embarrassed. Winema Riddle and Sarah Winnemucca were the first native women of courage and wisdom she had met. Their accomplishments made Maria want to prove herself their equal— to her family, to Mrs. Duniway, to Portland society.

If these women could advocate for their people, then surely Maria, who had all the advantages of wealth and education that being a McDougall gave her, could write a meaningful newspaper article. And not only did she have a responsible position at *The New Northwest*, but she had both Will and Amos courting her. Both were good men, respected both by Papa and by the Portland business community. For the first time in her life, she believed she was inferior to no one. But she wanted the rest of the world to see her talents as well.

Maria used her afternoons to work on her article about the family business. She didn't have enough information to finish the article, but she could outline what she wanted to say. Then she would know where the holes in her story were and where she needed to investigate.

She wondered if Will was distracted because of the business issues Mr. Zhuang had analyzed in the McDougall kitchen. Maria was certain Mr. Zhuang was there because the business had a problem, even if Papa and Will wouldn't tell her what it was.

"Papa," she asked one evening, "did Mr. Zhuang find the answers you needed?"

"Hmm?" Papa said, looking up from his paper. "No, not yet." Then he frowned at her. "Why do you think I need answers from Zhuang Li?"

"Well, something must have led him to take up space at our kitchen table."

"Don't worry," Papa said, burying his face in the paper again. "Will and I can handle our business issues."

When she tried to question Will, he was even less forthcoming than Papa. Something bothered them both, but they refused to tell her anything.

She made a chronology of the company's history from the time Papa returned from California. Then she realized she needed to know more about the Boston origins of the firm, and she would have to ask Papa or Will about that.

But as she wrote, she couldn't make the story come alive. To give her article the hook Mrs. Duniway would want to draw in readers, Maria would have to ferret out the current issues plaguing Papa and Will.

On Friday, March 21, as Maria left *The New Northwest* office, Amos Higgins fell into step beside her. "Good afternoon, Maria."

"Amos," she said, smiling. "Are you recovered from your travels now?"

"Yes, I am hard at work again." He took her arm and tucked it into the crook of his elbow. "But I'm not working so much that I can't enjoy an afternoon walk with you. Must you go straight home, or might I persuade you to take a cup of tea with me?"

"Tea would be lovely," she said, following him into the St. Charles Hotel. For a moment, she wondered why she felt comfortable dining with Amos, when the prospect of accompanying Ben Holladay made her feel dirty.

Amos was a gentleman, she decided. Ben Holladay, despite his wealth, was a scoundrel. Amos courted her openly and presumably would propose marriage if the two of them suited. Ben Holladay made his illicit proposition through innuendo and deceit.

But Ben Holladay had no place in her thoughts today, she told herself. She turned her attention to the man with her and let Amos seat her in the restaurant and order tea and cake.

"Tell me, Amos," she asked when the tea arrived. "What happened in California?"

"Hasn't your father told you?" Amos shook his head. "It was a most unfortunate situation. One of our branch managers was stealing from the company. There is no other explanation."

"How?" Maria asked. "Doesn't he have to report his results to Papa?"

"Yes, my dear," Amos said. "But reports can be falsified. With the distances involved, it's hard to audit our inventories and receipts. That is how I spent my time in California. The new manager and I went through every box and file in the warehouse." Amos described his work in California.

Maria wanted to pay attention because she might learn something she could use in her article, but the warm tea and heavy cake made her sleepy. She interrupted, "What did Mr. Zhuang find out from his audit while you were gone?"

"Zhuang?" Amos asked in surprise. "Zhuang Li? What was he doing?"

"I don't know," Maria said. "But Papa and Will had him reviewing all sorts of documents in our kitchen."

"Well, I shall certainly find out," Amos said. He looked angry. "Have you finished, my dear? Let me see you home so I can get back to work."

As they walked home, Amos's anger dissolved, and he again charmed Maria with his attentions. She wished Will paid her half the compliments Amos did.

As they turned the last corner toward home, Amos tightened his grasp on her arm. "Maria," he said, "I was most sincere in the Valentine's Day note I sent you. I want to deepen our acquaintance, and I hope you will let me escort you to the theater or a musical performance soon."

She smiled. "I would be delighted, Amos." She paused, then ventured softly, "I missed you while you were gone."

He smiled back. "And I missed you, Maria. I hope we will not part again." He bowed over her hand when they reached her door. "I shall inquire about theater and musical offerings in town and let you know. But first, I shall see whether your father is available for a brief meeting."

Maria ushered Amos to Papa's library, then almost danced as she climbed the stairs to her room. Amos truly was a gentleman. He made her feel beautiful and loved. She never felt sullied or inferior in his presence. Nor patronized.

Chapter 51: Meeting with Cassidy and Higgins

On Saturday morning, March 22, Pa summoned Will to the library.
"Higgins was here yesterday afternoon," Pa said. "Apparently, Maria told
him Zhuang Li was reviewing documents in our kitchen. Thank goodness
she didn't know what he was looking for. Higgins is upset. He questioned
me about what Li was doing."

"Higgins is sharp," Will said. "He'll put two and two together and get
something close to four. I told him Cassidy claims the San Francisco reports
were forged. Now he knows Li was working on something confidential. He
probably suspects Li was auditing those reports."

"I wish Maria weren't involved," Pa said, sighing. "She's determined to
make a name for herself at the newspaper, and she could land in trouble."

"Then we should keep her out of it," Will said.

"If we find out Higgins is implicated, we'll have to tell her," Pa said.
"He's courting her."

"Can't you warn her off him now, Pa?" Will pleaded. Maria wouldn't
listen to him about Higgins, but she would heed Pa.

"We have no proof against Higgins," Pa said. "But I will make sure she
doesn't make any promises to Higgins until we sort this out."

Will slumped in his seat. He hated to think of Maria marrying Higgins.
He thought of the ring he'd hidden with his journals. Maria's birthday was
a week away. Should he propose to her then? If she accepted, he wouldn't
have to worry about Higgins.

Pa broke into Will's reverie. "I told Higgins we'd meet with him and
Cassidy. It's time to have it out with them. Can you arrange it for Monday?"

"I'll send Cassidy a note. I'm sure he'll want to meet."

"Let me lead the meeting, all right, son? I don't want to frighten either of them off. One of them knows more than he's saying."

Will grimaced, but said, "Yes, Pa."

"Unless Zhuang Li is the thief."

Will sat up straight at that. "Li? But he's the one who first mentioned discrepancies back in December."

"Maybe so," Pa replied. "But he only came forward when Higgins was away and unable to defend himself. And in Higgins's absence, Li had access to the documents in question."

"I thought you trusted the Zhuang family, and Li in particular."

"But how well do I know them?" Pa said. "The Chinese are an insular group."

"Isn't that our fault, Pa? When have we ever asked Li or his family to dine with us? They stay in Chinatown because white society doesn't want them. Li is one of only a few Asians working in a white company. Maybe we should involve him in Monday's meeting, so the three of them can keep each other from lying."

"If I thought that would work," Pa said, "I'd consider it. But frankly, I think Higgins and Cassidy will cause enough fireworks without Li there, too."

Will sent a note to Cassidy, who confirmed he could meet Monday morning.

On Sunday, Will found Mama alone in her morning room. "Might I have a word?" he asked. At her nod, he perched on the edge of a small divan.

"What is it, dear?" she asked.

"I bought a ring for Maria."

Mama's face lit up. "Oh, Will. Has she accepted? She hasn't said—"

"I haven't asked yet. Maybe on her birthday."

Mama's expression turned neutral. "What do you think she'll say?"

"Obviously, I hope she'll say yes. She has been my dearest friend since she was a baby. And I've hoped to marry her since I returned last fall. But I truly don't know what she will say."

"Does she know you love her?"

"She should by now."

Mama laughed. "Whether she *should* know is not my question. I asked if she *does* know?"

Will stood and paced the room. "I've told her. Yet, she still seems taken with Amos Higgins. Who, by the way, might be a thief."

Mama sighed. "Mac and I have discussed the office intrigue. But as I understand it, there's no way of knowing whether anyone is stealing. And all of your suspects must be considered innocent until proven guilty."

"Not when it comes to Maria's heart, Mama." Will turned to his mother. "I couldn't bear seeing her get hurt in this mess."

"Then you and your father must get to the bottom of the business problems. And leave Maria out of it."

"But Mama—"

"I will pray for you and Maria," Mama said. "You are my children, and your happiness means everything to me. But if you marry each other, you must be prepared—the community will gossip because you were raised as siblings."

"That won't matter—"

"I fear it will," Mama said. "You and Maria both have difficult pasts to reckon with. Our local society will not help you escape our family's history."

Will had barely removed his hat and coat on Monday morning when Higgins stormed into his office. "Is your father here?" Higgins asked.

Will glanced at the clock—half past eight. "I came early to be sure I arrived before Cassidy. Pa's taking the carriage. He'll be here at nine."

"How do you see this meeting going?"

Will shrugged. "Pa says he'll handle it." Will wanted to question Higgins now—to spread out Li's findings and demand Higgins explain the discrepancies. But Pa wanted to hear each man out, let them debate each other, instead of Pa and Will confronting them. So, Will only said, "Pa hasn't told me more than that."

"Cassidy can make up whatever he wants," Higgins snapped. "How can we disprove him when the records are in California? All we have in Portland are his reports."

Higgins didn't seem to know about the ledger Cassidy had brought north. Maybe he hadn't done a thorough audit in San Francisco. Or maybe Cassidy had shown Will and Pa a false ledger, and the authentic books were still in California. Will needed to warn Pa about what Higgins had just said.

Will heard a commotion in the office lobby when the carriage driver helped Pa into the building. Will rushed to assist his father to his desk, then shut the door to Pa's office, leaving Higgins outside. "Pa, Higgins doesn't know about the ledger Cassidy brought us. All he knows is Li was reviewing documents for us."

Pa sighed as he eased into his chair. "Let me handle them. As I've said, if anyone is stealing, he'll hang himself soon enough."

Will had to trust his father, though every instinct told him to thrash Higgins. And maybe Cassidy as well.

When Cassidy arrived, Will escorted both Cassidy and Higgins into Pa's office.

"Well, gentlemen," Pa began, "there seems to be a disagreement between you. I authorized Mr. Higgins to end your role as branch manager, Mr. Cassidy, but I am prepared to hear you both out." He turned to Higgins. "Mr. Higgins, please begin by describing how we got to this point. Tell us what you divined from the reports we received from California."

Higgins recounted how Sacramento's profits exceeded those of San Francisco. He ended by accusing Cassidy of mismanagement.

Cassidy shot to his feet. "You called me a thief when you fired me. Do you retract that slander now?"

"It doesn't really matter, does it, Cassidy?" Higgins drawled. "You squandered our assets at best. And stole from us at worst."

Cassidy's expression darkened. "That's a damned lie. You forged the reports I sent."

"Forged?" Higgins scoffed. "How could I have forged your reports?" He turned to Will. "Where are the reports? Let's have a look at what I supposedly forged."

Pa nodded at Will. "Bring in the documents. Let Higgins have his say."

When Cassidy opened his mouth to protest, Pa held up his hand. With a grim face, he said, "You'll have your turn."

Will fetched the San Francisco reports and spread them out on Pa's desk. The three younger men leaned over them while Pa sat back in his chair.

"All right, Higgins," Pa said. "Prove your point."

Higgins went through his litany again, this time pointing to numbers in the reports as he spoke.

Cassidy shook his finger in Higgins's face. "Those are not my reports. I never saw these documents before arriving in Portland."

"Then where are your reports, Mr. Cassidy?" Pa asked.

"I mailed them to you. I don't know what happened after that."

"Do you have copies of what you sent?" Pa asked.

Cassidy's face flushed. "Not with me. Copies of my reports remained in the San Francisco office after Higgins threw me out. But the ledger I brought—"

"Ledger? What ledger?" Higgins stared at Cassidy, his eyebrow twitching.

"I had last quarter's ledger at my house when you fired me. I brought it here."

"You stole company property?" Higgins shouted.

"I brought it straight to the company's owner," Cassidy yelled back. "That's hardly stealing. Where's the ledger, Will?"

Pa nodded at Will, who retrieved the book.

"All right, Mr. Cassidy," Pa said. "Tell us what you think happened."

"I'm at a disadvantage, Mr. McDougall," Cassidy said. "I have not had the opportunity to compare the falsified reports with the ledger I brought, but I shall endeavor to show where they differ." Slowly at first, then with more confidence, Cassidy pointed out several of the discrepancies Zhuang Li found. Not all of them, but as Cassidy said, he hadn't seen the reports before.

Higgins sneered. "There's no way to prove what you say. First, there is no proof this book is the real ledger."

Will couldn't help himself. "Did you inspect all of last quarter's ledgers in San Francisco, Higgins?"

Higgins shrugged. "I looked at what was there. I can't possibly remember all the records I reviewed. And as I told you, I left everything in Beck's hands." Then, turning to Pa, he continued, "Second, even if this is a real ledger and there are discrepancies, Cassidy could easily have changed the reports himself. And third, as I said earlier, whether the low profits are because of poor management or theft is irrelevant. Cassidy was properly fired as branch manager. That is why you authorized his firing."

"But whether there is theft does matter," Will protested. "If someone is stealing, we must identify the culprit and have him arrested."

Cassidy made a sound of protest.

Pa held up a hand. "We will not resolve this matter today. Do either of you have any explanations for the discrepancies beyond what you have already said? Will is right. If there is a thief, he must be punished."

Cassidy stood, tugged down his vest, and said haughtily, "I have not stolen from your company, Mr. McDougall. And I will not have my integrity maligned. I will return to California tomorrow. All I ask is that you not slander my good name, so that I might find other employment to feed my family." He stalked out.

"Well," Higgins said, rubbing his temple. "Good riddance. Now, tell me what Li found. I assume that's what he was doing in your kitchen."

Pa placated Higgins, much to Will's dismay, then sent the head accountant back to work. When Higgins left, Pa said, "Higgins is a smart man. He deduced what Zhuang Li was doing, and he'll want every detail. He'll hound Li now, and you will have to make sure Higgins does not unfairly attack Li."

"If Higgins is the culprit, he'll do everything he can to discredit Li," Will said.

"Li himself could be the culprit," Pa said. "Either on his own, or in cahoots with Cassidy."

"You don't believe that, do you?" Will asked.

Pa shrugged. "I do not have a basis for believing anything. Cassidy claims he didn't know about the forged reports until he got to Portland. If someone forged them in Oregon, Li could have done it as easily as Higgins."

"Why would Li—?"

"Why would Higgins?" Pa said, interrupting Will. "Men will do anything for riches. Whether they are white or Asian or African or Indian. If they think it is in their self-interest, they will lie and cheat and steal. Every man has a breaking point."

Will had no response to that. But in his heart, he still suspected Higgins.

Chapter 52: A Birthday and a Letter

On Thursday, March 27, after hearing the knocker, Maria opened the front door to find Amos Higgins standing on the porch with a nosegay and a box of chocolates. "A little bird told me your birthday is this Sunday, Maria. I came to offer my felicitations."

She smiled. "Thank you, Amos." She took the flowers and candy. "Won't you come in?"

He shook his head. "I cannot stay. I simply want to wish you many happy returns and ask if you would accompany me to a theatrical on Saturday, April 5."

"Oh," Maria said. "I'm sorry, but that is Papa's birthday. After everything he's been through this year, our family will be celebrating."

With a rueful expression, Amos bowed. "Then perhaps we could try for Friday, April 4? I will see if I can switch the tickets."

"That would be delightful," Maria said. She tried again to get him to stay, but he declined.

She told Mama of Amos's invitation, and Mama confirmed, "We will certainly celebrate your father's birthday, but you must also enjoy your evening with Mr. Higgins."

"Now that I'm calling him Amos, Mama, don't you think you should as well?"

Mama smiled. "Before we celebrate Mac's birthday, we will celebrate yours. Would you like to invite Mr. Higgins to the noon meal on Sunday?"

"Yes, please," Maria said. "I will write him now to issue the invitation." She went to her room and soon had a note ready for the post.

Sunday after church, the family gathered for their dinner. Amos joined the McDougalls for a sumptuous beef roast and accompaniments, followed by angel food cake smothered in chocolate sauce. Amos toasted her with a wide smile, "Angel food for an angel."

"That is my line, Higgins," Papa said, also smiling. "I have told her that on every birthday since she was born."

Maria caught Will rolling his eyes, a sullen expression on his face. "Don't you wish me a happy birthday?" she teased.

"Of course," he said. But he did not smile.

Amos left in midafternoon. After Maria showed him out, Will followed her into the hallway. "Would you walk with me, Maria?"

"I'm still full after dinner," she said. "And it's cold."

"Just a stroll in the garden." He sounded strangely nervous. "I need to talk to you."

"All right," she said. "Let me fetch my cloak and hat."

She bundled into a wool cape and old bonnet, then met him at the kitchen door. They went outside, and Will sat beside her and heaved a sigh.

"What is it, Will?" she asked, wrinkling her brow. "Is something wrong?"

"No, Maria. Not wrong." He stammered, "I-I hope everything is *right*. Will you marry me?" He took a small package from his pocket and unwrapped a ring. A lovely ruby surrounded by small diamonds. "I bought this for you. For your birthday and as an engagement ring. Will you have me?"

She took it, her heart pounding. "Oh, Will, it's lovely." She closed her fingers around it, imagining herself married to Will. It felt comfortable. Familiar. Then she thought of her newspaper work and all she wanted to accomplish. She thought of Amos.

She swallowed back tears, not wanting to hurt her dearest friend. "I'm not ready. Not yet." She placed the ring back in his palm. "I'm sorry, Will."

"But Maria, I love you," he said, taking her hand. "I want to spend my life with you. I've thought so ever since I returned from Boston." He seemed to struggle with what to say, then continued in a rough voice, "I can't bear seeing you with Higgins. I want to be the one you smile at. I've waited. I've tried to be more than a brother to you. If you're not ready now, then when?"

"I don't know, Will," she whispered. "I love you. You've always been my best friend." She gestured helplessly. "But marriage? I don't know. I need to prove myself before I wed."

"We could be happy."

Maria smiled. "We have always rambled on well together. But marriage demands more."

"You've liked our kisses. Don't deny it."

"I have," she admitted.

"Isn't that enough?" He rubbed her fingers softly.

She shook her head. She'd liked Amos's kisses, too, but she couldn't tell Will that. "I'm just not ready."

At that, Will cursed and leaped to his feet. "Then there's nothing I can say."

"No." Her throat swelled shut with tears. "I'm sorry."

As Will strode into the house, Maria stayed on the cold stone bench, feeling bereft. She hated hurting him. His proposal was well-intentioned. He loved her. And she loved him. As a brother. And as more—perhaps.

But she also liked Amos, which was part of her reason for not accepting Will. She liked Amos's attentions—and surely, that must mean she wasn't ready to marry Will.

Still, her desire to prove herself was the biggest impediment to marriage. Will didn't seem to understand her need to show she was more than the daughter of a prostitute with native blood. She wanted to write as much as any man did. Only then would she feel worthy of being the wife of either Will McDougall or Amos Higgins.

She wasn't ready to accept any man's proposal. Someday she would be. But not yet.

Other than supper, Maria avoided Will for the rest of Sunday. Monday morning, she grabbed a biscuit in the kitchen and told Mrs. O'Malley she needed to get to the newspaper early. "Put some bacon in that, Maria," Mrs. O'Malley said. "You look peaked this morning."

Maria let the housekeeper stuff the biscuit with bacon, thanked her, and left for downtown. When she arrived at the newspaper office, only Daisy was there.

"What brings you in so early?" Daisy asked, peering at Maria above her heavy spectacles. "Did you enjoy your birthday?"

"It was memorable," Maria said, taking off her hat and coat.

"Tell me." Daisy folded her hands and waited for Maria to sit.

"Amos Higgins came to my birthday meal with the family. He was very courteous." Maria unwrapped her biscuit and took a bite.

"Then why do you look so harried?"

"Will proposed."

Daisy's eyes widened. "Will? You mean your brother Will?"

Maria nodded while taking another bite.

"He proposed marriage?"

Maria nodded again.

"But he's your brother."

Maria sighed. "I've told you I'm adopted. He isn't really my brother. I'm not related to any of the McDougalls."

Daisy visibly relaxed. "Yes, I remember. But everyone in Portland thinks he's your brother."

Maria shook her head. "My parents have always been open that I'm adopted. Papa was acquainted with my mother in California and brought me home with him after she died."

"And your father?" Daisy looked skeptical.

"No one knows who he was."

"But Maria," Daisy said gently, "is it possible—?"

"Papa says he isn't my father. And I believe him." Maria wouldn't go into Will's birth—Papa hadn't fathered either of them, so they couldn't be related. But no one outside the family needed to know about Will. Still, Daisy's reaction was a taste of what Maria and Will would get if she accepted his proposal.

She sighed. "I turned him down. I came in early this morning so I wouldn't see him. Plus, I want to work on my article."

"What are you writing about?"

"Something is happening in our family business," Maria said. "Embezzlement, I think. That is news, and I want to report it."

"But what will that do to your family?" Daisy said. "Does your father know what you're doing?"

"Not yet," Maria said. "But I will tell him before I give it to Mrs. Duniway."

Maria made little progress on her article that day. She needed more information—information that only Will or Amos or Papa could give her. She didn't want to talk to Will or Amos. That left Papa.

That afternoon as Maria walked home, she thought of Daisy's caution. Her friend was right—if she didn't let Papa know what she was planning, he would be hurt. And perhaps angry with her for interfering in the business. Another reason to speak with Papa, so she went to look for him as soon as she entered the house.

Instead, she found Mama in the hallway in a tizzy. "Look, Maria," Mama said, waving a letter. "It's from my mother."

March 1, 1873

Ma chère Geneviève,

Now that spring is nearly upon us, I have decided that Jacques and I should pay you a visit. Our farm is in grave distress, and I am hopeful Oregon will offer us more prosperity, as it has you and your family.

I will wire you when we are ready to leave Missouri, so you can prepare for our arrival. I assume we can begin our sojourn in Oregon in your home.

Your loving mother,
Hortense Peterson

"Why on earth is she coming to Oregon after so many years?" Mama wailed. "I must host her and Jacques, of course, but why? And why did Will ever stop to see them last fall? This is all his fault."

Chapter 53: Beck's First Report

Will didn't know how to treat Maria after she rejected him. He spent the days after her birthday grimly avoiding her. He ate breakfast after she left for the newspaper and tried to schedule his other meals with friends and business associates.

On Tuesday, April 1, Will ate supper at a tavern near the docks with Noah Pershing. "Why so glum, mate?" the steamboat captain asked. "Your sweetheart turn you down?"

Will grunted and gulped his whiskey.

Noah chortled. "So, she did?"

"I asked Maria to marry me. She refused." Will tossed back another gulp, bracing for Noah's kidding.

But his friend surprised him. "You didn't see it comin'?"

"If I had, I wouldn't have asked her. I even had a ring." Will relived his humiliation when Maria handed back the ruby ring he'd chosen. It was hidden again with his journals.

"Could she change her mind?"

Will shrugged. "I don't know. Amos Higgins is also courting her."

"He's the one you don't trust?"

"That's him," Will said. "He's too smooth by half. I think he's hiding something, but I have no proof. Pa and Maria both think he's an estimable fellow."

"What will you do next?"

Will plunked his empty glass on the table and signaled for another. "I'll keep watching him. And keep watching out for Maria. What else can I do?"

Will felt the tension every time he walked through the hallways at work. Zhuang Li spoke only when spoken to. Higgins barked orders at every employee he encountered. Except Li. Will thought Higgins avoided Li, and he wondered whether the two men had spoken after Higgins learned Li reviewed the San Francisco ledger.

No word from Cassidy. He'd checked out of the hotel right after their meeting. Will assumed he'd returned to California.

Meanwhile, Pa either didn't notice the tension, or the men hid their differences from Pa.

Late in the week, Higgins strolled into Will's office. "I'll be taking Maria to the theater Friday evening," Higgins said. "Thought you should know."

Will wondered if Higgins knew he'd proposed to Maria. "Enjoy the performance."

"And I'll be at your house for your father's birthday dinner on Saturday," Higgins continued. "Your mother invited me."

Was the accountant deliberately taunting him? Will looked down at the papers on his desk, willing Higgins to leave. "Delighted."

"Anything you want to discuss?" Higgins asked.

Will shook his head, then a thought occurred to him. "When do we expect Beck's first report?"

"Next week, I expect," Higgins said. "It takes time to reconcile the ledgers after month's end, then mail takes four or five days by steamboat."

"Any word from him? A wire or letter?"

Higgins shook his head. "Shall I request an early update?"

"Don't bother," Will said. "We'll know soon enough."

Will went to bed early the evening of April 4. He couldn't bear to watch Maria come home with Higgins. He didn't want to risk making a scene, as he had the last time Higgins took her to a theatrical. And he surely would, after the way she had rejected his proposal.

As if Maria and Higgins and the office tensions didn't give Will enough to worry about, Mama was on a tear. She'd received a letter announcing Grandmère Peterson and Jacques were on their way to Oregon. Every time Mama saw Will, she scolded him again for visiting them.

"Why did you want to meet them?" she asked for the hundredth time.

"You know how they treated me."

"She's my grandmother," Will said. "The only grandparent I'll ever know." Mama's father was dead, and they both knew why he'd never know his paternal grandparents.

She fussed, but she couldn't contradict him. "Tell me about Jacques—the half-brother I've never met."

Will shrugged. "He seemed a decent sort. Not well-educated. Their farm was in miserable shape, but I think he tried to make it prosper. The land needs more labor than they can afford."

Mama sighed. "Well, if they come, we will host them, of course. Mac and I will figure something out."

"She didn't say when they would arrive, did she?"

"No," Mama said. "I hope they wire before setting out."

The following Thursday, April 10, Beck's report arrived. "See?" Higgins waved the document at Will. "Earlier in the month than Cassidy ever sent his report."

"What does it show?" Will asked.

"San Francisco profits are up ten percent," Higgins replied. "And no drop in receipts from Sacramento. Beck is off to a strong start."

"He had you there to help him start."

"Yes." Higgins nodded. "And we must watch the California operation closely to be sure Beck continues at this pace."

"Will you have his report audited?" Will asked. "Maybe Zhuang Li can take a look."

Higgins raised an eyebrow. "There's little to audit. All we have is the report and the gold and bank drafts Beck sent north. The ledgers are in California."

"Li found discrepancies before," Will said. "Let him look."

Higgins hesitated, then shrugged. "All right. No harm in seeing what he finds."

Will looked around the office for Zhuang Li, but the clerk wasn't there. Another employee told Will Li hadn't shown up for work, so Will headed to Chinatown.

He found the Zhuang home on Second Street, a couple of blocks away from the Front Street docks. He knocked, and his former traveling companion, Zhuang Jin, answered.

"Good afternoon," Will said. "Is Zhuang Li at home?"

Jin frowned. "Li cannot see you."

"He wasn't at work. Is he ill?"

"You not hear?" Jin said. "He hurt."

Will doffed his hat and stepped forward, but Jin blocked him from entering. "How was he hurt?" Will asked. "Is that why he missed work?"

"Men beat him. You not know?"

Shocked, Will shook his head. "Who did it? Has he seen a doctor? Can I help?"

"Chinese doctor treat him. He better soon, but hurt lots now."

"Would you ask him if he will see me?" Will said. "I want to assure my father he'll be all right."

Jin ushered Will inside, then disappeared into a back room. Strange, savory smells wafted through the air as Will waited. An old man and two small boys sat on cushions, all of them staring.

Jin returned. "Come," he said. "Li talk to you."

Will followed Jin to where Li lay on a pallet, his face bruised, his ribs wrapped. An older woman knelt in the far corner. Will nodded to her, then squatted beside Li. "What happened?"

"I walk to work, men stop me," Li said in a raspy voice. "Hit face. Kick ribs."

"Who were they?"

Li grimaced as he shrugged. "Don't know."

"White men?" Will knew the answer before he asked.

Li nodded. "Maybe from docks." His eyes narrowed. "Maybe Higgins send them."

"Why would Higgins have you beat up?"

"He not like me. I not like him." Zhuang Li winced as he spoke.

Will blew out a breath. "He doesn't like me either, but he hasn't had me beat up."

"You not Chinese."

Will had no response to that. "The reason I came to find you was that we have Beck's first report from San Francisco. Higgins says the profits are up for March, which is what he expected when he replaced Cassidy with Beck. I would like you to review the report and any documents we have in Portland that could confirm or deny its accuracy. But that can wait until you're on your feet again."

"Monday," Li said. "I be ready Monday."

Will touched Li's shoulder gently. "Take care of yourself. I'll check on you again tomorrow."

Chapter 54: Maria Talks to Li

Maria tried to enjoy her evening with Amos on April 4, but her memory of rejecting Will's proposal haunted her. The musical performance at the New Market Theater was good, though not as memorable as the performance of *Bluebeard*. Amos was as attentive as always, complimenting her on her dress and hair. His hand at the small of her back as he guided her to their seats was possessive and protective. He seemed glad to be with her, unlike Will's stormy behavior in recent days.

"Might I kiss you good night?" Amos asked when he brought her home.

She smiled and nodded.

His lips were firm and a trifle urgent. She felt wanted, an unsettling feeling.

"Soon, Maria," he whispered. "Soon I hope we will be more to each other."

Maria tried to focus on her work for the next week. But her conflicting feelings for Will and Amos made concentration difficult.

Friday, April 11, was Good Friday. Maria stayed home from the newspaper to help Mama and Mrs. O'Malley with Easter preparations. Midmorning, Will entered the kitchen and asked, "Do we have any soup I could take to the Zhuang household?"

Mama looked up. "Why do the Zhuangs need soup?"

"Zhuang Li was beaten. I want to take him something to show our concern."

"How dreadful!" Mama said. "Of course, you must take him some food."

She nodded at Mrs. O'Malley.

"Got chicken stock," Mrs. O'Malley said. "I'll add vegetables and meat. Come back after the noon meal, and I'll have a pot of soup and some bread. If them Chinese eat good Christian food."

Will smiled. "Everyone eats chicken soup. Thank you."

Maria followed Will out. "What happened to Mr. Zhuang? Does it have anything to do with our company?"

Will shook his head. "I don't think so. The Chinese are often targets of harassment and violence."

"You don't think it's connected to us?" Maria frowned. Of all the Chinese in Portland, why had Zhuang Li been attacked? "May I come with you?"

"There's no need—"

"I know, but I like Mr. Zhuang. I'd like to see him."

Will agreed. After their meal, Maria and Will took Mrs. O'Malley's bundles and set out in the carriage for Chinatown. "Watch your step," Will said, as he helped her down from the carriage. Chinatown smelled odd, but the streets were no dirtier than those near the newspaper office.

He led her to the Zhuangs' door and knocked. Li himself answered. His face was bruised purple, but he smiled. "Mr. Will, Miss McDougall."

"How are you, Li?" Will asked. "May we come in? Our mother sent soup and bread."

"Thank you." Li bowed as they entered the house. He brought two chairs out from a corner, then groaned as he sat on the floor. "May I offer tea?"

"Not necessary," Will said, as Maria said, "Thank you." She hoped for an opportunity to ask Li why he'd been attacked. "Are you healing well?" she asked.

Li shrugged. "I hurt. Will hurt many more days. But I get better."

"And you still don't know who did this?" Will asked.

"No. Jin ask, but no one say."

"I have a friend, a steamboat captain," Will said. "I'll ask him to make inquiries."

Li nodded.

"Could your attack be related to your work for Will and my father?" Maria blurted.

"Not know."

An older woman brought in a tea tray, then left. Li poured tea into little cups without handles and offered one to Maria and another to Will.

"What were you working on, anyway?" Maria asked as she sipped.

Li glanced at Will, then shook his head. "Your father not want me tell."

Will did not respond, and Maria realized neither man would tell her anything. She and Will drank their tea, wished Li well, and left.

After their visit to Zhuang Li, Will seemed to thaw toward Maria. She knew her refusal of his proposal had wounded him. She wished she could have accepted, if only to spare his feelings, but she simply wasn't ready for marriage.

On Easter Sunday after church, the family gathered for a midday feast of roast lamb, potatoes, and greens. The mood was festive. Mama didn't mention her mother's possible arrival. Pa and Will didn't mutter about business troubles. Even Eliza humored the younger children. If only their home could be this peaceful every day.

"Will you walk with me, Maria?" Will asked when the meal was over.

Maria glanced at Mama, who shrugged. "All right," Maria said. "Let me fetch a shawl."

When she was ready, Will escorted her to the garden. "Shall we stay here or walk along the street?" he asked.

She glanced up at the sunshine. "Let's stay. It's a lovely day. The lilacs will bloom soon."

They walked a lap around the garden, then sat on a sunlit bench. Will smiled at her, like he used to, before she rejected him.

"I'm sorry, Will," she said again. "I never meant to hurt you."

"Is it Higgins?"

She lifted a shoulder, then dropped it. "I don't know. I'm just not ready for marriage."

"When will you be?"

"Mama says I'll know." She shook her head. "I hope she's right."

Will took her hand. "Then I still have hope."

She sighed again. "Maybe."

"What did you and Will talk about?" Mama asked Maria that evening after they put Evie and Eddie to bed.

"He wants to know if he has hope," Maria said.

"What did you tell him?"

"I said I'm not ready now. That's all I can say." Maria's eyes welled with tears. "How will I know who the right man is, Mama? And when the right time comes?"

"You'll know." Mama smiled with a faraway look. "When you can't imagine life without him. When being with him always brings you joy." Then her smile faded. "But don't wait too long. Sometimes, life interferes."

"You mean like when Papa left for California?"

"Yes," Mama said. "I thought I'd lost Mac forever. He said he was returning East. I didn't think I'd ever see him again." She hugged Maria. "But then he returned. With you. And my life has been mostly joy ever since."

"I don't want to hurt Will," Maria said. "He's always been my friend."

"I know," Mama said. "I don't want to see Will hurt either—by you or anyone else. But you can't let that determine your decision. You must follow your own heart and trust yourself."

Monday morning, the front doorknocker sounded as Maria was leaving for work. She opened the door to find Zhuang Li standing on the porch, hat in hand.

"I come like Mr. Will ask," he said.

"Will left for the office already," Maria said. "Was he expecting you?"

"I thought he want me work here again. Now I go there." Li turned to leave.

"You look much better today," Maria said.

Li turned back and bowed. "Much improved."

"What does Will want you to work on?" she asked.

"California report. He want me review."

"But the records are in California." Maria understood that much about the branch reports—the Portland office relied on what it received from the managers.

Li shrugged. "I do what I can."

"Will should be downtown," Maria said. "I am headed to the newspaper. Will you walk with me?"

"That not wise, Miss Maria," Li said. "People not like."

"Nonsense," she said. "Let me get my hat."

When she was ready, Zhuang Li waited on the porch. He kept a careful distance between them as they walked, stepping behind her whenever anyone passed them on the road. She realized he was worried about her reputation—or perhaps he feared another beating. She should have been more thoughtful. The Chinese and whites in Portland did not mingle.

She might have Spanish and Indian blood, but to the denizens of Portland, she was still a McDougall daughter. She would have to be careful, so no harm would come to Mr. Zhuang because of her.

Chapter 55: Zhuang Li Reviews Report

Will ushered Zhuang Li into his office. "I'm sorry, Li," he said. "I should have waited at home for you. But this way, we can gather the documents you need and take them back. You can work in our kitchen again."

"Mr. Higgins know I audit report?" Li asked.

"Yes," Will said. "We can't hide taking the ledgers and reports out of the office."

"Maybe I work here instead," Li said. "Then I not bother family."

Will shook his head. "No, I want you to have privacy. No one will remove records from our house. Who knows what could disappear here?"

Li nodded, but looked uneasy.

Will frowned. "What's wrong?"

"I not want another beating."

"Because you'll be walking between our home and Chinatown?"

"Yes."

"Then we'll put you up at the house while you work," Will said. "My mother can find you a place to sleep—if you're willing."

"All right," Li said. "I send word so my family know."

"Of course."

They gathered the ledgers showing receipts from California during the period covered by Beck's latest report. Higgins helped them collect everything.

As Will and Li prepared to leave, Higgins said, "Send word, Li, if you need anything else. I'll bring it myself."

At the McDougall house, Will led Li into the kitchen. "Mama will sort out your sleeping arrangements. And I'll send our stable boy with a note to your family. You'll join us for dinner, of course."

Once Zhuang Li was settled, Will went to find Pa in the library. "Li is here now."

"How is he?" Pa asked. "Healed?"

"He looks better. Still bruised, but ready to work."

Pa leaned back in his chair. "What do you think he'll find?"

Will shrugged. "I don't know. I hope we can figure out what's been going on in California. But I'm not sure if we have enough here in Portland for Li to ferret out whether we have a thief in our employ."

"Maybe there's a thief," Pa said. "Or maybe someone made careless errors. We may never know."

"Surely, the culprit will have left tracks." Will rubbed his neck. He refused to believe the mystery would remain unsolved. "If I have to go to California myself, I'll get to the bottom of it."

"Don't prejudge," Pa said. "If you have blinders on, you'll miss the truth."

"Blinders let a horse see what's in front of him," Will retorted. "If the records show what's in front of us, Li will find it."

Pa frowned. "You've had it in for Higgins since you met him. And for Beck, because you got off on the wrong foot with him last fall and because Higgins likes him. But now that Cassidy's gone, if the situation improves—which at first blush it has—then it's likely Cassidy is the culprit."

"Let's see what Li comes up with," Will said. He didn't want Cassidy to be a thief.

Monday evening, Will stopped by the docks to see Noah Pershing. "What do you know about dockhands beating up Chinese men?" he asked.

Noah shrugged. "It happens. Most of the captains stop their men when they see them. But some just turn a blind eye. Since the December fire, the number of incidents is growing."

"Even though there's no proof the Chinese started the fire," Will said. "Only rumor."

"Even though." Noah raised an eyebrow. "I've heard another rumor that might interest you."

"What's that?"

"Your man Higgins is in deep with Holladay."

"Higgins? What's he doing with Holladay?" Will asked. As far as he knew, the two men were acquainted, but had no dealings. "And what do you mean, he's in deep?"

"Holladay is seeking investors for his railroad project," Noah said. "I hear Higgins wants to be one of them."

"Who'd you hear that from?"

"A bartender at the Pacific Hotel," Noah replied. "Higgins has been trying to find someone to lend him money to invest with Holladay. But any man with money to invest would put his funds directly with Holladay. No reason for anyone to loan to Higgins."

Will spent Tuesday at home while Li reviewed the San Francisco report. He didn't want to hover, but he wanted to be the first to hear the result. Plus, he needed to mull over what it might mean if Higgins invested in Holladay's railroad scheme.

Tuesday afternoon, as Will prowled the house, Mama called him into her morning room. "Why are you so anxious, son?" she asked.

"Waiting for Li's audit. Pa told you why he's here, didn't he?"

Mama nodded. "I know you want answers, but breathing down his neck won't help."

"I know." Will sighed. "But I can't help myself."

Mama bit her lip, then peered at Will. "How are you doing?"

"What do you mean?"

"How are you doing since Maria told you she wouldn't marry you?"

"I'll be all right." Will paced in front of the window. "What does she see in Higgins, anyway?"

Mama was silent for a moment. "He's a respectable man with a responsible position. Your father trusts him. Amos treats Maria well. Why wouldn't she be interested?"

Will made a sound of despair. Neither of his parents believed Higgins could be a thief. "She was my best friend. We grew up together."

"Maybe that's why Amos intrigues her," Mama said. "He isn't someone she's always known. Sometimes too much familiarity isn't conducive to romance."

"But I've always loved her, Mama."

"And she loves you, Will. Maybe you and she can find your path to each other. But if not, you'll find someone else to love."

Will swallowed. Mama's assurances were no comfort.

Li finished his audit by late Tuesday. "Not many records," he told Will. "Only one month to review. Without California ledger, we can't be sure."

"What did you find?" Will asked.

"Not much. One error." Li shrugged. "One set of receipts added wrong. Looks like clerical mistake."

"How much was the error?" Will peered over Li's shoulder as the Asian man pointed to a column of numbers.

"One dollar." Li grinned. "Not even Chinaman steal so little."

"So, Beck's report seems honest?"

Li nodded. "Seem so."

"Then what's next?" Will said, as much to himself as to Li.

"Wait for next month," Li said. "Review report again."

"Even if someone's stealing," Will said, "he knows we're watching now. He'll be careful."

"Yes," Li said. "He be careful. Or they—maybe more than one man."

Chapter 56: Picnic in the Park

On Tuesday, April 15, Maria spent two hours setting type for this week's issue of *The New Northwest*. Typesetting was usually Robert's job, but he had broken his hand and was slower than usual.

"We've got to get the galleys ready by day's end," Mrs. Duniway fumed. "Except page two with my editorial. I won't finish it until tomorrow, so we'll have to do that page then. We print Thursday."

"I'll help," Maria volunteered. "I'm slower than Robert at his best, but I can match him today."

"But your work must be double-checked," Mrs. Duniway said. "Your accuracy isn't what Robert's is."

"I'll review her typesetting," Robert said. "I can still read type backward, even if I can't handle the fonts very well."

Maria and Robert worked until the page was set. Maria stifled a smile when she noticed Robert sneaking a glance at Daisy every chance he could.

Maria stayed at the newspaper longer than usual. By the time she left, she was famished. As she donned her hat and cape to leave, her mouth watered at the thought of the plate Mrs. O'Malley would have waiting for her.

She'd walked most of the way home when she encountered Amos Higgins.

"Maria," he said, doffing his hat, "I just left your house. Your mother expected you hours ago." He sounded disapproving.

"I had to work," she said. "Were you looking for me?"

"As a matter of fact, I was." His stern tone turned solicitous. "I hoped you would accompany me on a picnic this Saturday."

"A picnic?" Maria smiled. "Where?"

"To the new City Park. The city bought the land over a year ago, though it remains undeveloped. Still, the views are spectacular, and spring has finally arrived." Amos grinned. "I, for one, am eager to enjoy it."

"Who else have you invited?"

He hesitated. Surely, he hadn't expected she would accompany him on a picnic in the wilderness alone. "Why don't I leave that up to you?"

"Perhaps Will can join us," Maria said, and Amos's expression soured. "And Nate and Eliza. And my friend Daisy Wilson from the newspaper, if that isn't too many. Do you have anyone you would add to the group?"

"I think that will make a pleasant afternoon," Amos said, bowing. "Shall I call for you all at your house at eleven?"

"Mama will insist on providing the lunch," Maria said. "And we can take our carriage."

Amos shook his head. "No carriage. The roads are little more than trails. I will hire a wagon and team."

Maria beamed. "It's settled then. We'll see you Saturday at eleven."

Maria invited Will, Nate, and Eliza. Lottie insisted on coming as well, and Mama declared that if Eliza was in the group, Lottie should be, too. "It is becoming a family affair," Maria said. "I wonder what Amos will think of us all."

"I could invite Zhuang Li," Will said, grinning.

Maria frowned. "This was Amos's idea. We shouldn't impose."

Will grimaced. "We're not imposing. We're providing the food. What's one more person in the wagon?"

"You know Amos and Mr. Zhuang don't get along," Maria said. "I'll ask Robert from the newspaper, as well as Daisy. Robert is sweet on Daisy, though she doesn't know it."

At work the next day, Maria invited them. Daisy was delighted and gushed about how handsome both Amos Higgins and Will were. "Whichever one of them you don't want, I'll take," Daisy said. Robert's jaw clenched at Daisy's words.

On Friday, Abigail Duniway entered the office waving a telegram. "I've heard from Winema Riddle," she announced. "There was another battle in the Modoc War. Winema was almost killed."

Maria gasped. "What happened?"

"No details in the telegram," Mrs. Duniway said. "Only that the Army attacked and won. She says a letter will follow."

"Can we find out more from the Army?" Robert asked.

"I'll ask my brother." Mrs. Duniway sighed. "Harvey no longer edits *The Oregonian*, but he still has contacts there, and the Army tells their reporters more than they tell me." Her skirt swished around her as she bustled out of *The New Northwest* office.

Half an hour later, she returned. "Harvey says the Army received a dispatch from Major Mason, the commander at Stronghold, this morning. General Canby was assassinated several days ago. In response, the Army cut off the Modoc water supply, then attacked on the fifteenth. Apparently, the Modoc warriors retreated and escaped. Several soldiers died, and even more were wounded, but only one Indian boy and a few Modoc women were killed."

"What about Winema?"

"She is a heroine," Mrs. Duniway said, smiling. "During the skirmish that killed General Canby, she saved Reverend Alfred Meacham. The reverend was injured, but she prevented the tribesmen from scalping him. I have no more details, so I hope she tells me more in her letter. If not, I shall write to request the story."

"A heroine," Maria murmured. Even an Indian woman could be a heroine. She might never see battle, but perhaps her writing could benefit someone. Mrs. Riddle's bravery strengthened Maria's resolve to prove herself.

Saturday morning dawned cool but sunny. Maria helped Mrs. O'Malley prepare a feast that filled three large wicker baskets, then she gathered blankets and cushions for the group to sit on. Everything was ready in the kitchen when Amos drove his hired wagon to the side portico at eleven.

The group loaded their picnic goods and climbed into the wagon. "Will you sit with me, Maria?" Amos asked.

"Thank you," she said, smiling as he assisted her onto the wagon bench. Will sat behind them with the others and frowned. Maria was glad he'd agreed to come, though he would likely glower at Amos all day.

With a tap of the reins on the horses' backs, Amos headed west from town toward City Park on the bluffs above the Willamette River. As he had told Maria, the roads were rough and muddy, and narrow branches brushed the wagon sides as they passed. But Amos drove them to an open field on a hillside facing east with a view of Mount Hood in the distance.

Maria loved to stare at Mount Hood, which could be seen from many vantage points in Portland. It rose above the other Cascade peaks in Oregon. She remembered the mountain erupting in 1866, when smoke and steam were visible from their home in Oregon City. She'd feared lava would cover their home, as Mt. Etna had Pompeii centuries earlier. Fortunately, the Mount Hood eruption produced no lava, and the mountain maintained its majestic silhouette against the sky.

When they stopped, Amos and Nate released the horses to graze. Will and Robert spread blankets on the damp grass, and the women laid out food. With laughter and friendly bickering, the picnickers then ate their fill—chicken, meat pies, bread, apples, and cakes, all washed down with cider and mint tea.

"I'm stuffed," Nate moaned, as he reclined and rested his head on a cushion. "I'm taking a nap."

Eliza and Lottie searched for early wildflowers, and Robert asked Daisy if she would walk with him to the far side of the meadow. Daisy glanced at Maria, who turned to Amos and said, "Shall we go with them?"

Amos stood and offered Maria a hand to help her rise. "Of course."

Will looked like he was about to follow, but Nate, eyes closed, asked Will a question. Maria didn't hear Will's response, as she and Amos followed Daisy and Robert.

The damp grass soaked Maria's hem. She and Amos fell behind Robert and Daisy. "Might I speak plainly, Maria?" Amos said, when the other couple were out of earshot.

"Certainly," Maria said.

Amos took Maria's hand and opened his mouth to speak.

"Maria! Higgins!" Will shouted from behind them.

Maria turned and smiled at Will. "Are you joining us?"

"If I may," Will said, matching pace on her left side, while Higgins still held her right hand.

Higgins squeezed her fingers gently, then let her hand drop. "What is it, McDougall?"

"The view from here is spectacular, isn't it? You can see the whole Willamette Valley." Will gestured at the river ribboning its way from south to north. "And Mount Hood in all its glory."

The three of them made small talk, then joined Robert and Daisy. After a bit, they all returned to the picnic blankets, woke Nate up, packed the baskets, and headed home.

As Higgins drove the wagon up to the McDougall house, he murmured to Maria, "I'm sorry we couldn't speak privately. May I call on you tomorrow? Weather permitting, perhaps we might stroll in the garden."

"That would be delightful," she said. "Mama's daffodils are coming up. The iris won't be far behind."

After the picnic baskets had been returned to the kitchen, Will asked Maria, "What was that about? With Higgins?"

She frowned. "What do you mean?"

"His calling on you tomorrow."

Hands on her hips, she said, "Were you eavesdropping?"

"I couldn't help but hear. Even over Eliza and Lottie's chatter. What does he want?"

"He didn't say. I suppose I'll find out tomorrow."

"Is he going to propose?"

She sighed in exasperation. "How should I know?"

"Doesn't a girl know when a man wants to marry her?"

"I didn't know *you* were going to ask. And I certainly don't know what Amos has in mind." Though she suspected Will was right. If Amos proposed, how should she respond?

Will took her hand. "Maria, you know I love you. I want to marry you." He took a deep breath, then said, "But most of all, I want you to be happy." He paused. "If Higgins is the man for you, I'll dance at your wedding."

Maria swallowed hard. She'd never appreciated Will's friendship more than at that moment. But did she want to marry him? Or Amos? She still wasn't ready to accept either of them.

Maria barely slept that night, in a dither about what Amos might say. In the morning, she heard none of the Sunday sermon and hardly touched the noon meal.

She and the rest of the family were settled in the parlor when the door knocker sounded. Will answered it, then ushered Amos in. After making small talk with Papa, Amos turned to Maria and asked, "Would you walk with me, Maria?"

She stood, her knees quaking. "Of course."

They went outside and made their way to Mama's garden. "Lovely day, isn't it?" Amos said.

"Yes," Maria said. "We're fortunate this spring." She paused. "Thank you for arranging the picnic yesterday, Amos."

He made a small sound in his throat. "I'd hoped to speak with you then. The pretty setting—Mount Hood in the background—seemed suitable."

She stopped and inhaled deeply. His obvious nervousness gave her confidence. "Suitable for what?"

Amos took her hand in both of his. "I have hoped, Maria, I have dared to dream that you would look kindly on me. That you would agree to be my wife." He cleared his throat. "What I mean to say is—Maria, would you do me the honor of marrying me?"

Maria mutely thanked Will for preparing her. She'd had time to think about how to respond—she would tell Amos the same thing she'd told Will. "It is I who am honored," she said. "But this is unexpected. And I am not ready for marriage."

"Won't you take some time to consider?" Amos squeezed her fingers gently.

"I have thought about it," Maria admitted. "But I do not want to marry yet."

His grip tightened. "My future—dare I say, *our* future—rests in your hands. I will wait, of course, but I will ask again."

"I do not know whether—or when—I will reconsider," she said, her resolve growing. "I want to prove myself at the paper, which is why I do not feel ready for marriage."

"Is it Will?" Amos said.

"Will?" she asked in surprise.

"I've seen how he looks at you."

Maria pulled her hands free. "I told you—I am focused on my work."

"Are you in love with him?" Amos demanded. "You were raised as brother and sister, but I know you are adopted. Your heritage shows in your face. I asked your father about you soon after I began working for him."

"My heritage?"

"He told me your natural mother was of Spanish descent. He said he adopted you after her death."

"What else did he tell you?" Maria wondered whether Amos had looked down on her all this time. She'd felt no condescension from him, but he'd talked to Papa some time ago, so he'd had a while to school his behavior.

"That's all." Amos took her arm and led her along the garden path. "I see you as your parents' daughter. A true McDougall. But Will—how does he see you?"

She stiffened. "That is between Will and me."

Amos's jaw tightened, but he nodded and said nothing more until they were inside the house. He bowed as he left. "We will talk further," he said. "I hope to change your answer to yes."

Chapter 57: Planning Another Trip

Will spent hours puzzling over the discrepancies Zhuang Li had found in Cassidy's reports and the lack of such discrepancies in Beck's first report. The only way to uncover the truth was to go to California himself. He wondered whether to go alone or take Li with him.

On the Monday morning after the outing to City Park, Will laid out his plan for Pa.

"Why?" Pa asked. "What can you discover that Higgins didn't?"

"We don't know whom to trust," Will said. "You said yourself Higgins and Beck were close."

"True," Pa said. "And, of course, I trust you more than Higgins, Beck, Cassidy, or Zhuang Li. I suppose any employee could be guilty of negligence or fraud." He sighed. "When would you leave?"

"As soon as I can. If I get there before the April report is prepared, I can watch how the work is done."

"Damned weather." Pa grimaced as he shifted in his chair. "My bones hurt when it rains." He sighed. "Your presence will alert any thieves to our suspicions."

"Yes." Will nodded. "But if they know we're watching, perhaps they'll stop. Which would prevent our profits from bleeding further." He paused. "Should I take Li?"

"Why?"

"He spots errors much faster than I do." Will valued the Asian man's knowledge. But Li could be part of the fraud. Plus, he recalled the awkwardness of traveling with Li's cousin Zhuang Jin.

"Bring the records back with you if you think an audit is needed," Pa said.

"I want your perspective, not Li's or anyone else's."

"All right." Will had reached the same conclusion, but was glad Pa agreed.

"What about Maria?" Pa asked.

"Maria?" Will frowned. "What does she have to do with my trip to California?"

"Higgins proposed yesterday," Pa said. "She told Jenny last night."

Will swore.

Pa's eyebrows rose. "Maria didn't tell you?"

"No."

"Then you didn't hear it from me."

"And what am I supposed to do now?" Will said. "I can't hide my knowledge from Maria."

"Talk to your mother."

"You're letting Mama take the blame for you?"

Pa shrugged and grinned.

Will went immediately to find Mama in her morning room. Standing in the doorway, he asked, "Do you have time to talk?"

Mama sighed, turning around from her desk. "I thought you might come see me. Did Maria tell you?"

Will shook his head. "Pa let it slip."

"I told him not to." Mama gestured for him to sit. "Maria confided in me. Though I told her I wouldn't keep a secret from Mac."

Will dropped into the chair. "What did she tell Higgins?"

Mama frowned. "I won't break my daughter's confidence."

"Then he did propose to her?"

"You already know that much. But I won't tell you more."

Will slouched in the chair. "What should I do, Mama? I want to marry her myself."

"I know, dear," Mama said, her voice softening. "But you can't control what happens. You must let Maria find her own way."

"If she marries Higgins, she'll regret it." Will leaned forward, hands on his knees. "He could be a swindler."

"Mac says there's no proof. And you're biased because of Maria."

"We haven't found any records that show he's cheating. But I still think he could be involved. Zhuang Li says—"

"Mr. Zhuang seems to be a fine man," Mama said. "But he wouldn't be believed in court. Not against Amos Higgins. Not unless you have solid evidence."

Even his mother gave Higgins the benefit of the doubt. Will swallowed. How could he convince Maria to marry him? Or at least not to marry Higgins? "What should I do?"

"Tell Maria you'll love her no matter what." Mama leaned over and took Will's hand. "You are both very dear to me. I want you both happy. And neither of you will be happy if she marries you for the wrong reason. You can't pressure her into making this decision. She must decide for herself—and she may not choose either of you."

Mama's last statement was a reason for hope. "Then she hasn't accepted him yet."

Mama sighed. "I've already said too much. Just tell Maria you want her to be happy."

He had told her. Now he muttered, "She won't be happy when she discovers Higgins isn't the man she thought." He stood, kissed Mama's cheek, and left.

That evening after supper, Will knocked on Maria's bedroom door.

"Come in," she called.

As he entered, he caught the scent of her lavender soap. "I hear congratulations are in order," he said.

She stood from her dressing table, frowning. "Who told you?"

"Mama and Pa both know," he said. "And I could tell something was troubling you."

She shrugged. "It's not trouble. Amos has been very kind. I just need to decide if I want to marry him."

"Do you?"

She gestured helplessly. "I told him what I told you—I'm not ready."

"I want you to be happy, Maria. Just as I said last week." Will shut the door behind him.

Her lips trembled, but she said nothing.

"I love you. I want to marry you." He took a deep breath. "But not if you don't love me as a husband. I mean it." He paused and swallowed. The next part of his speech was difficult. "If Higgins is the man you love, I'll say no more. And if you don't want either of us, I still want you to be happy."

"Thank you, Will," she whispered.

"I'm going to California soon," he said. "You'll have time to decide without me hounding you."

"Oh, Will." Her voice caught. "Don't let me chase you away. It's been lovely having you home this winter."

"It's not you," he said, as he opened the door to leave. "It's business. And I won't be gone long."

Tuesday afternoon, Will purchased a steamboat ticket to San Francisco. The next boat south left on Thursday, and he meant to be on it. He told no one at McDougall & Company. Neither Higgins nor Zhuang Li needed to know—they could ask Pa if they wanted, but he hoped Pa wouldn't reveal anything until he was in California. He wanted to surprise Beck.

After he bought the ticket, a voice called his name. He turned, expecting to see his friend Noah Pershing.

To Will's surprise, Jacques Peterson, his mother's half-brother, came striding toward him. "Just the man I needed to find," Jack said. "Mama and I arrived on the steamboat today."

"I thought you were going to cable us first," Will said, then realized he didn't sound very welcoming.

"No time," Jack said. "We reached San Francisco, then caught the boat north the next mornin'. Mama was prostrate with fatigue, but we couldn't afford to rest in San Francisco. A damned shame—I liked what I saw of that bustlin' town."

"Where is your mother?" Will said. "I must take you both to my parents' home."

Jack pointed. Hortense Peterson sat on a trunk, fanning herself.

Will approached her and bowed. "Grandmère," he said. "It is good to see you again."

"Dear boy," she murmured. "Travel is so difficult. I am weary to the bone. Where is my dear Geneviève?"

"We didn't know you were arriving today," Will said. "Let me hire a carriage to take you home. I'll arrange for your trunks to be delivered later."

"Jacques must stay with the baggage," Grandmère said. "We have brought everything."

Will looked at the pile—five enormous trunks and several smaller bags. "I see," he said faintly. "I will help Jack make the arrangements. Then I'll escort you home."

He flagged down a porter and gave directions, promising payment when the luggage arrived. Then he secured a carriage and helped Grandmère inside. "Jack," he said, "the porter will handle the trunks, but you best watch over him."

"Will do," Jack said, with a small wave to his mother. "I shall follow shortly, Mama."

Will settled across from his grandmother in the carriage. "How was the journey, Grandmère?"

"I suffered greatly the whole way," she said. "The train was dirty. I couldn't sleep. And then the ship—I have never traveled the rough seas before. It is nothing like river travel in Louisiana or Missouri. At my age, it is too much."

Will murmured something soothing, and they rode in silence until they reached the McDougall house. Will leaped out, paid the driver, then helped his grandmother up the porch stairs. When he opened the front door, he called, "Mama, you have a visitor."

Mama entered the hallway as Will led Grandmère into the formal parlor. Mama gasped and stopped short. "*Maman!*"

"Geneviève," Grandmère said. "I am finally here. Take me to my room at once—I must rest."

"And her son Jack will be here shortly," Will said. "He's seeing to the luggage."

"Perhaps some refreshment first," Mama said, taking her mother's arm and casting a wild look at Will over Grandmère's head. "You must be parched. Will," she ordered, "please ask Mrs. O'Malley to bring tea and scones or cakes or something. And to have two guest rooms prepared."

Will nodded and turned toward the kitchen. "Order coffee for me, dear boy," Grandmère called after him.

When he returned to the parlor, Mama and Grandmère sat on a divan. For the first time, Will saw them side by side. Mama must take after her father, the man Will had been named for, because she bore little resemblance to Grandmère, other than her short stature.

"Did you talk to Mrs. O'Malley?" Mama sounded desperate.

"Yes. The tray will be here soon."

Grandmère chattered on, complaining about the journey, about Jacques's inattentiveness, about the poor state of their Missouri farm.

"How is Letitia?" Mama said, interrupting her mother at one point.

"She died a month before we left," Grandmère said.

"Oh, no!" Mama pressed her hand to her mouth, looking stricken. Will felt a pang of sorrow, too—he'd liked Letitia.

"We've been at sixes and sevens ever since she passed," Grandmère continued. "No one could cook for me like she did. No one left to keep house. We had to hire help from the village—can you imagine? No one would live in. Nothing has been the same since the War."

"Indeed," Mama whispered.

The tray arrived, and Mama busied herself fixing a plate for her mother. Will took a small cake for himself and sat beside Grandmère, listening as she prattled on about the hardships of running the farm, the cost of hired labor, and Jacques's failure to manage the farmhands.

He'd have to exchange his ticket to San Francisco—the trip would likely be delayed. He would have to help Mama settle Grandmère.

Chapter 58: Higgins Pleads His Case

Maria arrived home Wednesday afternoon to find the household in an uproar. "Our Grandmother Peterson has arrived," Eliza announced, flouncing on Maria's bed as Maria put away her hat and reticule. "And her son. She's nothing like Mama. Except she's short."

"Where are they now?" Maria asked.

"She insists we call her Grandmère." Eliza pronounced the word "Grand-mare."

"And her son is Jacques?" Maria asked.

Eliza nodded. "Our uncle is quite handsome, though he doesn't sound very educated. Not like Will."

"Well, they lived on a farm in Missouri." Maria sighed. "I suppose I should introduce myself." She checked her reflection in the mirror, smoothed her hair, and went downstairs. Eliza trailed behind.

"Good afternoon, ma'am," Maria said to the plump little woman in the parlor. "I'm Maria." She gave a little curtsy.

"This is the adopted one?" Grandmère asked Mama. "The Spanish girl?"

Mama's voice tightened. "This is my oldest daughter Maria."

"I've been at my job at *The New Northwest* newspaper," Maria said, sitting near her grandmother. "I'm sorry I wasn't here to greet you, Grandmère Peterson."

"No one greeted us." The old woman sniffed. "Will happened to be at the dock, or I don't know what I would have done. Jacques was of no use."

"When will I meet my uncle?" Maria asked.

"Your uncle?" her grandmother said. "Pfft, he is not your uncle."

"Maria is my daughter," Mama repeated with emphasis.

"Adopted. Her Spanish blood is quite evident, isn't it?" Grandmère waved a hand. "Of course, there were still some Spaniards in Louisiana when I was young, but that was long ago."

"I have Indian blood, too," Maria said, wanting to shock her grandmother. Let the old biddy react to that aspect of Maria's heritage.

Grandmère's eyes widened. "I'm surprised you're so candid, miss."

"I've met several prominent native women in my role for the paper," Maria said.

"Of course, Oregon is still the frontier, isn't it, Geneviève?" Grandmère turned to Mama, ignoring Maria.

Maria then noticed a man about Will's age sitting in the corner, away from the women. He smiled, walked across the room, and bowed to her. "I'm Jacques, Miss McDougall. Since I'm your half-uncle, may I call you Maria?"

She smiled and offered her hand. "Very nice to meet you. And may I call you Jacques? I don't think I can call someone so young Uncle Jacques."

He laughed. "Jacques or Jack. I answer to either. Tell me about your work at the newspaper, though I can't say I'm much for readin'."

He seemed sincere, so Maria described Mrs. Duniway's focus on human rights, including women's suffrage. Jack didn't protest the notion of women voting, though he said little at all. He seemed pleasant enough, but was not as polished as Will or Amos.

"And what are your plans now you're in Portland, Jack?" she asked.

He shrugged. "I ain't got much of a plan. It was all I could do to get Mama here, with her weak lungs and vapors. I suppose I'll find somethin' once she's settled."

"Will you be staying with us?" Maria asked.

"That is up to Geneviève," he said. "Though we can't afford anywhere else until I find work."

"Will told me you had a farm in Missouri."

Jack nodded. "But we lost it when we couldn't pay the taxes. Sold what we could to buy our tickets to Portland. Good thing Will invited us to visit last fall, or we'd have had nowhere to go."

Mama and Papa would have two more dependents. Maria hoped Grandmère would adapt to Oregon.

That evening after supper, the family gathered in the parlor. Maria mended Evie's torn pinafore while Eliza read aloud from Dickens. Will showed Andrew how to whittle a horse. The others—including Jack—played euchre or sewed.

Someone tapped the front door knocker, and Will answered. "Higgins," Maria heard him say, so she was ready when Amos stepped into the parlor.

Mama introduced him to Grandmère and Jack. Amos bowed over Grandmère's hand. "Mrs. Peterson, a pleasure to meet you." He gave the older woman the same bright smile he often gave Maria. "I can see now why Mrs. McDougall is such a lovely woman."

Maria raised her eyebrows—Amos had never remarked on Mama's looks before. Mama was still attractive, but Grandmère was plump and petulant. Maria saw little resemblance between Mama and Grandmère.

"And what is your connection to my family?" Grandmère asked.

"I am the head accountant at McDougall & Company," Amos said, nodding at Papa. "And I hope to make Miss Maria my wife."

"Your wife?" Grandmère exclaimed.

Amos turned his smile on Maria. "She is as lovely as you and her mother," he said. "And accomplished. Has she told you about her newspaper work?"

"I've heard something of it," Grandmère said with a sniff. "But, of course, she bears no resemblance to my daughter or me."

"In manner, she favors her mother," Amos said. "If not in appearance. Maria is a woman any man would be fortunate to wed."

Across the room, Will and Jack both stared at Amos with identical frowns.

"Shall we make up another table for euchre, Maria?" Amos asked. "Your mending can wait, can it not?"

"We'll make up the four," Will said, clapping Andrew's shoulder. "I'll partner you, Andrew. We'll whittle another evening."

Soon, Grandmère declared herself fatigued and ready to retire. Mama had given her the best guest room, leaving a smaller room for Jack. Maria hoped no more visitors would arrive. These two were already a strain on the house—and on the family.

The next day at *The New Northwest*, Mrs. Duniway showed Maria a brief letter from Winema Riddle. "She and her husband are still mediating between the Army and the Modoc," Mrs. Duniway said. "They hope to arrange a peace settlement. Unfortunately, she writes few details about the battle."

"What an achievement if she negotiates a peace treaty," Maria said. "Do you think the war will end soon?"

"Let's hope so," Mrs. Duniway said. "The Army has not fared well in the skirmishes to date."

As Maria helped set type for this week's editorial, she reflected on Winema Riddle's impact on relations between her tribe and the whites in Southern Oregon. Yet Grandmère sneered at Maria's Indian heritage.

Maria thought little more of Grandmère than the older woman thought of her. Grandmère clung to the past—a past that relied on one race owning other human beings. A past that had vanished with the defeat of the Confederacy.

For the rest of her shift, Maria reflected on her good fortune in being raised by Mac and Jenny McDougall, as well as on Mama's good fortune in being rescued by Papa before Will was born. Grandmère had not mentioned Will's father. Did she even care who had sired Will? Did she suspect Will and Jack might be half-brothers? As far as Maria knew, only her parents, Will, and herself were aware of the complete story of Will's birth.

These thoughts still occupied her when she arrived home that afternoon. She found Jack lounging in the parlor. "Where is everyone?" she asked.

He slammed shut the book he'd had on his lap—a copy of Chaucer's *The Canterbury Tales*, a tome usually kept on the top shelf to hide it from the younger children. Maria wondered whether he'd actually been reading it. "My mama's nappin'. Your family all seem to be occupied. I'm the only one with nothin' to do. Will you keep me company?"

"For a moment," she said. "Then I must help Mama and Mrs. O'Malley with supper."

"Is your family always so busy?"

"We try to be," she said. "Why not ask Will about a job? Perhaps he could find you something at McDougall & Company."

"I will do so," Jack said. "Thank you for the suggestion."

Amos joined the family for supper that evening. He sat near Maria, and when the meal was over, he asked if she would walk with him in the garden.

"Not for long, Maria," Mama said. "It will be dark soon."

Maria nodded, retrieved her shawl, and followed Amos out to the garden.

He took her hand. "Have you thought about my proposal, Maria?"

"I'm sorry, Amos," she said. "I have had little time to think since Grandmère and Jack arrived."

"What do they have to do with whether you will marry me?"

"The entire house is in a stir. It's difficult for Mama to cope with her mother after so many years apart. And Jack is a stranger to all of us."

"When will you have time to think about me?"

"I doubt my answer will change, Amos. I enjoy my work at the paper."

He cupped her cheek with his hand. "I will ask again. Soon I hope you will say yes."

Chapter 59: Will Hires Jack

Friday morning, Will was surprised to see Jack in his office doorway downtown. "You got time to talk?" Jack asked.

Will waved Jack toward a chair. "I'll make time." He liked the man, but thought Jack doted too much on his mother—Grandmère Peterson needed less mollycoddling rather than more.

Jack sat, looking unsure. "I'd like a job."

"Doing what?"

Jack shrugged. "What needs doin'?"

"What have you done besides run a farm into the ground?" Will tried to soften his harsh question with a grin.

But Jack stiffened. "'Tweren't my fault. Them damned Yankees freed the slaves."

"You won't win friends talking about damned Yankees in Portland," Will said. "There are some Southern sympathizers, but this is Republican territory. Grant won Oregon last fall in a landslide."

"You try runnin' a farm when your trained labor up and leaves."

"Labor you never paid a dime," Will replied. "So, what kind of job do you want now?"

"Hear tell your pa has a farm in Oregon City," Jack said. "Does he need an overseer? Or what about your warehouses here in Portland? I know how to manage inventory."

"Inventory." A light dawned in Will's head. "We have little inventory here. But you liked San Francisco, didn't you?"

Jack nodded. "What little I saw of it."

"I might have a job there. It's reconnaissance of a sort." Will explained

287

the situation with Cassidy and Beck. "I think Cassidy was blamed unfairly for the low profits, but I can't prove it. And I think Beck is hiding something, but I can't prove that either."

Jack grinned. "Then I would be your spy?"

"Does that bother you?"

"What would I have to do?" Jack asked.

"Keep your eyes and ears open," Will said. "Look for anything that seems odd—particularly with the movement of gold and goods. Watch who Beck meets with, who writes him or wires him."

"How'm I supposed to spy on Beck if I'm in the warehouse? He'd be in an office, not gettin' his hands dirty, I suppose."

"I'm going to San Francisco in a couple of days. Come with me. I'll introduce you to Beck. We'll try to meet with Cassidy also—if he'll talk to us. He can tell you what to watch for."

Jack hesitated. "What about my ma? I can't just leave her."

"Why not?" Will said. "My mother will care for her as well as you can."

"Mama tends to sulk," Jack said. An understatement, if Will had ever heard one.

"Mama can handle her." Of that, Will had no doubt—Mama could charm a snake. Mama wouldn't enjoy it, but she could certainly manage an old biddy like Grandmère Peterson. "We'll leave on Monday, assuming my parents agree."

That evening, Will spoke to Pa in the library. "Jack wants a job. I think he can help in San Francisco. I want to take him with me, and I'd like to leave on Monday."

Pa sipped the whiskey Will had poured. "Jack? What does he know about our business?"

"Nothing," Will said. "He claims to know warehouses and inventory, but he doesn't know our operation. That leaves him free to ask questions."

"You trust him?"

"I have no reason not to," Will said. "He's at least as trustworthy as Beck, in my mind."

Pa's voice turned harsh. "Remember who Jack's father was."

Will remembered—Grandmère's second husband was one of Mama's rapists. Possibly, the man had fathered Will as well as Jack. "Jack isn't Bart Peterson," he said. "You can't condemn Jack for his father's sins. Not unless you condemn me for those sins, too."

Pa's jaw tightened, but he dropped the subject. "What do you see Jack doing?"

"Learning the ropes. Looking for anything strange. Reporting to me what he discovers. He'll have to be careful, because Beck could get suspicious. But if I introduce Jack, Beck will know you and I are watching him."

Pa twisted his glass in his hands, round and round. Finally, he looked up. "All right. Let's try it. Assuming Jenny agrees to handle her mother."

Will grinned. "Mama will have the hardest job of all."

Jack was delighted when Will told him Pa had approved their trip to San Francisco. Will outlined Jack's responsibilities and pay, and Jack was agreeable. "We'll sort out the details when we speak with Beck," Will said.

When Jack expressed his gratitude, Will said, "Pa and I are counting on you to tell us the truth. And to report back to me regularly. Not to Higgins, only to me."

"You don't trust Higgins?" Jack asked.

Will shook his head.

"Even though he's courtin' your sister?"

Will decided to trust Jack. "You know Maria is adopted," he began.

Jack grinned. "Mama made sure to tell me. She don't like the Spanish. And Indians is worse."

"I've asked Maria to marry me," Will said.

Jack raised his eyebrows, and his grin widened. "You're a lucky man. When's the big day?"

Will grunted. "Not until she accepts me. And Higgins asked her, too."

Jack chortled. "Should I get in line?"

"You'd better not," Will warned. "But that's one reason I'm biased against Higgins. Still, if Maria accepts him, I don't want her hurt. I need to be sure of the facts before I do anything against Higgins. But all we will tell him is that I'm offering you a job in California."

Jack's expression sobered, and he nodded. "I won't let you down. I'm grateful for the chance."

That afternoon, Will bought two steamboat tickets to California for Monday. When he got home, he looked for Maria.

"Thank you for suggesting I hire Jack," he said. "I'm taking him to San Francisco with me."

"I like Jack," she said. "But why must you both go? Amos just returned from California."

"I want someone there with family ties," Will said. He thought she might believe that explanation. "Jack fits the bill."

"But he knows less than I do about the business."

"He'll learn," Will said, ignoring her hint that she should be told more about the company. "I like him. And I trust him."

Maria frowned. "You don't trust Amos, do you?"

"Pa does," Will replied. "But I'm not sure."

"Hmm," was her unsatisfactory response.

"You won't accept Higgins while I'm away, will you?"

"I've told you—I'm not ready to marry."

Will took her hand. "Do I have any hope, Maria?"

"Why won't either of you believe me? I simply do not want to marry now."

Will smiled. At least she hadn't said no.

Grandmère Peterson had a fit of the vapors when she learned Jack would go to San Francisco with Will. "Why must you leave me, *mon fils*?" she wailed at supper Friday evening. "My only son. Who will care for me?"

"You're livin' with your only daughter," Jack said.

"Pfft, I hardly know Geneviève," Grandmère sobbed. "She left me when I was carrying you, dear boy, and you have been my rock since you were born."

Will glanced across the table at Mama. Her lips thinned, but she said nothing. "I promise to take good care of Jack on our journey," Will told his grandmother. "He will earn good money, and when he returns, he can find a home for you."

"A home?" Grandmère looked surprised. "But I have a home. Geneviève has taken me in."

Will caught Maria's eye. Her lips twitched, and he could tell she was amused by Grandmère's contradictory responses.

Chapter 60: Maria's Next Response

Maria missed Will after he and Jack left for California. She hadn't realized how much she relied on Will's companionship. Although she'd grown used to his absence during his seven years in Boston, having him home these past months felt familiar. Comfortable. Sweet.

Now she felt like she was missing a part of herself. They'd argued since his return, but it was the affectionate sparring of long-time friends who trusted each other. Who loved each other.

She loved Will. She always had. But could their companionship turn passionate? Did she want it to?

She wasn't ready to commit to Will, but if he felt like a part of herself, she could never marry Higgins. It was time to tell Higgins how she felt.

Higgins called again on Sunday, May 4, and took Maria for another walk in the garden. "You've had two weeks since my proposal, Maria. Are you ready to declare?"

She stopped. "It's no, Amos. I can't marry you."

"No?" he shouted. He'd never raised his voice to her before. "Why not?"

"I don't want to marry now."

"Is it Will?" His grip on her arm tightened. "Are you going to marry him?"

She shook her head. "I have not accepted Will."

His eyebrow twitched. "Are you telling me 'not now' or are you telling me 'never'?"

She wouldn't leave room for doubt—that wouldn't be fair. "I do not want to marry you, Amos. My answer is 'no', and it will not change."

He bowed stiffly, then stalked out the back gate, leaving her alone.

Monday evening, Papa called Maria into his library. "Amos Higgins is upset," he said. "I understand you refused his offer of marriage."

"Yes," Maria said. "I had to. He kept pressing for an answer, even after I told him I wasn't ready. It wasn't fair to make him wait. I knew I could not marry him."

"What about Will?" Papa asked. "What have you told him?"

"I told Will I don't want to marry yet," Maria said.

Papa exhaled. "That is your right. But now I have an angry accounting manager. And Will isn't here."

"I don't have to marry any man," she said. "Not unless I love him. That's what you've always told me."

"And I won't tell you differently now," Papa said, though he sighed after he spoke.

"Do you think Amos will leave the company?" Maria asked. She didn't know whether she hoped he would or wouldn't. Her life might be easier if he were gone. But she liked Amos, even if she didn't want to marry him.

"I don't know," Papa said. "Losing him would be a blow—he knows my business backward and forward. But I don't think he is pursuing any other employment opportunities."

"I'm sorry, Papa."

"Don't be, Maria," he said, finally smiling at her. "You must follow your mind and heart. Even if it leaves your father in a lurch."

"Will's stay in California won't be long, will it?"

"No." Papa steepled his fingers. After a pause, he said, "I've been pondering whether to bring Nate into the business. He turns nineteen this week, and he has no interest in continuing his education. What do you think?"

Surprised that Papa asked her opinion, Maria said, "What does Will think?"

"I haven't asked him."

"Shouldn't you? I thought you planned on Will taking over the business someday."

Papa sighed. "I need to have a long conversation with Will when he returns. Between recovering from my accident, dealing with business problems, and now helping Jenny with her mother and brother, I have neglected Will. I imagine he feels uncertain about what I want him to do."

Maria patted his hand. "Will wants to work with you. But he isn't sure you trust him."

Papa's eyes widened. "Not trust Will? I've told him I trust him more than anyone in the business. He is sometimes naïve, but he's honest, capable, and devoted to our family."

"Will needs to know how you feel, Papa."

"I've rejected both of them," Maria told Daisy on Tuesday morning as they sorted through the newspapers in the day's mail. "Amos Higgins is angry with me. I've hurt Will. My father is worried. I can't make anyone happy."

"You've turned down two perfectly good suitors?" Daisy shook her head. "If Robert proposed to me, I'd say yes in a heartbeat."

"You must love him." Maria wondered if her two colleagues ever talked to each other—she could see they were in love, but did either of them know how the other felt?

"Yes." Daisy nodded. "But I'm practical, too. He ain't rich, but he makes a decent living. I could quit the paper and make a home."

"What would your mother do without your income?" Maria asked. "And your younger brothers and sisters?"

Daisy shrugged. "Ma knows I'll marry someday. Robert and I could put a little aside to help her. Maybe take my sister to live with us." She shook a finger at Maria. "If I had a rich man offerin' to marry me, I wouldn't wait for love. I'd snap him up right quick."

"But marriage is forever." Maria smoothed the newspaper in front of her, then set it aside.

Daisy picked up the paper Maria abandoned. "That's why I want to marry. I need to know I'm set. Makin' a man's home and bearin' his children is what a woman does. As long as the husband provides and the wife keeps the family, the marriage can work."

Maria sighed. Daisy's view of marriage was so different from hers. She wanted a man who made her as happy as Papa made Mama. She wanted a man who trusted her and could himself be trusted. She smiled, deciding to play matchmaker. "Robert loves you, Daisy. Anyone can see that. Perhaps he'll start courting you soon."

"I hope so," Daisy said. She placed a hand on Maria's arm. "I don't mean to dismiss your concerns. You said you can't make anyone happy—are *you* happy?"

"Me?"

"Yes," Daisy said. "It doesn't matter if your suitors aren't happy, or even your father, if you've done what you must."

"I have," Maria said. Saying the words aloud made her realize they were true. "I don't love Amos. I'm not sure about Will. And I want to write for the newspaper." She shrugged. "My father will find someone to replace Amos—or even Will, for that matter—if either leaves the company. It isn't my duty to marry for the sake of the business."

"Well," Daisy said, grinning. "If that's settled, then shall we get back to work?"

That evening, Mama weighed in with her opinion on Maria's decision. "Amos has been a fine employee for your father, and a courteous guest," Mama told Maria. "But if you don't love him, you shouldn't marry him. Marriage is hard enough, even with affection. Sometimes, the memory of past affection is all that carries a couple through difficult times."

"Have you and Papa had difficult times?" Maria asked. "It never shows."

"We try to keep our differences from our children," Mama said. "Though it isn't always easy."

"When was your hardest time?" Maria asked.

"When Mac left for Boston that February after we arrived in Oregon. I never thought I'd see him again."

"But you weren't married then. What about after you married?"

A sad smile flickered across Mama's face. "When we lost little Abram in fifty-nine. He was so small when he died, such a sweet baby. I grieved, and Mac grieved. But we could not grieve together. It took time for us to find our way back to each other."

"I remember Abram," Maria whispered. "I grieved, too."

Mama took Maria's hand. "I know, dear. And I hope you never suffer the sorrow of losing a child." She squeezed Maria's fingers. "I won't push you to marry. Not Amos. Not Will. Nor anyone else. But as you weigh your choices, be sure you aren't just delaying a hard choice. Whether that choice is between two men or between marriage and the newspaper. Only marry for love. If you love the man, the two of you will find your way to happiness, no matter how rocky the path."

Chapter 61: In San Francisco

The trip from Portland to San Francisco took five days. High winds off the Pacific made traversing the mouth of the Columbia River dangerous and slowed their initial progress. Will and Jack arrived in San Francisco on Friday, May 2.

It had been three weeks since Beck's March report had reached Portland. Now that April was over, Beck should have started the next report. Will wanted to watch the process firsthand.

During the voyage, he taught Jack as much as he could about McDougall & Company. It would have been easier to instruct Jack in Portland with the ledgers and contracts in front of them. But Jack seemed to be a quick learner. He asked good questions, though his lack of formal schooling meant Will often had to start with the basics.

"What's the use of a receivables ledger?" Jack asked. "I can understand writin' down money as you get it. But why write it down when you just think you're gonna get it?"

"Because we need to know what we're owed," Will said. "Didn't you keep track of who owed you money on the farm?"

Jack laughed. "No one owed us. We owed everyone else."

"But when you sold corn or hemp or tobacco, didn't people buy on credit?"

Jack shook his head. "We needed cash. Particularly after the War. I didn't sell nothin' 'less I got cash or goods in trade."

By the time they arrived in San Francisco, Will had taught Jack enough for the Missourian to know what to look for. "We want to know how someone might hide cash or gold or bank drafts, so they don't get recorded as income," he summarized again on the last morning as the ship breached the Golden Gate. "Or maybe someone isn't documenting receipt of goods to hide inventory—if it isn't recorded in inventory, then there's no way to track it, short of going back to bills of sale, which is tedious. And I also want to know how someone could record expenses twice. Or overstate them. And anything else you think looks suspicious."

Jack looked dubious. "That's a lot to watch for. I'm only one man. And I'll be new to the business. Why would Beck even let me near the books? Particularly if he's the one stealin'."

"He might be more likely to ignore you because you're new," Will said. "Or you could play the role of a disgruntled black sheep in the family." He realized Jack might think he was stating the truth. "Of course, you aren't— my parents and I trust you," he hastened to add.

Jack shrugged. "I don't know why. You don't know me well. You must be desperate to use me as your spy."

"I am desperate," Will said. "I trust you because I need to. But you and Grandmère need my parents, so I figure we're even."

They turned their attention to the approaching wharf. The green hills around the harbor gleamed in the sunshine, and San Francisco Bay sparkled as the waves rolled. "It's a fine city," Jack said, gesturing toward the buildings behind the harbor. "Bigger'n Portland, ain't it?"

"By far," Will said. "Though not as big as St. Louis."

"I ain't been to St. Louis but twice," Jack said. "It ain't half as pretty as California."

As they disembarked, Will clapped Jack on the shoulder. "We'll spend the weekend taking in the sights. And maybe looking for Cassidy. Then Monday morning, we'll surprise Beck."

Despite his promise to relax, Will was eager to get on with their business. He and Jack walked the city Friday afternoon, then dined at their hotel that evening with Cal, whom Will had cabled from Portland to meet them.

"You're still sure you don't want to join the business?" Will asked his younger brother.

"You have reinforcements now," Cal said, nodding at Jack. "You don't need me." Jack looked uncomfortable as the brothers argued.

"There's always a place for you, if you want it," Will said. But unless Pa insisted, Will realized Cal would never work for the family business.

Besides, Jack now knew as much as Cal did about McDougall & Company. Will dropped the matter, and he and Cal reminisced about their childhood for the rest of the meal.

Saturday morning, after Cal left for Oakland, Will took Jack to Cassidy's home. "Let's see if he's in," Will said.

They surprised Cassidy, but he welcomed them into his study. "What brings you to California?" he asked.

"Jack needs a position with McDougall & Company. I thought he could learn the ropes here."

"You trust Beck to teach him?" Cassidy asked.

"Jack will be my eyes and ears," Will said. "May he come to you if he has questions?"

Cassidy shrugged. "I have a new position with another export company. I don't owe the McDougalls anything."

"No, you don't," Will said. "But I think you're a man who cares about justice. You went out of your way to warn us about Beck. I doubt you will leave us in the lurch now."

Cassidy studied Will, then nodded at Jack. "All right. If you need anything, come by the house. But don't bother me at work."

Will leaned forward. "Where would Beck keep any records that show he's stealing?" For the next hour, Cassidy talked to Will and Jack about the San Francisco branch bookkeeping—where the ledgers were kept, how inventory was tracked, how the monthly reports for Portland were prepared. "Of course," Cassidy said as he finished, "Beck might have changed things since I was fired."

Monday morning, Will and Jack arrived at the McDougall & Company branch office before it opened. Only a night guard was on duty. "No one comes in till eight o'clock, sir," he said with a yawn.

"May we wait in the lobby?" Will asked.

The guard waved them in. "Just sit where I can see you."

Will watched as men trickled into the office, many giving him a wary look. One man in a coat and tie asked who he and Jack were. When Will gave his name, the man's eyes widened. He muttered an excuse and dashed out of the building.

"He's likely gone to warn Beck," Will murmured to Jack.

Around nine o'clock, Beck strode in. "McDougall," he said, offering his hand. "I didn't expect you."

Will shook hands and introduced Jack. "My uncle needs a job, and my father and I thought he could learn from you."

"Doing what?" Beck asked. "What's your background, young man?"

Jack hemmed and hawed about managing inventories in Missouri.

Will interrupted, "I want you to train him, Beck. Let's start with the reports you send to Portland. It's time for the April report, isn't it?"

"It isn't finished yet," Beck said. "Maybe by the end of the week—"

"Good," Will said. "Jack and I can watch your clerks prepare it."

"Then what?" Beck asked. "That won't take but a couple of days."

"Good to know," Will said. "Then you can put Jack to work managing the warehouse."

"I've got a warehouse manager," Beck said.

"I remember him," Will said. "I thought he said last fall he was close to retiring. Train Jack as his replacement."

Beck's eyes narrowed. He looked ready to argue, but only nodded.

"Then let's get started on the April report," Will said.

He and Jack followed Beck to the accounting area. They sat with the clerks all day, asking questions to understand the process. In late afternoon, Will asked, "Are these the only ledgers used for the report?"

"Yes, sir," one clerk answered.

"Then I'll take them back to the hotel," Will said. "Along with today's draft of the report. I'll bring everything back to you tomorrow."

The man hesitated. "But sir—"

"I'll clear it with Beck," Will said. "My family owns the business. He doesn't."

Will and Jack spent the evening comparing the report with the ledgers. They had noticed no inaccuracies as they watched the clerks compile the report. By midnight, they still had found nothing wrong.

Will rubbed his eyes wearily. "I can't find any issues. Tomorrow morning, let's find you a place to live. In the afternoon, we'll take the books back to the office. Beck can stew in his juices until then."

Early the next morning, they copied the key ledger entries for Will to take back to Portland. "I want to be sure what we get in Portland matches the original books, since these seem correct," he told Jack.

"You think someone in Portland is makin' the changes?" Jack asked.

"I don't know," Will replied. "But I want every bit of information I can get."

After they finished copying the ledger, they set out to find Jack a rooming house. They had recommendations from the hotel staff and soon found a clean and pleasant room with board included.

"It's nicer'n my room in our farmhouse," Jack said. "I'll be plenty comfortable."

"Good," Will said, grinning. "Now, let's get our noon meal, then go see Beck again."

When they returned to the office, Beck questioned them about what they'd found. "Everything looks fine," Will said, not going into any detail.

"How long do you plan to stay in California?" Beck asked.

"Just long enough to get Jack settled," Will said. "I want to walk through the warehouses with him. And maybe make a trip to Sacramento."

Beck clenched his jaw, but nodded. "As you wish."

On Wednesday, Will and Jack took a steamboat across the bay and up the American River to Sacramento. "It took my father days to travel on horseback around the southern tip of the bay," Will told Jack. "I've read his diary—no ferries or steamboats back then."

"Why'd he leave your ma in Oregon?" Jack asked.

Will shrugged. "I don't know that part of the story. Whatever happened, he was in California when gold was discovered in forty-eight. He started mining and made a fortune. So, in the end, I think Mama was fine with why he left her." He couldn't tell Jack the rest of the story, not without implicating Jack's father in the attack on Mama.

Jack liked Sacramento. "Feels more like Missouri 'n San Francisco does," he told Will. "It's got a river, it's got farmin' and ranches all around. And it's quieter." Though as he spoke, a raucous fight broke out in the bar where they sat after supper.

Will studied Jack. "Maybe you should work in Sacramento instead of San Francisco. Think about what you might like. Learn what you can in San Francisco, then we'll see."

Jack nodded and gulped his whiskey. "First, we decide if Beck is crooked. Then, I'll figure out where I belong. It'll have to be someplace Mama likes, too."

Will was glad he didn't have to find a home for Grandmère. But he would have to find a home that would suit Maria—if he ultimately won her heart and hand. Could they be happy in Portland, surrounded by people who'd known them as brother and sister?

Both Will and Jack sat in silence, lost in thought. A couple of times, Jack opened his mouth as if to speak, but he said nothing.

Chapter 62: Nate's Birthday

Maria missed her sessions helping Papa with his correspondence. Although he still walked with a cane, the stable boy drove him to the office most days. Both his improved mobility and Will's homecoming meant that he didn't need Maria to read him his mail.

But while Will was in California, Papa occasionally asked Maria for assistance, as he did on the evening of Monday, May 5. "My head aches," he said. "Help me sort the papers Higgins brought this afternoon."

"Of course, Papa," she said, following him into the library.

They went through the documents, and she wrote the responses he dictated. When they finished, he leaned back in his chair and said, "Since our conversation the other day, I've decided to offer Nate a job. Do you think he'll be interested?"

Maria's eyes widened. Papa seemed to truly want her opinion, even though he wouldn't talk to her about the business. She pondered his question. Nate had never spoken of joining McDougall & Company, but he didn't want to enroll in college, and he was restless. "I think so. What would you have him do?"

"He knows nothing about the company," Papa said. "He'd start at the bottom."

Maria laughed. "But he thinks he knows everything."

Papa laughed, too. "Doesn't everyone at nineteen? Maybe he could work for Higgins."

Maria froze. Did Papa want to rehash why she rejected Amos? To steer him away from that topic, she asked a question that had vexed her for weeks. "Did you ever think about offering me a position?"

He stared at her, frowning. "You're as intelligent as any of the boys. But business is no place for a woman. Didn't you learn that when you interviewed Holladay?"

"Not all men are like Mr. Holladay."

Papa waved a hand, dismissing her response. "Plus, when you marry, there'd be problems if you marry anyone in my employ. Your husband wouldn't want you working where he does."

"But what if I marry someone else? Or don't marry?" Maria asked.

"You'll marry someday. And then you'll need time with your babies."

Why couldn't she work and raise children? Mrs. Duniway had several children. But Papa wouldn't understand. "Won't you tell me about the problems at McDougall & Company?" she asked.

Papa looked away. "Someone's stealing from us. That's all I can say."

She asked half a dozen ways, trying to use what Zhuang Li had told her to get more information from Papa, to find out what he and Will thought about the thefts, but he wouldn't say more.

After talking to Papa, Maria returned to the parlor. Mama sat alone, sewing by lamplight. "Papa said he wants to offer Nate a job," she told Mama.

Mama nodded. "Mac and I discussed it. I think it would be good for Nate."

"I do, too." Maria sighed. "But Papa won't offer me a job."

"It's for your own good," Mama said.

"Doesn't he trust me?"

Mama set down her needle and the pillowcase she was hemming. "Of course, he trusts you. It isn't about trust, it's about what's best for you."

Maria paced. "I'm twenty-three years old. Can't I decide what's best for me?"

"Can you?" Mama countered. "You've turned down two marriage proposals."

"You told me to wait until I was certain. I'm not ready." She faced her mother. "I've worked at the newspaper for months now. Mrs. Duniway says I'm an excellent writer, but she won't give me a story she will publish."

"You started at the paper to support women's suffrage," Mama said, resuming her sewing. "Which you're doing. You've learned from Abigail and her staff. You've met interesting native women, like Winema Riddle.

You can build your career, or you can marry. Perhaps you can do both, but don't expect your father to make a place for you at his company—he worries too much."

Maria grimaced as she sat beside Mama. "Why is he so protective?"

Mama reached out and patted Maria's hand. "He has seen women hurt in this world—me, your birth mother. Even you, when you were at school. You can't ask him not to worry."

Maria huffed. "He says I'm as smart as the boys. But he won't treat me the same."

Mama shook her head and smiled. "And he never will."

The next day, Maria fumed to Daisy about her conversations with her parents, ending with, "They don't see me as a capable adult."

"Parents—especially fathers—never think their little girls grow up," Daisy said, pushing her spectacles up her nose. "Except for cleaning house and caring for young'uns. My ma had me diapering babies by the time I was seven. And cooking and scrubbing, too. I hired on with Mrs. Duniway as much to get away from housework as to earn a wage."

"My parents have plenty of help," Maria said. "They don't need me, not really. But they won't let me go. They wouldn't have dreamed of sending me to California in Will's stead."

"Of course not," Daisy said. "You might get hurt."

Since neither could change their elders' minds, they turned to more pleasant topics. "Has Robert talked to you recently?" Maria asked.

Daisy giggled. "He asked me to walk with him after work today. I think he'll buy me a coffee and biscuit at the tea shop."

"You must tell me all about it tomorrow," Maria said. She wished her relationships with Will and Amos were as simple as Daisy's seemed to be with Robert. Why was it so hard to find a man she could love? And to be ready for that love?

On Wednesday, May 7, the family held its traditional birthday dinner for Nate. Papa invited Amos Higgins to the meal. "I'm offering Nate a job," he told Maria. "I'd like Higgins to be there to second the offer. Will his presence make you uncomfortable?"

"It's your business, Papa," she said. "If you need Amos here, I'll manage.

303

I can be polite to him, even if I won't marry him."

"Good girl," Papa said, hugging her.

"I assume you've told Amos the plan," she added. "You're not surprising him, are you?"

"I've talked to him," Papa said. "He says it's my company, and he expects several of my sons to join us."

At dinner, Amos was quiet and spoke only to Papa and Mama, except to congratulate Nate on his birthday. When Maria caught his eye, he glared.

After the cake was served, Papa stood. "A toast to my son on his nineteenth birthday."

The others raised their glasses—water or wine, depending on age.

"Nate," Papa continued, "Mr. Higgins and I would like to offer you a position as inventory manager at McDougall & Company. It's an entry-level assignment, but you will learn the business—won't he, Higgins?"

Higgins grunted.

"So, come Monday, if you accept, you will be on the payroll."

"Really, Pa?" Nate's face lit up. "I can start working? No more school?"

Maria saw Mama hide a smile.

"You can keep the job if you work hard," Papa added. "But if you play hooky, I'll treat you worse than any teacher."

The younger children laughed, but Amos's face remained grim.

Chapter 63: Revelation in California

Will and Jack spent several days in Sacramento investigating McDougall & Company warehouses. Beck had not hired a supervisor to replace himself, leaving the Sacramento operations to a cantankerous old warehouse manager and a young bookkeeper.

"Mr. Beck comes 'round every month or two," the old manager told Will. "Seems he likes city life in San Francisco. Moved his family there quick as he could."

"Then you won't mind if Jack and I poke around in the inventory," Will said.

The old man shrugged. "Seein's how your name's McDougall, seems you can do what you want."

Jack and Will made copious lists of the warehouse contents, then questioned the bookkeeper about how records were kept—receipts of goods, sales to customers, transfers of inventory to San Francisco, where gold and bank drafts were secured, and how monies were sent north to Portland. "Most gold goes to San Francisco now," the bookkeeper said. "I don't know what Mr. Beck does with it from there."

"What did he do when he was based here?"

"He mostly sent packages to Mr. Higgins in Portland. He sent monies along with his reports to Mr. Higgins."

"Who reconciled the reports?" Will asked.

"Mr. Beck looked at the reports, decided what to send to Mr. Higgins, and counted out the monies from our vault here in Sacramento."

"And now?" Jack asked. "What do you do when you send gold and bank drafts to San Francisco?"

"I don't do nothin'," the man said. "Mr. Beck goes in the vault when he's here. He takes what he wants."

"Does he make a record of it?" Will asked.

"Aye," the bookkeeper said. "He gives me a note tellin' me what he took."

"Do you make a count afterward?"

"I do." The man nodded. "It's always been correct." He paused. "Well, 'cept once. One time, Mr. Beck was off by ten dollars. I told him, and he thanked me for correctin' him. Never happened again."

Over supper that evening, Will and Jack reviewed their findings. "Beck knows the Sacramento bookkeeper is watching him," Will said. "If he's stealing, it must be happening in San Francisco. I'm afraid you'll have to spend time there for a while if we're going to dig deeper."

Jack grinned. "I might like to settle in Sacramento eventually, but I'm happy to stay in San Francisco—at least while Mama's not here. I'll sow my wild oats afore she joins me."

Will frowned. "You're here to do a job."

"Us Missouri boys," Jack said with a wink, "we can do our work and play, too."

Will and Jack spent the weekend in Sacramento, then returned to San Francisco on Monday, May 12. They spent Tuesday talking to Beck about how he handled Sacramento receipts and how he sent monies to Portland.

"I've always dealt with Higgins," Beck said. "I write him what I need to handle payroll and operations in California. He writes back when Portland needs more funds from the branches. I send him what he asks for, unless I can't manage without the funds in California."

"Now that you handle both locations, do you move funds between San Francisco and Sacramento?" Will asked.

Beck nodded. "When I need to. Higgins doesn't seem to mind. I put it in my report."

"Oh?" Will was surprised. "I thought you were still sending separate reports for the two California branches."

"Well, yes," Beck said. "But I tell Higgins when I'm moving gold or bank drafts."

"Isn't it dangerous to move gold and paper around?" Jack asked.

"Wells Fargo provides armed protection," Beck said. "Their stages are safe. Obviously, I prefer not to move too much gold—their guards are expensive. But when I need to, I do. Or when Higgins orders it."

Beck and Higgins seemed pretty cozy, Will thought. "Where is all your correspondence with Higgins?"

Beck waved his hand. "In the files. Didn't you see it?"

Will shook his head. "There were a few letters, but not as many as it sounds like you've written."

Beck shrugged. "Some is done via wire. The bookkeepers can find what we have. I may have thrown away the telegrams once we acted on them."

Will and Jack finished their conversation with Beck, agreeing that Jack would ask the bookkeepers for Beck's correspondence with Higgins. Jack would also talk to Beck the next day to receive a work assignment in San Francisco.

"I'm leaving for Portland tomorrow," Will said.

"It's been a pleasure having you here, young man." Beck stood and shook Will's hand. "And I look forward to working with you, Jack." His words were unctuous, compared to his cold greeting when they first arrived.

That evening, Will and Jack dined at the hotel before Jack returned to his rooming house. "If you need to tell me something, send a telegram to our home. Direct it to my attention," Will instructed. "Don't wire the company offices. I don't want Higgins hearing about it."

"All right," Jack said. He hesitated, then said, "There's something I've wanted to discuss with you."

"Oh?" Will waited, turning his whiskey glass in his hand.

"I appreciate your kindness since Mama and I arrived. And your willingness to give me a chance to work." Jack paused, then continued, "I don't know if I'd be so charitable in your place."

"What do you mean?"

"Once, when my pa was in his cups, he told me somethin'," Jack said, looking down at the table. "He told me he hadn't been very kind to your mother before she left."

Will's hand stilled on his glass. "Go on."

"What do you know about why your mother left Arrow Rock?" Jack said.

"I think I know the full story," Will responded, unwilling to say more.

"I'm sorry for my father's conduct," Jack said. "He did not behave like a gentleman."

"Then you know the story as well?" Will asked.

Jack peered at the amber liquid in his glass and sloshed it gently. "He said he and two other men . . . assaulted her. He cried as he told me. He was sorry, if that makes any difference."

"Then you know we might be half-brothers?"

Jack nodded. "He was sorry. And so am I."

Will shook his head. "It's not yours to be sorry for. I have often wondered about your father—I hated him and the other men when I found out. I couldn't understand, and I ran away from home."

"I'm sorry," Jack repeated.

"But I soon realized Mac McDougall was my father in every way that mattered. He's been good to Mama and to all his children—whether or not they bear his blood."

They drank in silence. Then Will asked, "Does your mother know?"

Jack shrugged. "I don't think so. We've never spoken of it. Who knows in your family?"

"Only Mama and Pa," Will said. "And Maria and me. Maria was present when one villain came looking for us in Oregon City."

"What happened?" Jack tossed back the rest of his whiskey.

"Did you know Pa killed one of them in Arrow Rock? A sheriff. That's why he ran away with Mama. She shot the sheriff's son, who was another of them."

"Yes," Jack said. "My pa told me that."

"The sheriff's son survived. He later deserted from the Confederate Army. He ended up in Oregon City and found us. He broke into our house. Later, he killed a man and was hanged for it."

"Then all three of them are dead?" Jack asked.

"And good riddance," Will said. "I'm sorry you lost your father, but I can't forget—or forgive—what they did to Mama." Even though their actions had given Will life.

The next morning, Will boarded the steamboat alone, relishing the chance to spend a few days by himself. The trip to California had been useful, though it had proven nothing. But Jack was now in place to keep watch over the California branches—and on Beck.

While the boat headed north, Will studied Beck's final April report. He'd checked it against the copy of the Sacramento ledger he and Jack had made.

They hadn't been able to copy the San Francisco ledgers, not with Beck hanging over their shoulders.

Still, he could give Beck's report to Higgins without telling Higgins he'd copied the Sacramento ledger. Maybe Higgins would hang himself by altering the report. Will could ask Li to audit the Sacramento report against the ledger copy.

Will didn't trust the relationship between Higgins and Beck. The two men appeared to have private communications not reflected in the company's files. At least, they weren't in any files Will had seen. He'd searched Higgins's office and found nothing. He suspected Higgins kept documents related to the company at his apartment, but Will had no cause to search there.

By the end of the first day at sea, Will had thoroughly reviewed the business problems. His thoughts turned to Bart Peterson's drunken disclosure to Jack. All three men who could have fathered Will were dead— one killed before Will's birth, another hanged for his crimes, and Peterson dying a bitter and guilty old man.

How fortunate Mama had been that spring day in 1847 when Mac McDougall rode through Arrow Rock. And Will had been fortunate, too. Mac was a far better parent than any of the three men who might have fathered Will. He would spend his life repaying Mac for making him a McDougall.

Later that night, Will hungered for Maria. Every swell of the ocean brought him closer to her. But what good did proximity do if she would not have him? Ever since he'd returned from Boston, he'd dreamed of a future with Maria. She'd blossomed during his years away and was even more desirable now than she had been when they were young. No other woman had ever attracted him more.

What if she chose Higgins? Or someone else? Could Will let her go?

What choice would he have?

Chapter 64: Maria Misses Will

When Will had been in Boston, Maria hadn't thought of him often. But while he was in California, almost daily she had something she wanted to talk to him about—Papa's offering Nate a place at the company, Grandmère Peterson's latest insult, even how oddly Amos acted after she rejected him.

Discussing that last topic with Will would have been awkward. She'd turned Will down, too. She didn't regret it—she wasn't ready to marry. But Maria could imagine herself married to Will, though not to Amos.

When they were children, Maria could talk to Will about anything. She hadn't had a real confidante in the family after he left for Boston. Cal and Nate teased her unmercifully. Eliza made everything a competition and grated on Maria's nerves, and Lottie was too young and silly.

Mama always offered gentle and practical advice. But these days, Grandmère Peterson's venomous remarks put Mama in a dither, and Maria hated to add to Mama's concerns.

How had Mama come from such a mother? Maria wondered about Mama's long-dead father, the old Virginian Army officer who died as a sickly and impoverished Missouri farm owner. He must have had a strong character to endure Grandmère Peterson's self-absorption. Or perhaps circumstances after his death made Grandmère the way she was.

Whatever the past, now Maria had to listen to Mama fume about Grandmère. Maria suspected she was the only person Mama could talk to other than Papa. Mama and Papa rarely kept secrets from each other.

Which brought Maria's thoughts back to Will. He was keeping secrets from her about McDougall & Company. She didn't think he'd kept many secrets from her in the past, and she wished he wouldn't now. She needed information to write her article. And his lack of trust made her doubt him as a suitor.

If only he were home. Maybe then she could sort out her thoughts.

With no one at home to confide in, Maria brought up her worries to Daisy at work. One afternoon, the two of them were alone in the office searching for material to reprint in the next issue.

Maria sighed deeply as she put one paper down and reached for the next.

"What is it?" Daisy asked.

"I don't know where my life is headed." She must have sounded melodramatic, because Daisy laughed.

"What do you have to fret over?" Daisy said through her chuckles. "You have a lovely family, a fine home, and Mrs. Duniway dotes on you."

"She does not," Maria protested.

"She told me I need to work as hard as you do," Daisy said. "And to improve my penmanship so it's as neat as yours."

"That hardly means she dotes on me."

"What's troubling you?" Daisy reached for the next paper in the stack between them.

"Will. I miss him."

"So?"

"I feel so discombobulated when he's gone. I want to talk to him, and he's not here."

"Do you love him?" Daisy asked, peering over the top of her spectacles. "Like a husband?"

"I think I might."

"Do you want to marry him?"

"I don't know." Maria looked at her friend. "Shouldn't I be sure? Mama says I should."

Daisy smiled gently. "You have time, Maria. Take the time to be sure."

Will returned late Saturday, May 17. Only Maria and their parents were still awake when he walked in. Mama jumped up to hug him, and Papa shook Will's hand and clapped him on the back. Maria simply smiled.

"How was your trip, son?" Papa asked.

"I'll tell you in the morning," Will said. "I'm too tired now." They all retired for the night.

Sunday morning, the family went to church—all except Will, who slept through the service. That afternoon, Will and Papa closeted themselves in the library. When they finished, Maria finally had her turn.

She told him everything—about Papa's offering a job to Nate, about her frustration that Papa didn't see her as part of the business, and about Mama's tears over Grandmère. "I don't understand why Grandmère is not grateful," Maria complained. "She and Jack have nowhere else to live."

"Jack told me about their difficulties," Will said. "They couldn't manage the tobacco and hemp crops without slave labor, so the War ruined them."

"Then why doesn't Grandmère treat Mama better? She almost cast Mama out all those years ago, yet Mama is gracious to her now."

Will shrugged. "Jack told me his mother refused to accept any changes to their lives, even when the slaves left. Only Letitia stayed, and she grew too old to handle the house."

"What do you think of Jack?"

"He's a good fellow."

"Can he help McDougall & Company? As much as you or Nate can?"

"Too soon to tell," Will said. "But he's made a good start."

"What did you learn about the business problems in California?" she asked. But Will was no more forthcoming than he'd been before his trip to San Francisco.

Monday morning, Maria edited Daisy's article on the merits of linen and cotton for summer clothes. Mrs. Duniway called Maria into her office and said, "I have an assignment for you."

"Yes, Mrs. Duniway?" Maria said, smiling. Maybe this would be her opportunity.

Mrs. Duniway handed her a letter. "Read this."

May 14, 1873
Dear Mrs. Duniway,
I am taking a moment to update you on the hostilities between the Modoc and the Army. Negotiations are underway, and my husband and I interpret for both sides in the conflict. I

*do not know what will come of our efforts, but
we hope for an end to the fighting soon.*
Cordially,
Winema Riddle

When Maria looked up after reading, Mrs. Duniway said, "I want you to write an article on the war—what led to it, the rights and wrongs on both sides. You seem interested in native affairs."

"I am," Maria said. "But shouldn't we wait? It sounds like more will happen soon."

"Oh, we won't publish it right away. But your draft can be updated as soon as the hostilities end. We'll only need to add the result of the negotiations."

"But what if the outcome makes my draft irrelevant?"

Mrs. Duniway frowned. "Do you want the assignment or not?"

"Yes," Maria said quickly. "I'll get started right away."

"Leave the ending open," Mrs. Duniway said. "We'll need to edit it later, but write what you can now. Can you have it ready in two weeks? Go through all the Oregon papers since the conflict began and summarize the causes of the war."

"May I include the wrongs done to the tribes? The way Mrs. Riddle has described them to us?"

"If they are necessary to the conclusion you reach after doing the research, then you must include them." Mrs. Duniway waved Maria off. "Now, finish today's work, then get started on this assignment."

Chapter 65: At Work in Portland

Still weary from his travels, Will went to the office on Monday, May 19. He asked Zhuang Li to come to the McDougall house that evening. He didn't want to bring the California documents into the office for Higgins to see—not until Li reviewed them. That evening after supper, Will took Li into Pa's library. Will had already told Pa everything he'd learned in California, but Pa joined them anyway.

Will recounted what he and Jack had done in California—their discussions with Beck, Cassidy's cautions, their tours of the San Francisco and Sacramento operations. Will showed Li Beck's April report and said, "Jack and I reviewed this as it was prepared, and we didn't see any errors. We copied the ledgers from which the information was taken. Will you check everything again?"

"Mr. Higgins see yet?" Li asked.

Will shook his head. "I wanted to show you first. But Higgins knows I have it. I told him I forgot it this morning, but I'll have to give it to him tomorrow."

"I copy tonight," Li said. "May I use kitchen again?"

"I made an extra copy while I was on the ship," Will said. "Take what I have, and review it all at your home, then come see me when you're done."

Li nodded.

"You know I don't trust Beck," Will continued. "But Jack and I didn't see any obvious problems. He's sloppy recording the movement of goods and gold between San Francisco and Sacramento, but we found nothing missing."

"I look." Li stood to leave and bowed to Pa. "I finish by end week."

Tuesday morning, Will handed Higgins Beck's report. "Here's the April report," he told the accountant. "I watched the preparation, and I didn't find any discrepancies between this and the records in California."

"Just as it should be," Higgins said. "Thank you for carrying it north. Though I could have had it two weeks ago, if Beck had sent it directly to me."

"I'm sure that's true," Will said. "But I was glad for the chance to review the records. I think we need to do so more often. Perhaps one of us should go to California every few months."

"If we find any reason to doubt Beck, that would make sense," Higgins said. "How is Jack working out in California? He's uneducated and inexperienced."

"Yes, but he's a quick learner," Will said. He and Pa had not told Higgins that Jack would be watching Beck.

On Thursday, as Will and Pa drank whiskey after dinner, Will asked, "Now that Nate's working for the company, shouldn't he join our evening conversations?"

Pa grinned. "What do you think of your younger brother joining us?"

"If he's happy, then I am, too." Will swirled the amber liquid in his glass. "But Maria seems discontent."

Pa shook his head. "She asked if I'd considered hiring her." He sighed. "Of course, that would be impossible. Though she could run rings around half the men in the office."

Will chuckled. "Only half?"

Pa lifted his glass in salute. "You're right—she's brighter than most of them. But to your point, I will start inviting Nate." Then Pa turned serious. "Have you heard from Li yet?"

"No," Will replied. "He said by week's end. I'll follow up tomorrow."

"I hope the California problems are behind us," Pa said. "Whether Cassidy was stealing or merely negligent, his departure should have settled things."

"And if the discrepancies weren't his fault?" Will asked.

"Then whoever the culprit was is now on notice," Pa replied. "And Jack is watching for fresh trouble."

That evening after talking with Pa, Will started upstairs toward his bedroom. He paused at the sound of crying coming from Mama's morning room.

He followed the sound and found Maria sitting at Mama's desk, her head in her hands. "What's wrong?" he asked.

"I'm working on an article for Mrs. Duniway," she said, wiping her eyes on her sleeve. "About the Modoc War. I'm struggling with what to say."

"Why?" Will pulled up a chair. "You're a talented writer."

"I don't know what she wants." Maria sniffed. "Winema Riddle says the war may end soon. Mrs. Duniway told me to write a piece with all the background, so we're ready to publish something as soon as hostilities end. All my research focuses on the Army's reasons for fighting. There's nothing on the Modoc perspective—only what Mrs. Riddle has told us in the past."

"Isn't that enough?"

Maria sighed. "Who will believe an Indian woman over Army officers?"

"Have you talked to Pa? Maybe he knows someone who can help you."

"I want to do this on my own. And I want it to be good."

"Isn't part of being a reporter finding sources wherever you can?" Will asked.

"You're right," Maria said, gathering up her papers. "And it's too late to do anything more tonight. Maybe the problem won't seem so impossible tomorrow."

Will took her hand. "You'll figure it out. I think the Modoc article could be a great story."

"If you'd let me write about McDougall & Company, I wouldn't have this problem," she said as they climbed the stairs. "I'd have plenty of sources within the family."

As Will readied for bed that night, he considered his discussion with Maria—which felt like many of their long-ago conversations. They'd listened to each other's confidences then, sometimes teasing in response, sometimes encouraging. Tonight, Maria felt like his best friend again.

If that's all he could have from her, it would have to be enough. But to keep even that much of Maria in his life, Will realized he would have to support her, the way he had so many years ago.

Still, as he fell asleep, he hoped she would change her mind about him. He wanted more than friendship.

Friday morning, Will found Li at the office. "Have you analyzed the documents yet?" he asked.

Li nodded. "I tell you later."

"I'll take you to lunch at the hotel," Will said. "We can talk there."

Li shook his head. "Should not be seen with you alone. We talk at your house tonight."

"All right," Will said, realizing Li feared another beating. "I'll see you there."

When Will and Li were settled in the kitchen that evening with mugs of tea, Li said, "I look at report. I look at ledger copy. Everything match."

"That's good news," Will said. "Though it doesn't help us find out who was stealing before."

"No." Li slurped his tea. "But we must watch."

"Watch what?" Will asked.

"Certain accounts," Li said. "Easy to cheat. Like inventory. We can't know what really in warehouse."

"That's why I left Jack there," Will said.

Li raised an eyebrow. "How you tell Jack what look for?" He sipped more tea. "And what Beck do with gold he move? Who weigh it both in Sacramento and in San Francisco?"

Will sighed. Li was right. There was too much they could not know. "I'll write Jack. I'll ask him to track inventory. But Beck won't let him see everything. Beck thinks Jack is a new underling. If Jack snoops too much, Beck will know he's being spied on."

Will spent the weekend writing Jack a long letter, detailing all the places Li thought someone could steal without detection. But if Beck was the thief, he'd surely hide his misdeeds from.

Chapter 66: Evie's Birthday

Evie's seventh birthday fell on Sunday, May 25. The little girl giggled and wiggled all week in anticipation. Every evening, Evie had some new wish for the family celebration.

"I want to sit in Mama's seat," she requested one day. "At the end of the table from Papa." Then she added, "And I want to wear a crown."

When her siblings laughed, she pouted. "But I'm the birthday queen." They only laughed louder, which made her cry.

Mama soothed her. "You may wear a paper crown while we sing to you. But it would be too hard for you to eat your roast and potatoes with it on." And Mama switched the conversation to a discussion of moving Maggie and Evie into a bedroom of their own, as she had promised months ago.

As Evie's excitement grew, Grandmère Peterson became more petulant. "I don't know why you cater to that child," she fumed at Mama. "In my day, children were seen and not heard. Certainly, until they had better manners than your Geneviève." Only Grandmère called Evie by her full name.

"She's a good child," Mama said, smiling. "And I've grown more indulgent in my old age, haven't I, Maria?"

Maria laughed. "You were always indulgent about birthdays, Mama."

Grandmère sniffed. "She's not your mother," she muttered.

Mama stood, her short frame straight and stiff. "Maria is my daughter as much as Evie is." Her voice was icy. "I raised her. And raised her well. Just as I have all my children."

"Here? In this wilderness?" Grandmère said, gesturing around the elegant parlor as if it were a shack. "Oregon cannot compare to the Louisiana of my girlhood. Everything we had came from France, not hacked out of the forest."

"I won't have you disparaging my home or my children," Mama retorted. "Particularly when you have no home of your own."

"*Tiens*," Grandmère said, switching to her native Créole French as she continued to berate Mama. She spoke so rapidly Maria could barely understand her. But despite long years away from speaking French regularly, Mama answered just as rapidly, her tone sharp.

As both women's voices rose to shouts, Maria tried to calm them. "Shall we call it an evening?" she said. "Grandmère, may I help you upstairs? I'll ring Mrs. O'Malley to bring you some chocolate to help you sleep."

It took a while, but Maria finally settled Grandmère in her room. As always, Grandmère treated her like a servant.

Still, as Maria tucked Grandmère into bed and arranged her pillows, Grandmère said, "For a Spaniard, you've turned out all right. You have a gentle hand."

"Thank you, Grandmère." Maria turned to leave.

"You know I can't abide you calling me that," Grandmère said. "You must call me 'madame.' "

Maria met her gaze. "You heard Mama. She is my mother, which makes you my grandmother, does it not?"

"Not in my mind. You're still a Spaniard."

"And an Indian," Maria shot back. "You know my natural mother had native blood."

Grandmère's cheeks reddened. "How can you taunt me so? I come from the finest family in Louisiana—"

"You should be grateful my parents have taken you in," Maria said. "Mama opened her door to you, though you treated her abysmally before she left your home."

"Whatever do you mean?" Grandmère's face flushed more, and her eyes flashed.

Hands on her hips, Maria said, "You were about to throw her out because of her situation—"

"I know of no situation," Grandmère retorted. "She was my daughter, yet she abandoned me to run off with a man I'd never met. The man you call your father, though he is not."

"You know why she left," Maria said. "She was abused—"

"I don't know what you're talking about," Grandmère insisted. "She abandoned me."

Maria realized Grandmère would never admit the truth—about Mama or about Will. Perhaps she knew, and perhaps she didn't. But Maria would not find out tonight.

On Saturday, Maria frosted Evie's birthday cake for their Sunday celebration. Then she spent the afternoon making sure all her siblings had presents for Evie. She helped Eddie draw a picture of a queen with a crown, then showed Andrew how to sand the horse he'd whittled. As she assisted Andrew, she remembered the horse Will had carved for her years ago—Cal had hidden and broken it, so Will made her another one. That second horse still sat on her dresser, where she fingered it every time she brushed her hair.

Grandmère stayed in bed all day, and Mama had a headache. Both seemed shaken by their argument the day before. "I can't think why she hates me so," Mama whispered when Maria brought her a cup of tea. "I was the best daughter I could be."

"Perhaps she knew what her husband did to you," Maria said, laying a cool cloth over Mama's forehead. "She might have blamed you, though it was not your fault."

"Perhaps," Mama murmured. "I keep telling myself I was better off leaving. Mac gave me a wonderful life. A wonderful family. I would not have had this life in Missouri. I *was* better off," she emphasized. "And so was Will. Let alone you." She patted Maria's hand. "You are a fine daughter, and I have loved you from the moment Mac brought you to me."

Maria leaned over and hugged Mama. "And I don't remember a time when I didn't love you," she whispered.

By Sunday morning, Grandmère Peterson still hadn't left her room. Before the family went to church, Maria knocked. At the feeble, "Come in," she entered.

"Oh, it's you," Grandmère said. "I thought it might be Geneviève. Where is she?"

"She's getting ready for Evie's party this afternoon." Maria closed the door behind her and said in her firmest voice, "We are celebrating a seven-year-old's birthday today. You may join us, or you may stay in your room.

But neither Mama nor I will wait on you. We will be wishing my youngest sister—your granddaughter—many happy returns."

"My nerves—"

"Your nerves can wait a few hours," Maria said. "We are going to church now—"

"But not to Mass," Grandmère declared. "Your mortal souls—"

"—and I will check on you when we return. Do not expect Mama, as she will be busy." Maria turned to leave. "Rest now. I hope you feel well enough to join the celebration."

She left and heaved a deep sigh.

After church, Maria kept her promise. Grandmère was at her dressing table, fully dressed, brushing her hair.

Maria smiled. "May I help you?"

"Yes, child, that would be nice," Grandmère said. "I'm sure your stint at church, regardless of denomination, has improved your attitude."

Maria took the brush and stroked the older woman's hair, then pinned it into coils. "You look ready for a birthday party," she said as she secured the last pin. "Will you join us?"

"If I'm going to eat, I suppose I must." Grandmère rose and preceded Maria out of the room. She remained on good behavior through the meal, the cake, and the presents, though Maria saw her frowning petulantly at Mama from time to time.

Maria spent every spare moment working on her article about the Modoc War. She struggled to balance the tribes' perspective with that of white settlers and the Army. The Modoc had lived for generations in Oregon before the Americans from the East ever arrived. But the settlers had developed the land into productive farms and timberland. Should the hereditary rights of the Modoc tribe outweigh the prosperity brought by the white pioneers? Maria sympathized with both sides.

One evening, she tried to explain her dilemma to her parents and Will. "The newspapers only describe the settlers' perspective. And the Army's."

"I've always thought the West was large enough for all of us," Papa said.

"I agree," Maria said. "But how do I make white readers empathize with the Indians?"

"You told me Winema Riddle's grandfather was a famous chief who welcomed whites when they came," Will said. "Perhaps you could urge your readers to return that welcome."

"Perhaps," Maria said, though she doubted many Oregonians would cede productive land to the tribes. "All most farmers see is good land left fallow for hunting and fishing, when they could farm it or harvest the timber."

"A lot of the tribes' traditional land is not suitable for farming," Will said. "You haven't seen Southern Oregon. Much of the area where the Modoc and Klamath tribes have been penned up is barren volcanic rock. I saw it when I was with the militia in sixty-four."

"Your heart will tell you what to write," Mama murmured. "And now, we should all go to bed."

As Will and Maria walked up the stairs, he caught her hand. "Mama told me how much help you were in planning Evie's party—especially with Grandmère." He squeezed her fingers gently. "Even though you're working so hard on your article."

"It's been a challenge." Maria sighed.

"You're appreciated here at home, Maria," he said. "And I'm sure Mrs. Duniway appreciates you, too, or she wouldn't have given you this assignment."

Will's praise warmed Maria's heart as she prepared for bed. She fell asleep hearing his words, "you're appreciated."

Chapter 67: Telegram from Jack

Will wrote a long letter to Jack that included Zhuang Li's instructions for what Jack should look for in California. Will wondered how long it would be before he heard back—it would take close to a week for Jack to receive the letter, then Jack might need time to learn the answers to Will's questions. Even if Jack already had information, it would be at least two weeks before Will received a response.

He ended it,

> *Please send word as soon as you have anything to report.*
> *A telegram to let me know it is on the way, followed by a*
> *detailed letter.*
>
> *Will*

Will posted the letter on Monday, May 26, and immediately began fretting about Jack's response.

To his happy surprise, the following Monday, June 2, he had a telegram from Jack waiting for him when he got home in the evening.

DATE: 2 JUNE 1873
FROM: JACQUES PETERSON SAN FRANCISCO
TO: WILLIAM MCDOUGALL PORTLAND
BECK RETURNED SACRAMENTO WAGONFUL
UNKNOWN GOODS LETTER TO FOLLOW

What did that mean? Will wondered. Had Beck returned to Sacramento with goods or returned from Sacramento with them? The brevity of telegrams was often confusing. He could wire Jack for more details or await Jack's promised letter. It didn't seem as if Jack had learned much, so he might as well wait.

Will showed the telegram to Pa after supper. He'd asked Pa not to include Nate in this meeting—they hadn't told Nate about the suspected theft. Will didn't trust his younger brother not to tell Higgins and others in the office if Jack learned who might be stealing from them.

"What's this mean?" Pa asked after reading the telegram.

Will shrugged. "I have no idea. But it sounds as if Jack suspects Beck of something."

Pa grunted. "But we don't know what. Damned telegram."

Will grinned. "That's what I thought when I read it."

"There are plenty of valid reasons for Beck to move goods between Sacramento and San Francisco." Pa threw the telegram onto his desk.

"But it could mean Beck is moving inventory for his own purposes," Will argued.

"It could. But we don't know." Pa frowned at his whiskey glass. "Nothing to do but wait for Jack's letter." He turned his frown on Will. "You trust Jack, don't you?"

Will nodded. "I do. We don't have any choice but to trust him. But I do."

Even though Jack's letter wouldn't arrive for several days, Will puttered around the house more than usual, coming home for the noon meal and waiting for the afternoon post to arrive.

One afternoon that week, he came upon Grandmère Peterson alone in the large parlor. She appeared to be dozing when he entered the room, so he tried to back out quietly.

"Is that you, William?" she said sharply, opening her eyes.

"Yes, ma'am."

"You look so like your grandfather. My William." She sighed mournfully.

Will sat near her. "What was he like, Grandmère?"

"So tall and handsome," she said, with a faraway look. "And he sat a horse well. Cavalry, you know."

"I ran away with the Oregon militia cavalry." Will wondered if his grandmother had heard the story.

She looked at him sharply. "Why would you run away? Your parents dote on you."

Will remembered why he'd run away, and he didn't want to tell her that part of the story. "Just one of those things young boys do, I suppose. Tell me more about my grandfather."

She went through the history of their courtship. When William Calhoun served as an officer under Andrew Jackson in the War of 1812, he'd spent time in New Orleans and visited the plantation where Hortense lived. They'd fallen in love, as she told it, and married after the war. William and Hortense lived on their own plantation. They also owned a grand house in New Orleans until he lost the land. She was vague about how that happened.

"So, my father purchased a farm in Missouri for us, and we moved there," she said. "I was devastated to leave Louisiana and my family. But we had a daughter to raise."

"What happened then?" he asked.

"William loved his books. And he loved his daughter Geneviève. But he didn't love farming. Our overseer stole from us and absconded. We were left with only the land. And the slaves." Her lips bent in a bitter line. "Then William died, and Geneviève ran away." She gestured. "You know the rest."

"I'm sorry, Grandmère."

She brightened. "But I married Mr. Peterson and bore him a son. My beloved Jacques." Her eyes narrowed as she looked at Will. "Whom you sent to California, though I need him with me. He is the only one who understands my ailments, who cares for me."

"Maybe you could join him soon in California," Will said. "Would you like that?"

"I don't know." Her frown deepened. "Are you trying to send me away from my Geneviève? I've only just found her again. I enjoy the time with my daughter after so many years apart."

"We'll see how Jack does in California. I don't know yet whether he will be better suited for a role there or in Oregon."

"But you think he can support me in my old age?" she asked querulously.

"I see no reason he couldn't," Will said. Though he wondered if Jack could ever earn enough to satisfy Grandmère Peterson.

325

After talking to Grandmère, Will walked past Mama's morning room, where Maria sat hunched over Mama's desk. He paused. Should he disturb her or leave her be? He knew she struggled with the article she was writing.

His affection for Maria won. He asked, "How's your article going?"

She sighed. "It should be easy. You and Papa were very helpful. You gave me a more objective point of view than what I read in the newspapers."

"What is *your* point of view, Maria?"

"Mine?"

Will nodded. "You have a unique perspective. You were raised in a white family, but people outside the family sometimes treat you as an Indian."

"But I know so little about the native experience. If I knew more, perhaps this would be easier."

"You haven't lived in a native community," Will said. "But I dare say you have tried to imagine it. That's more than most of your readers will have done."

"Yes," Maria said, frowning. "I have tried to imagine what it must be like. To have your homeland stolen. To be herded and penned up like animals. To be starved of the foods you have eaten for generations."

Maria's vehemence surprised Will. "Is it that bad, do you think? The Bureau of Indian Affairs gives them food and clothing."

"But never enough." Maria stood and paced the room. "Often, half of what is set aside for the tribes is stolen, sometimes by the very people whose job it is to protect them. No wonder they attack." She whirled to face him, her skirts swishing around her legs. "Wouldn't you attack if your family was starving?"

"I suppose." Will thought of the native camps he'd seen in southern Oregon in 1864. Some had been impoverished. Others had contained goods Indians had stolen from whites. As always, there were two sides to every story. "Have you written the article to show the good deeds and the sins of both sides?"

"I've tried." Maria collapsed in her chair again. "It's hard. I sympathize with both sides, and that's what makes it hard."

Will grinned. "You should have gone to law school, like I did. We were trained to argue both sides." He stood, leaned over, and kissed Maria's cheek. "You'll get it. You are a smart woman and a talented writer. You can do it."

Chapter 68: Modoc War Is Over

After talking to Will, Maria felt better. His confidence in her ability to portray both the Modoc and white perspectives gave her a freedom she hadn't felt before. As a result, she tackled the piece with renewed energy and excitement.

Maria began writing from scratch, though she had her last several drafts spread around her on the floor and desk. She started with what Papa and Will had told her about the historical background of the conflict. She included the facts she'd gleaned from the papers and from Winema Riddle's letters to Abigail Duniway. But she didn't stop with history and facts. She let her own emotions color the text, both to emphasize the suffering of the Modoc after the whites invaded their territory and to show the courage and fortitude of settlers seeking new homes and opportunities.

There was wrong on both sides, she concluded, but there was right as well. Both races deserved a home, and, as Papa often said, there should be room in Oregon for everyone.

By Wednesday evening, Maria was pleased with her draft. She put it aside, planning to take it to the newspaper office in the morning to edit. Then she went to bed and slept soundly for the first time since Mrs. Duniway had given her the assignment. She smiled as her head hit the pillow, thinking of Will's earnestness in helping her.

Maria was at work early Thursday morning. She went through her article line by line, then copied a clean draft to give to Mrs. Duniway. The editor would surely mark it up, but Maria was proud of what she had for Mrs.

Duniway to review.

"Maria," Mrs. Duniway said when she came into the office. "Have you heard? The Modoc War is over."

"Over?" Maria dropped her pen, spattering ink on her neat page. "When? How?" Her stomach sank. All her hard work might be for nothing.

"I just heard. Telegrams arrived in Portland last night from the Army officer in charge. Captain Jack has been captured. General Davis, of course, is taking full credit."

Captain Jack was the leader of the Modoc renegades who had left the reservation. The tribes thought him a hero, though the Army called him a reprobate. "How was he captured?" Maria asked.

"I don't know the details, but I'm sure *The Oregonian* reporters are writing about it. How is your article coming along?"

"I'm finished," Maria said. "But the war's end means I'll need to rewrite it."

"Go talk to *The Oregonian* reporters. See what they know."

Maria wondered whether spending any more time on the article was worth it. "Will we be able to publish anything?"

"I won't know until we learn more," was Mrs. Duniway's unsatisfactory answer.

Maria left *The New Northwest* newsroom and headed upstairs to where *The Oregonian* reporters sat. She found three men hovering over telegrams from the Army outpost, but the telegrams said little. "We're likely to get dispatches tonight or tomorrow," one man told her. "We'll have an article for Saturday's paper."

"Will you let me see the dispatches?" Maria asked.

"Not until after your paper is published this week," the reporter told her. "We can't let you get a scoop on us."

Maria returned to tell Mrs. Duniway what she had learned.

"Let me see what you have so far," Mrs. Duniway said.

The editor marked up Maria's draft, then returned it, saying, "Find out the end of the story, and start there. Remember, in newspaper writing, you tell the end of the story first."

"Then you will publish it?"

"It's a powerful piece," Mrs. Duniway said. "But circumstances might overtake it. Go edit it as I suggested."

Saturday, June 7, *The Oregonian* printed the story of the capture of Captain Jack. Maria hadn't been able to learn any information from *The Oregonian* reporters, so she read the Saturday paper avidly.

She took a copy to *The New Northwest* offices, slapping the paper down on Daisy's desk. "Look," she said, pointing at the article in the middle of the front page. "Our friends at *The Oregonian* call Captain Jack a renegade. And an outlaw." She didn't even mention the epithet "redskins" which also featured in *The Oregonian*'s article—too many whites disparaged the native population by seeing only the color of their skin.

"At least one of their sources calls him brave," Daisy pointed out.

"Yes, but the entire tone of the article suggests the Army heroically captured the dastardly natives." Maria paced in the limited space between desks. "I think Captain Jack was the hero—he held off the Army for months. How I wish I could speak with Winema Riddle."

"What would she tell you that you don't already know?" Daisy asked.

"I'm sure she'd have sympathy for the Modoc."

"But you also have that sympathy. So, write your article with that in mind."

Maria stopped pacing. "You're right," she said, snatching up the paper. "I have been too focused on taking a balanced approach. I will write the article showing how the Modoc have stood up for their land and their customs."

She sat at her desk, began with the capture of Captain Jack, then rewrote the rest of the article with a focus on the wrongs done to the Modoc. She dashed it off, not caring about the ink spots on her pages, and ended with a hope of peace—"But peace shall not be possible unless the white settlers recognize the losses of the natives who came before them."

When Maria finished her new draft, she took it to Mrs. Duniway. "I've rewritten it," she announced. "You might not like it, but this is what I believe."

Mrs. Duniway frowned. "You didn't believe what you wrote before?"

"The facts were true," Maria said. "But I tried to balance both perspectives. I didn't tell the full truth as I see it. I told a good story, but I didn't focus on the human rights behind the facts. Isn't that what you want this paper to do? When the injustices by both sides are weighed, human rights favor the Modoc."

"I know you think I am too concerned about women's rights," Mrs. Duniway said. "That I only care about how women can make a place for themselves in the world while still managing their homes. But all peoples have innate rights, as our Declaration of Independence says." She reached out her hand. "Let me read what you have written. I'll talk to you again on Monday."

Maria handed the article to Mrs. Duniway, then left for home. She would have to wait through the weekend to know whether Mrs. Duniway would publish it.

Chapter 69: Letter from Jack

As Will predicted, Jack's letter didn't arrive until Saturday, June 7, almost a full week after the telegram. Will tore it open and read:

June 2, 1873
Dear Will,

The wagon of goods from Sacramento was gold dust! Beck got to San Francisco with the load on Sunday. But I didn't see where he stashed the bags in the warehouse, so I spent Sunday night snooping around.

I found the bags in a far corner of the cellar, back where old crates are stored. The bags was covered with boxes and burlap, and I almost missed them. I opened one up and it was full of gold. I filled an envelope with some flakes, just to have proof. I ain't stealing. I've saved the envelope for you.

Monday morning, I asked Beck what the bags was for. I didn't tell him I'd found them, nor that I seen they was full of gold. He was honest and said they was gold from mines north of Sacramento. He'd traded with miners, he said, and got the gold in payment for wares he sold them.

I asked why he needed gold in San Francisco, trying to seem like I just wanted to learn how the business works. He didn't want to say, but I pestered him. Finally, he said he bought a shipload of goods from China that's coming soon, and he needs gold to pay for the goods.

I ain't heard nothing about a load of Chinese goods, but I

*don't know everything what's done here. Maybe you know
about it up in Portland.*

*After I talked to Beck, I wired you. Then I wrote this letter,
and I'll put it in the post for the next boat north.*

I'll write again if I learn more.

Give my love to Mama,

Jack

Goods from China? The McDougall & Company branch managers had a lot of leeway to fill the warehouses with whatever they thought would sell. But a shipload of goods that required several bags of gold to pay for? Will thought he or Pa would have heard about that.

He needed to talk to Pa.

As Will headed toward the library to find Pa, he saw Maria coming through the front door. She looked worried. "What is it?" he asked her.

"Did you see *The Oregonian* today?" she asked, taking off her hat. "About the capture of Captain Jack of the Modocs?

Will nodded. "Quite a story."

"Yes, and it changed my perspective on my article. I rewrote the whole thing and gave it to Mrs. Duniway. But I don't know if she'll publish it."

"Why wouldn't she?"

"I took the side of the Modoc. I didn't like the Army bragging about Captain Jack's capture."

"What did Mrs. Duniway say to that?"

"She hadn't read it when I left. I don't know."

"Still, it must be a relief to have turned in the article."

"It is," Maria said, sighing. "But now I have nothing pending."

"What do you want to write next?" Will asked. Even as he spoke, he guessed her response.

"You know I want to write about our family business," she said.

His instinct had been correct. "I need to talk to Pa," he said. "I'll ask him."

She smiled, the first smile he'd seen since she arrived home. "Then you're not saying no?"

"I'm not," Will said. "Though I can't say yes. Not on my own. Pa will have to agree, too."

Pa wasn't feeling well that afternoon, and Will wasn't able to talk to him about Jack's telegram until Sunday after church services. As soon as the Sunday dinner was over, Will closeted himself with Pa in the library and showed him Jack's letter.

"Gold, hmm?" Pa said after reading the letter. "Beck's story is plausible. He could have purchased Chinese silks and teas and the like. There's a big market for such products all up and down the West Coast. We could sell a shipload here in Portland if we had access to some of the merchandise Beck bought."

"If that's what happened," Will said. "Or Beck could be siphoning off gold from those bags to fill his own pockets."

Pa grinned. "Much like Jack did?"

Will frowned. "Jack was upfront about taking the gold out of the warehouse, unlike Beck."

"Maybe so," Pa said. "But we still don't have proof Beck is doing anything wrong."

"The problem with gold as payment is that there's no standard." Will moved to stare out the window at the afternoon sun. "Even if the bags are weighed, the exchange rate varies. It's whatever the parties agree to."

"That's true," Pa said. "And a thumb on the scale easily changes the weight."

"How do we track down Beck's tale about a shipload of Chinese goods?" Will asked. "Has Beck or Higgins told you about such a purchase?"

"No," Pa said. "And Beck should have told you, me, or Higgins. You and I are in the dark, so that leaves Higgins. We need to talk to him."

"Are you feeling well enough to go to the office tomorrow?" Will asked. "We should talk to Higgins together."

"I think so," Pa said. "My bones tell me when it's going to rain, but the skies were clear today. We'll see what the morning brings."

Will remembered Maria's request. "Maria still wants to write about the company," he said. "She turned in her article about the Modoc and is looking for a new subject."

"This isn't a good time," Pa said, leaning back in his chair. "There are rumors about the Northern Pacific Railroad. Wherever they decide to put the western terminus will affect our business in the Northwest."

"It won't be Portland," Will said. "I read they've committed to putting the terminus on Puget Sound."

"Yes," Pa said. "But the spur line from Portland north toward Seattle is already being built. Portland will need to connect wherever the line ends. And I want to open a new branch wherever that terminus is."

"What are you hearing?" Will asked.

"Tacoma."

"Tacoma?" Will was surprised. "I would have guessed Seattle. Who told you it will be Tacoma?"

"Seattle is the bigger town," Pa said. "But men are buying up land around Tacoma. I suspect the purchasers are railroad insiders seeking to make a profit. No one has told me anything—it's only my speculation."

"What does the railroad's plan have to do with Maria?"

"I don't want her getting ahead of whatever decisions we make on investments in Washington Territory. And I certainly don't want her mentioning possible theft from our business."

"So far, she's focused on our operations in Portland and California."

"Yes," Pa said, nodding. "But as soon as she hears the rumors about the Puget Sound terminus, she'll want to include that in her article." He stood. "Let's talk to Higgins. Then we can decide what to tell Maria."

Monday morning, Pa and Will took the carriage downtown. Pa called Higgins into his office and asked with no preamble, "Do you know anything about Beck purchasing a large order of goods from China?"

Higgins looked startled. "No, sir," he replied. "How did you hear that?"

Will couldn't tell if the man genuinely knew nothing, or if Pa's question about a matter Higgins believed he'd hidden from Pa and Will simply surprised him.

"Will had a letter from my brother-in-law Jack," Pa said. "He mentioned talking to Beck about the order from China."

"Well, Beck knows the California market better than we do," Higgins said, rubbing his temple. "If he thinks he can sell Chinese goods at a profit, I'm not surprised he'd place a big order."

"Could be," Pa said. "But he should have cleared a large expenditure like that with you or Will or me."

"Yes," Higgins said. "I'll wire him and ask for the specifics." His eyes narrowed. "Just what is young Jack Peterson doing in San Francisco, anyway?"

"He's learning the business," Will said. "He needs to support himself and his mother. And we'd prefer him to be in California rather than Oregon."

Higgins raised an eyebrow and grinned. "Family differences?"

"Something like that," Will said, then pursed his lips to indicate the subject was closed to Higgins.

"Jack's an eager learner," Pa said. "His letter to Will was full of questions."

"Should I answer it?" Higgins asked.

"Don't bother," Will said. "I'll handle it."

Higgins stood to leave. "I'll wire Beck and let you know his response."

Chapter 70: The Article Is Finished

When Maria arrived at work Monday morning, Mrs. Duniway still was not there. "She's late today of all days," Maria fumed to Daisy.

"What's so important today?" Daisy asked.

"I gave her my article on Friday, and she said she'd talk to me this morning."

"Oh, that's all." Daisy busied herself with the work in front of her. Then she heaved an enormous sigh.

Maria frowned at her friend. "What are you upset about?"

"Robert didn't call on me yesterday."

"Has he been calling regularly?" Maria was surprised—Daisy had only mentioned Robert's visits once or twice.

"Every Sunday. At two in the afternoon. Like clockwork." Daisy sighed again.

"Have you seen him yet this morning?" Maria asked. She looked around, not seeing Robert.

"No," Daisy wailed. "I don't know where he is."

"Maybe he's sick."

"I hope so," Daisy said. "At least that would explain why he didn't call yesterday." She put a hand over her mouth. "Is it dreadful of me to wish him ill?"

Maria chuckled. "Yes, but I understand."

"Should I visit him after work today? Or is that too forward of me?" Daisy's fingers clenched the paper she held.

"Yes, it is," Maria said firmly. "You must wait to hear from him. If he doesn't come to the office today or tomorrow, I'm sure Mrs. Duniway will send a boy to check on him. We have to get this week's issue typeset."

"Will you be sure she does?" Daisy said, grabbing Maria's arm.

Maria glanced at the clock. "It's only nine now. Maybe he just overslept."

The door opened, and Mrs. Duniway bustled in. "Maria," she said, "please come see me." And she swept past Maria and Daisy into her office.

Maria squeezed Daisy's hand, then followed the editor. "Yes, ma'am?" she said, closing the door behind her.

"Have a seat," Mrs. Duniway said. "Let's discuss your article."

As Mrs. Duniway questioned Maria about several points she'd made, Maria's heart sank. Mrs. Duniway hadn't liked it. She wouldn't publish it. Nevertheless, Maria did her best to answer the questions and to argue for the positions she'd taken.

"All right," Mrs. Duniway said after about fifteen minutes. "Clean it up, based on my margin notes." She handed Maria the copy. "We will publish it on Friday."

"Do you mean it?" Maria said, clutching the pages to her breast. "You liked it?"

"It is not what I would have written," Mrs. Duniway said. "But you state your arguments persuasively. Your theme is consistent with the purpose of our newspaper, and your views deserve an airing. We will publish it."

Maria stood. "Thank you, Mrs. Duniway. Thank you."

Back at her desk, she realized Friday was the thirteenth of June. Was it a curse to publish her first feature article on Friday the thirteenth?

Maria revised the article to Mrs. Duniway's specifications and gave it to the editor that afternoon. "Here it is, Mrs. Duniway. I copied it over neatly. If you need anything more, please let me know."

"Robert will typeset it tomorrow," Mrs. Duniway said.

"Where is he today?" Maria asked.

"He told me Saturday that he would not be in today. I didn't pry," Mrs. Duniway said without looking up from the papers in front of her.

"It's just that Daisy—"

At that, Mrs. Duniway glanced up with a grin. "Tell Daisy not to worry. I'm sure Robert will return tomorrow."

Maria passed the message along to her friend, then headed home, eager to tell her parents and Will about the article.

She found Mama first and told her the good news, then Papa. "Where's

Will?" she asked her father after he congratulated her.

"Ben Holladay called a meeting downtown this afternoon," Papa said. "Will is representing us."

"Mr. Holladay? What about?" Both Will and Papa had made their dislike of Mr. Holladay clear.

"There is talk about how the Portland community can hasten the development of the rail line north to Puget Sound," Papa said. "Of course, we don't know where that line will end, so it is difficult to plan. But Holladay thinks he knows something."

"Did Will tell you I still want to write about McDougall & Company?" Maria asked. "Perhaps the new rail line is a reason for me to pursue the topic now."

"Just because you have one feature article soon to be published doesn't mean you should write another immediately," Papa said. But he smiled as he spoke. "I am proud of you, but you should take your direction from Abigail Duniway, not your own desires."

"But Papa—"

"Yes, Will mentioned your intention. I don't think writing about our family business right now is a good idea," Papa said.

"Why not?"

"Will and I will answer your questions about the company's history," Papa said. "But there are things happening that we don't want to make public. We can't discuss current transactions or developments."

"What's so secret?" Maria asked. "Don't you trust me?"

"It is easier if Will and I keep the matter to ourselves," Papa said. "I haven't told Nate what's happening either."

"I bet Amos knows," Maria guessed.

"Amos Higgins knows some of it," Papa said. "But I haven't told him everything." He frowned at Maria. "And that is another reason for me not to tell you. I don't want you telling Higgins—"

Maria opened her mouth to speak.

Papa put up a hand. "The less you know, the easier it will be for you."

Papa's words took some of the glow away from Maria's sense of achievement over her Modoc article. She recalled Papa saying her husband should be open about his business with her, but apparently Papa didn't think that applied to his dealings with his daughter. Not even Will's effusive praise that evening brought back her euphoria from her conversation with Mrs. Duniway.

"I knew you'd get it published," Will said. "Congratulations." He pulled her close and kissed her cheek.

He'd made no romantic overtures in several weeks now, and the kiss surprised Maria. Rather than remark on it, she simply smiled, then asked him about his meeting with Ben Holladay. "What did you learn from Mr. Holladay?"

"Pa doesn't want you writing about the company's current dealings," Will said.

"He told me." She sighed. "I won't submit anything to Mrs. Duniway about McDougall & Company until Papa and you tell me I may, so just tell me what you'd tell Mama or Nate."

"Holladay is fairly certain the rail line from the East will go to Tacoma," Will said. "Which is closer to Portland than Seattle, so that is good for us. He is soliciting funds to complete the spur line from Kalama to Tacoma."

"Hasn't our company invested in that line already?" Maria asked.

"I can't tell you our current investments or our plans," Will said. "We have some money invested in rail developments. But we haven't invested big anywhere—not on the northern line, not on the line to California. We've mostly kept our money around Portland and Oregon City."

"Why is that?" she asked.

Will shrugged. "Ask Pa. He'll tell you if he thinks you should know."

"Do you have to deal with Mr. Holladay?" Maria gave a slight shudder, remembering her meeting with the man.

"Are you sure you told me everything about your meeting with him?" Will asked, frowning.

"I told you as much as you're telling me now," she said. "All you need to know."

As Mrs. Duniway predicted, Robert was back at work on Tuesday. Daisy was in a dither watching him, and Maria had to make up for Daisy's distraction.

On Wednesday morning, Robert handed her a galley of her article. "I thought you might want to see it before we print the whole page."

"How kind of you, Robert!" she said, taking the still damp page. "May I read it?"

"Of course," he said. "But it's too late to make any changes."

That afternoon, Maria ran an errand to *The Oregonian* reporters' office. "Miss McDougall," one man called out. "Did you see our article about the Modoc? They ambushed some settlers last night and shot a rancher. This war ain't over."

"What?" She rushed over to the man's desk. "May I see?"

He handed the morning paper to her. She skimmed the article he pointed at. A band of Modoc had come upon ranchers who had captured several of their fellow tribesmen. When the Modoc warriors tried to free the captives, they killed several whites. She wondered what Mrs. Duniway would do with her article now. "What more do you know?"

He grinned at her. "You'll have to read our paper tomorrow."

"May I have this copy?"

He shrugged. "Why not?"

She took the paper directly to Mrs. Duniway. "Look," she said, waving *The Oregonian* issue. "Have you seen this?"

"Yes," Mrs. Duniway said. "I read it this morning."

"Will you still publish my piece on Friday?"

Mrs. Duniway leaned back in her chair and sighed. "The events this week make it harder to justify your opinion that the Modoc are the victims in this dispute. But the latest skirmish does not change the history between the tribe and the settlers." She frowned at Maria. "Has your opinion changed?"

"No."

"Then we will run your article."

"Thank you, Mrs. Duniway." Maria exhaled and turned to leave.

"This should teach you, however," Mrs. Duniway said. "Being a newspaper writer means you sometimes write without knowing the end of the story. You must come to your convictions strongly enough to hold them, even if events turn against you."

Maria nodded. "Yes, Mrs. Duniway."

"Sometimes," Mrs. Duniway said, with a faraway look in her eye, "we write the story not knowing whether it will ever end. Like my battle over women's suffrage."

"Surely, you will be successful."

"I hope so, Maria. But will it be in my lifetime?"

Chapter 71: What Does Higgins Want?

Maria was on tenterhooks all day Thursday, hoping nothing more would develop that would affect how readers perceived her article. It was too late for Mrs. Duniway to change her mind about publication, because *The New Northwest* was printed on Thursday. But Maria worried events might prove her a fool.

Once Robert had the first copies of the issue, she picked up a copy. "May I take this home?" she asked.

He smiled at her. "Your first big story, Maria? Of course."

She tucked it under her arm and left the newspaper office.

Amos Higgins was waiting for her outside. "Maria," he said, "I came to walk you home."

"How nice, Amos," she said. "I haven't seen much of you recently."

He bowed and offered his arm. "Your father and brother have kept me busy. They have some notion of foul play in California. Have they told you about that?"

She took his arm. "No, they tell me very little about the business. Though I understand there is talk about investing in the railroad with Ben Holladay." She showed him her copy of *The New Northwest*. "Look, I have my first feature article published in tomorrow's edition."

"How wonderful," he said. "What did your father or brother tell you about Ben Holladay's plan?"

"Only that he wants investments in the rail line between Kalama and Puget Sound. But until the Northern Pacific announces where the line will end, he may have trouble finding financiers. Have you heard any more about the railroad?" she asked.

"No, no," he said. "Might we stop for tea or ice before you go home?"

"Well—"

"We must celebrate your achievement," he said, smiling. "Please."

"All right."

He escorted her into a small tea shop nearby. After he ordered tea and two dishes of vanilla ice cream, he smiled and said, "Let me read your article properly." He took the paper from her, then frowned as he read.

"Don't you like it?" she asked.

"You are quite sympathetic toward the Modoc."

"Yes," she said. "My investigation led me to believe the white settlers and the Army have treated the tribe poorly."

"But you must see the progress farmers and ranchers bring to our state. Why, the savages—"

"The Modoc are not savages, Amos," Maria said. "They have different customs. But their way of life suited them for centuries before the Americans arrived."

"Never mind," Amos said, putting down the paper. "We should not argue. I am pleased you have your name in print now."

"Yes," she said. "I have wanted this since I started working on the paper."

"Perhaps now you will turn your mind to other matters."

"Such as?" she asked, smiling at the waitress who set their ice cream in front of them.

"Such as marriage," he said, taking her hand. "I have resisted renewing my proposal, knowing you were focused on your work. But after this milestone—" He pressed her fingers gently. "Will you reconsider? Will you do me the honor of marrying me?"

Maria wondered why he had chosen this setting to ask her again. She could hardly walk away, though she had no more interest in marrying him now than she had when he asked before. "Amos, I—"

"Is it too sudden?" he said. "Do not answer now, then. But give it some thought, please. I want us married soon. As soon as you will have me."

Maria bit her lip and nodded.

Maria was eager to see her article in the stores, so she left for work early on Friday. To her surprise, Amos waited for her on the street outside her home. "Amos," she said, "what are you doing here?"

"I came to walk you to work," he said, offering her his arm as he matched his pace to hers.

"I want to stop by the mercantile near the office," she said. "To buy a copy of the paper."

"You had a print of your article yesterday," he said, smiling. "But you want an extra, don't you?"

"Yes," she said. "I will keep it forever."

He laughed, then said, "Have you thought any further about my proposal?"

"No," she said. Her family's congratulations on her article the evening before hadn't given her any time to think about Amos. "I haven't had a moment alone."

He took her hand. "Please answer me soon, Maria. Because I have thought of nothing other than making you my wife."

"My opinion has not changed, Amos." She tried to pull her hand away, but he clasped it more tightly. "I have no more to say."

"Please rethink your opinion. I am ready to settle into marriage, and you are the woman I love."

"Love?" she said, stopping on the boardwalk. "This is the first you've mentioned love."

"Surely, you must know how dear you are to me." He pressed her fingers. "Men are more reluctant than women to express such emotions. But you are the woman I want to spend my life with."

Did his avowal of love change her opinion? "I will consider what you say," she said. "But I most likely will say no again."

His eyebrow twitched, but he nodded. When they reached the mercantile, he ushered her inside. "Let me buy you a copy of your paper. And I will buy one for myself as well. I, too, treasure your accomplishment."

He paid for the copies while Maria smiled at the compliments from the storeowner's wife. "How courageous you are," the woman said. "You have voiced your opinions most forcefully."

"I hope to persuade the citizens of Portland—" Maria began.

"Well," the woman said, "I don't agree with what you wrote. Not about the Indians. But it is brave of you to take up their cause."

Amos walked Maria to the door of the newspaper office. He kissed the back of her gloved hand, then handed her the paper he'd purchased for her. "Again," he said, "congratulations on your success. And I hope you will give me your answer to my proposal soon."

Once inside the office, Maria put the paper down and sighed as she removed her hat.

"Why the huge sigh?" Daisy asked. "You should be dancing with happiness at your success."

"Oh, I am," Maria said. "At least about the article." She sat next to Daisy and whispered, "Amos proposed again."

"How wonderful!" Daisy clapped her hands. "A second chance. Have you accepted him?"

"No." Maria sighed again. "But I told him I would consider it."

"Do you mean to accept him?"

"No."

"Well, I would if I were you," Daisy declared, pushing her spectacles up her nose. "Amos Higgins has a splendid position and must have a good income."

"But I don't love him."

"Do you love Will?" Daisy asked. "And if you don't love either of them, then which will you accept?"

"I'm not ready to marry either of them," Maria said.

"Why ever not?" Daisy put down her pen and stared at Maria. "You have to marry someone."

"No, I don't," Maria said. "I can live with Mama and Papa as long as I want. Or even find my own rooms in town, though that would require some persuasion on my part."

"But marriage," Daisy said, a faraway look in her eyes. "Your own home. Your own husband and babies. That's what gives a woman security in life."

"Perhaps."

Mrs. Duniway entered the office and came to congratulate Maria. "Your article is the talk of the town, my dear," she said. "I am very proud of you."

"Thank you, Mrs. Duniway," Maria said. "Though the clerk at the mercantile told me she didn't agree with me."

"It doesn't matter if people agree with you," Mrs. Duniway said. "What matters is that you have spoken—and written—your mind. If readers then discuss the issues you raise, you have done your job well."

By Saturday afternoon, Maria could no longer keep Amos's proposal to herself. Mama was busy catering to Grandmère's demands, but Maria pulled her mother aside and asked, "May I speak with you in private?"

"I have only a moment, dear," Mama said. "I have invited some of the older ladies from church over to meet my mother. I am hoping she will make a friend or two to give her other people in Portland to socialize with."

"This shouldn't take long," Maria said.

After they settled in Mama's morning room, Maria blurted, "Amos proposed again."

"My goodness," Mama said. "What did you tell him?"

"I didn't know what to say," Maria confessed. "I told him no before. But he caught me by surprise and pressed me. So, I told him I'd think about it."

"Are you considering him seriously?" Mama asked, seeming surprised.

"No," Maria said. "But he is persistent. He walked me to work this morning."

"Without coming in to greet your father or me first?" Mama said, her eyebrows rising.

"He says he wants us to marry soon."

"There is no reason to accept him, and certainly no reason for urgency," Mama said, pressing Maria's hand. "You have a home with us. You do not need to marry, as some women do."

"That's what I told Amos," Maria said. "And Daisy. But Daisy thinks all women should marry. She hopes to marry Robert, but she would take almost any man, even if she didn't love him."

"Daisy is in a very different position than you are. Daisy and her mother are responsible for raising younger children, and they have little money. If she and Robert decide to marry, she will have a good man who will help her with her family. You have no need of anything from a husband, other than his love, respect, and fidelity."

Maria thought. Would Amos give her those things? Did it even matter if he would? "I don't want to marry Amos," she said. "I respect him, but I don't love him."

"Then tell him no," Mama said, pressing her hand again. "But be sure of how you feel. Because when you talk to him, you should be definite. Do not give him false hope. When you reject him, you don't want him asking again."

Chapter 72: Rumors About Railroads

On the evening of Monday, June 16, Will sat in a smoky private room at the St. Charles Hotel with Ben Holladay and several other Portland businessmen. Holladay's invitation specified he wanted to discuss the future of railroads connecting to Portland.

When Will arrived, Holladay bellowed, "Just you? Where's your father? Where's Higgins?"

Will was surprised at the mention of Higgins, but he replied only, "My father still tires easily after his accident. He rarely goes out in the evening. I will certainly tell him of this evening's developments."

During the meal, Holladay expounded at length about the need for more rail lines both around Portland and between Portland and other towns. "And the Northern Pacific will end somewhere in the Puget Sound area," he said. "They have not declared where the western terminus will be, but the railroad's owners and board members are buying up land around Tacoma."

"How do you know that?" another man asked.

Holladay puffed his cigar, then grinned. "I make it my business to know."

"The line on the Washington Territory side of the Columbia starts in Kalama and heads north toward Tacoma already, doesn't it?" Will asked. "Surely, someone must have some reason to think it will end there."

Holladay grinned again. "Someone must."

After the hotel waiters cleared away the meal and left the men to their brandy and port, Holladay leaned forward and said, "And now, gentlemen, it is time for civic-minded citizens of Portland to declare our support for the rail lines. We must put together sufficient capital to sway the Northern Pacific—and the California railroads as well—to hurry their rail construction to connect our city to the rest of the nation."

"What do you have in mind, Holladay?" someone called from the far end of the table.

"We must build our own rail conglomerate." Holladay pounded the table. "Those of us present this evening have the funds to influence decisions in Washington. We cannot let the Eastern tycoons push us around."

"How much will it take?" Will asked.

"If each of us around this table put in fifty thousand dollars—" Holladay began.

"That's seven and a half million dollars!" came a cry from someone. "Why, we could buy a fleet of steamships for that."

"But steamships won't get us into Eastern markets," Holladay said. "And what I'm asking from you is only a fraction of the cost of tying into the Northern Pacific line. Other communities will also seek to become rail hubs. But we in Portland must become the biggest hub between San Francisco and Puget Sound. We need spur lines to transport our timber and grain to the East Coast—that's why I need your commitment. If Oregon doesn't get a rail connection to the East soon, California will take all the profits."

"Fifty thousand is a lot of money," Will said.

Holladay pointed his cigar at Will. "Surely, McDougall & Company can raise the funds."

Will felt put on the spot. He couldn't commit without talking to Pa. "I'll talk to my father—"

"I thought you were past your leading strings, boy," Holladay sneered. "Are you sure you belong at this table?"

Will stifled the urge to clench his fists. He had to follow Pa's lead. "My father and I discuss all major investments. This certainly qualifies as major."

The conversation continued, though Holladay ignored Will for the rest of the meal. As the party broke up, however, Holladay called Will over for a private word. "Your man Higgins has invested his own funds with me," he told Will. "A substantial sum, though not enough yet to be a full partner in my conglomerate. He told me he could raise the entire fifty thousand. He also said McDougall & Company would contribute the same to become another full partner. Have you not talked to Higgins?"

Higgins had said nothing to Will about investing in railroads. Given what Noah Pershing had told Will, he was surprised Higgins had raised enough money to court Ben Holladay's favor. And if Pa was aware of Higgins's investments, he would have told Will. "I'll involve Higgins in the conversation with my father," Will said. "But Higgins cannot speak for our family—only my father and I can. Higgins speaks only for himself."

As soon as he got home, Will went to find Pa, who sat in his library reading. "Not in bed yet, Pa?"

"Almost, son." Pa shut his book and asked, "How was the meeting?"

"Full of surprises." Will sat across from Pa. "Holladay is a pompous ass, isn't he?"

Pa grinned. "A braggart and a sly dog. But he has done a lot for Portland. His purpose is to line his own pockets, perhaps, but the city still benefits."

"He's planning a syndicate to invest in railroads, this time to connect Portland with the Northern Pacific. And he seems confident the line will end in Tacoma."

Pa nodded. "That's what I have heard as well."

"A full partnership will cost us fifty thousand dollars."

Pa whistled.

"And he says Higgins is also raising the funds to be a partner. Separate from McDougall & Company."

Pa's mouth gaped. "Amos Higgins?"

"Yes. Where does Higgins get that kind of money?"

"I have no idea." Pa swore. "Unless he thinks he'll get it from me by marrying Maria. He proposed to her again."

"What?" Will jumped to his feet. "She wouldn't . . . . You wouldn't. . . ."

"No, I wouldn't." Pa said. "I might make Maria and Amos a gift if they marry. But I would tie it up, so she is protected. This venture of Holladay's is speculative at best. No place for Maria's funds. All his ventures are risky—and often more of a risk to his partners than to him."

"I thought Maria turned Higgins down."

"She did. But he might still hope to persuade her."

That would never happen. Or so Will hoped. Pa's response that he'd tie up any wedding gift didn't satisfy Will, but there was no use arguing that point until Maria accepted the man. "So, what do you think we should do about Holladay's request?" he asked.

Pa shrugged. "I'm not inclined to give him fifty thousand dollars. My experience in California was that the men supplying goods to the miners made more than the miners themselves. I suspect the same will be true now.

Let others build the railroads—our company is better off serving the rail workers." He looked Will in the eye. "And I think you should go to Tacoma to buy land suitable for a warehouse."

"You don't think we should invest at all with Holladay?"

"I didn't say that. I think we should make a small investment. Enough to stay informed about what Holladay is doing. But not enough to bankrupt our company if his enterprise is a failure."

"And how will we know where to buy in Tacoma? Or if Tacoma is even the terminus of the Northern Pacific."

Pa chuckled. "You're smart enough to figure that out. You've wanted a role in the family business. Dealing with our expansion in Tacoma is a start."

Will left the library determined to find out whether Higgins had any source of funds other than his prospects if he married Maria. He didn't like Higgins, and he didn't want to think Maria had been duped by a scoundrel.

Tuesday morning, Will walked into the dining room to find Maria eating breakfast with some of the younger children. "Aren't you off to the newspaper?" he asked her.

"In a bit," she said, seeming distracted.

"Congratulations again on getting your article published," he said, helping himself to several slices of bacon and a pile of scrambled eggs. He sat next to her. "Please pass the salt."

She passed him the pepper shaker.

He grinned. "I asked for the salt, please." He took the other shaker when she handed it to him. "What's wrong with you?" Could she still be considering Higgins?

"Just a lot on my mind." She took a bite of toast, then put the bread on her plate and sipped her coffee.

"Pa thinks I should go to Tacoma."

"Hmm." She sipped the coffee again and pushed her plate away.

"If you're not going to eat that toast, may I have it?" he asked.

She pushed the plate toward him.

"Aren't you going to ask me why Pa wants me in Tacoma?"

"You and Papa never tell me anything," she said. "Why would today be any different?"

"But you keep asking." Will frowned. "What's wrong, Maria?"

"Just a lot on my mind," she said again. And she wouldn't say more.

Will needed to get to work, but immediately after breakfast he went to find his mother.

"Mama?" he said, knocking on her morning room door, then entering. "What's wrong with Maria?"

"I swear," Mama said, looking up from the menus she was writing. "If my mother doesn't find something to do with her time, I might have to run away from home again."

"What has Grandmère done now?" Will asked, sitting in a chair near Mama's desk.

"She has decided none of my linens are adequate, and I must buy new. I hemmed all the sheets we have within the last five years. And Maria, Eliza, and Lottie embroidered all the pillowcases. I cannot throw those out. They are perfectly suitable."

"Perhaps you can distract her," Will said.

Mama sighed. "I'm sorry to vent my frustrations on you. My *maman* has always wanted new and better, even when she did not have the money to spend. Now she wants to spend my money."

"Was your father like her?" Will asked.

"He liked nice things," Mama said, smiling. "But I don't think he noticed when his sheets and towels frayed. He was more interested in his books." Then she frowned at Will. "What did you need from me?"

"Everything, Mama," Will said, leaning over to kiss her cheek. "But specifically, I wondered why Maria seems so out of sorts. Is it Higgins?"

Mama's frown deepened. "I don't know if I should tell you. She got mad at me the last time—"

Will muttered a curse.

"Why are you surprised?" Mama asked. "Amos has been pursuing her for the better part of a year."

"But she told him no."

Mama sighed. "He's a persistent man."

Will wondered if he should have been more persistent with Maria. "How did she respond?"

"She told him she'll think about it."

"Why? She rejected him the last time." Will frowned. "Has Pa told you about Higgins's involvement with Ben Holladay?"

"Mr. Holladay?" Mama stared at him in surprise. "What is Amos doing with Ben Holladay?"

"Holladay says Higgins has invested in his latest railroad scheme. Holladay wants McDougall & Company to be a partner in the project as well. But according to Holladay, Higgins made a substantial individual investment. And Pa and I don't know where he's getting the funds." Will paused. "Pa thinks he's counting on getting money from us if he marries Maria."

"Oh, dear," Mama murmured. "Do you think he'd really do that?"

"I don't know," Will said. "Pa and I haven't decided how much to invest. But I don't want Maria's money to be tied up with Holladay. Even if she marries Higgins, she needs the protection of funds set aside for her in something conservative."

"Surely, your father will see to that."

"Yes," Will said. "Pa will protect Maria. But perhaps Higgins has other ideas." He touched Mama's arm. "Please, Mama, tell Maria to be careful. I'll tell her, too, but she'll pay more attention to you."

Chapter 73: More from Jack

Will watched for an opportunity to talk to Maria about Higgins's renewed proposal. He didn't know what he would say, but somehow he had to warn her away from Higgins without it looking like sour grapes on his part.

On Thursday evening, June 19, when Will returned home from the office, he found a letter from Jack waiting for him. He took it to his room and tore it open.

June 13, 1873

Dear Will,

I have much to report, though it is mostly rumor, and I ain't got many facts to back it up. First, there's an old man by the name of Jackson in the warehouse here in San Francisco. He used to work in the Sacramento warehouse, but moved to San Francisco at Beck's request. I've taken to having a beer with him after work some evenings. Last night, Jackson told me he'd heard Beck kept a second set of books in Sacramento. He records purchases and sales and movement of goods that ain't shown in the ledgers he writes his reports from. Jackson suspicions Beck now does the same thing in San Francisco. The old man was in his cups when we talked, but he seemed pretty sure.

I asked why he was so sure, and he said because the gold you and I seen in the San Francisco warehouse ain't on the official ledgers. I questioned him about how an old warehouseman would know this, and Jackson said his son-in-

law works in the accounting office. Jackson asked him how much the gold was worth. His son-in-law snooped around, then told him there ain't no gold listed in the inventory log.

I'll look for a second ledger, but I don't get much time in the office, being stuck in the warehouse most of the time.

Second, I hear tell Beck wired Higgins on Tuesday last, the 10th. Jackson heard Beck tell a delivery boy to take it right quick to the telegraph office. Jackson heard Beck say it was to a Mr. Higgins in Portland, and it needed to get sent that day. And he told the boy he shouldn't say nothing to no one. I don't know what the telegram said—Jackson ain't heard nothing about that.

I hope this is the kind of information you want from me. I wish I could be more specific, but I don't hear much from the warehouse. And I don't know the men in the office who work with Beck.

I'll write again if I learn more.

My love to Mama,

> *Jack*

Will read the letter again, then showed it to Pa. "We need to get a man in the front office in San Francisco," Pa said.

"But who? And how quickly can we make that happen?" Will asked. "I should tear the Portland office apart, looking for whatever Higgins might have from Beck that we haven't seen."

"I don't think Higgins would keep anything at the office," Pa said, rubbing his chin. "Most likely, Beck sends the telegrams to Higgins's lodging. And we can't get in there."

"Do you agree now, Pa, there's reason to suspect Higgins? And to stop Maria from marrying him?"

"There's reason to investigate further." Pa looked at Jack's letter again. "But Jack admits he only has rumors about both Beck and Higgins. Is Beck working alone? Is Higgins in cahoots with Beck in keeping the gold and other assets off the official ledgers? Are the two of them involved in some side business? Or is it something totally innocuous?"

"We know Higgins needs money to invest with Holladay," Will said.

"But that doesn't mean he's stealing," Pa argued. "Maybe he is. Or maybe he and Beck have another venture on the side. I wouldn't be happy with either man if that's the case—I want them focused on McDougall business. But working two jobs isn't illegal."

Will didn't see any innocent reason for Higgins and Beck to be communicating in secret. "I'll look through Higgins's office again."

Pa glared at Will. "Don't make a scene, son. Don't alert Higgins we have new suspicions."

"We have to tell Maria what's going on," Will said, ignoring Pa's admonition. "We can't let her entertain his proposal. Not now, and not ever."

Will and Pa agreed that McDougall & Company would contribute up to ten thousand dollars to the rail enterprise, but only after the announcement of where the western terminus of the Northern Pacific line would be. "I don't want to finance a rail line to nowhere," Pa told Will. "And I'd prefer we invest our dollars in the Portland area on lines that will be useful no matter where the Northern Pacific builds."

"Shall I tell Holladay that?" Will said.

"Yes," Pa said. "Set up another meeting with him and try to do it quickly."

"Do you still want me to go to Tacoma?" Will asked. "If so, I'll need to get a ticket soon."

"Yes, I want to know what's happening in Tacoma," Pa said. "I may not want to put a lot of money into railroads. But we know how to buy and sell goods people want. If men are investing in land in Tacoma and the area will grow in population, we could open a branch there. Or Seattle. You might look at that town as well, while you're in Washington Territory."

"It sounds like I could be away for several weeks," Will said. "I'd rather be closer to home, so I can see Jack's correspondence as soon as it arrives."

"Tell Jack to communicate with me in your absence," Pa said. "And while you're away, I'll open any mail he sends you."

Will met with Holladay on the morning of Monday, June 23, and passed along the McDougall & Company position.

"I'm disappointed in your family, McDougall," Holladay said. "Particularly given what Higgins told me. He said you'd readily support my investments."

"Higgins is an accountant," Will told the rail baron. "He does not speak for McDougall & Company on strategic matters."

"He is also an investor in his own right," Holladay said.

"Has he fully funded his investment?" Will asked, wondering if Higgins had come up with the money he'd been lacking the week before.

"Not yet," Holladay said. "But he promises it soon."

"Has he said where he'll get his funds?"

Holladay laughed. "If he had, I wouldn't tell you. It ain't none of your business where Higgins gets his money, as long as he ain't stealing from you. Is he?"

Will grinned. "I wouldn't tell you if he were. Would you tell me?"

Will bought his ticket to Tacoma at the dock, then went to McDougall & Company and then went to see Higgins in his office. "Pa is sending me north next week," Will told the accountant. "Is there anything you think I should know before I leave?"

"Why north?" Higgins asked. "Is this to check out the Tacoma situation?"

"Yes," Will said. "We told Holladay we won't make a large investment in his venture now, though we will invest enough to stay in the discussions."

Higgins grimaced and scratched his temple. "That's a mistake. If you're not in at the beginning, McDougall & Company stands to lose influence in the development of both Oregon and Washington."

"What about you?" Will asked. "I hear you are investing."

"I will do what I can," Higgins said. "I take a long view of railroad development in the area, as I thought your father did. But unlike him, I will sacrifice now to get in on the ground floor with Holladay."

"You must have made earlier investments that panned out to have funds to give Holladay now," Will commented.

Higgins shrugged. "I've done well here at McDougall & Company. And I am grateful to your father for that. Plus, my mother's uncle left me a small inheritance."

"Bully for you," Will said. There was no way to verify whether Higgins had received an inheritance, as he claimed. "Have you heard from Beck recently?"

Higgins shook his head. "Not a word since his last report. Shall I wire him to ask for an update?"

"No need," Will said, sure the accountant was lying. "We'll hear soon enough."

"Have you heard anything from your uncle Jack?" Higgins asked, examining his fingernails.

"He writes me occasionally," Will said. "But he has said nothing noteworthy." If Higgins was going to lie, then so would Will.

That evening, Will found Maria and asked her to join him in Mama's morning room. "Of course," she said, smiling. She brought her knitting and took it out of her bag once she was seated.

"I hear Amos Higgins proposed to you again," Will said.

"Yes," Maria said, continuing to knit.

"You must turn him down," Will said.

She raised her eyebrows as she stared at him. "I thought you said you'd dance at my wedding."

Will knelt beside her and took her hand. "I want you to be happy, Maria, but there are things you should know about Higgins."

She frowned and pulled her hand away. "I've been asking you for months to tell me what's going on at McDougall & Company, and you've refused."

"I'll tell you." On the spot, Will decided to tell Maria everything—she needed to know to keep her away from Higgins. He stood and paced. "Pa and I suspect Higgins is stealing from us."

Maria gasped.

"Admittedly, we don't have any firm proof. But there are rumors both here and in California that there are two sets of books. Cassidy told us that when he was here."

"Is that why you met with Mr. Cassidy in Oregon City?" she asked.

Will nodded. "And Jack and I met with him again in California last month. But we have found nothing to verify Cassidy's claims." He paced another length of the small room. "Zhuang Li suspects the same thing here in Portland."

"How can Amos be involved in keeping a second set of books in California?" Maria asked. "He doesn't know what's happening there except what the branch managers tell him."

"I think Higgins and Beck are in it together," Will told her. "We can't prove anything. But while this is pending, you shouldn't accept Higgins's offer."

"I'd already decided against it," Maria said. "I won't marry Amos."

"Will you promise me that?"

"I won't promise you anything. I'm telling you—I don't love Amos, and I won't marry him."

Relief filled Will's heart. "Thank goodness for that."

"Now," she said. "What evidence do you have that Amos and Beck are stealing?"

Will told her what was in Jack's letter, as well as what Cassidy had said months earlier. "But you can't print any of this in the newspaper," he said. "We have no proof, and at this point, it would be libelous. But I trust you, Maria."

Chapter 74: What About Love?

On Wednesday, June 25, Maria accompanied Papa and Nate to see Will board the steamship for Tacoma. As they rode to the docks in the carriage, Papa gave Will lengthy instructions about the prospects he might find for the family business in the Puget Sound area.

"Keep your eyes and ears open," Papa told Will. "If it looks like the Northern Pacific will not end in Tacoma, but elsewhere, head to that location and see what property might be available at a reasonable price. Our goal is to profit from rail traffic."

"Yes, Pa." Will rolled his eyes at Maria with a grin. "I evaluated lots of parcels in Boston with Uncle Owen. I can handle this."

Papa clapped him on the shoulder. "I'm sorry, son. It's hard for me to give up control. I wish I could go with you."

Before he boarded the boat, Will hugged Maria and said to her quietly, "Take care, Maria. Remember, I want only your happiness. But watch out for Higgins. Whether or not he's stealing, I don't think he means our family well." Then he shook hands with Papa and Nate and carried his bags up the gangplank.

Maria was surprised at the lump in her throat as she waved goodbye to Will. He'd been away for so many years in Boston, and she had adjusted. Why did his travels now affect her so deeply?

"Come, Maria," Papa said. "Nate and I will drop you at the newspaper office on our way to work."

That afternoon as she walked home, Maria fretted about her conversation with Will earlier in the week, as well as his parting comment to her that morning. Was Amos Higgins a thief? What did he want from their family? And from her?

It was time to give Amos a firm answer to his proposal. She would not marry him. She could not marry him. She should never have agreed to even consider it again. But she'd been flustered when he confronted her in the tea shop and then pressed her again outside her home.

Maria also decided she should tell Papa that Will had talked to her about the possible thefts from McDougall & Company. It didn't feel right that she had the information, and Papa didn't know. Plus, she wanted more specifics. She would promise Papa that she wouldn't publish any articles until he gave her permission to do so, but she wanted the details.

That evening after supper, Maria followed Papa into his library. "May I speak with you, Papa?"

He glanced at Nate, who had also followed him. "Maybe tomorrow night, son." Then he turned to Maria and said, "Of course, my dear."

Papa poured himself whiskey. "Would you like sherry, Maria?"

"No, thank you, Papa," she said as she took a seat. She rarely drank spirits, and she needed a clear head to speak now.

"Is this a personal matter or are you going to interview me about the business again?" he asked with a smile.

"Some of both."

He sat near her. "Go ahead."

"First," she said slowly, "You know Amos proposed to me again."

Papa frowned. "I thought you told the blackguard off."

"Why do you call him a blackguard?" she asked, puzzled. "I thought you liked Amos."

"He's been an excellent accountant, or so I thought," Papa said. "But lately I have had reason to question some of his actions and motives."

"Then Will was right," Maria said.

"Will? Right about what?" Papa asked.

"Will told me he suspected Amos and perhaps others were stealing from McDougall & Company."

"I told Will to keep you out of it." Papa sounded angry.

"He meant well in telling me," Maria said. "He wanted to protect me from

Amos."

"Well, I do, too." Papa rubbed his forehead. "But Will and I agreed the best way to protect you was to leave you out of it."

"Don't blame Will."

Papa sighed. "I don't. But you can't accept Higgins. Not now."

"No," Maria said. "I'd already decided to reject him completely. I don't love him, and I don't like the way he pushes me to change my mind."

Papa set down his glass and took her hand. "You will tell me if he tries to intimidate you, won't you? I won't have him frightening you."

"I will tell you," Maria said. "I mean to refuse him as soon as I can, and I will let you know when I do."

"Why don't you come to his office?" Papa suggested. "That way, there will be men around you can trust. Me. Nate. Zhuang Li. Anyone at the firm would surely keep you from harm. And Higgins is less likely to make a scene at his place of work."

Maria didn't think Amos would physically harm her, but Papa's idea made sense. Amos might get angry and shout. "All right," she said. "I will visit him at work tomorrow afternoon." She smiled. "Now, what will you tell me about the suspected theft?"

Papa frowned.

"I promise I will not give any information to Abigail Duniway or anyone else outside the family until you tell me I may," she said. "But I think the story of how our family business grew would inspire many Oregonians— the decisions you made through the years, the crossroads we find ourselves at now—all of it."

It took a little more persuading, but Papa at least answered her questions about the past, even if he wouldn't go into any detail about the current problems.

The next afternoon, after she finished her work at *The New Northwest*, Maria walked to the McDougall & Company offices. She entered the building, nodded at the clerk nearest the door, and headed for Amos's office. She stopped at Nate's desk and greeted him. He grinned at her. "Take care, sister." So Papa had told Nate about her purpose. She smiled at him and continued down the hall, also nodding at Zhuang Li as she passed his desk.

Her hands trembled, and her legs were weak. She was glad Nate and Zhuang Li had seen her—if Amos became angry, they would hear. Papa's office door was open, but she didn't look in before knocking on Amos's door next to Papa's.

When she heard him say, "Come in," she entered.

"Amos? May we talk?" Her heart beat harder as she spoke.

He frowned, then his face cleared. "Why, Maria, what a pleasant surprise." He escorted her to a chair in the corner, then sat in another chair beside her. "To what do I owe this honor?"

"I have your answer," she said bluntly. "I will not marry you. And I ask that you no longer pay me any attentions of that sort."

If he had frowned before, now he glowered. "That saddens me, Maria. I had every hope—"

"I have given you no reason to hope," she said. "Not since I refused you before." She rose.

He stood as well, blocking her exit from the office. "I wish you would reconsider."

"I will not change my mind," she said. "Please excuse me."

He paused for a moment, and she feared he would start shouting. But he stepped aside and let her go.

Maria looked inside Papa's office, but he was not there. She nodded at Nate as she walked past his desk. "All is well?" he asked.

She smiled. "All is well."

She left the building and headed down the boardwalk toward home. Her hands still trembled. She was relieved the encounter with Amos was behind her, but now she wanted only to hide in her room for the evening. Or to talk to Will, but he was gone.

Maria compared Amos's new reaction to her refusal to Will's. Will had been disappointed she hadn't accepted him on the spot. He pouted at first, but now he told her he only wanted her to be happy. By contrast, Amos had been furious this afternoon.

If Will were here, he would cheer her up—he usually did. He often knew what she was thinking, even before she told him. He was always the one she wanted to talk to first after any crisis. He understood her. She loved that about him, as she loved so many things.

She loved him.

At that thought, Maria stopped suddenly on the boardwalk. She loved Will, and he loved her. She respected him, and his behavior in recent weeks had shown he respected her as well.

She remembered cuddling with him on the train home from Oregon City, the comfort he'd given her. She thought again of his kisses. Both gentle and passionate. Her body warmed, even more than the summer sun warmed her.

She wanted his comfort. She wanted his kisses. He could make her happy, and he said she would make him happy as well. He had offered marriage. All she had to do was accept. Was she ready to do so?

Yes, she thought. Yes. She wanted to spend her life with him.

Chapter 75: Exploring Tacoma

By the time the ship passed the mouth of the Columbia River, the rough seas off the Olympic Peninsula, and the currents of Puget Sound, the steamboat trip to Tacoma took the better part of two days. Will had plenty of time to reflect on his conversation with Maria.

He'd done his best to convince her to reject Higgins. Despite the lack of hard evidence, Will was convinced the accountant was stealing. He also believed Higgins wanted to marry Maria only to get money from Pa.

But beyond his suspicions of Higgins, Will didn't believe Maria could be happy with the man. Higgins displayed a certain indifference and arrogance toward the office staff. Such behavior would surely spill over into his personal relationships. It would destroy Will to see Maria suffer at the hands of her husband.

Whether Maria married Will was of less importance now than keeping her from marrying Higgins. Though once she rejected Higgins, Will would certainly renew his efforts to win her. He'd told Maria about the McDougall & Company business problems not only to dissuade her from considering Higgins but also to show his confidence and trust in her.

When he'd arrived in Portland, Will had wanted Maria because she was beautiful and had been his best friend during childhood. He'd assumed she would be the same the girl he'd always known. But over the last several months, he'd discovered how she'd matured—through her work at the newspaper, her concern over Zhuang Li, her support of Mama in caring for the rest of the family. Maria deserved happiness, and Will aspired to be the man to make her happy. He wanted to earn her trust and love.

But first, Will had to figure out where Tacoma might fit in the McDougall business. He believed the company needed to prepare for the future of railroads. Soon, rails would connect the Pacific Northwest to the rest of the nation. The Pacific Northern Railroad line would be as significant to Western development as the completion of the first transcontinental line.

Indeed, Will thought, the rail connection would be as monumental as the blazing of the Oregon Trail over a quarter century earlier. Already, the railroad to California had reduced the importance of the Trail. Wagons took four to six months. Via rail, traveling the same distance could take as little as six days.

Pa believed the McDougalls should not be major investors in the railroads themselves. He believed the company should support the men who constructed the lines, who settled at the stations along the way. The first step in expanding that vision was an investment in Tacoma, and he'd made Will responsible for deciding the family's place in that city. Will hoped Pa would accept his recommendations—Pa's comments on the dock in Portland showed he still fretted about ceding control to Will.

The steamship arrived in Tacoma in late afternoon on Thursday, June 26. As the boat docked at the wharf and passengers disembarked, Will scanned the shoreline. The town on the edge of Commencement Bay was a small frontier settlement. It smelled brackish from a large marshy area south of the wharf. Much of the bay frontage was undeveloped, but scattered buildings rose on a bluff above the shore. From what Will could see, the town was only a few blocks deep. The population couldn't be more than a hundred people.

Once Will was on dry land, he asked a dockhand where he could find a hotel.

"The Steele Hotel is all we got," the man said. He nodded toward a two-story building nearby.

Will took his bag and walked toward the hotel. His observations of the sparsely settled township did not improve his assessment of Tacoma's commercial potential. The streets near the wharf were little more than muddy tracks. Both Portland and Oregon City were many times bigger than this pioneer town.

The Steele Hotel was a simple wooden building, plain boards on the outside, no shutters on the windows. Will climbed the stairs of a small porch, went through the door, and set down his bag. The interior seemed clean, though as plain as the outside. A clerk stood behind a tall desk in the corner, and Will asked, "Do you have a room available for a few weeks?"

The man nodded. "One room left. It's small. Dollar a night, five dollars a week."

"I'm sure it will be fine," Will said.

The clerk turned a registry book toward Will. "Where you from?"

"Portland." Will signed the registry.

The clerk handed Will a key and gestured to the dining room in back. "Breakfast and supper included. Supper is served at six on the dot."

Will grinned. "Then I'm in time to eat tonight?"

"Yes, sir."

Will found his room on the second floor, washed at the bowl in a corner, then returned to the main level to eat. Five or six other men waited as well. Will introduced himself, and he learned most of the men were in Tacoma because of lumbering or shipping. One well-dressed gentleman named Thomas Mitchell said he was looking at land in the area, but he was close-mouthed about his purpose. Will decided to remain silent about his own interests until he learned more.

After the meal, which was plain but adequate, Will returned to his room. As he settled in for the night, he wondered what Maria was doing that evening. Had she rejected Higgins yet? If not, when would she? Will took out a pen and paper and wrote:

> *June 26, 1873*
> *Dear Maria,*
>
> *I am registered at the Steele Hotel in Tacoma, and I hope you and the family will write. I do not know how long I shall be here, but the town at first glance offers little in the way of amenities. Perhaps there is an opportunity for McDougall & Company, but I cannot yet say.*
>
> *This next is meant only for you, dear Maria. I hope you will send Amos Higgins packing for all the reasons I gave you. Of course, I am biased by my deep affection for you, which I hope you will return in time. In any case, my dear, please give your heart only to a man who warrants it. I fear Higgins is not that man. And I pray that I am.*
>
> *Will*

The next morning, Will was downstairs for breakfast not long after dawn, which came early so soon after the summer solstice. The only other man at the table was Thomas Mitchell.

"You said last night you were looking at land," Will said. "What do you plan to use the land for?"

"Whatever makes me a profit."

"Tacoma seems an unlikely place for any business establishment," Will said, helping himself to another slice of ham from the platter on the table.

"We shall see, young man," Mitchell said with a grin.

Taking a guess that Mitchell's purpose was similar to his own, Will asked, "Do you think the railroad will put its terminus here?"

Mitchell's eyes widened. "What have you heard?"

Will shrugged. "The railroad will end somewhere on Puget Sound. I assume Tacoma is a possibility."

Mitchell's lips narrowed. "I couldn't say."

Will wouldn't get anything more out of the man, so he finished his breakfast and headed out to inspect the town. He returned to the wharf, thinking land close to the dock would be best for a warehouse. He was surprised to find little development near the docks. There was a grain mill, but not much else.

Of course, he did not know where the railroad would put its station, assuming the terminus would in fact be in Tacoma. He could only speculate.

The air was dank, even in late June. Tacoma was even more overgrown with vegetation than the undeveloped portions of Portland. But when the clouds lifted, the majestic Mount Tahoma, much larger than Mount Hood, dominated every vista to the east.

Will found an undeveloped field a block inland from the grain mill. It was on a bluff above the wharf, but the field itself was flat and large enough to build a warehouse. He wondered how to find out who owned it.

Will returned to the hotel and asked the clerk where land records were kept. "You might try the post office," the man said. "Job Carr's the postmaster. He was the first settler in these parts. Used to own a lotta land 'round here."

After getting directions, Will found the post office in a small wooden house. A man sat rocking on the porch and smoking a pipe. "Are you Job Carr?" Will asked.

"I am."

"I'm William McDougall. I saw a field near the grain mill, and I wondered who owns it."

"Which field might that be?" Carr puffed his pipe.

Will described the land as best he could. Carr got to his feet slowly, and said, "Might be we should have a look."

The two men walked through the muddy streets, Carr gnawing on the end of his pipe. When they passed the mill, Will pointed out the parcel.

"That land ain't for sale," Carr said. "A speculator bought it recently."

Disappointed, Will asked, "Do you know of any flat fields for sale that aren't too far from the wharf? My family operates warehouses, among other endeavors. We might expand into Tacoma."

"Why here?" Carr's eyes narrowed and he bit his pipe.

"We have a branch in California already. It only makes sense to expand north of Portland next."

"Not till there's a railroad, it don't," Carr said.

"The Northern Pacific Railroad is coming to Puget Sound," Will said.

"They ain't said where they's gonna build. What you hearing?"

"I've only heard rumors," Will said. "Nothing certain."

"This piece ain't for sale." Carr clamped his teeth over his pipe stem.

Carr had been no help. Will spent the rest of the day traipsing through Tacoma, but no other sites appealed to him.

On Saturday evening, June 28, after another fruitless day searching for property in Tacoma, Will sat at the supper table, again with Thomas Mitchell.

"Why such a glum face?" Mitchell asked.

"I was hoping to find land for a warehouse near the dock," Will said. "But the only place I liked isn't available, according to Job Carr."

Mitchell guffawed. "Carr would know. He used to own half the town. He came to Tacoma in sixty-four and filed a land claim. Since then, he's sold most of it. Now he's like the rest of us—waiting to hear what the Northern Pacific will do."

"What's your interest?" Will asked.

Mitchell glanced around at the other diners. "Let's have a drink after dinner. I'll tell you what I can."

When the meal was over, the two men took their whiskey glasses to a small table by the fire. A fire in late June. Will shook his head as he settled into a chair. But the heat was welcome in the damp air.

Once they were seated, he asked Mitchell, "What's your business here?"

"Tell me more about your operation in Portland first," Mitchell said. "It might be we could partner well together, but I can't disclose what I know unless I see a possible connection."

Will gave him an overview of McDougall & Company—Pa's Boston origins, the California operation Pa started after the Gold Rush, the later expansion into Oregon, where Portland was now the Western headquarters. "We are mostly a supplier and exporter of merchandise with warehouses in Portland, San Francisco, and Sacramento," he said in summary. "Though my father also invests in steamboats and railroads, when the opportunity seems right. And he's lent money to farmers and merchants in Oregon as well. Most of them are families he met when traveling the Oregon Trail."

"We might have interests in common," Mitchell said, adding in a hushed voice, "I represent the board members of the Northern Pacific owners."

Will raised his eyebrows—Mitchell must know the railroad's plans. "I see."

"I am scouting a site for the railroad terminus building, and I am also seeking amenities for the railroad in Tacoma—"

"Then Tacoma will be the terminus," Will said.

Mitchell shrugged off Will's conclusion without responding to it. "We have not decided on the exact site. I'm not satisfied that the current town location can suit our needs. I think the station should be south of town."

"South? But don't you want to be near the wharf?" Will asked.

Mitchell shook his head. "Not the existing wharf. It can't handle bigger steamboats. One amenity the Northern Pacific will need is a new wharf. A deepwater wharf."

"And you think a suitable wharf can be built south of town?"

"Ain't decided yet." Mitchell squinted at Will. "Would you like to inspect the area with me tomorrow?"

"Of course," Will said. He wondered whether he could trust Mitchell or whether the man was another flimflam speculator like Holladay.

"Obviously," Mitchell said, "I am talking to you in confidence. But for the railroad to be successful, there will need to be warehouses to store the goods transported between sea and rails. We could develop a profitable partnership."

"I cannot make any commitments on partnership yet," Will said. "But I am happy to inspect land with you to determine if there is a location that would benefit us both."

Early Sunday morning, the muddy streets of Tacoma were empty. The bell of a small church tolled as Will and Mitchell left the Steele Hotel. They rented horses at the only livery in town, then rode south along the cliff above Commencement Bay until they reached a flat area above the water.

"Water's deep out there," Mitchell said, pointing at the bay. "A wharf here could accommodate large ships."

Will looked around. The cliff where they stood would need a road down the hill to the water. It was steep, but it could be done. But this location would only make sense if both a wharf and the railroad terminus were nearby.

"But who would build the wharf?" Will asked. "Will the Northern Pacific Railroad handle construction, or would you want another operator to run the shipping operation?"

Mitchell shrugged. "We haven't decided how much the Northern Pacific will take on. Our first priority is the rail line. We are committed to building the line to Tacoma, as well as connecting it to the line from Kalama."

"What would you want from partners at this stage?" Will asked. He would have to write Pa about Mitchell's proposal, and he wanted to be clear on the railroad's expectations.

"All we seek now is a commitment to build a warehouse near the terminus building. We would need to work out details, such as how much inventory your enterprise can handle. If you're interested, I will contact my principals about the level of investment we would expect."

"I will contact my father about the possibility of working with you," Will responded. "McDougall & Company would also seek certain guarantees of volume to make our operation profitable."

Will returned to his room and wrote Pa a long letter. He described Mitchell's prediction the Northern Pacific terminal would be located south of Tacoma, the need for a deepwater wharf and warehouses nearby, and the probable need for an investment from McDougall & Company to make this all happen. He urged Pa to respond quickly.

On Monday morning, Will sealed his letter and took it to the dock. "Can this letter go out on today's steamboat?" Will asked. "And when will it reach Portland?"

The dockmaster nodded. "Should be there tomorrow night or Wednesday."

"Thank you." Will paid for the letter, then returned to the hotel. There was nothing to do now but wait for Pa's response. Even if Pa wrote back immediately, his answer wouldn't arrive until the end of the week. Tacoma was not a pleasant place to be stranded. But Will had no choice.

Chapter 76: Terminus Announced

Over the next few days, Will tried to negotiate with Thomas Mitchell. But Mitchell had other deals in the works as well, and he had little time for Will. Plus, Will couldn't make any final decisions until he heard from Pa.

While he was at loose ends, Will rented a horse and explored the area. The existing town of Tacoma had little to recommend it. Plus, if Mitchell were correct that the terminus would be south of town, the commercial area would expand south as well. Will rode along the shore to the south, then into the hills behind the town. The land was pretty, though almost completely undeveloped. It must look like Oregon had when Mama and Pa arrived. The vegetation was lusher and more overgrown than around Portland. And everywhere he looked, Will saw water—if not Puget Sound, then streams trickling down from the mountains to Commencement Bay.

Behind it all stood Mount Tahoma, which loomed over both the town and the surrounding forest and fields. Sometimes the massive mountain seemed friendly and protective, other times its presence felt ominous. Will wondered what legends the natives told about the mountain.

When he asked Mitchell about Mount Tahoma, the railroad agent said, "I know little. It's a dormant volcano, I think. Sure is big, ain't it?"

A volcano. Will had been in Boston when Mount Hood erupted in 1865. But he'd heard the stories. Would Mount Tahoma spew smoke and rocks as well?

Despite the damp and the mountain, the region's beauty grew on Will. On Wednesday afternoon, July 9, he rode through an open meadow dotted with wildflowers and surrounded by evergreens. The field sloped gently down a hillside. From the top of the meadow, he could see the water of

Commencement Bay to the west, while Mount Tahoma rose behind him in the east.

It would be an ideal location for a house. When McDougall & Company expanded into Tacoma, he could manage the new branch—he could shape it to suit his vision of the company, as Pa had in Oregon and California. He would talk to Pa about taking on the Tacoma operation when he returned to Portland.

If he moved to Tacoma, he would need a home. A home for Maria, if only she would marry him.

Will brooded all evening about the field he'd seen and the home he wanted to build on that hillside. He could see Maria smiling at him from the front door of their house. He could hear children laughing as they frolicked in the wildflowers.

The next morning, he found Job Carr and inquired who owned the land where he envisioned the house. "Most places south of here are open for homestead, far's I know," Carr said.

"How might I file for a homestead?"

"Ain't no good way. Most men just stake out the land they want, then worry about gettin' the land patent later." He squinted at Will. "You got a specific plot in mind?"

"I do," Will said. "It's south of here, and a bit inland."

"Why you wanna be south?"

Will shrugged. "I like the looks of it. I could build a house there."

"You know about the new Timber Culture Act, don't you?" Carr asked.

Will recalled reading about this expansion of the Homestead Act. Effective in March of this year, Congress added one hundred sixty acres to the amount of land that could be claimed, if the settler agreed to plant forty acres of trees within ten years. "The land I have in mind doesn't need more trees. I don't even know if I want one hundred sixty more acres."

"Well, you could stake out the timber claim and worry about trees later. When you file for the land." Carr grinned. "One thing we got plenty of around Tacoma is empty land."

Not for long, Will thought. Once the Northern Pacific announcement was made—and Mitchell assured him that would be soon—people would flock to Tacoma. Men were likely to claim land south near the terminus, rather than land near the present town of Tacoma.

"Would you help me stake out a parcel?" Will asked Carr. "I need to return to Portland, but I aim to be back in Tacoma soon."

Carr grinned again. "Why not? I can't protect the land from squatters while you're gone, but I'd swear to anyone you was the one what staked it out."

Will finally received a letter from Pa on Thursday, July 10. Pa authorized Will to make the best deal he could with Thomas Mitchell.

Over and over, Will read what Pa had written:

> . . . I agree with you that McDougall & Company should be one of the Northern Pacific's partners in Tacoma. Our improved ability to trade in Asia and throughout the United States will be profitable for everyone involved.
>
> I have confidence, son, that you will keep the best interests of our family and our business in mind. You have proven yourself to have a level head over the past months since you have returned. . . .

Pa had confidence in him.

Will's intuition told him Tacoma offered an excellent opportunity for their company. Seattle might be the more populous town now, but Tacoma was closer to Portland, and the Northern Pacific would make Tacoma prosper.

Secure in the knowledge Pa would support him, Will met with Mitchell on Friday and hammered out their arrangement—McDougall & Company would build a warehouse to store freight shipped on the Northern Pacific railroad and would transport goods between the rail line and the wharf. The Northern Pacific would sell McDougall & Company a lot for the warehouse at a nominal price. The lot would come from the land grant the railroad received from the federal government. The railroad would also guarantee the McDougalls a certain amount of freight business for several years.

The timing of all this was uncertain, given that the Northern Pacific had not yet announced the line would end in Tacoma. "Don't worry," Mitchell told Will. "The announcement will be soon. But then, there is no firm schedule for building the tracks. That depends on our investors."

When they agreed on terms, Will and Mitchell shook hands.

That afternoon, Will met with Job Carr again. They returned to the field in the hills south of Tacoma. Carr shook his head when he saw the parcel. "It's purty, that's for sure," he told Will. "But it's far from town."

"My family began outside Oregon City in forty-seven," Will said. "We lived there until my father built a house in town a few years later. I don't mind the distance from town. And Tacoma will grow."

"That's my bet, too," Carr said. "You might as well claim as much land as you can. You can sell off what you don't need when the town do come out this way."

They staked out a parcel encompassing a full three hundred and twenty acres. Will made sure that the field where he wanted his house—his and Maria's house—had plenty of land around it. He would decide how to develop the land and where to plant trees in the years ahead. His first goal would be to build a home for himself and Maria.

On Saturday, Will wrote up a description of the parcel he had staked. He had Job Carr sign it, attesting that Will was claiming the parcel. "I'll file this in Oregon when I return," he told Carr. "There's a land office in Oregon City, which used to cover the whole West Coast. Now there's an office in San Francisco, too. But I believe Oregon City still handles land claims in Washington Territory."

"Nothin' much built in Washington Territory yet," Carr said. "Which is why we don't much worry about filin' our claims."

On Sunday morning, Will drafted a contract documenting the agreement he had reached with Mitchell. That afternoon, he explored the area further from town. But he ended the day riding through his claim, thinking again about the house he would build for Maria. If only she would have him.

Monday morning, from the Steele Hotel, Will heard the church bell clang. He went downstairs. "What is it?" he asked the clerk.

The man grinned broadly. "Telegram from the Northern Pacific. They're puttin' their terminus here in Tacoma."

"It's official then?" Will asked.

"Seems to be."

Thomas Mitchell entered the hotel waving a piece of paper. "I told you it wouldn't be long," he crowed. He handed the paper to Will.

Will read the single line in the telegram: "WE HAVE LOCATED

TERMINUS ON COMMENCEMENT BAY." He grinned.

"Them folks in Seattle, I bet they're fit to be tied," the hotel clerk said.

"This calls for celebration," Mitchell said to Will. "I'm hosting a banquet this evening for the men who have helped the railroad. You'll join me, of course."

"Of course," Will said. "Let's sign our contract, so we have even more to celebrate. Then soon, I must return to Portland and begin fulfilling our firm's side of the agreement."

"It'll be months before the land grants come through," Mitchell said. "But you and I can plan for the warehouse."

That night, after the contract was inked, Will and Mitchell celebrated, along with others in Tacoma.

On Tuesday, Will packed his belongings and said goodbye to Job Carr and Thomas Mitchell. "I will return soon," he told Mitchell. "And if there is anything you need from me or from McDougall & Company, please contact me. Telegram or letter. I am eager to move ahead with our firm's expansion to Tacoma."

On Wednesday, July 16, Will boarded the steamboat heading south to Portland. He had been away from home for only three weeks, but they had been eventful weeks. He had found a new business venture and a new home. He looked forward to the opportunities ahead. All he needed was for Maria to join him.

Chapter 77: Maria's Next Article

Maria hugged her decision to marry Will close to her, not even confiding in Mama. She needed to talk to Will first. But she spent her last waking moments every evening wondering how marriage to Will would fit into her hopes and dreams. She wanted so many things—to be a successful reporter, to be a cherished member of the McDougall family, to find a man to love for the rest of her life, to be a wife and mother.

She was on her way to succeeding at *The New Northwest*. Mrs. Duniway relied on her and had assigned the Modoc article to her. Now, Maria was working on a piece about the McDougall business. She didn't know if Mrs. Duniway would print it, but she wanted to show Papa and Will she understood the business. She hoped to persuade them to include her in their conversations about McDougall & Company. Even if they wouldn't hire her, Maria wanted to be involved. Mama relied on her at home, and Maria wanted Papa and Will to rely on her as well.

Given her experiences at the newspaper, Maria now realized her Spanish and Indian heritage did not make her less than others in Portland society. Her classmates at school might have treated her poorly—both then and since they'd grown up—but Maria could hold her own with Abigail Duniway, Winema Riddle, and Sarah Winnemucca. She was as well-educated and as knowledgeable and talented as any woman in Oregon.

Which left her with the desire to find a man she could love and respect, a man with whom she could raise a family. Will was such a man. She smiled to herself as she fell asleep, dreaming of Will's return home.

While Will was away, Maria spent every minute she could drafting her article about McDougall & Company. She traced the company's origins from Papa's time in California during the Gold Rush, then circled back to describe his family's Boston roots in banking and law.

By the time she wrote about the years when the business expanded from Oregon City to Portland—and now the plans to move into Washington Territory—she was pleased with the piece. She described Papa's influence on settlers in Oregon City and Portland, his support of farming and transportation, his focus on the coming importance of the railroads. The words flowed from her pen until she neared the end of the article.

Then she paused. There were challenges ahead for the company. At the very least, Will and Nate and others in her generation would take over from Papa. If and when Papa let them. The business also suffered growing pains from its expansion and the lack of trustworthy agents outside the family.

What should she say about the likely thefts? What about the coming of the Northern Pacific? What lay ahead for McDougall & Company? She could not predict the future any more than Papa or Will could.

Stymied at how to proceed, Maria made a clean copy of what she had written thus far to show Papa. She would listen to his input, and as she had promised, she would not submit it to Mrs. Duniway until he approved.

When she finished copying her draft, Maria took the article to Papa and said, "Here is what I've written based on the stories you've told me and what you've taught me since last autumn. I want to offer it to Mrs. Duniway to publish. But I will not do so without your permission."

Papa frowned, but held out his hand. "I told you there wasn't much of a story here."

"But there is, Papa. You built this company from nothing into a flourishing enterprise. Perhaps you had the support of your brothers in Boston, but you started alone in the West. It was only years later that you joined forces with them."

"We are in the middle of a complicated situation at the moment," Papa said. "Both because of the suspected thefts and because Will is pursuing opportunities in Tacoma."

"I hope you will tell me more, Papa," Maria said. "And I hope you will let me show it to Mrs. Duniway. But I will not hurt the family business. And if you tell me this is not the right time to publish the story of McDougall &

Company, then I will abide by your decision."

Papa grunted. "Let me read it."

Maria left Papa's library and went to the parlor to spend the rest of the evening with Mama, her sisters, and Grandmère Peterson. The older woman held a recent issue of *Harper's Monthly* in her lap, but she gazed out the window instead of at the magazine.

"Good evening," Maria said as she settled into a chair and pulled out her mending.

"What do you have there, girl?" Grandmère asked.

Maria smiled. "Andrew's trousers. He ripped another hole in the knee. The pants have already been patched twice."

From across the room, Mama sighed. "He needs new pants—he outgrows everything so quickly. But he'll just rip new garments as well. I will wait until the new school term begins. For the summer, when he's playing outside, he can wear patches."

Grandmère sniffed. "My Jacques never ripped his trousers."

"I bet he did, Grandmère," Eliza said.

"Well, I never mended them."

"Letitia probably took care of it," Mama said. "She mended my clothes when I was small. Until she taught me to do it myself."

"You spent so much time with that old woman," Grandmère said. "More time than you did with me."

Mama was silent. Letitia had probably been nicer to Mama than her own mother had been, but Maria also chose not to confront Grandmère.

Grandmère looked at Maria. "How is your newspaper work coming?"

Maria looked up in surprise at the question. "Very well, thank you."

Grandmère's hands fidgeted with the fringe on her shawl. "What are you writing? You've been closeted in your room all week. This is the first evening you have deigned to spend with us."

"I've written an article about McDougall & Company."

Mama took a sharp breath and frowned at Maria.

"I just gave it to Papa to read," Maria told her mother. "He knows I won't publish it unless he approves. And I want all his suggestions and corrections."

"I read what you wrote about the Modocs," Grandmère said. "You portrayed the heathens too sympathetically. But the piece read smoothly."

"Thank you," Maria said. She managed not to respond to Grandmère's remark about heathens.

Papa said nothing about her article for the better part of a week. Maria bit her tongue every evening at supper, wanting to ask his opinion. Did he dislike it? Did he want to reflect on the consequences of its publication? She was so curious, but she would get a better response if she waited for him to raise the subject.

Finally, on Thursday, July 3, Papa called her into his library after supper. "I've read your article, Maria."

She sat silently.

"It is well written," he said. "Though I expected nothing less."

"Did you have any corrections?" she was brave enough to ask.

He nodded. "I marked it up." He handed it back to her. His black scrawl covered some of her sentences, but he hadn't edited her writing as much as Abigail Duniway did. "And I added a few details to flesh it out."

A quick glance revealed there were more additions than deletions in his comments. She smiled. "Thank you, Papa."

"But about publication . . ."

Her heart sank. "You don't want it published?"

"Not now," he said. "The company is on the brink of expansion. I had a letter from Will yesterday. I want to wait and see what happens in Tacoma."

"Oh."

He smiled at her. "Don't despair. If all goes well, you'll have a better ending to your story. Will thinks there is potential in Tacoma, and he wants to negotiate an agreement with a railroad man there."

"I see."

"He asks for my advice. What do you think I should tell him?"

Was Papa really asking for her opinion? "What does Will say?"

Papa explained the railroad terminus was still uncertain, despite the promises the Northern Pacific representative had made. "Will is confident the railroad will end up in Tacoma, and I agree. But not where people in Tacoma expect it."

"Then the land south of town is likely to become more valuable?" Maria asked.

"Yes." Papa nodded.

"You should tell Will you trust him," Maria said. "Tell him he is on the scene, and it seems he understands the situation. Tell him you will abide by his decisions in the matter."

Papa smiled. "Then that is what I shall do. Because I agree with you."

The next morning was Independence Day. Mama and Maria prepared a picnic to take downtown so the younger children could watch the parade.

"Did you talk to Mac?" Mama asked as they made sandwiches and poured lemonade in jars.

Maria nodded. "He doesn't want me to publish yet."

"Give him time," Mama said. "He's worried about the business. But he's proud of what you wrote." Mama turned from wrapping sandwiches. "I read your article as well. You did a wonderful job capturing the growth of Mac's ventures over the years."

"Thank you." Maria smiled at Mama's praise.

"Let your father come to the realization your article will help him."

"You really think it will?" Maria said. "He seems to think it will hurt."

"The likelihood that someone's been stealing from him makes him fret. He doesn't want any extra attention on McDougall & Company at the moment." Mama sighed. "But he intends to expand, and the publicity could help."

"He asked me for my opinion about expanding," Maria said. A note of pride crept into her voice.

"I'm glad," Mama said, smiling. "He appreciates your talents, you know."

"I told him to trust Will's opinion."

Mama looked at her sharply. "Have you given any more thought to Will's proposal?"

Maria nodded. "I love him, Mama. I miss him."

"Do you want to marry him?"

"I will talk to him when he returns. We need to speak candidly."

"Oh?" Mama asked.

"Will seems to take my writing more seriously now than he did last fall. But I want to be sure he won't stifle me."

"Do you intend to keep writing for the paper after you marry?" Mama sounded surprised.

Maria sighed. "I'm not sure. But I want the option. And I want to know Will supports my doing so."

"Then you're right—the two of you must talk," Mama said with a nod.

The family rode downtown in their carriage, all except Papa, who decided he didn't want to spend the day outside in the heat.

After the parade, they ate the sandwiches and other foods Maria and Mama had prepared. The lemonade tasted refreshing, even though by then it had warmed in the July sun.

Maria saw Daisy and Robert walking along the main street, and she hailed them. They joined the McDougalls for a glass of lemonade.

Daisy drew Maria aside and whispered, "Robert proposed. Just as the guns were saluting our soldiers."

"I'm delighted for you." Maria smiled. "I assume you said yes."

Daisy laughed. "Of course, I did. Then he kissed me. Right there where the whole town could see."

"How bold," Maria said, grinning and squeezing Daisy's hand.

"We will marry soon," Daisy said. "No reason to wait. Though I need to talk with my ma. I don't know how she will cope without me, but we'll figure it out."

"Then you and Robert won't live with your mother?"

Daisy shook her head. "Robert has found us a little house. Not too far from the newspaper office. He can walk to work."

"Will you keep working at *The New Northwest*?"

"For a bit." Daisy's voice lowered to a whisper. "Until I'm with child."

Daisy could have a baby soon. A pang went from Maria's heart to her belly. She missed Will. When would he return? What would they decide?

The following Monday, Maria was late leaving for work. As she walked out the door, Amos Higgins approached. "I'm here to see your father," he said. "But since I've found you, might we talk?"

"I have nothing to say to you, Mr. Higgins," Maria replied, and she tried to walk around him to the street.

He stepped in front of her. "Please give me a moment to plead my case."

She stopped and stared. "There's no need, Mr. Higgins. As I told you, I do not wish to marry you."

"But—"

"If you do not step out of my way, I shall tell my father of your interference."

Amos glared, but moved aside.

Maria kept an eye out for Amos for several days after their encounter, but she saw nothing of him. On Wednesday morning, July 16, Papa had a telegram from Will—he had made a deal in Tacoma and was returning to Portland.

She expected Will on the afternoon of July 17, but he didn't arrive. Finally, the following afternoon, he walked in the front door. She heard him from the parlor and rushed into the hallway to greet him.

"Will," she exclaimed, hugging him. "We thought you'd be home yesterday."

He returned the hug and kissed her cheek. "I'd hoped to be here then. But the currents at the mouth of the Columbia were wild. The steamboat had to wait for calmer weather. The wind didn't shift until this morning. Only then could we head upriver."

The rest of the family fell upon Will with greetings as well. Maria had no further chance to talk to him alone. That evening after supper, as Maria left the parlor to go to bed, Will took her aside and said, "I'd like to speak with you, Maria. Alone. But now is not the time."

She smiled. "And I want to speak with you, too, Will. We'll talk tomorrow."

Chapter 78: Will Explains His Decisions

Will had no time alone with Maria the evening he returned from Tacoma. Mama took him into her morning room to tell him of Grandmère's behavior. She beseeched him to placate his grandmother. "She's been very difficult," Mama said. "And you're good with her, Will. I think she listens to you because you look like my father."

Will promised to do his best with Grandmère.

After the rest of the family had gone to bed, Will and Pa sat in the library. Will described his exploration of Tacoma, ending with his explanation for why he'd settled on building the warehouse south of town. "Thomas Mitchell is certain the railroad station will be built near a new wharf."

"And that's where you leased land for us to build?" Pa asked.

"Yes," Will said. "It's a good parcel, and Mitchell has agreed to terms that are advantageous to both our business and the railroad. McDougall & Company will make money transporting the railroad's cargo from rails to the wharf, and we can also store and sell our own inventory to ship east via the railroad on favorable terms."

"Good work, Will," Pa said.

"There's more, Pa." Will took a deep breath. He didn't know how Pa would react to what he would say next. "I staked out land for myself as well—a homestead claim. I want to manage the Tacoma branch and build a home there."

Pa frowned. "You don't want to stay in Portland?"

Will shook his head. "I think I can better serve the company in Tacoma. Your health has improved, and you can tutor Nate in the operation here in Portland. I want to build something on my own. I can do that in Tacoma."

"There's more I could teach you here," Pa said.

"I don't doubt that, Pa," Will said. "And I want to learn from you. But I also want a piece of the business to manage on my own. I can grow more if I'm the man in charge."

"You could manage the California operations."

"Yes," Will said. "But we will need someone in Tacoma. And I can build the branch there from the beginning. It will be mine."

"And you want to build a home," Pa said. "Does this have anything to do with Maria?"

Will nodded. "I'm going to ask her again to marry me. If she'll have me, we'll build the house together. If not . . ." He didn't want to think of the alternative. "If not, then I need to get away from her for a while."

"She turned down Amos Higgins," Pa said. "But he's still sniffing around."

Will clenched his fists. "Do I need to speak to him?"

"I don't think so," Pa said. "I'm likely to fire him soon. I expect he will push me into it, even if we never prove he stole from us. I suspect he only wanted to marry Maria to stay close to me."

"Do I have your blessing to speak to Maria?" Will asked.

Pa smiled. "I gave you my blessing before. You still have it."

Will found Maria at breakfast on Saturday. "After you've eaten, shall we take a walk?"

"I'd like that," she replied with a smile.

A short while later, as she put on her hat and gloves in the front hall, he asked, "Would you prefer to walk toward town or in the garden?"

"Let's go to the garden," she said. "It's quieter."

He escorted her outside toward the carriage house and stables. They stopped to pet the horses, then entered the garden.

"I want to tell you about my trip to Tacoma," he began, just as she said, "I turned Amos down. For good."

Will stopped and took her hands. "I'm glad you turned him down," he said. "How did he take it?"

She shrugged. "He wasn't happy. But that is not my concern."

"Before I tell you about Tacoma," Will said, "let me say my feelings have not changed. I love you, and I want to marry you."

"And I want to marry *you*," Maria said, squeezing his fingers. "That's what I wanted to tell you. I love you, too."

Will couldn't keep from grinning. "You do? You will?"

"Yes." Her grin mirrored his.

"Then we will work the rest out," he said, drawing her closer and kissing her deeply. She molded her body to his.

After a bit, he pulled away from her reluctantly. "Now, let me tell you about Tacoma. I've bought land. We'll build a house—"

"A house? In Tacoma?" She put further distance between them. "Why?"

"McDougall & Company is going to open a branch there to support the Northern Pacific Railroad. And Pa and I have agreed I will manage our operations there."

"Away from Portland?"

"Yes." Will looked at her, puzzled. "Don't you think it would be nice to start our marriage in a fresh place?"

"But our family," Maria said. "I've never lived away from them, other than when I helped run Mrs. Duniway's school. And I wasn't happy then."

Will's heart sank. He'd dreamed of such a lovely future in Tacoma— Maria as his wife, him leading the McDougall & Company expansion. "But I'll be with you. We'll build our family along with the business."

"I-I-I need to think about it," Maria murmured, looking at the ground. "I love you, Will. But this isn't the future I imagined."

"Did you think we would continue to live with Mama and Pa?" Will asked, waving toward the house.

"No." She shook her head. "I thought we'd have our own house. But in Portland. Where we could see family every day." Now she looked at him. "And what about my job? Did you expect me to quit the newspaper?"

Now it was his turn to stammer. "W-w-well, I hadn't thought about it. I don't mind you writing for the paper. But it would be hard to do from Tacoma."

She made a sound in the back of her throat. "I need to think about it," she said again. "Let's not tell the family anything yet." She turned and rushed into the house.

Will didn't speak alone with Maria again for the rest of the weekend. On Monday morning, he headed into the company offices for the first time since his return from Tacoma.

Zhuang Li came to his office shortly after he arrived. "Mr. Will, we need talk."

"Come in," Will said, ushering Li to a chair.

"Mr. Higgins mad," Li told him. "I don't know why. He search files last week."

"What was he looking for?" Will said.

Li shook his head. "I not know. I not ask. He not like me, wouldn't tell."

"Let me know if you find out anything," Will said. He couldn't get too upset about Higgins snooping around in the files. Not when his future with Maria was in limbo.

Will went to the hotel for the noon meal because Holladay had called a meeting of his investors. Will thought he would see Higgins there, but the man was not present.

"What happened to Amos Higgins?" he asked Holladay.

"Where've you been, McDougall?" Holladay's voice boomed out. "Higgins is out. He couldn't raise the funds he committed."

"He told me he had a sure thing," Will said. "An inheritance."

"Guess it wasn't so sure. Word around town is he gambled to get his stake." Holladay chuckled. "But he lost everything."

"Have you talked to him?" Will asked. He wondered what Higgins's losses would mean for the accountant's role in McDougall & Company. Will would have to tell Pa, and Pa might well fire Higgins sooner rather than later.

"Nah," Holladay said, chuckling again. "I won't rub a dog's nose in his own manure. Won't do it to a man neither."

That evening, Will met with Pa and Nate in the library. "I had an interesting conversation with Ben Holladay today," Will began.

"Oh?" Pa poured them each a whiskey, Nate's glass only one finger deep.

"He says Amos Higgins gambled away the stake he'd planned to invest in the railroad."

"That explains it," Nate said.

"What do you mean?" Pa asked, turning to Nate.

"Higgins was prowling through the office like a panther while you were gone." Nate grinned. "The boys in the office laughed about his bad mood until he lambasted one of them for snickering at him."

"At this point, he's still our head accountant," Pa said, frowning. "I don't want him disrespected."

"Is he mistreating anyone in the office?" Will asked.

Nate shrugged. "Billy—the boy he yelled at—he deserved it. But I'm glad old Higgins won't be my brother-in-law."

Will glared at Nate. "What do you know about that?"

Nate grinned. "Everyone in the family knows Higgins proposed to Maria. How could something like that stay quiet?"

"What else do you know?" Will said through his teeth.

Nate held up his hands, his glass in one, the other with fingers spread wide. "Nothing, big brother. I know nothing more."

"Now, boys," Pa said. "This is serious. If Higgins is desperate, he might take risks in the business. Or worse. Watch him."

"I'll warn Maria, too," Will said, afraid Higgins might harm her. "She needs to know."

True to his word, before he left for work Tuesday morning, Will searched for Maria. He found her sitting alone in Mama's morning room. "I learned yesterday that Amos Higgins lost a lot of money gambling," he told her.

"Mr. Higgins is of no concern to me," she replied. "I don't need to know."

"If he has nothing left," Will said, "then he has nothing left to lose. He might act stupidly, even criminally."

"I have no interest in anything he does," Maria said. "There's no need for you to be jealous any longer."

"I'm not jealous, Maria," Will said. "I'm warning you. Don't be alone with him."

"Why would I be alone with him?" She smiled. "But if it makes you happy, Will, I will be careful."

"That's all I ask." He leaned over and kissed the top of her head. "Have you thought any more about our conversation on Saturday?"

"I've thought of little else," she said with a wry smile. "It's a lot to absorb. But I love you, Will. I'll get used to the idea of living in Tacoma. If you'll let me try to continue working for the newspaper."

He shrugged. That hadn't been part of his vision of their future. "If you think you can."

"All I'm asking is that you let me try."

He nodded. "You can try." He took a breath. "Should we announce our engagement now?"

She shook her head. "Give me another day or two. There's no hurry."

Chapter 79: What Zhuang Li Finds

Once again, Maria was caught up in preparations for a sibling's birthday. Lottie would turn sixteen on Sunday, July 27. Maria spent hours placating Eliza and Grandmère Peterson so Mama could focus on Lottie. Eliza and Lottie, less than two years apart in age, hissed at each other like angry kittens. Adding Grandmère to the mix made family meals even more volatile.

"Remember, Eliza," Maria told her sister. "You had a lovely celebration at the theater last fall. Now it's Lottie's turn."

"She's too young to go to the theater," Eliza scoffed.

"And all she wants is to have a Sunday dinner with her school friends and Mama and Papa," Maria said. "Which Mama and Mrs. O'Malley have agreed she can do."

"But that means the rest of us have to eat in the parlor or go on a picnic." Eliza heaved a sigh worthy of an actress. "I should have been included in Lottie's supper party. I go to school with her, and I know all those girls."

"Lottie didn't go to the theater with you."

"But you did." Even months later, Eliza acted miffed that Maria had been included in her birthday celebration.

Maria knew better than to react to Eliza's whining. "Will is taking anyone who wants to go for a picnic in the park. You enjoyed that earlier in the year."

"But now it's so hot," Eliza grumbled. "My hair will frizz."

"Would you rather stay home with Grandmère Peterson?" Maria asked. "Evie and I will be keeping her company. Or stay in the nursery with Eddie?"

"Gracious, no," Eliza said. "The old biddy never says anything nice to anyone."

Privately, Maria thought Eliza took after Grandmère, but she said nothing.

When Sunday came, Maria took plates of food to the parlor for herself, Grandmère, and Evie. Evie's young cheerfulness brightened the mood, but Grandmère was in a snit. The older woman hated being left out of anything, and missing both the birthday dinner and the picnic made her grumpy. Maria did her best to engage Grandmère in conversation, but Grandmère's monologues made Evie fidget.

Still, Maria had worked out a detente with Grandmère. She placated the older woman, who alternated between treating Maria like a servant and a favored granddaughter. Grandmère had little use for Eliza, whom she considered selfish, or Lottie, whom she said was silly. The boys, other than Will, gave her headaches. Only Will, Maria, and Mama could ever please her—and then only rarely.

When the picnickers returned, Maria helped Will empty the picnic baskets. The dinner party was over, and Mrs. O'Malley was cleaning up. "How was your afternoon?" Maria asked.

"Nate teased Andrew and Maggie mercilessly, and Eliza refused to leave the shade of an oak tree." Will shook his head. "I think I prefer Amos Higgins's company to that of my younger siblings."

Maria laughed. "I know that's not true."

"And how was your time?"

"Evie was a delight, and Grandmère was Grandmère."

Will grinned. "Then we're even. Though you manage Grandmère beautifully."

"She still prefers you." Maria smiled. "Everyone does."

"Give yourself credit—you've earned her respect." Will took her hand. "Walk outside with me?" He nodded at Mrs. O'Malley, who stood at the sink scrubbing pots.

"All right." She left to get a hat to shade her face, then hurried back.

They walked to the garden, and Will held her hand again. "When shall we announce our engagement?"

She said, "I'm ready. After today, I've had enough family. Maybe it would be nice to start fresh by ourselves."

"Are you ready to tell the family?"

"Has Papa said you can manage the Tacoma branch?"

"He said you and I needed to decide. But he'll let me go if you agree you'll go with me. As my wife."

She tightened her grip on his fingers. "I want to marry you, Will. Let's talk to Mama and Papa. Make sure that they agree with the plan."

Will turned her to him, leaned over, and kissed her. He tasted of lemonade from the picnic.

That evening, most of the family retired early, tired after the celebrations. Will and Maria met with Mama and Papa in the library. Will's ring was back on Maria's finger, and she squeezed her hand to feel its presence.

When the four of them had settled—Papa in his usual chair, Mama beside him, and Will and Maria on a sofa facing their parents—Will said, "Maria and I have agreed to wed."

Mama rose and hugged Maria first, then Will. "I am so happy," she said, and Maria heard the joy in her mother's voice.

"Is this true, Maria?" Papa asked. Though his words seemed skeptical, he sounded pleased, and his face held a broad grin.

"Yes, Papa. I want to marry Will."

"We shall plan a wonderful wedding," Mama said, taking her seat again.

"Where will you live?" Papa asked.

"We want to go to Tacoma together," Will said. "To open the McDougall & Company branch there."

"So far away," Mama murmured.

"I don't want to tell anyone yet," Maria said. "I've agreed to go with Will. But I don't want a lot of fuss. Mama and I can talk about the wedding. Will and Papa need to decide the timing of the move to Tacoma. Then we can make our announcement."

"It will all work out," Mama said. "Do you want a quick wedding, or do you want to wait?"

Maria looked at Will. "We haven't talked about that."

"Mama is right," Will said, taking Maria's hand. "It will all work out. But the sooner, the better, for me."

Over the next several days, Maria and Mama discussed the wedding and what Maria would need to set up a new household. Mama repeated her concern about Will and Maria being so far away.

"At least we won't have to listen to the gossip here in Portland," Maria said. "You've said people will talk."

Mama sighed. "Perhaps it is best for you to start your lives somewhere else. When do you want to tell the rest of the family?"

"Soon, Mama." Maria needed to get used to the idea herself. She was glad Mama and Papa had taken the announcement in stride. But she wasn't ready to have Grandmère and all the children talking. And she certainly wasn't ready for all of Portland to know.

On Thursday, August 1, Will traveled to Oregon City to check on the family property there. Because Papa still wasn't comfortable making long trips by train or carriage, Will went in Papa's stead.

Friday morning, Zhuang Li came to the McDougall residence. Will was absent, and Papa was resting, so Maria spoke with him.

"I must talk your father or brother," Li said. "Very important."

"What is it?" Maria said. "Might I help?"

"When Mr. Will be back?" Li asked.

"Not until tomorrow afternoon," Maria said.

"I must see him." As they spoke, Li turned a piece of paper over and over in his hands nervously.

"Do you have something for him?" Maria asked. "Could I give it to him?"

Li hesitated, then said, "I not want this. You keep secret. Give Mr. Will soon as he home."

"What is it?" What Li gave her looked like a loose page from a ledger like those she'd reviewed with Papa.

"I find mixed with invoices." Li lowered his voice to a whisper. "It show Mr. Higgins steal."

"What do you mean?" Maria looked at the document in her hand.

"You tell Mr. Will," Li said. "He will know."

"But how do you know this document is Mr. Higgins's?" Maria asked.

"His handwriting," Li said. "I know it."

"Are you sure?"

Li nodded. "You show Mr. Will. Ask him see me. Must be more records like this. I look."

Chapter 80: Another Telegram from Jack

Will grew bored with all the whispering between Mama and Maria about their future nuptials, and he was glad to escape to Oregon City for a couple of days. His business with Pa's tenants and debtors proceeded without a hitch, and on Friday afternoon he headed home.

On the train ride back to Portland, Will daydreamed about his future with Maria. She'd agreed to everything he wanted—marriage, moving to Tacoma, a house on the land he'd bought. He could see it now—their home, Maria waving at him as he returned from the warehouse. A dog barking as it raced to greet him, a child or two toddling behind. Maybe she would give up newspaper work once she had a baby to tend.

He was glad their parents were amenable. He'd worried Pa would not let him start the Tacoma branch or that Mama would not want Maria so far from home. But all his fears melted away.

Soon, he would need to make another trip to Tacoma to plan the warehouse construction. Perhaps he should hire an architect in Portland to draw plans for a house. He wanted something like his parents' current home, though he remembered Grandmother McDougall's house in Boston as well. Some fine touches like hers would make the Tacoma house more genteel, as would befit the manager of the newest branch of McDougall & Company.

It would be many years before Tacoma rivaled the company's other West Coast branches. But Will would make the Tacoma branch profitable. Having the Northern Pacific in town would ensure that.

How far the McDougalls had come from when Pa brought Mama to Oregon the year Will was born! Every time Will thought of how the West had developed during his lifetime, he marveled. And he and Maria would be part of future developments.

When Will reached home, he greeted his family. Everyone was present except Maria. "Where's Maria?" he asked.

"She must still be at work," Mama said. "She hasn't returned home yet."

She rarely stayed downtown all day. When she attended an evening meeting of a women's suffrage group for Mrs. Duniway, she let the family know.

"Zhuang Li was looking for you this morning," Nate said. "He stopped me at the office first thing. He said he had something for you and would bring it here."

"What was it?" Will asked.

"I don't know, and I didn't ask," Nate said.

"Maybe I should seek him out." Will didn't really want to go to the office late on a Friday afternoon, but Zhuang Li wouldn't have come to the house without good reason. "Then I'll walk Maria home."

Just then, the front door knocker sounded. Nate answered it, then returned with a telegram he handed to Will. "From Jack," Nate said.

> DATE: 1 AUGUST 1873
> FROM: JACQUES PETERSON SAN FRANCISCO
> TO: WILLIAM MCDOUGALL PORTLAND
> PROOF HIGGINS AND BECK STEALING LETTER
> FOLLOWS

"Look, Pa," Will said. He read the telegram to his father. "Jack doesn't explain. I'm going to the telegraph office to wire him for more information. Then I'll bring Maria home."

Will hurried downtown and sent the following message:

> DATE: 1 AUGUST 1873
> FROM: WILLIAM MCDOUGALL PORTLAND
> TO: JACQUES PETERSON SAN FRANCISCO
> WIRE DETAILS IMMEDIATELY EVEN IF LONG

After paying for the telegram, he walked to *The New Northwest* office. But Maria wasn't there.

Robert was still working, setting type for the next edition. "She left in midafternoon," Robert said. "She seemed upset."

"Where was she going?" Will asked.

Robert shrugged. "I don't know."

Will headed home. "I can't find her," he told his parents when he arrived.

"Oh, no," Mama cried.

Pa's face turned grim.

"I'm going to Zhuang Li's house," Will said. "Maybe he knows what's going on. He can at least tell me what he wanted me to see."

By now, the sun was low in the sky, and Will was exhausted from his travels. He had the carriage rigged, then drove to Chinatown to the Zhuang residence. He left the sleepy stable boy with the carriage and pounded on the Zhuangs' door.

The old woman who'd tended Zhuang Li's injuries opened the door and bowed.

"Where's Zhuang Li?" Will asked.

She said something in Chinese and ushered him in. She bowed again, then went to a back room.

But Li did not appear. Instead, his cousin Jin entered the room and said in surprise, "Will, why you here so late?"

"I'm looking for Li." Will ran a hand through his disheveled hair. He must look like a wild man.

"Li not here," Zhuang Jin said. "He not come home tonight."

"He wanted to give me something," Will said. "And Maria can't be found."

"You not think—"

"I don't know what to think," Will said. "But I need to find Maria. I've looked everywhere."

Jin bowed. "If Li come, I tell him you here."

"Do you know what Li wanted to give me?" Will asked.

Jin shook his head. "I not see Li all day."

Will sighed. He wouldn't find any answers here. He nodded at Jin. "Thank you." And he turned and left.

Chapter 81: In Higgins's Office

After her conversation with Zhuang Li, Maria spent Friday morning at the newspaper. She worried about what Li had told her. She didn't doubt his sincerity, but how did the document he'd given her prove Amos Higgins was a thief? She wished Will were home—he could figure it out.

She grew so anxious she left *The New Northwest* in midafternoon, hoping Will had returned from Oregon City. She walked to the McDougall & Company offices. "Is Will here?" she asked the clerk at the front desk.

"I'm sorry, Miss McDougall," the man replied. "Will has not been here today."

"And my father?"

"He also has not been in."

"Nate?" Perhaps he would know whether Will was home yet.

"I haven't seen Nate either," the man said. "Mr. Higgins—"

She was afraid to talk to Amos. What if what Zhuang Li said was true? And she had promised Will she would not meet with Amos.

"No, thank you," she said. "I'll head home. I'll find them there." She turned to leave, then turned back. If Zhuang Li were at work, perhaps he would explain further. "Is Mr. Zhuang Li here?"

The man smiled and nodded. "Yes, miss. Shall I get him?"

Maria shook her head. "I know where he sits." She went to the accounting department and found Li at his desk.

"Mr. Zhuang," she began.

He looked up, and his eyes widened in horror. "Miss, you shouldn't be here. Where Will?" He stood and took her arm. "We go now."

"But—"

"Mr. Higgins. He here. In office."

"I'm not afraid of Mr. Higgins." But she'd promised Will she wouldn't meet Amos, so she followed Li out of the building.

"I take you home," he said.

She pulled away from Li's hand on her arm. "Don't be silly. I'm looking for Will."

"You not see him yet?"

She shook her head.

"Then he not know what I tell you this morning?"

"No," she said. "He must still be in Oregon City."

"I take you home," Li repeated. "You not stay here." He took her arm again and led her down the street.

"Wait," Maria said, stopping on the boardwalk. "You said there were more documents like this one. Where are they?"

"Not safe to look," Li said. "You go home."

Maria was tired of every man she encountered trying to protect her. "Let's have tea," she said. "I want you to explain why this document is so important." She took it out of her reticule.

"You carry it with you?" Li said, his voice rising. "Why you not hide?"

"You didn't tell me I needed to," she said. "Please. I need to know what this is about." She didn't think Li would make a scene on the street. An argument between them could lead to his arrest.

Li sighed and nodded. "I tell you."

They entered a tea shop in the next block. After they ordered tea and cake, Maria handed Li the document. "Now, please explain what this shows."

"Look," Li said as he pointed to a column of numbers. "Here. These amounts not on our books. Here entry for one hundred dollars. Says received from Mr. Beck in California. Then shows subtraction—minus twenty dollars. Leaves eighty dollars. Date here. I check our ledger for that date. Ledger only shows eighty dollars received."

"What does that mean?" Maria asked.

"Someone steal twenty dollars." Li ran his finger down the column of numbers. "Every entry here show money not recorded in company ledger. Only less money in ledger."

"But how?" Maria asked. "If there were an audit, wouldn't the differences show up?"

"If good man audit." Li pointed at the numbers again. "But Mr. Higgins control audit. I only man checking him."

Maria frowned. "And why have you been checking on Mr. Higgins?"

"I not trust him." Li blew on his tea, then took a sip. "Must be more documents like this."

"Where?" she asked, then sipped her own tea.

"Probably his office. I find this paper in stack he give me. He make mistake to give me. But I think he have more documents."

Maria took another sip, thinking. There was only one way to find out what was happening. "Then we shall have to look."

His eyes widened. "No, Miss Maria. Too dangerous."

"You have a key to the McDougall offices, don't you?"

He nodded. "Yes, but—"

"My father owns the company," she said. "You work there. We won't get in trouble for being in the office."

"But Mr. Higgins—"

"I can handle Amos Higgins," Maria said. She thought briefly of Will's warning, then shrugged it off. Amos might bluster, but he wouldn't hurt her. After all, the last thing he'd said to her was he wanted to marry her.

It took Maria until they finished their tea and cakes to convince Zhuang Li to return to the McDougall & Company offices with her. She needed him, because he knew what they were looking for. And he had the key.

As she talked to Li, she convinced herself she was not violating her promise to Will. She had no intention of meeting Amos Higgins. In fact, she hoped to avoid him. And Li would be with her, so she wouldn't be alone with Amos.

They waited until after closing time at McDougall & Company, then returned to the building. Zhuang Li led her to the back alley door and unlocked it. They crept inside. Early evening light filtered through the windows—at the beginning of August there was plenty of light to see. They would be gone before dark fell.

Li led the way to Amos's office. They encountered no one in the halls, and she was relieved Amos was not working late.

"We look now," Li said in a hushed tone.

"What are we looking for?" she whispered back.

"More pages like what I show you." Li began rifling through papers on

Amos's desk.

"Where should I look?" Maria asked.

He pointed to a stack of papers on a file cabinet. "You start there. Loose papers. Then drawers of cabinet."

Maria and Li worked in silence. Maria's hands grew grubby as she thumbed through dusty files. Finally, she and Li had looked at all the papers and files they could see.

"The only thing left is the drawers in his desk," she said.

"I search already," Li said. "Will did, too. Only one drawer locked. Will say Higgins keep whiskey there."

"So that's the only place we haven't searched tonight?" Maria said.

Zhuang Li nodded. "No key."

She tugged on the drawer. It didn't budge. She stared at it, then took out a hairpin. "Let me try this."

She stuck the hairpin in the lock and jiggled it. Nothing. She pushed harder. It clicked. "Voilà!" She grinned and pulled the drawer open.

Inside were two tumblers and a silver flask. But behind the flask was a ledger. Maria pulled it out and handed it to Li.

He opened the book. "This it." The ledger pages looked just like the one they'd discussed in the tea shop. "Start last year. Then this year. Can't tell everything, but I think it show money taken."

"Why would he record all his thefts?" Maria asked. If she were stealing, she wouldn't write it down.

"He and Beck. They split money maybe."

"Honor among thieves," Maria murmured. Was it really that simple? "All right," she said. "Let's take this to my home. Surely, Will or Papa will be there by now." She turned to leave.

Amos Higgins stood in the doorway.

"I think not, my dear," Amos said, waving a pistol at them.

Maria gasped. Beside her, Li uttered what sounded like a Chinese curse.

"Perhaps you should have a seat, Maria," he said, gesturing with the gun toward a chair. "And you, Li, you've been a problem ever since you started working here."

"You've been stealing from my family," Maria said, recovering her outrage. "For years, it seems."

"I wouldn't have to steal if you married me," Amos said. "Your father would settle a large sum on me, I'm sure."

"You only wanted to marry me for my money."

Amos's glance swept down her body. "You're attractive enough," he said. "Despite your blood. It wouldn't have been a bad fate for either of us."

Li made a sound low in his throat.

"What will you do now?" Maria asked.

"That is a problem," Amos said. "I hadn't planned to kill anyone. But I can't let you go free. And I need the ledger back. It's the only way I can keep Beck honest."

"He steal with you." Li sounded like he was stating a fact, not asking a question.

"He has been very useful," Amos said. "In fact, Beck was the first to siphon profits from the California operation. When I went to inspect the Sacramento branch and discovered his thefts, he showed me his methods. We agreed we could take twice the amount if we worked together. It's been a very profitable enterprise."

"Then why did you need me?" Maria asked.

"Insurance," Higgins said. "Eventually, we would have been found out. But your father wouldn't have me arrested if I were married to you. Then Holladay offered me a stake in the railroad. I needed more funds to invest. So I tried to speed our courtship along." He leered at her. "It might not be too late."

At that, Li launched himself at Higgins. Higgins shot, and Li fell to the ground.

Chapter 82: Kidnapped

Maria screamed and dropped to her knees beside Li. Blood gushed from the unconscious man's side. "You've killed him," she cried.

Amos tapped Li with his foot, and Li groaned. "He's harder to kill than that." He jerked Maria's arm. "Come on. We're leaving."

"I'm not going anywhere with you," she said, struggling.

Ignoring her words, Amos pulled her to her feet. He grabbed the ledger she and Li had found and shoved it at her. "Bring this." Then he gripped her arm and held the pistol against her side. "Let's go."

His firm grip gave her no choice. Clutching the ledger, she stumbled out of the office beside Amos. She glanced back at Li, who lay silently on the floor. Amos marched her out the back door where she and Li had entered, then down the alley for a few blocks. They passed the rear of a furniture store, which Maria recognized by its loading dock. She and Mama had bought a divan there last year.

As Amos yanked her along the alley, a dog slunk along the opposite side and a small boy bounced a ball against a wall in the late evening twilight. She opened her mouth to call to the boy, but Amos shoved the pistol into her ribs. "Keep quiet," he said, tightening his grip. "I'll shoot you, then the kid."

A block past the furniture store, Amos dragged her up a metal staircase in the rear of a building. At the top of the staircase, he opened the door and pushed Maria into a dim hallway. He led her down the hall to a door. Keeping one arm around her neck, he unlocked the door with his other hand, then pulled her inside. He slammed the door shut behind them and leaned against it, panting as he shoved her away.

She stumbled into the center of the room—which appeared to be the sitting room of an apartment. At the far side of the room, she saw a door to another room, in which she glimpsed a bed.

" 'Will you walk into my parlor? said a spider to a fly,' " Amos hissed. "I would have preferred to bring you to my parlor under more favorable circumstances, my dear. But needs must when the devil drives."

"What's next, Mr. Higgins?" she asked. "Surely, you don't think you can get away with this. My family will be looking for me."

"You didn't give me any choice, Maria. I can't let anyone see that ledger. Hand it over."

She looked down, surprised she still carried the account book. Amos grabbed it.

"Why do you keep it?" she asked.

"As I said, I don't want Beck stealing my share. He has easier access to the California assets. And he probably has a ledger of his own to keep me from taking more than my share."

"Then Mr. Cassidy was right," Maria said. "He told Will there were two sets of books."

"We had to be careful of Cassidy until we got him fired. He's an honest son of a bitch."

"I'm thirsty," Maria said. "And it's late. Do you have anything for supper?" Anything to keep Amos from shooting her.

Amos frowned. "Are you offering to fix me a meal?"

"If you have food and drink, we should sustain ourselves." Mama's admonition to catch flies with honey flashed through her mind.

He waved the pistol toward a cupboard.

Maria opened it and found tea and bread with a rack to put on the fire for toast. "Will you build up the fire, please?" she asked, scanning the cupboard to see if there was anything she could drug his tea with. Nothing.

Amos kindled the fire but kept an eye on her. When she found a knife to slice the bread, he left the fire and trained the gun on her. "Don't do anything foolish," he said.

Maria sliced the bread, then Amos took the knife from her. She crouched by the fire and put the teakettle on a hook and the bread in the rack, which she turned carefully. When the bread was toasted, she slathered it with jam. She wondered how to keep the bread knife, but Amos watched her too closely.

"Aren't we the picture of domesticity?" Amos said. "If you're so eager to play the wife, why did you reject me?"

"I don't love you, Amos."

They ate their small repast in silence. When they finished, Amos beckoned to her. "Come here."

She approached, but stood out of his reach. He grabbed her and tried to force a kiss on her lips. She struggled and turned away.

"Your reputation will be ruined anyway," he said. "Once people know you've spent the night with me. You might as well enjoy it."

She struggled again.

"You don't think sweet William will want you now, do you?" he taunted. "If he was ever any more serious than I was."

She glared at him. "Oh, you were serious. You needed Papa's money." Maybe she could bargain with him. "I can still get you something from Papa if you let me go."

Amos laughed. "He won't give me a penny now. I'll have to leave Portland."

"Perhaps you won't," Maria said, trying to think how to persuade him. "We still could wed. Papa wouldn't have you arrested if you're my husband."

Amos shook her. "And why would you marry me?"

She shrugged. "As you said, I'm ruined."

Amos pulled her close again. "Then we might as well enjoy ourselves."

"No!" Maria tried to hide her revulsion. "Papa will kill you if you rape me. And if I'm going to marry you, I'd rather wait until we're wed."

Amos chuckled. "You think you can put me off?"

"I may not be able to stop you, Amos," she said. "But I can probably hurt you before you succeed. Is that what you want? Or do you want Papa's money?"

"Holladay ridiculed me when I couldn't come up with the funds he wanted."

"Well, then," she said, "let's go talk to Papa. Perhaps he'll give you your stake for the railroad if I'm safe and whole. But you'll get nothing from him if I'm hurt."

He gestured toward a chair. "Sit," he said, rubbing his temple. "I'll decide in the morning."

Amos tied Maria to a chair in the bedroom with her hands fastened behind her back. The cravats he used were painfully tight around her wrists and ankles, but he didn't touch her any further. He lay down on the bed, and soon he was snoring, but she was too uncomfortable to sleep. A nighttime breeze wafted through the bedroom's cracked window, chilling her.

Her bladder grew so full it burned, and she finally woke Amos. "Please, Amos, I need to use a chamber pot."

He groggily undid her bindings and gestured toward a screen in the corner. He had the gun in his hand again. "Be quick about it."

As Maria used the chamber pot, she saw a cake of shaving soap and his razor. She wrapped the razor in a towel and slid it inside her skirt pocket. Would he find it?

But Amos was too sleepy to notice, and he tied her arms and legs again without searching her.

Maria dozed fitfully through the darkest hours of the night. As dawn approached, she roused, smelling smoke. She glanced at the fireplace in the other room, but the embers had burned down—it was not the source of the odor.

The smell grew stronger, and within a few minutes, smoke wafted through the cracked window—the fire was outside. She heard the clang of a fire bell.

"Amos," she shouted. "Fire. We must leave."

He startled awake. "What?" He looked around.

"There's smoke. Something's burning. We have to get out of here."

He frowned. "You can't fool me."

"Amos, go look," she urged. "The smell is getting stronger. And I hear the fire wagon."

He opened the window wider and peered out, then cursed. He opened the door to the apartment. More smoke billowed from the hallway. "Christ," he said. "Let's go."

"I'm tied up," she said. "Papa won't give you anything without me, remember?"

He untied her, grabbed the gun and ledger, and pulled her into the hallway.

Chapter 83: Where Is Maria?

Will stormed into the house after his fruitless search in Chinatown. Though well past midnight, Nate and his parents sat in the parlor, wide awake and waiting.

Will ran a hand through his hair. "I couldn't find Zhuang Li or Maria," he said. "I don't know where she is."

Mama's sobs filled the room, and deep lines of worry etched Papa's face. Nate swore under his breath.

"Where haven't you looked?" Papa demanded.

"The newspaper office," Will said. "I'll go there now. Then the Zhuangs' house again."

"I'm coming, too," Nate said, already on his feet.

The brothers raced downtown to *The New Northwest* office. The building loomed dark and silent. Locked.

"We have to get in," Will said. "Come on." They scrambled into the back alley, and Will hurled a rock through a window. He'd pay for the damage later. After knocking out the glass, Will boosted Nate through the opening, then Nate unlocked the door for Will. But the office was deserted—no pressman or guard, no sign of Maria.

"The Zhuangs' house. Now," Will ordered, and they sprinted toward Chinatown.

Will pounded on the Zhuangs' door until Jin answered, dressed in a Chinese robe. "Li still not here," Jin said.

"Have you seen Maria?" Nate asked. "She's not at the paper, and she hasn't come home."

Jin shook his head. "I see no one. Where else you look?"

"Let's try our company offices," Will said. "If Zhuang's there, he might know where she is."

"I come, too," Jin said.

The three men hurried to the McDougall & Company building in the early dawn hours. Once inside, they fanned out to search. After a minute, Will heard Nate shout, "Higgins's office. Li's hurt!"

Will ran through the hall to find the others. Li lay on the floor of Higgins's office, blood pooling beneath him. "What happened?" Will demanded.

"Shot," Jin replied, using his robe to press the wound in Li's side. "But alive."

Li groaned, murmuring something in Chinese.

Will touched the wounded man's shoulder. "Li, where's Maria?"

"Higgins," Li moaned.

"Higgins has her? Where?" Will asked.

Li spat out a string of Chinese words.

"He not know," Jin translated. "Higgins stealing. Li has proof."

"Why did Higgins take Maria?" Will couldn't fathom it.

"She find book," Li whispered. Then another burst of Chinese.

"He know nothing more," Jin said. "Must take him home."

Will spun toward Nate. "Help Jin get Li to Chinatown. I'm going after Maria."

"Where?" Nate asked.

"Higgins's apartment." The accountant had pointed out his building when they watched the December fire together. "It's a block north of the furniture store. Find me after you get Li home."

They left the newspaper building, Li supported between Nate and Jin. Outside, the smell of smoke hit Will. Loud bells clanged in the distance.

Will swore. "Another fire. Get Li home. I'll find Maria."

Will ran toward Higgins's apartment, heart pounding. Flames flickered from the tops of buildings, casting an ominous glow over the street. Surely, Higgins wouldn't trap Maria in this inferno.

Glass exploded from windows as flames engulfed one building after another. The entire block became a blazing deathtrap. A storefront collapsed in Will's path, bricks crumbling into a smoldering heap. He darted into an alley behind the buildings, sweat streaming down his face.

He almost turned back. Then he spotted two figures struggling halfway down the alley.

Maria.

And Higgins.

"Maria!" Will roared, his voice raw from smoke and fear.

"Will!" she cried. "He has a gun." She strained away from her captor, dropping something—a book, it looked like.

Higgins hooked his left arm around Maria's neck, a pistol in his right hand. Heedless of the risk, Will charged toward them.

Maria screamed, then slashed Higgins's left arm.

Higgins's gun fired, a wild shot. He dropped the weapon with a cry of pain and grabbed his bleeding arm.

Maria held a bloody razor.

Will crashed into Higgins, both men slamming to the ground. As they tumbled across the alley, burning embers rained down, searing Will's face and hands. "Maria, go home!" he yelled.

"I won't leave you," she cried.

Higgins's right fist connected with Will's jaw. Pain shot through his head, and he fought to stay conscious. "Run!" Will bellowed, heaving his body to pin Higgins beneath him.

Higgins groaned, clutched his wounded arm, and writhed to escape Will's weight. Seizing his chance, Will punched Higgins in the nose, feeling a satisfying crunch of bone.

Higgins grunted as blood streamed down his face. He flung himself upward, and the men pummeled each other as they rolled toward a burning building—the Kellogg Hotel, Will thought, though he'd lost his bearings. Finally, Higgins managed a blow to Will's ear, staggered to his feet, and reeled toward the flames.

His head pounding, Will stumbled after Higgins, but stopped at the hotel entrance. "No, Higgins," he shouted. "It's too hot."

Without looking back, Higgins plunged deeper into the inferno, heading toward a staircase.

Will gasped sobbing breaths as he watched in horror. He couldn't pursue the villain—with Maria away from her captor, he wouldn't risk his own life.

The staircase collapsed over Higgins and sent him plummeting into the cellar.

A wave of heat forced Will to retreat. "Maria!" he rasped as he lurched toward her, wheezing. "We have to get out of here!"

"Wait," she said, scooping up the book she'd dropped. "It's proof Higgins was stealing."

Will grabbed it from her, as she batted at embers scorching her skirts. "Let's go," he urged.

They worked their way from the alley to a wider street. Will shuddered as he realized their narrow escape. He and Maria dodged falling bricks and wafting cinders as they wended through downtown. Will wrapped his arm around her, his grip unyielding. He would never let her go again.

The fire seemed to go on for miles, but it was probably only five or six blocks wide. Mansions as large as the McDougall home had burned to their foundations, as had many commercial and industrial enterprises. Finally, they reached an unscathed block not far from their home.

"Do you think the company's offices are safe?" Maria said, gasping.

"Doesn't matter," Will said, his voice hoarse. "You're safe. That's all I care about."

Maria smiled, teeth gleaming against her soot-covered face. "We're both safe," she said. Then her eyes filled with tears. "Zhuang Li—Amos shot him."

"He's alive," Will assured her, holding her tighter. "Nate and Jin took him to Chinatown."

Her brow creased with worry. "Did they make it?"

"We'll find out soon enough," Will said as he led Maria up the front steps of their home.

Chapter 84: Aftermath

Papa himself opened the door and grabbed Maria into the tightest hug she'd ever felt. "Maria, Maria," he said, over and over.

"Papa, I'm all sooty," she whispered against his chest. But she gripped him as closely as he held her, relishing his solid strength.

"As if I care, my dear girl," he said in a choked voice. "You're safe." Then Papa turned to Will. "And you, son." He gathered Will into his arms as well.

"We're both fine, Pa," Will said, thumping Papa on the back.

By this time, Mama was in the front hall, too, crying as she embraced them all.

They made their way to the parlor. "Where's Nate?" Will asked.

"He hasn't come home," Papa said, his voice rising with concern. "Wasn't he with you?"

"I sent him to take Zhuang Li home," Will said.

"What happened to Li?" Papa asked.

"Amos shot him, Papa," Maria said.

"But he's alive," Will added. "And conscious when I left him."

"We'd better hear the whole story," Papa said as they all sat. Maria nestled close to Will on a sofa, ignoring the soot and cinders in their clothes.

Mama asked Mrs. O'Malley to bring hot chocolate and sandwiches, and Papa poured them all whiskey while they waited. At the first sip, Maria felt the alcohol burn her already aching throat. "Water," she gasped. "I'd better have water."

Will hurried to pour her a tumbler.

The parlor door burst open, and Nate rushed in. "Downtown's aflame," he cried. "I couldn't find—" Then he halted. "You're safe," he said to Will. "And Maria, too."

"You're just in time to hear the story," Papa said, pouring a full measure of whiskey for Nate.

For the next hour, Maria and Will and Nate recounted what had happened—Maria finding the ledger, Amos shooting Zhuang Li, Amos taking her to his apartment (at which Mama moaned and Papa's expression turned flinty), Will searching for her, Nate finding Li, Nate going to Chinatown, Will fighting with Amos, and their final frightening journey home through the flames.

"How much of the town burned?" Mama asked. "Is it as bad as last December?"

"Worse," Nate said. "There are blocks and blocks burning. It may take days for the firemen to put it out."

"Nothing has been done to improve our firefighting capabilities since the last blaze," Papa said. "It's morning now, but there's no sign of the sun. The city will be a long time recovering." The skies outside the parlor window were gray with soot.

"What happened to Amos, do you think?" Maria asked Will. "He couldn't have survived, could he?"

Will shook his head. "I don't see how. I watched him fall into the cellar, then burning timbers collapsed on top of him. But we won't know until the flames are out."

The fire raged for over a day, and it stopped only because it ran out of fuel when it reached the part of the city burned the prior December. Not until Sunday afternoon were citizens allowed into the charred area. Even then, the police warned people to be careful. "Might still be hot pockets and smoldering coals," one constable told Maria, Will, and Nate when they ventured downtown.

They could only skirt the perimeter of the fire, which had burned from Morrison Street on the north to Market Street on the south, and from the Willamette River west to Third Avenue.

"But McDougall & Company is safe," Will said.

"And so are the newspaper offices," Maria said. "And our family's home." Tears came to her eyes as she thought of the burning mansions they'd seen as they made their way home. Now, those houses were only skeletons, and whole families roamed their blackened yards to salvage anything left unscathed in the debris.

Late Sunday, Will and Maria and Papa sat down with the ledger Maria had retrieved from the alley after Amos fell. "I can't make heads nor tails of it," Will said. "Can you?"

Papa shook his head. "You two should take it to Zhuang Li. See how he is doing. If he is able, ask him how he interprets this book."

"Did Li tell you anything about his findings?" Will asked Maria.

"Yes," she said. "But all I understood was that it proves Amos was stealing. It shows the receipts from California and the portion he took."

Monday morning, Will bought a copy of *The Oregonian*, which had managed to publish a paper, though the editors had missed the Sunday issue. Twenty blocks burned, it reported. Many people dead.

Amos's body still had not been identified. A corpse had been found in the cellar where Will saw him fall. The McDougalls assumed it was his body, but as yet there was no confirmation.

That afternoon, Will, Maria, and Nate ventured into Chinatown. Parts of that neighborhood were charred beyond recognition. "Firefighters spent little time here," Nate commented.

"The money was in the mansions and businesses on First Street," Will said. "That's what they tried to save. Not Chinatown."

The Zhuang house had not burned, and their street looked much as it had before the fire. The old woman who'd greeted them on prior visits opened the door, bowed, and went to get Li. Both Li and Jin joined their visitors.

"How are you feeling, Li?" Will asked.

"Some better." Li bowed to Nate. "Thank you, Mr. Nate, for bringing me home."

"He lose much blood," Jin said. "But doctor say he be all right."

"I'm so glad," Maria said.

"Tell us about the ledger Higgins had," Will said, spreading the book out in front of Li.

"This book show how Mr. Higgins steal money from company," Li said. "I not trace every entry, but many."

"How did he do it?" Maria asked.

"Sometimes he transpose numbers. Company get less, he take difference," Li said. "Sometimes he write wrong digit. Sometimes he not record one bank draft in list of many. Looks sloppy, but always in his favor. Sometimes inventory not recorded. Or too little inventory."

"And he kept a record of everything?" Will asked incredulously. "Why?"

"Beck involved, too, I think," Li said. "See telegram." He pulled a telegram out of an envelope in the back of the ledger.

"I hadn't noticed this," Will said. He took the telegram from Li. "It's from Beck." Will read, " 'Deposited two hundred dollars in our account this month. What is your take?' "

Maria gasped. "Then they were working together."

"So it seems," Will said. "It's time to fire Beck." He turned to Li. "Can you show us more details?"

Li went through the ledger line by line to show which transactions he'd audited and which he hadn't deciphered yet. "Total he steal over ten thousand dollars," he concluded. "That what I find so far."

"Enough to cover Higgins's initial investment with Holladay," Will murmured.

"But not if he had to split it with Beck," Maria said.

"When you are able," Will said to Li, "please come to our house so you can show this to my father. We need to get rid of Beck as soon as we can."

On Tuesday, Maria returned to *The New Northwest*. She couldn't justify staying home any longer, not when there was work to be done. Word of her capture by Amos Higgins had reached Abigail Duniway and the rest of the staff.

"Are you all right, my dear?" Abigail asked, stepping out of her office to greet Maria.

"Yes, Mrs. Duniway," Maria said. "My throat is still scratchy, and I'm coughing. But I'm fine."

"You could have been killed," Daisy said. "How did you get away?"

"I hid a razor in my skirts," Maria said, shuddering as she remembered the blade slashing Amos's arm. "Then Will fought with Amos."

"And now he's dead," Robert said. "Good riddance, from what I hear."

"What are people saying?" Maria asked. She worried that her reputation would be tarnished if the full story were known.

"That a man who worked for your father held you for ransom," Daisy said. "Was that true? Did he want money?"

Maria shrugged. She didn't know how much of the story Papa would want told. "I'm not sure what he thought he would gain by holding me," she said. "But I am fine now."

"Maria," Mrs. Duniway said, "would you please join me in my office?"

When Maria had taken a seat in the editor's office, Mrs. Duniway said, "I won't ask you for more than what your family is comfortable making public, but I would like for you to write the story of your abduction and escape. It would make for thrilling copy."

Maria hesitated, then said, "I have been working on an article about my father's business. Amos had been stealing from us. But I promised my father I would not publish the story until he agreed."

"Will he agree now?" Mrs. Duniway asked.

"I'll find out."

That evening, Maria told Papa of Mrs. Duniway's request.

"Now that we know who the thieves were," he said, "I can't see the harm in the story. But you cannot publish it until Will has gone to California and fired Beck."

"Is it safe for Will to go?" Maria asked.

"Someone must," Papa said grimly. "And Will volunteered."

Chapter 85: What the Future Holds

Later that evening, Will and Maria wandered hand in hand in the garden. The sun was setting, and the sky glowed orange and purple. The smoke from the fire had dissipated, but a sooty odor still wafted through the air.

Will gently squeezed Maria's hand, drawing her closer. "I want to be sure of you," he said. "Will you marry me soon?"

Maria nodded happily, her smile radiant. "As soon as Mama and I can arrange it."

Her answer filled his heart with joy, but he continued with the speech he had prepared. He wanted to be sure she understood his feelings. "I don't care if you continue to write for the paper—for *The New Northwest*, or for a paper in Tacoma if one starts publishing there. I'll even stay here if you don't want to go to Tacoma. I just want you as my wife."

She reached up and covered his lips softly with her fingers. "Will, shush. I said I'd marry you."

He turned her into his embrace. "I want you to be happy, Maria."

"I am happy." She rested her head on his shoulder. "Or I will be if I know you're safe. Do you have to go to California?"

"Yes." He didn't want to leave her, but Pa still couldn't travel so far, Nate was not mature enough, and Jack wasn't yet fully integrated into the business. "It's got to be a family member who confronts Beck. I'm the best man for the job. Pa agrees." Will had a steamboat ticket to San Francisco for the following Monday.

Maria's face fell at his words, but she nodded. "I understand," she said.

"We will marry as soon as I return," Will promised.

Maria's laughter rang through the garden. "I think Mama will have something to say about that."

"What do you mean?" he asked, confused.

"She is planning the wedding." Maria grinned. "And she means it to be a grand affair."

At that, Will's shoulders slumped. "Do we have to?"

"Yes." Maria's voice was firm. "We have to keep Mama happy."

On Wednesday, firefighters retrieved a body from the Kellogg Hotel cellar. There was an onyx stone near the corpse in a pool of melted gold. "It's Amos Higgins's ring," Will declared when the coroner asked him about it. "He always wore it."

With that confirmation, the coroner declared the body to be that of Amos Higgins. Higgins had no family in Portland, so Pa and Will took it upon themselves to arrange the funeral for the following Saturday. Will attended along with his parents, Maria, and Nate.

As the minister spoke, Will reflected on the past year. From Boston to Portland, California to Tacoma, his life had taken unexpected turns. He'd discovered new family members, forged lasting friendships, and persuaded Maria to be his wife. He took Maria's hand and held it through the rest of the sermon.

When the congregation rose to sing "Amazing Grace," Will felt a wave of emotion at the familiar hymn, almost always sung at funerals. The fourth verse touched him deeply,

> *Yea, when this flesh and heart shall fail,*
> *And mortal life shall cease,*
> *I shall possess, within the veil,*
> *A life of joy and peace.*

At the words "A life of joy," Will squeezed Maria's fingers. She looked up at him with loving eyes.

He leaned over and whispered, "That's what we will have here on earth—a life of joy."

"But not peace?" she whispered back with a smile.

"That I cannot promise," he said. "But I promise you joy." His smile was as much a vow as the words he hoped to say soon.

That afternoon, Will received the detailed letter Jack had promised in the telegram he'd sent on the day of the fire. The several-page letter recounted what Jack had found in a journal kept by Beck.

"It seems Beck had records similar to what Higgins kept," Will told Pa. "But I will see for myself next week."

"Be careful, son," Pa said, worry showing in his eyes. "Beck will be cornered. And a trapped animal lashes out however he can."

"I'll be careful, Pa." But he knew he was facing a difficult confrontation.

When Will arrived in San Francisco on Thursday, August 14, Jack met him at the dock. "We'll talk to the bastard tomorrow, won't we?" Jack said.

"Yes," Will replied. "The sooner the better."

Early the next morning at the McDougall & Company office in San Francisco, Will and Jack fired Beck. Beck blustered and swore, his face contorted with rage and fear. "I've done nothing wrong," he spat, his eyes glinting. "You have no reason to give me the axe."

"That's not what Higgins said," Will said. He didn't know if word of Higgins's death had reached Beck.

Apparently, it had not. "That thieving crook?" Beck scoffed. "He's just covering his own hide."

"It doesn't matter, Beck," Will said. "You're fired. Effective immediately. And if you don't leave quietly, I'll have you arrested." Will held out his hand. "I'll take your keys now, and we will change the locks both here and in Sacramento to be sure you cannot return."

Beck's eyes narrowed to slits as he sneered, "Who'll you get to run the place?" He nodded at Jack. "He ain't ready to take over."

"That is my problem," Will said. "Not yours."

Beck stormed out, cursing, and Will sighed in relief.

They next went to see Samuel Cassidy and offered him the job of managing both San Francisco and Sacramento, on the condition that Jack serve as his second in command. "Train my uncle well, Cassidy," Will said. "He's been helpful as my eyes and ears here."

"You won't be taking over the California operation yourself?" Cassidy asked.

Will shook his head. "I'll be heading up our new Tacoma branch. We'll be ready when the Northern Pacific reaches Puget Sound."

Over the next two weeks, the three men worked together from dawn until dusk. They uncovered many inventory discrepancies and the same types of errors in the company ledgers that Zhuang Li had found in Portland. "It'll take a while to sort through it all," Cassidy said. "But Jack and I will get to the bottom of it. And you'll have accurate reports from here on, I promise."

On Thursday evening, August 28, Will and Jack ate supper together for the last time before Will steamed north to Portland. "Are you comfortable working for Cassidy?" Will asked.

Jack nodded. "He's a straight shooter. I never could cotton to Beck. You was right about him."

"Are you ready to bring your mother to San Francisco?"

At that, Jack laughed. "I suppose I must. You done me a favor, puttin' me in this job. I like the work, and I can make a decent livin'. Now I'll do you and Jenny the favor of gettin' Mama outta your hair."

Will grinned. "It's for my mother I ask," he said. "Maria and I'll be in Tacoma. But I don't think Mama can tolerate Grandmère under her roof much longer."

Chapter 86: Tacoma

Will had an easy journey back to Portland, but the next few months were far from smooth sailing. He and Maria announced their engagement in *The Oregonian* on September 16, the birthday Will shared with their brother Andrew. But their joy was short-lived. Two days after the announcement, the stock market in the United States crashed. The McDougall & Company business in Boston suffered major losses, and the strain reverberated all the way to the West Coast.

"Should we delay opening the Tacoma branch, Pa?" a worried Will asked a few days after the crash.

"What do we hear from the Northern Pacific managers?" Pa asked.

"So far, they are continuing their plans," Will said, though he wondered whether the railroad investors could weather the financial downturn. "Construction of the rail lines will probably be delayed. The timing depends on whether they can get financing."

Pa's brow furrowed. "Can we pursue other business opportunities in Tacoma?"

"I believe so. We'll have to venture into Seattle, too, I think, to make a branch in Washington Territory profitable until the Northern Pacific terminus opens," Will said, more optimistically than he felt. "But I believe we can turn a profit."

"And are you ready to take on that extra work?"

Will nodded. He still wanted a chance to work on his own. "I'd like to build the branch from the ground up. I'm ready."

Pa placed a hand on Will's shoulder. "Then you should do it. If anyone can make a success of it in these times, you can."

Will spent the autumn months planning both the new warehouse and a new home. He traveled back and forth between Tacoma and Portland, relishing whatever time he could spend with Maria.

Will and Maria were wed on Christmas Day, 1873. Mama insisted they wait until then to put distance between Maria's kidnapping and their marriage. "I don't want your reputation tarnished by anyone thinking you were forced to marry quickly," Mama told Maria privately.

Although Maria was eager to marry Will, she acquiesced to Mama's wishes. Besides, she was busy with the newspaper. She had written the story of what had happened during the fire, not naming her assailant, but making it clear that he had been a thief who had stolen from McDougall & Company.

Jack came to Portland for Christmas, and he would take Grandmère back to San Francisco after the wedding. "I've found a nice house," he told Maria. "Big enough for Mama and me both. And I hired her a French maid and a Chinese cook. She should be happy."

The wedding was a large affair, though less grand than Mama originally wanted. "Don't go overboard, Jenny," Papa told Mama. "Many people here in Portland are suffering after the fire and the market crash. We are comfortable, but we must think of our neighbors."

"Of course, Mac," Mama said. "But our neighbors must see that we support Will and Maria. Their circumstances are unusual, and I want everyone to know they have our blessing."

Christmas Day dawned cold and gray, and by late morning as the family left for the church, a rare snow was falling. "It's beautiful," Maria breathed as she rode in the carriage with Papa.

"And so are you, daughter," he said. "Are you happy?"

"Very happy, Papa!"

"I remember you as a wee mite when you were first born. So many years ago, though today those years seem like minutes." Papa's eyes held a sheen of tears. "And when I brought you home to Jenny, there was never any question for her—you were her daughter."

"I am so grateful for the life you've given me," Maria murmured. "I have always loved you and Mama so much. And Will. And I will love you all for the rest of my days."

They arrived at the church, already full of friends from Portland and Oregon City. Eliza and Lottie helped Maria smooth the skirts of her white lace dress and spread her veil over her face. Maggie and Evie wore white as well and sprinkled hothouse rose petals as they walked toward the minister and Will. Lottie and Eliza, dressed in blue, followed the younger girls, then Maria walked down the aisle on Papa's arm.

The wedding ceremony passed in a blur. All Maria saw of the church was Will's face grinning at her. He couldn't say his vows without smiling, though his words were strong and clear.

As she said her vows, staring into his eyes, she found she couldn't keep from smiling either. Surrounded by family and friends, amidst the falling snow and the promise of a new beginning, Maria knew that this was where she belonged. With each word of commitment, she felt a deep-seated certainty that she and Will were embarking on a journey that would last a lifetime.

Two weeks later, Will and Maria boarded a ferry bound for Kalama on the north side of the Columbia River. The leg of the Northern Pacific from Kalama to Tacoma had opened in December, so in Kalama they would transfer to the train. The whole family saw them onto the ferry in Portland.

"We're on our way home, Maria," Will said when at last they reached their private compartment on the train. "Of course, our house isn't finished yet. But Tacoma will be our home."

"Home is where you are," Maria said. She nestled her head on his shoulder. Her first two weeks of marriage had been filled with happiness and passion, a testament to the deep love she shared with Will. She hoped that soon Will's child would take root in her womb, and their family would grow.

"If you want to visit Portland, it's not too far," he said, brushing a strand of hair from her face after she removed her hat.

"Home is where you are," she repeated. She reached up to cup his chin and kissed him tenderly.

"A life of joy," he promised in a husky voice against her lips, then deepened the kiss.

THE END

Author's Note

A Life of Joy is the last book in my series about the McDougalls and Pershings. I could write many more novels about my characters from the 1847 wagon train to Oregon, as well as characters from the second generation, like Will and Maria. These characters are very real to me, and a part of me wants to make them real to readers as well.

But the arc of my series is complete. The series starts in the early years of the Oregon Trail migration and ends with plans for a railroad to connect the Pacific Northwest with the rest of the nation. In fact, after the first Transcontinental Railroad was completed in 1869, travel by wagon across the plains and mountains dropped off considerably. It would almost end completely by the time the Northern Pacific tracks were opened in 1883. Thus, the story line of my series embraces the history of the Oregon Trail.

Another reason to end the series is that *A Life of Joy* resolves the mysteries that brought Mac and Jenny McDougall to Oregon. Jenny's attackers are dead. She and Mac have reestablished communications with their families. Will and Maria have overcome their parents' pasts, and they are poised to expand the McDougall business in the West. (Although, in fact, the Panic of 1873 ushered in many years of financial hardship in the United States.)

I tried to be realistic in plotting the route and travel times of Will's transcontinental train trip. The journey could be made in as little as a week, and I read of one train that made it from Omaha to San Francisco in 89 hours. But I didn't find any actual train schedules, so my departure and arrival times are fictional.

My friends in Kansas City will wonder if I should have referred to the town by its official name in 1872, which was City of Kansas. However, it was already often called Kansas City, and the newspaper of the time was called *The Kansas City Times* (founded in 1867). The city's name was officially changed to Kansas City in 1889, and I have used Kansas City in this novel for simplicity.

The fires in Boston and Portland described in *A Life of Joy* were historical events, though their impact on the McDougall business is as fictional as the McDougalls. These fires were described in vivid detail in newspapers of the time, and I have adapted those descriptions in this novel.

The announcement of the Northern Pacific terminus coming to Tacoma is also factual. Seattle lobbied hard for the railroad, but Tacoma won. It took the Klondike Gold Rush in the 1890s to help Seattle outpace Tacoma in growth. The Northern Pacific Railroad subsidized Tacoma's development, though I do not know specifically how the Northern Pacific supported warehouses and other businesses necessary for the railroad's growth.

Several historical characters walk through this novel. Abigail Scott Duniway and her brother Harvey Scott were both prominent newspaper editors in Portland. Abigail Scott Duniway has been a character in several of my earlier novels. In this novel, set in the years when she published *The New Northwest* in Portland, she mentors my fictional character, Maria McDougall. Abigail started the newspaper to advocate for women's suffrage after her experiences with women customers as a milliner in Albany, Oregon. That era of Abigail's life is described in my novel, *When Heart Shall Fail*. Abigail frequently traveled around the West to champion women's suffrage, and I may have placed her in Portland at a time when she was promoting her cause.

Harvey Scott edited *The Oregonian* for many years, but in the fall of 1872, he had differences with the new publisher of the paper, and he left *The Oregonian* until 1877. My novel does not state when he left *The Oregonian* that autumn and may depict him as its editor after he left the paper.

The New Northwest shared offices with *The Oregonian* at some point, but Abigail also described starting her paper in a building at Third and Washington in Portland, where she employed a pressman. At another point, she mentioned that her sons helped set type. Robert Taylor, the typesetter in my novel, is a fictional character.

Although some of the newspaper stories mentioned in this book appeared in *The New Northwest*, all the scenes with Abigail are fictional. She did attempt to vote in the 1872 presidential election, and that event is described in *The Oregonian*. For more information about Abigail, read *Path Breaking: An Autobiographical History of the Equal Suffrage Movement in Pacific Coast States*, by Abigail Scott Duniway (1914). It is available online at https://www.google.com/books/edition/Path_Breaking/LYtJAAAAIAAJ.

Winema Riddle and Sarah Winnemucca were also historical figures. I have tried to depict these two Native American women as they really were, though all their scenes are fictional. Winema Riddle played a major role in resolving the Modoc War, as I have described.

Benjamin Holladay is another historical character. He was a prominent investor in stagecoaches and railroads in California and Oregon from the 1850s until his death. I have taken as many liberties with his character as he tried to take with Maria, and none of the events involving Holladay in *A Life of Joy* are factual. However, Holladay was described by his contemporaries as "illiterate, coarse, boastful, false, and cunning," and as "wholly destitute of fixed principles of honesty, morality, or common decency." Also, Holladay reputedly owned a house of prostitution in Portland. So I don't think I've gone too far in my depiction of the man.

Job Carr was the first permanent settler in Tacoma and an early promoter of the area. He'd sold most of his land by 1873, but he remained postmaster in Tacoma when Will visited.

Mount Tahoma is one of the traditional Native American names for Mount Rainier. Although the mountain had been named Rainier before Lewis and Clark's journey, people around Tacoma in the 1870s preferred the indigenous name, so I call it Mount Tahoma in this book.

As always, any errors or historical inaccuracies in this novel are my own, and I take full responsibility.

Discussion Guide

These questions are intended to help book clubs and other reading groups discuss *A Life of Joy*. They might also make good essay topics for students reading this novel for the classroom.

1. How does Maria's story reflect the challenges women faced in the 19th century? How do Abigail Duniway and *The New Northwest* newspaper influence Maria's development?

2. What does the novel suggest about the power of journalism in shaping public opinion and social change? How has the role of journalism changed in the electronic age?

3. How does Maria's mixed heritage shape her experiences and ambitions? In what ways does she challenge societal expectations, and how does her identity influence her choices?

4. How does the novel portray racial discrimination, particularly toward Native Americans and Chinese? Do you think the novel portrays race relations in the 1870s realistically?

5. How do Mac and Jenny McDougall's concerns about Maria's career reflect the values of the time? Do you think their parental worries are justified?

6. Maria struggles between pursuing her journalistic career and her romantic relationships. Do you think she can successfully balance both? Why or why not? What do you think she will do as a writer after the end of this story?

7. Given their complicated history, do you think Maria and Will's

relationship is appropriate for the 1870s? How might their relationship be perceived today?

8. Who are the villains in this story? Do you see any redeeming qualities in their characters?

9. How did delays in communications impact the plot of this novel? For readers who have read earlier books in this series, how have communications improved between 1847 when the series began and 1873 when *A Life of Joy* ends?

10. Which character was your favorite in *A Life of Joy*? How did this person change and develop through the story?

11. In what ways do historical events and social norms of the Pacific Northwest in the 1870s influence the characters' decisions?

12. The title, *A Life of Joy*, suggests themes of happiness and fulfillment. Do you think Maria and Will ultimately achieve a life of joy? Why or why not? How does the novel define joy in the context of ambition, love, and family?

If you enjoyed **A Life of Joy**, *you might also enjoy the earlier novels in this series.*
All books are available on Amazon and Barnes & Noble, or find them here:
https://www.amazon.com/Theresa-Hupp/e/B009H8QIT8

Acknowledgments

Since 2012, my writing critique group, the Sedulous Writers Group, has been an important part of my writing process. The members of this group have edited all my novels before publication. Their input has improved my writing in so many ways—from plotting to character development to polishing my language. My series about the development of the American West, including *A Life of Joy*, would be far less readable without their suggestions.

My thanks as well to beta readers of this book, specifically Carol, Dane, Debby, Mary Beth, Sally, Sylvia, and Tresia. I appreciate the time these friends have spent (some of them as beta readers for many of my books) catching my mistakes and plot holes, though any errors that remain are my responsibility.

Writers can only succeed with a community of support behind them. I am grateful to these friends and colleagues and to so many others who have helped me along the way.

About the Author

Theresa Hupp grew up in Eastern Washington State and the Willamette Valley in Oregon, and her ancestors include 19th century emigrants to Oregon and California. She lived and worked in Kansas City, Missouri, for many years, but she and her husband recently moved back to Washington State and now reside in Seattle.

Theresa is the award-winning author of novels, short stories, essays, and poetry. Before her writing career, she worked as an attorney, mediator, and human resources executive.

Lead Me Home (2015), a #1 bestselling novel about the Oregon Trail in Amazon's Kindle Store and winner of the Missouri Indie Author Project award for adult fiction, tells the story of Mac McDougall and Jenny Calhoun on their wagon journey along the Oregon Trail. *Now I'm Found* (2016) follows Mac and Jenny through the early California Gold Rush days. *Forever Mine* (2018) portrays the difficulties of the Oregon Trail trek from other travelers' points of view. *My Hope Secured* (2019), a Mid-America Romance Association Carla Award finalist, gives Zeke Pershing from the wagon company his own love story. *Safe Thus Far* (2021), a Thorpe Menn Award finalist, continues the family saga into the next generation. *When Heart Shall Fail* (2023), winner of the Missouri Writers Guild's Best Fiction Award, describes the fate of more travelers in the original wagon train. Finally, *A Life of Joy* (2025) completes the series with plans for a transcontinental railroad coming to the Pacific Northwest—which effectively ended travel along the Oregon Trail.

Theresa has also published two corporate thrillers under a pseudonym, as well as an anthology titled *Family Recipe: Sweet and saucy stories, essays, and poems about family life*. In addition, Theresa has published short works in several *Chicken Soup for the Soul* anthologies, as well as for *Mozark Press* and *Kansas City Voices*. She has been a member of the Historical Novel Society, the Missouri Writers Guild, Oklahoma Writers Federation, Inc., the Kansas City Writers Group, and Write Brain Trust.

You can follow Theresa on her website and blog, https://TheresaHuppAuthor.com, on her Facebook Author page, https://facebook.com/TheresaHuppAuthor, and her Amazon page at https://www.amazon.com/Theresa-Hupp/e/B009H8QIT8. You can also subscribe to Theresa's monthly newsletter through her website.

Readers' Praise for Earlier Books

Lead Me Home:

> *. . . on the challenging Oregon Trail of 1847 . . . the going is slow and scary and dusty behind a team of oxen. . . . [Hupp] takes us on this journey and shows how her characters cope and grow under these difficult circumstances.*

> *. . . an incredible story, amazingly and beautifully written.*

Now I'm Found:

> *Hupp has done extensive research on . . . traveling the Oregon Trail and prospecting for gold in the California mountains. The descriptions of those closely related periods of history are exciting backgrounds for a tender love story.*

> *. . . Hupp does history and fiction well!*

Forever Mine:

> *Hupp researches her books with care, plots them well, describes the land beautifully, and makes the people of these books come alive with vivid characterizations.*

> *For any true lover of the western and the hardships of the pioneers who were willing to put their life in danger. . . .*

My Hope Secured:

> *Historical fiction done right! The author does an amazing job of researching the time period. . . . If you are interested in pioneer history this is something you should not miss.*

> *. . . A wonderful story of finding love and family in the frontier of Oregon.*

Safe Thus Far:

This latest installment is such a natural progression of the story line. . . . Those of us who appreciate historical accuracy will see how much time and attention the author devotes to being true to history.

. . . [Hupp's novels are] compelling, page-turners, all of them. The newest, SAFE THUS FAR, maintains the same high standard for readability and entertainment.

When Hope Shall Fail:

This is how historical fiction should be written! The author does her research. The reader is transported to another place and time. . . . This book focuses on two people trying to figure out how they got to where they are. It's a great addition to the series.

Once again, Theresa Hupp has delivered a book that . . . has it all. Struggles in settling the old American West; refreshing old-fashion romance; hard-to-put-down thriller; everyday life of early pioneering craftsmen with historical accuracy; hardened characters with soft-spots; noble characters with flaws; and gentle characters who find strength and courage when it is most needed. It's all there.

All Theresa Hupp's books are available online at Amazon or Barnes & Noble, in paperback or ebook formats.